D0193252

ALSO BY DEXTER PALMER

Version Control
The Dream of Perpetual Motion

Mary Toft;
or,
The Rabbit Queen

MARY TOFT;

or,

The Rabbit Queen

DEXTER PALMER

PANTHEON BOOKS   New York

Copyright © 2019 by Dexter Palmer

All rights reserved. Published in the United States by Pantheon Books,
a division of Penguin Random House LLC, New York, and distributed in Canada
by Penguin Random House Canada Limited, Toronto.

Pantheon Books and colophon are registered trademarks of
Penguin Random House LLC.

Library of Congress Cataloging-in-Publication Data
Name: Palmer, Dexter Clarence, [date] author.
Title: Mary Toft; or, the rabbit queen / Dexter Palmer.
Description: First Edition. New York : Pantheon Books, 2019. Includes
    bibliographical references.
Identifiers: LCCN 2019013815. ISBN 9781101871935 (hardcover : alk. paper).
    ISBN 9781101871942 (ebook).
Classification: LCC PS3616.A33885 M37 2019 | DDC 813/.6—dc23 |
    LC record available at lccn.loc.gov/2019013815

www.pantheonbooks.com

Jacket image: *Credulity, Superstition, and Fanaticism,* engraved by Thomas Cook,
    after William Hogarth (detail). Private Collection. The Stapleton Collection/
    Bridgeman Images.
Jacket design by Janet Hansen

Printed in Canada
First Edition

9 8 7 6 5 4 3 2 1

But when a man's fancy gets astride on his reason, when imagination is at cuffs with the senses, and common understanding as well as common sense, is kicked out of doors; the first proselyte he makes is himself, and when that is once compassed the difficulty is not so great in bringing over others, a strong delusion always operating from without as vigorously as from within.

—Jonathan Swift, *A Tale of a Tub*

Contents.

Mary Toft;
or,
The Rabbit Queen

PART ONE.

CHAPTER I

The Exhibition of Medical Curiosities.

The convoy of nine decrepit coaches and wagons that constituted Nicholas Fox's Exhibition of Medical Curiosities rolled into the village of Godalming on a Friday in early September 1726, soon after sunrise. Its herald, careening headlong before the horses that pulled the lead coach, was a young blond girl whose face was half covered by a port-wine stain, one of her sky-blue eyes peering out of an inky blotch of burgundy. "Tomorrow, witness a series of physiological wonders of which I am the very least," she proclaimed to passersby, the men and women trudging out of town to begin the day's harvest of the hop fields. "For the meager price of sixpence, gaze upon the horrific consequences that occur when the Lord God stretches out his mighty finger and lays a curse on Man. Educational for the mind; edifying for the soul." The windows of the coaches had their thick black curtains pulled, proof against stray glimpses of their passengers. Education and edification would not come for free.

Zachary Walsh, at age fourteen the proud apprentice of Mr. John Howard, Godalming's finest (and only) surgeon, stood before the window of his loft in the Howards' home and watched the procession roll by on the street beneath him, imagining what grotesque secrets and horrors might stuff the carriages. Was it not his duty as an initiate into the surgeon's craft to be medically curious? It was. Granted, even after four months of learning the trade, the sight of blood still turned his stomach. (Just last week he'd tasted bile at the back of his throat while watching Howard patiently stitch shut a gash in a farmer's calf, laid open by the blade of a wayward scythe. Howard had punched the needle back and forth through the man's torn flesh as easily as if it were burlap, seeing the blood and not seeming to care. "You'll be as hardened to this as I am, soon enough," he'd said, his voice infused with an unexpected melancholy that Zachary couldn't understand.)

But Zachary's squeamishness did not preclude a love of mystery, and the drawn curtains of the coaches promised more profound alterations of the human shape than mere swollen stomachs or broken bones. Knowledge of strange, unknown anatomies, yes; sights to steel the spirit against sin as well. But also: nightmares. The most delicious nightmares, the kind that one has only after the wall between the mundane and the magical is breached directly before one's eyes; nightmares that make you smile as you shiver in your sleep.

As if sensing the turn of Zachary's thoughts from a distance, the girl with the birthmark spattered across her face left her place at the head of the parade of vehicles and ran back along the train, coming to a stop beneath Zachary's window. Standing in the street, the last dust clouds that trailed behind the convoy swirling about the hem of her pale yellow skirts, she impishly cast her gaze around her; then she looked up at Zachary, screwed her face into a grimace, and hissed at him as if he were a disobedient cat. *"Sssst! Sssst!"* Zachary involuntarily stepped backward, briefly fearing some kind of malediction, then feeling foolish because his fear had shown on his face, and she had seen it.

Then, giggling, the girl scampered away, to announce the exhibition's coming.

*

Zachary had first met his master John Howard last fall, when his mother had brought him to the surgeon as a patient: the boy had been suffering a constellation of troubles that included a throbbing headache, a throat so sore that each spoonful of porridge he tried to swallow pricked at it with a hundred tiny needles, a voice that had gone half an octave deeper even as he'd become unable to pronounce most words with any clarity, and breath that smelled like the interior of a newly disinterred coffin. Howard listened to Zachary's mother, Clara, describe the symptoms, then unceremoniously clamped his hand on Zachary's jaw, commanded him to open his mouth as wide as possible, and peered down the dark tunnel of his throat, involuntarily wrinkling his nose at the dank odor rising from it. "Quinsy," Howard said to Clara. "There: an abscess beside the tonsil. I don't think I've come across a case like this in two years or more. It calls for scarification, immediately: it won't disappear on its own. I hope your son is not given to nervousness." Zachary had a strange pride in contracting a disease that was at least on speaking terms with mortal peril, with a name that had such peculiar music. "Kinthy," Zachary said, and his mother wiped a glistening strand of drool from his lip with a handkerchief secreted in her sleeve.

Howard dosed young Zachary with a small glass of gin from a clear, unlabeled bottle, instructing him to drink it quickly and pouring him a second as soon as he had forced down the first. It was Zachary's first experience with strong liquor, and though he suspected that it would have stung his throat only slightly less were he not ill, the mellow fire in his stomach, and the cheerful light-headedness that ensued soon after, began to endear him greatly to John, and quinsy, and the medical profession.

Fifteen minutes later, the boy found himself stretched out on the long, wooden table in the room in Howard's offices where the surgeon stored his implements and practiced his art. Late-afternoon sunlight shone down on his face through a nearby window. "This will only take a few moments," Howard said, bending over him, "but you must be still. Open your mouth as wide as possible, once more." With his left hand, Howard inserted a thin piece of wood into Zachary's mouth, pinning down his tongue; then, as the boy's tongue involuntarily squirmed against its restraint, the scalpel in Howard's right hand slipped past Zachary's teeth and back farther still, deep into his throat, farther than it should have gone. Zachary felt himself trying to gag, wanting to struggle; he tried not to imagine the only tongue he'd ever had lopped out of his mouth by a clumsy slip of the blade, flopping mindlessly around on the floor like a fish just pulled out of the sea.

"Be still," Howard commanded in a low voice, and in the few seconds that Zachary was able to relax himself, Howard made three short, sure strokes with the knife. Zachary's mouth flooded with the sour taste of pus. "Don't swallow," Howard said, withdrawing the blade and the stick and offering Zachary a small wooden bowl. "Spit." Into the bowl went a thick, yellowish-white fluid, shot through with threads of crimson.

"The worst is past, I think," Howard said to Zachary's mother, "but the disease may return, in which case the tonsil will have to be removed and the child will have to be bled. Now, Zachary, hold this in your mouth: don't swallow, as much as you might wish to." He handed him a third glass of gin. "Spit it out when you return home. Then, twice a day for the next two days, do the same with white wine. One shilling, please."

*

Early one morning two weeks later, Howard heard a knock on his front door, faint and timid. He opened it to see Zachary standing there before him, alone.

"I'm well," Zachary said. "I did what you said, with the gin and the wine. My throat and my head don't hurt." His voice had returned to normal, with only an occasional warble that signaled an impending transition to adulthood.

"Then the rarest of specimens darkens my door," Howard said. "Neither ill nor in the company of the ill. Were it not for those two types of people, I and all my kind would be invisible." He beckoned Zachary inside.

Howard had found himself unoccupied so far that morning—though a calamity was surely due by soon enough—so he had been keeping himself occupied by struggling with a particularly thorny chapter of John Locke's *An Essay Concerning Human Understanding.*

Like many men in England who fancied themselves of a certain class and intellectual capacity, he owned a copy; like most of those copies, the majority of the signatures in his had never been split by a blade. Sitting on his shelves, the volume had come to seem to him over the years like a fraudulent prop. It squatted there in accusation; it called him a pretender.

And so as of late he'd taken up the habit of working his way through a paragraph or two each morning, before his first patient arrived. For all Locke's stated love of clarity, Howard found his prose to be a challenge, with his winding sentences and invented definitions—his "simple modes" did not seem simple at all. But Howard felt as if he was at last getting somewhere with it: his own mind, at least, occasionally seemed as if it were making more sense to itself, which justified the labor and the boredom.

Nonetheless, Zachary's arrival was a welcome distraction, though Howard had no idea what to say to him, or what Zachary might want. Howard's conversations in his role as a surgeon usually followed a predictable pattern—the description of the symptoms; the identification of the illness; the sure performance (one hoped) of a quick and effective remedy—and so this situation left him at a loss. There was a small room just off the main hallway of the house where Howard offered consultations, with a few comfortable chairs and shelves that held a few dozen volumes necessary to the practice of the surgeon's craft; he ushered Zachary inside. Zachary sat in a chair placed against a wall; as Howard sat in the larger chair behind his desk, he could see Zachary leaning over slightly, to peek through the doorway at the operating room directly across the hall.

"Well," said Howard, leaning forward with his hands clasped together on the desk in front of him, "state your business. I hope you're not nosing around here for another cheering dram of Madam Geneva—that's only for my special guests."

Zachary hesitated, and Howard feared that his attempt at levity had come off more stiffly than he'd intended. Then Zachary said, quietly, "The quinsy."

"Yes?"

"The thing in my throat. What was it like?"

Of course: no child visits a surgeon expecting to have a knife slipped down his gullet. He was still disturbed by the experience; he needed reassurance. "It wasn't a bad thing at all," Howard said. "Perhaps two hundred years ago the consequences might have been more dire, but medicine has much advanced since then. If you are feeling well by now, you almost certainly have nothing further to worry about."

Howard was puzzled by Zachary's reaction—he and his wife had not been blessed with children of their own, and so to him the behavior of the young was often a cipher. But he suspected that Zachary felt he was not getting what he had come here for, whatever that was. At the news of the positive prognosis the boy had slumped in his chair slightly, and was now staring at the floor as his cheeks bloomed red.

"It might have been worse," Howard said tentatively, making a first careful guess.

Zachary looked up again, a light dawning in his eyes, and Howard considered the matter.

"If you had not come to me when you did," Howard continued, more sure of his direction now, "and if you had let the abscess be, it might have turned gangrenous."

The corners of Zachary's mouth twitched, as if he was attempting to restrain a smile.

"Then," said Howard, "the incisions I made would have wounded you further, instead of providing relief. For your mouth would have begun to rot from the inside. Your tongue would have turned black and threatened to choke you; you would have suffered unbearable pain, followed by a numbness even worse than pain. And death often comes on gangrene's heels. I have seen such cases." *Though only in books,* Howard added to himself.

"That would have been awful!" Zachary said gleefully. "You must have seen all manner of completely *awful* things!"

This may be good fortune, Howard thought.

Leaning back in his chair, he steepled his fingers. "Just this past week, a drunkard was carried in here by two of his colleagues, his arms slung across their shoulders. The toes on his right foot had swollen to the size of sausages; they'd turned lovely shades of green and violet. The foot—"

"Yes?" Zachary was close to jumping out of his chair.

"It had to be amputated."

Zachary breathed in sharply.

"I can amputate a foot in three minutes," Howard said. "Faster, if I have an assistant."

*

Howard sent Zachary home with what would become the first of several loans from his library: a heavy, well-thumbed copy of *A General System of Surgery in Three Parts,* luxuriously appointed with plates that depicted wide-eyed boys with harelips, and tools whose ends had blades and knobs and bulbs, and corpses of women whose skin was flayed from throat to navel, peeled back to reveal the organs packed neatly beneath. The biblical mysteries with which Zachary's cleric father Crispin attempted to entrance his son were feeble competition; for Zachary, the medical texts were just as enchanting as tales of donkeys speaking or flesh transforming to salt, and the lists of body parts in Heister's *Compendium of Anatomy* had all the beauty of a psalm. Crispin was soon forced to put an end to his dreams of the Gospel becoming a family business.

By the following spring, just past the boy's fourteenth birthday, John Howard and Zachary's parents had come to an arrangement, and a contract was signed to bind Zachary over to the Howards as an apprentice for a period of seven years. The agreement was amenable to all, though Crispin still harbored regrets—Zachary suspected that there were times in the past when he and John Howard had been at odds, but their professions required them to maintain a certain cordiality, since there were regular occasions, invariably unfortunate, when a Godalming citizen might need both their services at once. The cleric's reservations aside, Crispin and Clara had managed to secure a rare opportunity for the child that lodged him in one of the more prosperous homes in Godalming, guaranteed his livelihood, and promised him prestige; the Howards received a fifty-pound premium that would cover the expenses of Zachary's room and board; and Zachary would be able to indulge a fascination that would, John hoped, be the genesis of a genuine love of the profession. (Though John had a few unvoiced doubts about the boy, and his eagerness for tales of injury and sights of ruptured bodies—he found himself wondering if Zachary wanted to become a surgeon not merely because he wanted to do good, but because he wanted to witness the evil done to human bodies by disease, chance, or the willful malice of others. But the Lord uses all people for his instruments, and John often felt the need for an extra pair of hands. Best not to question; best not to judge.)

Soon thereafter, Zachary moved into the loft in the Howards' home, a dim but capacious room that only rarely caught a sliver of sunlight from its lone window. Amid the single-story structures on the street, the towering house seemed extravagant and labyrinthine; its spaces suggested a future that its owners had once imagined as newlyweds, but had mostly failed to come to pass. Zachary's loft sat above the rooms that constituted the surgeon's offices on the floor below, which had a separate entrance from that of the domicile proper; it was the only room on the second floor that was occupied, and in the mornings he could hear John's wife, Alice, locking and unlocking the doors to empty chambers, for no reason he could fathom. When he ate his midday dinner with the couple who had effectively become a second set of parents, John sat before his plate of broiled pilchard or chicken roasted with cucumbers in a high-backed chair at the head of the long dining table, while Alice and Zachary perched on the ends of benches at his left and right hands, leaving room for five more at the least; settings at the opposite end of the table lay coated in a thin layer of dust. At night the house's darkened corners ate the candlelight; sounds hit the walls and fell dead.

By entering the Howards' lives, Zachary felt as if he'd walked in on a tale halfway through its telling; after John and Alice's years together, they shared a language that he did not speak and that they could not teach him, what with it being built upon their store of

shared memories. When Alice looked at John with a particular nar-
rowing of the eyes, it somehow did the work of a paragraph; John
could make Alice laugh with a barely noticeable tilt of the head. Even
at fourteen Zachary could tell that the secret language of the Howards was born out of a love that was merry, weathered, and earthy.
They touched, in a way that his parents never did—Alice sometimes
quietly reaching out to graze the tips of her fingers across the back of
her husband's hand—and they conversed in a manner that suggested
that they saw each other as equals (while Crispin Walsh, who felt his
rumbling baritone was backed by the authority of God, was given to
making pronouncements to which his wife and son were expected to
assent in silence).

Zachary also sensed that his new caretakers would be permissive in
a way that his parents were not. With little prior experience with children, they could not be expected to know what sort of trouble youths
were apt to get into; they also seemed to be unworried about the ideas
that Zachary might encounter, whereas his own father thought that
some concepts ought to be self-evidently shunned, as they would turn
good people from a good path. Crispin Walsh was deeply suspicious
of Locke and his like, though he too possessed a copy of the *Essay* that
had barely been read past its introduction; he thought all that professed love of man's unique ability to reason was an excuse to smuggle
atheism into the public discourse, despite Locke's *pro forma* protesta-
tions to the contrary. ("Beware the sentiment that a man's thoughts
alone are enough to let him understand the world," he'd said once to
Zachary at dinner between mouthfuls of mutton, gesturing at his son
with quick stabs of his fork. "It is a *fraudulent* idea, the product of the
devil himself, who wishes us to cover our own eyes rather than behold
the wondrous sight of the Lord.") John Howard, on the other hand,
though not inclined toward atheism, seemed at least willing to accept
the argument that the exercise of man's reason could only redound to
the glory of God, and so one's curiosity ought to be indulged whenever possible.

And so Zachary felt less trepidation than he would have otherwise
when broaching the possibility of attending the Exhibition of Medi-

cal Curiosities. He mentioned it over supper, a dish that Alice had prepared of peas and lettuce, heavily seasoned with salt and pepper, stewed and thickened with egg yolk. "Have you heard of the Exhibi-tion of—"

"Monstrous Calamities," Alice finished.

"Medical Curiosities," Zachary corrected, as Alice raised a ques-tioning eyebrow.

"I've heard it mentioned," said John. "Mrs. Glasse has colic and paid an early-morning visit—while you were still abed, Zachary," he finished pointedly. "She talked of it no end; her excitement could not be contained. She said that the passengers in the caravan that arrived this morning have taken up every room in the Silver Hart, across the street from her home; that some of them must be sleeping three to a bed. That when they alighted from their carriages and entered the inn, all but the proprietor of the exhibition and his young herald had black velvet cloths draped over their heads, so that their faces could not be seen. Zachary, what do you think I prescribed for Mrs. Glasse this morning?" A chance to atone for his indolence; a test, on which permission hinged.

Zachary thought for a moment. "The *Rheum Quinquinatum*," he said, stumbling only slightly over the tongue-twisting Latin. "To purge the stomach."

John offered Zachary the smallest nod of approval. "Mrs. Glasse said that one of the travelers was terrifying to lay eyes on, even with her head concealed by the velvet cloth," he continued. "From the neck down she appeared to have the shape of a young woman, but the way the cloth hung on her head indicated such a grotesque form beneath that Mrs. Glasse wondered if she were not looking on some kind of chimera. Without the covering, she must be quite a sight to behold. Zachary, what are the ingredients of the *Rheum Quinquinatum*?"

Zachary paused again, longer. "Canella bark, ground into powder. Bitters; aromatics. Roasted oranges infused in wine." He looked up at John, who only stared back placidly, saying nothing. Then: "Rhu-barb!" Zachary blurted.

"I might have eighteen pence to offer this Nicholas Fox, so that we might view the exhibition that he's been so kind to bring to us from London," said John. "In the interest of your education."

"You'll only need twelve," said Alice. "I want no part of it."

*

Nicholas Fox's traveling caravan had employed an advance scout to secure locations for his exhibition as it migrated from town to town along the River Wey; in Godalming, the display would take place late Sunday afternoon in an enormous barn on the north edge of town, with large doors on either end that let in the sunlight. It had once been used to store wool—even after two years of sitting empty, the musty odor of sheep still imbued its wooden panels. But the industry that had kept the town alive for centuries had been decimated at last by competition from the Continent: the sturdy Hampshire kersey cloths that were once the pride of the village were no longer wanted by the French, and evidence of Godalming's once lucrative clothing trade had nearly vanished. In the midst of prosperity, driven by the formidable economic engine that was London, England still nonetheless possessed a few scattered patches of blight. It was a testament to the exhibition's enchanting nature that so many were willing to spare sixpence—more than it would cost the largest of men to get dead drunk on gin—to see what wonders Fox had to offer.

John paid his and Zachary's fees to the man waiting at the barn's front door, and the two of them entered. Zachary was surprised to see his own father, Crispin Walsh, in the crowd just ahead of him, out of place in his cassock and peruke tied back with a black silk ribbon, half a head taller than all those around him. John gently touched Crispin's shoulder to get his attention, and when he turned to look down at Zachary he offered one of his rare sallies at humor. "I've caught you here, as I might have expected," he said. "But it seems you've caught me here as well."

"My master suggested we attend in order to further my education," Zachary replied, in a performance of doe-eyed innocence all the more brazen for its transparency.

"Would that my church had been as full this morning as this barn is this afternoon," said Crispin. "I feel compelled to inform myself of the true nature of my competitor."

A platform of wooden planks had been erected on the opposite end of the barn, on which a pair of musicians stood in front of a gauzy scrim that hung from a frame that was slightly askew. The musicians were dressed in matching suits that had once been white but that time and repeated wear had tinted a dingy pale yellow. They were seeming brothers, both with thick heads of curly black hair, both sporting unruly beetle brows above dark eyes; as they improvised intricate melodies on a recorder and violin, swaying their portly bodies in tandem, blurred shadows moved behind the scrim, which was lit from behind by the afternoon sun.

"Alice is well?" said Crispin, as he and John and Zachary wedged themselves forward through the press of spectators, jockeying for a good view of the stage. The flat delivery of the question suggested that if John and Alice had been in church this morning, he would not have had to ask it.

"She is," John answered. "She felt that attending an event such as this would . . . not be to her taste."

"This is as it should be," said Crispin. "I would not have allowed Clara to attend, had she requested. Such sights are not for women's eyes." He proclaimed this with certainty, despite the fact that no one had much of an idea of what the gathered audience was about to witness; indeed, almost all of the people in the barn were men, and the air was filled with the low susurration of their collective chatter and grumble. The few women who had entered in the company of their husbands looked around themselves with evident discomfort, occasionally catching each other's eyes across the barn with worried glances.

Soon, the front doors of the barn were closed, dimming the space as the only illumination came from the other set of open doors behind the platform. The musicians ceased their improvisations, bowed to the audience, and stepped to either side of the scrim as it parted. As the crowd quieted to a murmur, Nicholas Fox stepped onto the stage.

Zachary found Fox comical at first. He was a tiny man, and his clothing made him seem even smaller; his red, cherubic face was swallowed up by the ivory locks of the wig that tumbled down the sides of his head and the voluminous frills of the jabot fastened beneath his chin, which seemed to somehow produce still more frills as Zachary watched. He wore a suit of ditto, his waistcoat, coat, and breeches all of the same emerald green. But his ridiculous figure was counterbalanced by his unexpectedly deep and resonant voice, which brought on a stunned silence from the audience as soon as he spoke.

"Welcome, friends," said Fox, "to my Exhibition of Medical Curiosities! What a glorious chance is yours, for you are about to witness the most wondrous, terrifying alterations of the human form, brought to you from all the corners of the British Isles! When I look out at you, I cannot help but envy your innocence. For those of us who are no longer young, who've become jaded by the sight of ten thousand sunsets, is it not the rarest of pleasures to find oneself once again on the edge of the unknown? To truly encounter the new? Do I not tease you mercilessly with my curtain and my preamble; do you not smack your lips at your own delicious impatience? You do! A-ha: I see your smiles!" Nicholas Fox grinned with a delight that was genuine, and infectious.

But then his countenance darkened. "But is it not true that not all is worth knowing? Are there not many mysteries best left as such? Are there not certain truths that live in the black spaces of your mind that you would claw out of your own head if you could? I cannot speak with surety on whether what you will witness in just a few moments will bless or curse you, but know, as you stand here, that you take a risk, and that risk is one that some would be wise to avoid. Some forms of ignorance are gifts. In fact, before we begin," Fox continued, "I must ask: are there any women in the audience who are with child? If so I must, with regret, request—no, insist—that you leave. My assistant stands at the exit to refund your entrance fee, with all good will."

Leaning forward with his hands on his hips, he surveyed the crowd as it turned restless, and Zachary realized that this was part of

Fox's performance, to yank the audience from one emotion to another without notice, leaving them disoriented. "No women who are soon to become mothers? You must be *certain*. Such sights as will soon be revealed to you may have an especially adverse impact on those with delicate conditions. I swear to you that this is not a boast, that this is not theater. I give you this final chance: leave, and you may save your future son or daughter from a life of misery; remain, and the blame for any harm that comes to the child will fall on your head."

Near Zachary, a woman turned with an audible sigh, face turned crimson, and began to work her way back through the audience, toward the thin crack of light now spilling from the opening front doors of the barn. Her husband followed behind her, hand placed on the small of her back, gently urging her forward, scowling at the gawkers surrounding him. ("Well, there's some news," Zachary over-heard a man next to him say.)

Fox waited until the barn doors had shut once more and the audi-ence's tittering had died down, then continued. "Did such a precau-tion seem excessive to you? I assure you that it was not—by this exhibition's end I guarantee that you will find yourselves thoroughly convinced! Some of you have already seen the first piece of evidence in the face of the young woman who announced our arrival yesterday, whose poor angelic face was blighted by a birthmark: no one who truly understands the intricacies of human anatomy would be sur-prised to learn that her mother had an unusual love of *wine,* and of *strawberries.*"

"I seem not to understand human anatomy," John mumbled, as other people in the audience nodded their heads after a moment of confusion.

"But the phenomenon I will describe can lead to yet more tragic deformations," said Fox. "Consider our first subject, the son of a woman who, when with child, had an insatiable love of the practice of *bear-baiting.* Several times a week she would pay a visit to a London bear garden, to watch packs of slavering bulldogs tear at the flesh of a chained ursine prisoner, to see the maddened creatures knocked back with a single swipe of the giant beast's paw, their bellies ripped clean open, the pink strands of their guts spilling forth! Oh, I assure you, she found the carnage quite a delight! She would greet each death of a dog with merry applause; her cheeks would turn just as red as if she'd spied a swain across the street! And when the bear was at last felled, robbed of its life by a thousand bites, she would chew her own lip hard enough to taste her blood. But witness the sad result. Caleb?" he called offstage. "You may come forward."

The man who stepped through the parted curtains was shirtless, wearing nothing but a threadbare pair of breeches; his head hung forward, so that his damp, stringy brown hair obscured his face. He seemed to be in decent health, though perhaps a little thin and wiry to Zachary's eye: despite what could not have been the best of living conditions for him, he was tall, and ropy muscles rippled beneath his skin. He shifted his weight from one bare foot to another in nervousness, clenching and opening his fists.

"Turn, Caleb," Fox said gently.

He stood still, shaking his head *no,* and Zachary realized that Caleb was quietly weeping.

"Turn, Caleb," Fox said again, quietly but insistently. "You know that you must."

After a last moment of hesitation, Caleb did as Fox requested, whimpering as he shuffled around to present his back, and the audience gasped as one. For a large ovoid patch of Caleb's back, from one shoulder blade to the other, from the nape of his neck to the base of his spine, was covered in a tangled mat of thick, dark, dirty fur. Lodged within the fur were strange anatomical anomalies: a single staring eye, the color of a currant; a pointed, protruding tuft of hair in the shape of an animal's ear; and, with its teeth bared, a bear's snout, the tip of its black nose wet and glistening.

Zachary squinted at the man before him as his jaw dropped open. Did that lone black eye in the middle of the poor man's back—did it move? Did it *blink?*

"No!" Crispin Walsh cried as the bear's mouth embedded in the middle of Caleb's back pried itself open ever so slightly and emitted an anguished, wordless whine, in a voice that seemed weirdly, troublingly human. (Did Zachary actually hear that, a sound like a naked child's wail in the wilderness, so soft and distant that he might have confused it with a memory?)

*

As the exhibition continued, Nicholas Fox explained the medical theory that accounted for the parade of monstrosities that marched before his audience, one that seemed to Zachary to have the ring of truth to it. According to Fox, a principal influence on the shape of a newborn child was the state of mind of its mother during the months of her pregnancy: just as the daughter of a woman with a strong taste for wine might have a face with a birthmark like a glass of Burgundy spilled across a tablecloth, a woman who had expressed a fascination with bear-baiting might give birth to a son whose back advertised her depraved love of the cruel sport. Fox accompanied the reveal of each of his subjects with a tale of a mother's obsession, sin, or failure: the woman who never missed a chance to join the cheering crowds on Tyburn's hanging days as the necks of thieves and murderers were stretched at the gallows, whose son had half of his brainpan sheared off as neatly as if it had been done with a surgeon's saw; a woman who had an insuperable aversion to the taste of meat no matter the care taken in its preparation, whose daughter was born without a single bone in her body (Fox brought this unfortunate young lady out on a giant silver serving platter, a quivering, gelatinous mass of pink flesh topped with curly blond tresses). A shirtless man who propelled himself forward on crutches, the bones of his vertebrae visible through his brittle, mottled skin, his legs withered and bent backward like a dog's, was the supposed son of a woman who, said Fox with a leer, had an "unnatural affection" for a spaniel; a bearded giantess who towered over Fox, broad-shouldered and flat-bosomed in her frilly dress, hunched and growling with a simmering anger, was the product of a mother who "spent an undue time in the sole company of men, carousing in pubs as if she were one of them, heedlessly accepting their embraces once made sufficiently dizzy by the demon drink."

With each example, Crispin Walsh nodded with quiet grunts of understanding, while the divot between John Howard's eyebrows carved itself in deeper. Zachary himself felt torn between father and master, and was not sure what to think—though he'd been initially convinced of what he saw, and the logic behind it, he felt that there was something missing from the presentation. All of it was, for lack of a better word, grotesque.

As the sun descended in the late-afternoon sky, dimming the barn further still and lighting the scrim on the stage in shades of gold and red, Fox took the stage alone to introduce his final exhibit. "This last example is one with which I must take care," he said. "Both for her sake and for yours, I cannot bring her in front of the curtain to be seen with the naked eye: she must remain behind it, so that you may only view her silhouette. She takes no pleasure in the gazes of strangers, which may either make her weep violently or send her flying into a rage; as for you, were you to see her face-to-face, you might vomit, or go temporarily mad. Even the most adventurous, curious mind has its limits on what it can bear to know before it breaks."

Behind the scrim, Zachary saw a shadow, oddly shaped but suggestive of a human form, taking on definition as it approached. As his mouth went dry, he recalled John's words from the day before: *Mrs. Glasse wondered if she were not looking on some kind of chimera.*

"Consider," Fox said, "the woman with child who *reads*. Who seeks to occupy her mind with matters of art and science at a time when she is intended to embrace the role assigned to her by God, that of a wife, and of a mother. Who spends her days in the company of imaginary folk such as Moll Flanders and Roxana the Fortunate Mistress, while her belly swells and her needle goes neglected. Who fails to meditate on her responsibility to the new life that grows inside her. Such a woman's thought is *torn in two directions*—is it no surprise that if she were to give birth to a child in such an afflicted state of mind, that it would assume the most hideous of manifestations?

"Behold," Fox said, "the *woman with two heads*."

As the audience collectively drew in a breath, the translucent scrim billowed forward slightly as the woman behind it pressed her face—no, no, her *faces*—against it. She seemed to be roughly five feet tall, and her proportions beneath the waist, as indicated by her silhouette, appeared to Zachary to be close to normal, but her shoulders were disturbingly broad, and the two heads atop them were wedged tightly against each other. The leftward head was perfectly vertical, while the one on the right canted away from it, as if it were forever attempting to escape. Zachary tried to imagine what that must be like for her (for them? He didn't understand, and couldn't decide): another ear constantly brushing against your own ear; another mind in another brain, eternally so close to yours, always forcing its own troubled thoughts upon you; the pace of your own heart speeding because of another person's panic. Or perhaps there was only one mind shared between them; perhaps one of the woman's skulls held only dreams, or fog, or nothing at all.

Silence fell in the barn as the woman stood behind the rippling scrim, its hem lifted tall enough to display her feet, clad in a pair of pointed green silk brocade shoes, fastened with red ribbons. Fox's gaze swept back and forth across the audience, his shoulders squared, his jaw set in pugnacious challenge, daring someone to speak. Crispin Walsh closed his eyes and covered his face with a trembling hand; John Howard looked at the woman behind the curtain, and at Fox, and at the reactions of the audience members, and back to the woman again, as if he were contemplating a particularly difficult conundrum.

"Every woman is a wonder," Fox said, "and every woman carries within her the capacity to be the conduit for one of God's miracles. For what else is the birth of a human being but the sure confirmation of God's grace and power? But a woman who does not take care of her own mind during the time of her pregnancy, who does not fully accept the role with which God has chosen to favor her, presents"— and here his voice rose—"a *danger:* not merely to herself, or to her offspring, but to the public. For such poor creatures as you have seen before you today become the public's burden, even as they are outcast from society; they are forbidden to darken the doors of those of us who are not malformed, and yet they have no homes of their own."

Fox looked down at his feet as if in prayer; when he lifted his head again, his eyes glistened. "The exhibition that you see before you today is, I believe, my calling, and my moral duty," he said. "The few pennies that I collect from you allow me to give these people a domicile and occupation for some months out of the year, where they might not have had one otherwise and been reduced to charity. If you can find it in your heart to favor us with an additional donation, my assistant will receive your gift at the exit; even the smallest of coins will help.

"And with that, my exhibition ends. Good day to you all."

Behind the curtain, the woman dipped in a brief curtsy and retreated, her silhouette dissolving into a blur with each slow step backward.

*

"I am glad I attended that event," Crispin Walsh said, once he had left the barn with Zachary and John. (He had given an extra penny to the girl with the birthmark who stood at the door, collecting coins in an upturned three-cornered hat; John, on the other hand, had distractedly walked past the girl as if she hadn't even been there. As Zachary had passed, the two of them had briefly locked eyes, and the girl had grimaced and wrinkled her nose at him in a manner that inexplicably made him wish for her to do it again.)

"That was . . . surprisingly salutary," Crispin continued. "A reminder that not all of God's messages are to be found beneath the roofs of chapels, or between the covers of sacred texts." Zachary somehow had the feeling that he was intended to take this as a concession in an argument that he and his father had once had, long ago.

Crispin favored John with the briefest of bows, as if men of God could only be expected to bend so much. "Good day to you both," he said, turning to take his own path home. Zachary felt a brief tugging at his heart as his father walked away, but after a single misplaced footstep, he righted himself and fell in line with his master.

John was quiet, striding along with his hands clasped behind his back, and Zachary thought it best to leave him to his contemplation. Then, finally, he spoke. "Zachary."

"Yes, sir."

"Did you believe all that you saw today?"

Even as he recalled the bear's monstrous eye buried in the man's back, fixing him beneath its stare, Zachary hesitated: the fact that the question was even asked suggested that there was at least one wrong answer. "I don't know," he said, after a pause that, in his own ears, went on too long. "I know that I saw things, but . . . it is hard to truly say what they were."

"I don't know, either," said John. "I do know that we were . . . restricted, from fully observing, through means that were perhaps circumstantial, perhaps sly. This raises suspicions."

"What do you mean?"

"Did you notice? The exhibition was arranged so that the afternoon sun would shine into our eyes. And we could not see as well as we might have in broad daylight. What we believed we saw may have been what Nicholas Fox said it was; or it may have been fraud from beginning to end; or a mixture of the two, truth and falsehood blended together. The fellow with the ursine affliction may have had a rug attached to his back with some sort of glue, made for the purpose of deception; there may have been some rudimentary puppetry involved, some throwing of voices. The so-called 'boneless girl' may have merely been a pile of poultry with a wig on top. The man whose mother had a supposed love of viewing hangings may have had the shape of his head altered in the past, through some kind of necessary surgery. An illusion of a two-headed woman might be accomplished through any number of means—perhaps a second false head, attached to the pretender's shoulder, crafted from a substance light enough for her to support it. She may have stood behind the scrim so that we could fill in the silhouette we saw with our own imaginings, taking them as fact."

Zachary found this train of thought strangely deflating, and his realization of the truth of John's reasoning was laced with a resentment that he thought it wise to disguise.

"And I am inclined to dispute Mr. Fox's . . . theories of generation," John continued. "If it were fully true that the bodies of children are shaped by their mothers' minds, what about the children of mothers who are more innocent than most? Shouldn't the daughters of sinless women sport angel's wings, or possess eyes that sparkle in darkness? Did it not seem strange to you that the transformations we witnessed today were always monstrous? That they were always meant to punish?"

Suddenly Zachary wished he'd never seen the exhibit that he'd been so excited to attend. "I suppose, sir," he said, and heard a sadness in his own voice.

They trudged along together in silence as night began to fall. Then John said, his voice just above a whisper, "I believed it."

"Sir?"

"The two-headed woman. When I saw her, for the first time, behind the curtain, I believed in the truth of her, and the reason for her existence. I had no doubt. Only when I had left the barn did I start to question, to consider alternatives. It was as if a spell had been lifted once I had come into the open air."

Zachary nodded.

"Here is another question," John said. "In the moment when we were in the barn, looking at the woman as she stood behind the curtain. If all of us believed in her, would not her existence be a matter of fact, and not a fraud?"

"I don't understand."

John's pace slowed as he wrestled with the idea. "The truth of the matter. Is it a thing that exists outside of our minds, waiting for us to perceive it and know it as true? Or is truth a thing that collectively resides within the minds of all men, a matter of consensus, subject to debate, subject to alteration? The world outside our minds neither true nor false, but merely there?"

"I—" Zachary shook his head. "I am uncertain, sir."

"As am I," said John. "I am led to consider that the latter possibility may be the case; that our world has some secret horror that I cannot fathom if so, controlling the minds of men though it is impossible to perceive with our senses alone.

"But put such thoughts aside: they will keep you awake at a time when you need rest, for tomorrow. We are home."

CHAPTER II

THE ROYAL TOUCH.

A few days later, Mrs. Phoebe Sanders paid a visit to John Howard's practice, towing along her shy and lanky son Oliver, who had begun to display symptoms of the king's evil. Phoebe was more or less the parish's *de facto* Overseer of the Poor—it was her husband, Archibald, who had been elected under duress to the unpaid position last Easter, but after a month or so, his wife had discovered that the duty of deciding which members of the parish were deserving of poor relief dovetailed nicely with her hard-won and diligently defended status as Godalming's preeminent gossip. It soon enough became evident to all the town that Archibald was more interested in discovering what mysteries lay at the bottom of a glass of beer than in considering the welfare of the town's citizens, and would dispense funds to needy families only after a word from Phoebe in his ear. This fact gave her the chance to inquire with shameless relentlessness into the lives of the townsfolk under the guise of a woman whose only aim was the determination of the proper amount of charity, and to carry the news to people like John Howard who might not hear it otherwise, delivered along with stern pronouncements of the moral worth, or lack thereof, of the temporarily indigent.

The scrofulous boy's tumor lurked behind his right ear. As Howard folded the ear back to examine the lesion, Zachary sensed an uncommon tentativeness in his behavior: he leaned backward slightly and squinted at it, rather than bringing his face close to the affliction as was his usual habit. "Its color is uniform," he said. "It hasn't yet ruptured. A single cluster of kernels, and it hasn't spread." He looked at Oliver's mother. "This could be much worse. How is his health otherwise? A lassitude, I'd expect."

"He sleeps half the day if we let him," said Phoebe. "And his food goes untouched unless we threaten to punish him. It's gone on like this for longer than a week—I only noticed the lesion just now."

"You are nonetheless fortunate, I believe," John said. "The distemper is still in its early stages. Removal by incision should cure it fairly easily.

"Zachary," said John as Oliver's eyes widened in terror and he looked at his mother with a barely audible whimper, "pour a glass of gin for our young guest, and lay out my tools."

*

In the room across the hall in which John would perform the operation, Phoebe looked at the array of scalpels on their wooden tray, neatly aligned parallel to each other and equidistant, as Zachary had quickly learned that John preferred. "Knives," she said.

"These are knives, yes," said John. "And knives bring blood: if you are squeamish, it will be best for all involved if you do not watch."

Phoebe edged closer to John. "There is . . . no other way? An unguent of some sort? Might you mix up some manner of healing balm?"

"The only other way is for the disease to spread: across his neck, onto his face. It will turn an angry purple; it will scar. And members of the sufferer's family are more likely to contract it, the longer it persists."

Frowning, she retreated. "Knives seem so . . . primitive. I don't like them; neither does he."

"To bear illness when we have the wisdom and the method to relieve it is even more primitive, I would hazard. Mrs. Sanders."

Oliver entered the room with Zachary just behind him; the afflicted boy's cheeks glowed bright pink, and he seemed not to have a care in the world. John patted the operating table with his hand. "Up here. Lie on your stomach."

"Fifteen years ago," Phoebe said, "I would have taken him to a minister, instead of you. I would have taken him to *this* boy's father." She motioned toward Zachary, the lackadaisical gesture suggesting that she saw him as a poor stand-in for a genuine cleric. "He would have identified the disease just as well as you did—I knew it when I saw it myself; the diagnosis needs no *expertise*—and then I would have journeyed to London, with a certificate in hand that would have gained me admittance to a healing ceremony performed by Queen Anne herself. Think of it!"

"This will hurt for a few moments," John said, leaning over Oliver, scalpel poised. "But it will be over soon enough. Breathe slowly; breathe deep. Think of nothing other than your breaths, in and out."

"The queen would have cured the boy with a *touch,* for no cost at all, and placed a golden medal around his neck in the bargain. But those days are past. That England is gone."

"Zachary," said John, "hold him still. Pin back his ear. And don't touch the lesion."

"Now we are ruled by a *German*," said Phoebe, drawing out the word in contempt. "Who chooses not to exercise the gift that God has granted to all true kings and queens of England since time immemorial. Have you ever stopped to consider why King George of the House of Hanover would choose to forgo to use the royal touch? Unless—"

With a sigh, John turned away from his patient to face Phoebe. "I offer you two choices, before you warm to your chosen theme," he said. "Either continue your political carping, in which case I will cease my efforts here and leave you to ship this child off to Rome, where I believe the Pretender still performs the service you describe. Perhaps young Oliver here will come back cured, and a Jacobite.

"Or you may close your mouth, and let me work."

Phoebe closed her mouth.

*

Once the surgery was complete, and John had cleaned his hands by standing outside and having Zachary douse them with two buckets of well-drawn water, John left Zachary to bandage Oliver, and escorted Phoebe into his sitting room. He felt a twinge of guilt for snapping at Phoebe in the midst of the operation, and though he was the only surgeon available in the parish and could therefore have forced his clientele to put up with any of his changes in mood, he did not want to acquire a reputation as a curmudgeon: soothing small talk was called for, in advance of the presentation of the bill.

Phoebe sat across from John's desk, fidgeting and angry, but as soon as John asked her if she knew of any interesting events that had occurred in town in recent days, she relaxed and turned voluble, as if she'd at last received the signal for which she'd long been waiting. "Well. I *had* to give Mrs. Mitton a small bit of money," she said, the practiced hushed voice and cocked eyebrow presumably signaling a secret relayed in confidence. "When I saw her with such poor posture I knew what had gone wrong, but I thought it polite not to let on that I noticed: it was only a matter of moments before she confessed to me in a whisper that she'd had to pawn her only stays. Why, I believe she'd convinced herself that none of us could tell! But she's no longer nineteen. Right away I said, 'Here, have a couple of coins to fetch them out, you don't look yourself without them. I'll settle with Archie later.' The poor woman looked so grateful, I tell you. And I gave two shillings to the Tofts: I don't think Mary's seen a single day without melancholy since her miscarriage, and her husband seems to know no cheer either. Joshua must sit idle half the time—Lord knows there's no money in cloth. Mary's work in the hop fields might bring in a few pennies a day, but what will they do for the winter? It's a year of bad fortune for them. I said, 'I want you to put this toward socks for yourself and your child. I'll settle with Archie later.' Come November the poor fund will be stretched thin, but for now we will do what we can—"

Phoebe cut off her monologue at Oliver's timorous entrance. Zachary had a steadying hand on Oliver's shoulder, though the patient seemed to be in no danger of falling; Zachary also appeared to have used a bandage for Oliver's ear that was more appropriate for a compound fracture of the leg, tying it with knots that sailors had yet to discover. Half of young Oliver's face was eclipsed, and he peered at his mother out of one downcast eye. John sighed. It would do.

"I don't expect that the scrofula will recur, with the proper treatment," he said, pushing back his chair and standing. "As I said, we detected the distemper before it could progress. Change the bandage regularly until the wound heals; you need not be as . . . thorough as my assistant has been. His diet should promote digestion: mutton; poultry; corn bread. A broth of marjoram and mint, morning and evening. Avoid food that causes winds and vapors: onions, leeks, beans—"

"No more *farting*," Oliver said sorrowfully.

"It is indeed a tragedy to rob you of what I gather is one of your greatest pleasures," John replied, "but it must be done for your health; that of your family will, I presume, be a beneficial secondary effect. One shilling, Mrs. Sanders."

*

Over supper that evening, an asparagus ragout prepared by Alice, Zachary said to John, "I didn't understand what Mrs. Sanders said today. About the queen curing scrofula with a touch."

"You were but a babe in those days," said John, "but it is as she said. The late queen embraced a ritual that had been practiced by England's rulers for centuries. It is why another name for the disease is the 'king's evil': because it is thought by many that the king has—or had—a special ability to cure it. After the Restoration, Charles II alone touched tens of thousands. He gifted each supplicant with a golden touchpiece inscribed with the figure of an angel, signifying that the glory of the cure was to be credited to God alone, and not to the king. But once King George took the throne after Queen Anne's death—before your third birthday, Zachary—he abandoned the practice, for reasons known only to himself."

"That sounds selfish to me," Zachary said, frowning. "If I could cure the sick just by touching them, I would touch all the people I could."

"It is a complex issue," said Alice. "John is perhaps too circumspect to spell this out for you, so the duty falls to me. It may be that King George no longer offers the royal touch not because he chooses not to, but because he secretly fears that he does not have the ability to perform it, and will therefore not risk the attempt. The events that led to George's ascension would require a lecture, but let it suffice to say that in decades past, the powers that be decided that to have a Catholic seated on our throne would be the worst of all possible fates. So members of Parliament performed a close examination of the royal family tree while standing on their heads with their left eyes shut—"

"Alice exaggerates, Zachary."

"Not by much. As I was saying: through the use of soul-corrupting dark arts, Parliament deduced that the proper king of Great Britain is one Georg Ludwig von Braunschweig-Lüneburg, a Lutheran who speaks not a word of the native tongue of the nation he rules. If King George tried and failed to execute the royal touch, it would bring unwanted additional attention to an already vexing question of legitimacy—it would suggest to those who are foolish enough to give credence to such things that God confers the talent only on Britain's true ruler, who in this instance might be the Catholic Pretender James, now in exile on the Continent. Then we'd be in for yet another nuisance of a Jacobite uprising, yet another feeble failed invasion. Perhaps George thinks it best to let the issue lie. And I cannot blame him."

"There are other possible explanations that are . . . not so political," said John. "It may be that King George does not practice the royal touch not because he believes he lacks the power to heal, but because he believes that *no one* has the power to heal with a touch, whether a king or no. He may think, as many now do, that the time of miracles is past. The practice of the royal touch has its skeptics, with louder voices in recent years, and knowledgeable people have offered other explanations for its seeming efficacy. Daniel Defoe has claimed that the gold in the touchpiece that was given to scrofula sufferers had occult properties—that is, it was the touchpiece that healed the disease, not the king. Others think that the cure was effected through the power of the sufferer's imagination—that the momentous experience of breathing the same air as the monarch caused the sufferer to believe that he was being healed, and so he was."

"It's just like the stories we heard at the exhibition last week," said Zachary. "How the imaginations of the mothers changed the shapes of their children, and made them strange."

"It is . . . somewhat similar," said John as Alice sighed in an exasperation she could not be troubled to conceal.

"But what difference does it make if someone has the king's evil and they're cured of it through the powers of their own mind, instead of by the king touching them?" asked Zachary. "Is that bad? If that was what King George believed about how the royal touch worked, wouldn't he have only stopped the ceremony if he thought that what he was doing was bad?"

"It would be a deception," said Alice. "Much as, I would hazard, the audience of which you were a part a few days ago was deceived by that Nicholas Fox fellow."

"But it is incorrect to claim that what the kings of past centuries did was deceptive," said John. "Certainly, the monarchs themselves believed in the practice. We have the published testimonies of the sufferers themselves, and of surgeons of good reputation, who professed that their patients were cured by the royal touch when no other means was effective. Though perhaps it's the case that what the sufferer generously described as a 'cure' was in fact only a coincident reduction in symptoms, or an increased willingness to tolerate those symptoms, granted by the experience of the ceremony. Or perhaps the ceremony led the sufferer to engage in a persistent act of self-delusion, so that a sick man who wore the king's medal would look in a mirror and see a healthy man looking back. It is difficult to say without resorting to conjecture. We simply do not know enough about the matter to speak with confidence."

John pushed back his chair and stood. "But what happened in

the presence of past kings and queens is no concern to us. If a patient comes to me with the symptoms of scrofula, or any other distemper, I will use the tools available to me to effect a cure: my eyes; my hands; my expertise; my books; and my knives. These are all I have. Leave the patient's mind to the patient; leave the king's beliefs to the king; and leave God's thoughts to God."

CHAPTER III

A CONCERNED HUSBAND.

T he colors began to fade from the world as September slipped into October. With each passing day the sun struggled a bit more to lift itself above the horizon, its light cutting feebly through hazy clouds as it lumbered across the sky; afternoon gusts of wind played with coat lapels and hinted at the coming winter; night came on faster and lasted longer, and those who wandered Godalming's streets after dark looked like ghosts of themselves, pale in the icy starlight, slow-footed and enervated.

The hop season had neared its end, the sticky green cones plucked from their bines and dried and baled; a faint smell of beer still lingered on the hands of the harvesters, and yellow powder tinted their finger-nails. Wives weighed purses in their palms and asked themselves if the coins inside were sufficient to keep a larder stocked through the coming winter. In past years, the town's women would have commenced the steady knitting of woolen socks, a pair a day extruding from their needles as their fingers flew, hands temporarily divorced from bodies and acting of their own free will. But with the local decline in sheep-herding, the necessary yarn would be too difficult to come by, and too dear to allow a decent profit to be turned. And even Londoners now preferred to import their woolens from the Continent—those once desirable English socks, even if they were made, were nearly certain to go unwanted. Families without sufficient reserves would have to make ends meet through other means.

Neither Zachary's master nor his father had any cause for concern: a mere change of season would not alleviate the constant need of the people for medical treatment or spiritual comfort. Over a supper of Alice's simple roast chicken, which had quickly become one of Zachary's favorite dishes, John Howard told Zachary that he expected a change in the nature of the duties required of him in the coming months. "Fewer wounds and broken bones," he said. "Less time spent outside at work, in the close company of hammers and blades; less of a chance for boys to find mischief, falling from trees and roofs. More illnesses of the chest and throat. More need of my services as a man-midwife, this month and the next."

"Fire's not the only means of heat that families resort to in winter," Alice said, in response to the evident confusion on Zachary's face. "October is when women pay the bill for January's warmth."

"I . . . see," Zachary said, nodding with what he seemed to believe was an expression of sagacity.

Exasperatedly, Alice made a circle with the middle finger and thumb of her left hand and inserted the index finger of her right, in and out, in and out. "Alice!" said John, as Zachary's eyebrows raised and twin blushes appeared on his cheeks.

"Well, we're supposed to teach the boy; it's in the contract that *you* signed," said Alice. "Clearly he's learned little about the ways of the world from that cleric father of his. Is he not fourteen? Should he not at least have stumbled across those passages in the Bible that address the subject of fucking, the topic that any healthy fourteen-year-old thinks of more than any other? The poor thing's been kept in the dark his whole life, to no good end."

"Alice!" John cried again, the pitch of his voice uncommonly high. His hands twitched as he began to lift them toward his ears and stopped himself.

Alice smiled. "I'm pleased to know that you have not forgotten my name after all these years of marriage, dear husband."

*

Autumn was the season when Crispin Walsh's sermons tended to drift toward the subject of hellfire, as if he, too, wished to do what he could to provide warmth for others. "It is easy enough for a man to follow God's precepts in days of clear skies and sunlight," he said to Zachary during one of the boy's increasingly infrequent visits to his parents' home. "A man is most likely to strive to enter heaven if he feels he already has one foot through its gates. But in times of darkness, the fear of damnation is a more useful means of keeping the flock on its proper path than the promise of salvation. Summer days call for the carrot; winter days warrant the stick."

At times, it seemed to Zachary as if his father's God was constituted entirely of the commands that he had given, or that he had created humans solely in order to give himself beings over which he could exercise control. (And perhaps it was also true that Crispin Walsh saw this God as worthy of emulation. More often now, when Zachary was in the company of his father, they didn't have conversations: instead, Crispin gave Zachary orders to complete chores that Zachary felt were beneath any fourteen-year-old boy, never mind one that was a budding surgeon. Zachary suspected that the chamber pot whose foul, murky contents sloshed against its edges had been left to stew until the last moment, in the hope that the son would return, convinced of his own wretched prodigality even if it was not the case, asking for forgiveness and a place as a servant, even if such forgiveness was unneeded.)

Zachary had little idea of what John Howard thought of God; he wasn't sure that Howard himself had much of an idea, either. His best guess was that, if Crispin's God made humans in order to have subjects, John's made humans in order to be surprised by their actions, or perhaps bemused. John seemed surprisingly comfortable with *not knowing,* in a way that Zachary's father did not; John seemed paradoxically secure in his uncertainty, while his father would have seen the display of such uncertainty as a sign of weakness, an absence of faith.

What did Zachary himself think of God? His thoughts were difficult to articulate to himself. Even the mere idea of "believing in God" was, he thought but was afraid to say, strange: though he was surely not an atheist, the word *God* held no meaning for him in the way that words did for things he could see or touch, like chairs, or knives, or chamber pots. But the adults with whom he spent his life all seemed to "believe," even if the God in which they placed their belief seemed to wear a different face for every person, no two completely alike: to one man, a giver of rules; to another, a capricious and inscrutable judge; to still another, a distant observer of mankind's foibles and grasping attempts to make sense of the world. Even Alice, in her occasional joyous blasphemies—he recalled her clear delight at getting the chance to speak the words *Bible* and *fucking* in the same sentence—seemed to confirm her belief that there was Someone to blaspheme against (and who presumably was relaxed enough to find that blasphemy as amusing as Alice herself did).

Yet all of them probably thought that they all believed in the same God, who had the same shape in the minds of others as he did in their own. What sort of God could that be, who appeared in different guises to every person, but who had no presence here in the world, except in tales of long-ago miracles? Why, if he wanted to ensure that his followers would believe in him with certainty, would he not manifest in some manner that all could see with their own eyes, and agree on what they saw? What benefit could God gain from concealment, or from secrecy?

*

On October 13, 1726, the first day of the year that was chilly enough to compel John Howard to light a fire in his office, his first visitor was one Joshua Toft, a journeyman in the cloth trade.

The man was hulking and hirsute, and stood at the threshold of Howard's office, a faded, weather-beaten cloth cap clutched in his hands. His slumping posture suggested a diffidence at odds with his frame: with his stooped back and drawn-in shoulders, he seemed as if he genuinely believed he was half his actual size. His eyes were at odds with the rest of him, twin glints of silver twinkling in the shadows cast by his hooded brows.

John closed the volume of Locke on his desk, putting it aside with a mixture of relief and regret: he was finding Locke's pedantic definition of infinity to be deeply befuddling, but unpleasant as it was, his confusion had a cast to it that signaled an impending enlightenment. It would take him another morning to pick up the thread of reasoning once he dropped it. Alas: too late. "May I help you?" he asked, stifling a sigh, feeling the flickering flame in the back of his mind go cold.

Joshua Toft took two timid steps forward, eyes on the floor. He mumbled something John couldn't catch: a stuttered sibilant, a word that sounded like "wife," and little else. "Speak up," John said, becoming aggravated.

"My wife!" Joshua fairly shouted, then cringed as if startled by the sound of his own voice. "My wife," he said again. "Sh . . . she's. She's . . . she's with child. It's time."

He looked away from the floor and at John, who was leaning back in his chair, staring up at Joshua in puzzlement. "It's time," Joshua said again, his voice now steady and even, though his posture still suggested an instinctive supplication. "We need you. Today. Certainly before nightfall. Perhaps now."

Slowly, John pushed back his chair and stood. He looked at Joshua, then down at the book before him, as if some secret were hidden between its covers that needed urgent deciphering, then back at Joshua again. "That cannot be," John said quietly; then, again, louder: "No. That cannot be."

"I tell you, it is," said Joshua. "Perhaps I am not the expert in human anatomy that you are. But I know my wife, and I trust my eyes."

"Sit," said John, gesturing toward an empty chair.

"We don't have—"

"Sit, I said."

With slow steps Joshua found his way toward a chair and collapsed into it, the joints crying out as his formidable weight settled. He began to wring his cap in his large, meaty hands, as if he intended to tear it in two.

"Mr. Toft," John said, sitting down behind his desk once more and attempting to infuse his voice with a warmth and gentleness that he did not at all feel, "it has not even been six months since your wife's . . . untimely exclusion, in the spring. The blessing of a pregnancy, even one that might appear to have progressed far along, is easily within the realm of probability: I grant you that. But to suggest that my services are needed urgently? That the birth is mere hours away? This defies belief—my apologies, but there is no other honest way to state it."

The silver in Joshua's eyes brightened. "I know what I see," he said, his voice rising. "We have had three children before this—James, and the girls Clara and Bridget, both taken by the smallpox two years back. I am no fool. *Sir.*"

"I did not intend to suggest you were," said John. "I offer you my sincerest apologies, once again. But you do see the problem here, all the same? The situation presented to me requires either strange biology, or new mathematics; I refuse to ponder the latter, and cannot find any justification for considering the former. There must be some mistake; the facts must not be as they seem."

Joshua became still more anxious, twisting his cap in his hands, biting his lower lip, knocking his knees against each other. "There is . . . something else," he said. "This is a matter of shame for me; when I tell you of it, I fear you will come to the wrong conclusion, and call me the fool I say I'm not."

"Speak freely, Joshua: I am a doctor, not a judge. And these walls have overheard more confessions than you can ever know, from patients who contracted their illnesses through sins beyond most men's ability to forgive." John spread his arms in magnanimity. "I promise you: your secrets will remain within this room."

Joshua sat in silence for nearly a full minute, and John thought it wisest to stay silent as well, and wait. Then, with a long, heavy sigh, Joshua said, "Since the . . . exclusion . . . I have not . . . lain with my wife. But I tell you: I am no cuckold, either, and Mary is not one for adulterous intrigues. I know her mind as I know my very own."

John frowned. "Whether or not this is the case—"

"It is *not!*"

"I believe you. As I intended to say—whether or not this is the case, adultery would not resolve the basic impossibility of what you claim. Though it is true that the lack of adultery makes the situation even more confusing."

"There is . . . still more I might reveal," said Joshua, his voice barely above a whisper.

"Friend, you need not parcel out the details of this case in such a parsimonious manner," John replied. "The knowledge only has value after I've received it."

"You may perhaps not find this credible, sir. My wife . . . these past few months, she . . . talks in her sleep. Mumbling, but also . . . curses. The foulest language. I can't bring myself to repeat it. And, a few weeks ago, she began to weep in her slumber. Each night, without fail, I am awakened by her sobs. In the morning I ask her about her troubled sleep, and she remembers nothing."

"It seems that the two of you have failed to put the past behind you," said John. "All of what you describe to me—the illusion of a pregnancy by which you are both convinced; the ceasing of your marital relations; the woman troubled by dark dreams—all this suggests to me that neither of you has brought yourself to accept the unfortunate loss of your child a few months ago. I fear, Joshua, that you and your wife have indulged in a mutual comforting fantasy, in an attempt to recover—"

Joshua leaned forward. "Sir. She weeps not tears, but blood. In the morning I see the evidence on her face: twin tracks of red, leading back from the corners of her eyes to her ears. And spots of blood on our bedding as well."

John Howard stared at Joshua in silent shock.

"For months now," Joshua continued, "I have attempted to turn a blind eye to these details, for they were too bizarre for me to comprehend, and I could only hope that they would somehow vanish just as they came. Her restless sleep; her bloody tears; her complaints of the symptoms of pregnancy, despite the fact that relations between us have grown cold, and her belly has not swollen. But she tells me, this morning, that a child is ready to come, and I believe her. I do not understand what I see, but I can no longer pretend that I do not see it.

"And sir—I am terrified."

*

"Remain here for a moment," John said to Joshua; then he stood, left the office, and crossed the hallway to his surgery room, where Zachary was perched on the operating table, reading a small, leather-bound copy of Tauvry's *A New Rational Anatomy.* (John glanced at the chapter title on the open page, "On the Sense of Love," and reminded himself that he would have to explain to Zachary that just because certain parts of the body did not have functions that made for sala-cious reading did not mean that they were unimportant. It would be good for the boy to spend as much time contemplating spleens as he did testicles.) "Did you overhear our conversation in the other room?" he said.

"Much of it," said Zachary, which of course meant *All of it.*

"It is . . . quite unusual. I have as little understanding of this as the man who has paid us a visit—perhaps even less. But you and I will attend this woman. I expect that this mystery will resolve itself the moment I lay eyes on her, and that treatment of the mind and soul are required here, rather than ministry to the body.

"But one never knows." John sighed, and then a wry smile bloomed on his face. "Perhaps we will witness something wonderful today."

CHAPTER IV

A BIRTH.

The Tofts' home was a mile and a half distant from Godalming's center, a thirty-minute journey on foot. Joshua Toft had a long, lurching stride, kept a brisk pace, and wasn't one for idle conversation, and so he soon drew far enough ahead of Zachary and John for the two of them to speak together in low voices without concern for being overheard.

The worn leather satchel that contained the tools of the surgeon's profession bounced against Zachary's leg as he carried it. Concealed among them was one of the rarest of medical implements, which John Howard kept under lock and key apart from all his others, only bringing it out in circumstances such as these: "midwifery forceps," which Howard had obtained through means that he refused to describe. The forceps had been a tightly held secret of the legendary Chamberlen family of surgeons for, Howard guessed, sixty years or more; Howard judged that the tool was the key to the Chamberlens' famous skill in matters of difficult births. "It is a sin to keep such valuable knowledge to oneself, to invent a lifesaving device only to use it to procure oneself an advantage in trade," he'd said, though Zachary could not help but notice that Howard himself did not choose to advertise his ownership of the forceps, preferring instead to let his local reputation as a veritable miracle worker grow through word of mouth. That Joshua had chosen to solicit Howard's services instead of those of a conventional midwife spoke well of the forceps' quiet effect.

"Are you nervous?" John said. "I understand. The event that we are about to oversee was, until recently, considered one at which only women ought to be present. Women preferred to keep their mysteries and rituals to themselves; men preferred not to trouble their minds with them. An agreeable situation for all. But times have changed. The advanced knowledge of childbirth that we have acquired in recent years now places it more clearly in a surgeon's purview, and makes it the duty of men, no matter what noises midwives might choose to make about the ruination of their womanish ceremonies. The word *man-midwife* is a tortured locution, and somewhat embarrassing, but I accept it."

Zachary nodded, eyes resolutely on the road ahead of him.

"I suppose I should speak to you plainly, as Alice would," John said, dropping his voice lower still as they left the town center, veering from the main road that cut through Godalming as they followed Joshua's path. "This is knowledge you should perhaps not be granted until you are older, but it is the fate of the surgeon's apprentice to be initiated into secrets before his time."

Zachary looked up at John and offered a quick nod, his lips pinched, his face already gone bloodless.

No reason not to be honest, John thought. "Witnessing the delivery of a newborn terrifies men," he said. "It can be as difficult to watch as a death. All our lives we see the features that differentiate women's bodies from our own as sources of our pleasure; then, in the moment of birth, their true purposes are revealed. A human head emerges from the place that once served as a sheath for your yard. It is one thing to know it in theory; another thing entirely to see it. And so we speak of the process of birth in the language of miracle and mystery, to avoid confronting the fact that women's bodies are profoundly different from ours, and are *not our own.*

"I say that to say this: do not be deceived by any high-flown rhetoric you may have heard in the past about the magic of childbirth. Whatever is about to happen, as strange and even frightening as it may seem to you, will not be a miracle. It is a biological process, as much as digestion, or voiding of the bowels. It is a thing that animals do, and though we stand upright and wear garments and discourse on human understanding, we are, all of us, animals still. To believe that some sort of magic beyond our ken is occurring before your eyes may lead you to unfairly discount your own knowledge, and fail the patient in a moment of crisis. Do you see?"

"I do," said Zachary, the quiver in his voice signaling that, in fact, he did not. Well, best to see for himself: perhaps the only way for the boy to truly comprehend.

*

A small boy, perhaps two years old, was waiting in the yard outside the Toft home when the party arrived, lying on his back in the patchy grass, gazing up at the late-morning sky. Joshua reached the house ahead of Zachary and John, and from a distance, Zachary saw Joshua's quick, sharp gestures, his large, fleshy hands like ax blades cutting, signaling commands and criticism; at that, the child slowly roused himself, standing with the slouch of one who shouldered an adult's burdens and harbored an adult's resentments, or who at least had already learned to imitate such posture by example. "James," said Joshua with a desultory wave of his hand as surgeon and apprentice approached, introducing the boy with the inflection one might use for a cow in which one had a small but not undue amount of pride. James looked up at Zachary and grinned, his frock threadbare and dingy, his eyes shining in a face coated with a meticulously acquired patina of dirt.

"Stay outside, James," said Joshua, "but don't go far." He pushed the front door open and entered the house, with John and Zachary trailing behind.

It took a moment for Zachary's eyes to adjust to the dim interior. The front room was sparsely furnished, and held few if any signs of a leisure life for its occupants: three chairs and a three-legged footstool, all of wood; a tiny table with a few cups and a stack of plates; a teetotum, lying in wait on the floor to carve its autograph into a parent's unshod foot sole; no books, unlike the homes of the Walshes and the Howards, where the spines of library volumes advertised the natures of their owners as soon as guests set foot inside. The smell of the house tangled itself in Zachary's nostrils and wouldn't let go: the persistent mustiness of unwashed people forever in close proximity; the lingering smoke from hearth fire and scorched food; and, beneath that, a faint tang that put Zachary in mind of new blood, the butcher's-shop odor of meat just stripped of its pelt. He winced, blinking, and looked up to see that John was doing the same.

The bed in the back room, expansive with a wooden bedstead, spoke of better financial times for the Tofts in the past. But it was in bad shape, canting at a slight angle and sagging in the middle, with straw poking through a rent in the ticking. The sallow-faced woman who lay in its center, head propped up on a pillow, bedsheet pulled up to her neck, stared up at the ceiling in silence.

Zachary stood beside John, looking at the woman on her back in the bed as she breathed laboriously through her gaping mouth. It immediately occurred to him, with a certainty of which he was almost ashamed, that she was stupid. She had the face of a dullard: a large, sloping forehead; wide glassy eyes beneath heavy eyebrows; a lumpy, bulbous nose; fleshy, crooked lips; a double chin. Sweaty strands of sand-colored hair peeked out from beneath her faded lace cap. It seemed clear that this was a woman condemned to forever see the world through fog.

"Mary," said Joshua, nodding at the bed; then, indicating a woman whom Zachary had not yet noticed, standing next to the bed in the shadows: "My mother. Margaret." Except for Joshua, she was the tallest person in the room, slender and meager, face long, eyebrows thin and arched, dressed in the faded black of someone who had found mourning a suitable habit, and continued it long after it was warranted. She nodded once in turn, her gaze positioned halfway between John and Zachary, as if greetings were best doled out parsimoniously, and this one was expected to be shared.

John Howard stood at the foot of the bed for a minute, looking down on Mary Toft, his forehead furrowed; Margaret and Joshua Toft watched him in silence. "Zachary," he said at last, in a voice that Zachary found strangely absent of John's usual surety, "would you retrieve the stool from the other room? And after that, bring a chair for yourself. Just sit and watch today." He took the leather satchel from Zachary and extracted a bundle from it, wrapped in linen.

From outside came a cheerful squeal from James, the young boy playing at some kind of secret game he'd perhaps just invented.

By the time Zachary had brought the stool for John and the chair for himself, John had pulled Mary down closer to the foot of the bed, her knees bent, the bedsheet draped over her legs to make a sort of tent into which John could peer while seated. Silently, John pointed at the chair in Zachary's hands and at a space near the head of the bed, next to Margaret, and Zachary carried the chair over and seated himself. He could see John's face as he continued to look beneath the sheet, though what John himself saw as he examined the patient was left to Zachary's imagination, filled in by the woodcuts he'd pored over in medical manuals. *The place where a man sheathes his yard.* But preparing to transform, to become another thing not meant for men's pleasure.

He felt Margaret Toft touch him as she stood beside him, the tip of a single outstretched finger gliding back and forth along his right shoulder. The gesture was, Zachary assumed, meant to be taken as friendly, but nonetheless it made him break out in goose bumps from head to toe.

"This is . . . unusual," said John, after a few more moments. "There is bleeding here, but . . . from abrasions. There appear to be several small cuts and bruises. But I see no evidence of what I came here to—"

Mary suddenly screamed then, her left leg kicking in seizure, striking John Howard in the chest and jolting him backward.

"Labor pains," Margaret said, her finger still gently stroking Zachary's shoulder. "Since well before sunrise."

"Strange," said John, rubbing the sore spot opposite his heart, where a bruise was sure to develop.

From outside they heard the young boy's wavering wail, as if in answer to his mother's call.

John continued to examine the woman, as all in the room kept silent. At last, he looked up and at each of the others there in turn:

Joshua, Margaret, and Zachary. Then he stared into the space before him, mouth half open in confusion.

After a brief pause he returned to himself, straightening his back and shaking his head as if to clear it. When he spoke his voice was deeper and a little more imperious than usual, as if to compensate for the short moment of displayed weakness, unbefitting of an expert in his profession. "I know of nothing to do but wait," he said.

*

They did not have to wait much longer, not more than a quarter of an hour: that evening, John Howard would ruefully joke to his wife that he wished all of the deliveries to which he was summoned would be so considerately prompt.

Joshua Toft had taken to pacing back and forth between one room of the house and the other, head bowed in meditation, his broad-shouldered, gigantic back stooped. His wife continued to lie supine, knees bent, eyes on the ceiling, her body occasionally shifting slightly beneath the sheets as if to ease herself, but otherwise unmoving.

Zachary dearly wanted to fidget, and knew he could not—he was, after all, a professional, or at least aspired to wear a professional's mantle, and a professional would not jiggle his knee, or wring his hands, or hammer out a drumbeat on the floor with his feet. He tried to make eye contact with John, who was still seated at the foot of the bed, but John continued to focus solely on Mary. John was silent for the most part, forgoing the patter he usually employed to put patients at ease while he wielded his knives—his one quiet question to Mary about how she was feeling was met with a wordless mumble from the woman that nonetheless managed to convey a deep irritation, as if she had no patience for questions that John ought to have been able to answer for himself.

Zachary had almost convinced himself to slip into a reverie that he was sure would go unnoticed, sinking down in his chair, his eyes half lidded, when he felt Margaret Toft's hot breath on his ear as she stood behind him, bending over him. Its odor put him in mind of freshly turned soil, or a moldy, waterlogged book.

"Do you want . . . *tea?*" she asked, her voice a hiss just above a whisper. "It is *refreshing.* The water: it *boils.*"

"N . . . no, ma'am," he replied, sitting up straight again, not daring to turn to look at her.

Slowly, Margaret pulled back from him and rose. "You may soon wish," she said, her hand oddly heavy on his shoulder, "that you had accepted my *generous* offer."

Joshua rambled into the room, peered at each of its inhabitants in turn, swiveled, and strode out once more. John took no notice of him—he continued to watch the woman lying before him, as if attempting to will some kind of change with his mind, wishing for something to happen within her.

"Ma'am?" said Zachary over his shoulder, having second thoughts. "M-may I have some tea?"

"No," Margaret replied flatly. "You were a *foolish boy,* and now your chance is gone."

Unnerved by the exchange, Zachary briefly found himself alert once more, but his mind soon started to drift again. He wondered whether this vigil would make him miss a timely dinner—whether Alice would think to prepare something that could be left to eat cold as soon as he and John returned home, or whether he'd have to starve until supper. (Or perhaps—horrors—they'd still be here come suppertime, and through the night, and into the next day, waiting, waiting, in unending silence.) He thought about the girl with the port-wine stain on her face, from the Exhibition of Medical Curiosities: though he had only seen her twice, she had appeared in his mind ever since at the most unexpected times. Despite the birthmark, or perhaps even because of it, she had almost been pretty, and admittedly, her impish insouciance had held an inexplicable allure. When she entered womanhood, the man who could look past the blight on her face might find a kind of love with her. Perhaps beneath her clothes her skin would be of flawless porcelain; perhaps she'd be secretly piebald from head to toe, which itself might be a peculiar kind of beauty, heretofore unheard of, reserved for a lucky husband's eyes alone—

Mary Toft screamed.

She sounded as if devils were driving nails into her palms. She began to thrash wildly in the bed, kicking and moaning, arms flailing as she grimaced and punched the mattress with her fists, sending straw flying from its unstitched rent. Her wayward foot nearly caught John Howard across the jaw. "Joshua!" he shouted into the other room, clamping his hands on the surgeon's tools arrayed on the bed to stop them from spilling. "Come in here! Hold her down—calm her."

Joshua barged through the door as one of the legs at the foot of the bed gave way, splintering and shooting out from under the frame. The bed dropped with a loud *thump,* bouncing Mary and coming to rest at an angle, the sheet covering her body flying away, and as Zachary turned his head and closed his eyes, he heard a piece of crockery hit the floor and shatter in the other room.

He saw the soft flesh of a breast; he saw a pale expanse of thigh; he saw a tuft of hair in a crevice.

Joshua ran over to Mary, grabbed both her arms, and wrenched them down, pinning them at her sides; as her legs continued to kick, he bent over, placing his forehead against hers. "Be still," he whispered as she struggled, his voice even, and unexpectedly tender. "Be still. Be still." She began, slowly, to settle down, her breaths coming in hitching rasps, and John retrieved the bedsheet from the floor, shook it out, and draped it over her body once again.

Slowly, Joshua released his wife and stood. She kept her arms at her sides, teeth clenched, eyes squeezed shut and leaking tears. Then she grunted something that Zachary couldn't make out, though it sounded unpleasantly like a curse in another language.

"She says it's coming," Joshua said.

John looked up at Joshua, puzzled. "I don't see—"

Mary grunted again, louder, more clearly this time: "It's *coming.*" She threw her head back and shrieked, her body contorting beneath the sheet into a posture almost inhuman, as if her muscles wanted to snap the bones that gave them shape.

Leaning to the side and hunching to examine Mary on the lowered, crooked bed, John Howard shook his head; then, tentatively, he reached with one hand beneath the sheet that covered Mary's bent knees. He probed gently, his head cocked and his eyes closed; then, as a look of distress suddenly appeared on his face, he made a noise that was somewhere between a yelp and a bark.

He snatched his hand back, bloody, as if he'd been stung. "No," he said. *"No."*

Zachary felt both of Margaret Toft's hands on his shoulders now, pressing him down in the chair, moving close to his throat.

"No, no, no," John said, reaching toward Mary again. "No. No, no, no."

"Sir?" said Joshua, his voice remarkably placid. "What's wrong?"

"No. No." Both of John's hands were beneath the sheet now as he worked, taking deep, irregular breaths, biting his lip. Beads of sweat broke out in a line along his forehead.

Zachary felt his heart rattling against his rib cage.

John leaned toward the bed, farther than Zachary could understand, as if something beneath the sheet was grasping at the surgeon's hands, catching him, dragging him in. As Mary brought forth a larynx-tearing screech, John pulled back, nearly losing his balance and falling off his stool.

John looked at the little thing he held pinched between his thumb and forefinger, and began to weep.

It was a severed rabbit's foot.

Zachary heard the young boy James's gay laughter from outside the house, immersed in his own private amusements.

"Mary?" Joshua said, his voice barely audible. "Mary." His wife was glass-eyed, still as stone.

"No," John whimpered. "No. No." He deposited the blood-matted hunk of fur and meat with its four tiny black claws on the bed next to Mary with a strangely ceremonial reverence, as if he had no idea what else to do.

Wiping away tears with the back of his hand, John reached beneath the sheet once again.

A hind foot followed to match the forefoot; then John pulled out a thin, glistening rope of intestine, flinging it angrily to the floor. "God damn us all!" he shouted.

Zachary leapt up and tried to run, but Margaret grasped his shoulders and slammed him back down into the chair with an unexpected strength. She pressed her lips against his ear, her spittle coating it as she said, *"You should have taken the tea.* Now, sit and watch. *Boy."*

The rabbit's head came last, one of its ears broken and listing, its jaws frozen open to reveal teeth seemingly bared in a snarl, the marble of one of its eyeballs popped free from its socket, dangling from the hole by a tendril of muscle. John's initial shock and horror seemed to have given way, at last, to an uncanny reserve. Carefully, he placed the decapitated head on the bed, next to the two severed feet. He silently performed a last examination of the patient, withdrew, and covered Mary's legs neatly with the sheet.

Then he stood, nodded once at Zachary, and sprinted from the room, covering his mouth.

Zachary slapped aside Margaret's hands and followed, colliding clumsily with the wall as he ran. The acrid smell of puke hit him in the face as soon as he burst out of the front room of the house into daylight. He bent, hands on his knees, and joined John in retching, gagging as his guts twisted in his stomach and wrung themselves dry, his half-digested breakfast spattering on the ground.

The boy James stood before them in his dirty frock, pointing at John and Zachary and cackling, dancing an irregular jig to music only he could hear.

Out of breath, Zachary looked over at John, who was wiping a thread of bile away from his mouth with the back of his hand. "Sir?" he said. "I have a question."

The ghost of a smile flitted across John's face, and his red-rimmed eyes crinkled. "Yes?"

"What fee will you charge for this?" said Zachary, rising. "A shilling or two seems, somehow, too little."

CHAPTER V

Aristotle's Masterpiece.

The hours following that first horrific delivery, through the afternoon and evening and into the next day, were a blur in Zachary's memory, as if he'd somehow contrived to imbibe a few stiff doses of gin without realizing it. He remembered that he and John Howard had managed to return home, though after they'd walked a quarter mile down the road from the Tofts' house, John had realized that he'd forgotten his satchel and his implements, and shamefacedly had to turn back to retrieve them—after vomiting in tandem they'd both felt an instinctive compulsion to flee, consequences and professionalism be damned. Zachary remembered that John had closed his practice for the remainder of the day, secluding himself with his books, leaving the sick and injured to look after themselves or travel to another parish—fortunately, no one with a serious condition arrived at their door that day, and John was left in peace. He remembered sitting before the supper that Alice served, a salmagundi whose ingredients she must have been quietly collecting for days—roast chicken and potatoes and capers and onions and olives and currants and who knew what other wonderful things, all mixed together. He remembered leaving the dish almost completely untouched, asking for permission to go upstairs to his room after a few polite bites.

He remembered lying in bed, moonlight shining through the window of his loft, listening to the conversation of John and Alice below—though he could not make out the words, he could clearly discern the tenor. John's voice crept up in volume the longer he spoke, in tones of alarm that soon shaded into anger and frustration; Alice's responses were occasionally interrupted by a high ringing laughter of raillery, to which John would respond sulkily, as if wounded. (Why the mockery, so insensitive and undeserved? If only she had been there, to see for herself what he and John had seen! The vision of the rabbit's severed head with its broken ear and dislocated eye floated in the field of black behind the boy's closed eyelids.)

He remembered the dream he had had just before he slipped under—in it, he'd just gotten married hours before, and he stood with his bride beside their wedding bed as rose petals rained from the sky. She was the woman with the port-wine stain on her face, and she was naked—he knew this, even though she still wore her wedding veil and her body from the neck down was obscured by a pale, swirling mist, so that it seemed as if he were looking at an oil painting left incomplete.

The time had at long last come for the revelation of secrets, of curve of hip and shape of breast, destined to be known by him alone, for all eternity. Eager and full of ardor, breath quickened, yard standing, Zachary carefully took the veil in both hands and lifted it, to reveal the burgundy blotch that almost entirely covered the woman's face, the startlingly long incisors that protruded from beneath her top lip, the long white whiskers that drooped below her merrily twitching nose, and her blinking, shining eyes, a matched pair of inky black marbles. Then he woke.

*

Three days later, on a Sunday afternoon after services had ended and the congregation had dispersed, Zachary's father, Crispin Walsh, performed a shorter second ceremony, in which Mary Toft was churched. Seated on the front pew were the few witnesses to the ritual: the Toft family, Joshua, Margaret, James, and Mary herself, face concealed by a moth-eaten lace veil; John Howard and Zachary Walsh; and Phoebe Sanders, the wife of the Overseer of the Poor, who had decided, and which one might have reasonably predicted, to make the churching her personal business. She sat in the middle of the Toft family as if she were a well-loved cousin just arrived from a nearby town, head held high, an inappropriately wide smile worn on her face as a shield, impervious to the frequent stabs of Margaret's practiced scowls.

Crispin, still in his vestments, stood before Mary and beckoned: at the gesture Mary knelt in front of the pew on a pillow placed before her, head bowed. The cleric placed his hand on her head (and Zachary caught his father's quick glance at John Howard, who returned the look expressionlessly, even as Phoebe eagerly leaned forward in her seat in an undisguised attempt to interpret John's face).

Crispin's voice assumed the stentorian tones he used to suggest that powers greater than his own were speaking through him. "Give hearty thanks unto God," he said, "for your safe deliverance from the great danger of childbirth." Mary, in response, said nothing: she merely nodded, tentatively at first, then vigorously, until Crispin's gentle tap on her shoulder brought her to a stop.

" 'I love the Lord, because he hath heard my voice and my supplications,' " Crispin declaimed, eyes closed. " 'Because he hath inclined his ear unto me, therefore I will call upon him as long as I live.' "

This all seems so normal, Zachary thought—it seemed incredible to him that what most would consider the most salient fact of the matter was being left unaddressed. But then, why was he himself not speaking up? He had been there, after all; he'd seen it all firsthand. But at this moment, this ritual and its quick and orderly accomplishment seemed to be more important than the declaration of the truth in its entirety, for reasons he could not quite discern.

Crispin continued to recite the psalm, his right hand still on Mary Toft's head. " 'Gracious is the Lord, and righteous; yea, our God is merciful. The Lord preserveth the simple: I was brought low, and he helped me.' "

Who here knew? All of the Tofts, except perhaps for the child, who would not know what to do with such knowledge if he had it; John Howard; Zachary himself. Phoebe, with that grin plastered on her face, clearly did not. Did his father know—did he understand that the circumstances that occasioned the ceremony he now performed were most unusual? When he'd spoken of the "great danger of child-birth," had there been the smallest of quavers in his voice?

"'I said in my haste, All men are liars,'" Crispin said. "'What shall I render unto the Lord for all his benefits toward me?'"

Perhaps this ritual, performed in the same manner as all the ones before, was meant to make the past a thing that *had not happened,* by consensual agreement. Zachary's memory—of the bloody rabbit's foot retrieved; the surgeon's sudden tears; the string of guts and the mangled head that followed—would become a dream, and then that dream would dissipate as all dreams do, shredded by morning sun-light, carried away on the wind. The ceremony would convey to all who participated a welcome permission to forget, granted by the mer-ciful God who spoke in his father's voice.

"'I will pay my vows unto the Lord now in the presence of all his people, in the courts of the Lord's house, in the midst of thee, O Jerusalem. Praise ye the Lord.'" As Crispin finished the psalm and removed his hand from Mary, she stood and, head still bowed, offered the quaint suggestion of a curtsy, no more than a small dip and a bend of the knees.

From farther down the pew on which he sat, Zachary heard Phoebe Sanders's derisory snort.

*

After the ceremony had ended and Zachary began to make his way down the central aisle between the pews and out of the church (his father and John Howard a few steps behind him, heads inclined toward each other, whispering in restless consultation) he felt a hand on his shoulder—not Margaret Toft's pinching grasp, but a lighter touch. He turned to see Phoebe Sanders smiling at him. He was young, but not too young to be unaware that when adults address youths in such a familiar manner, as if they themselves are also adults, they are often in search of loose tongues. Phoebe's smile shrank slightly at his look of suspicion, then returned, more brightly still. "Isn't this so *unusual?*" she said.

"Yes, it is," said Zachary, instincts telling him to change the subject or back away, but Phoebe was too quick for him. She approached; she pounced. "I mean," she said, lowering her voice, "that if she had another miscarriage, no one wants to *say.*" She quickly counted out the months on her gloved fingers. "April was when I was here for poor Mary's last churching. May, June, July, August, September, October: barely six months—"

"Zachary!" He turned to look up at John advancing on him rapidly, his father just behind. "Do you remember those chores I asked you to finish?"

He nodded, slowly, though he did not recall any mention of chores at all.

"Well, you'd best return home and take care of them," John said, his tone uncommonly brusque.

Zachary was nonetheless glad to have been excused from Phoebe's interrogation. As he turned to go (and as Phoebe glanced sideways at John Howard, giggling sheepishly), he looked up at his father, and the expression he saw on his face was one he would never have expected there—it wavered between undisguised confusion and undiluted terror.

If he hadn't known before he churched the woman, he surely did now.

*

The next day was Monday, and Monday mornings were always quiet for John Howard's practice, as if the predictable, sedate routines of Sabbath evenings warded off the kinds of accidents that might require his attention. Zachary was awake early, for once—recent events had robbed him of his inclination to sleep in, since lying abed gave his mind too much of a chance to wander. He polished all the tools in John's operating room, then examined them once again to ensure that his work was thorough. He leafed through Heister's *Compendium of Anatomy,* the book that had been one of his first steps on the path to his apprenticeship. He looked at the illustrations, but did not see them; his eyes slid over the paragraphs uncomprehending, while his mind hummed its own dark melodies.

Eventually, heart pounding, he walked across the hall into John's office, where John was, as expected, reading *An Essay on Human Understanding.* He sat opposite John's desk, watching him read, and he waited.

John turned over a page and stared at it for some time, frowning; then he looked up at Zachary, his face downcast. "I suppose you have little interest in hearing what Locke has to say about the distinction between active power and passive power," he said.

"No, sir; I don't, really."

John sighed and shut the book before him. "I thought as much."

"We haven't talked about . . ."

"The . . . incident," John said. "I know."

"We haven't talked about it at all and it's the worst thing I've ever *seen,*" said Zachary, tears flowing freely now that had been corked up in him for days.

"I feel that I owe you an apology," said John, his own eyes watering in sympathy. "Had I known we were to encounter a sight so heinous, I would have spared you."

"I heard Mrs. Howard *laughing* at you. The night it happened. Why was she—"

"She thinks, not unreasonably, that I must be . . . mistaken, in what I saw. The tale is, indeed, difficult to accept as truth. Incredible as the story is, it shrinks in the telling—I could not make my words convey the horror of the details. And my own mind declines to consider the matter, even if I beseech it to do so. Whenever I attempt to think on last week's event, to try to form a hypothesis concerning its cause, my thoughts . . . refuse to proceed. Until I resign myself to ignorance, and move on to another, more comforting subject."

John leaned back in his chair, rubbing his eyes. "I don't know," he said. "Perhaps the incident will vanish into history and be forgotten.

I, for one, will confess that I am happy to let it do so, and I would hazard that everyone else involved would agree. Wouldn't you say?"

"I would, sir," said Zachary. "I don't ever want to have to think about it again."

John gave a single sharp nod of paternal approval. "Very well, then. A shared moment of collective delusion, here and gone. In later days we might whisper of the legend between ourselves—perhaps over the drink that will celebrate you becoming my colleague, rather than my apprentice."

"I look forward to that day, sir," Zachary said, as the two of them heard three staccato knocks on the front door.

"As do I," said John. "Now. Would you please welcome our first guest of the day?"

Zachary had barely gotten out of his chair when they heard the clanging rap of the knocker again, louder, more insistent. Wiping his eyes, he left the office to answer the door.

And when he returned a few moments later, his face was white— for behind him was Joshua Toft, his posture that of a supplicant, head lowered, hat in hand.

"Sir," Joshua said to John, "I may as well speak quickly, and plainly. The event we all witnessed, last week—I believe it's about to happen again."

"It can't be," said John.

"It is. The signs—they're all the same."

"You lie." John seemed surprised that the accusation had instinctively slipped out of his mouth.

Joshua stepped backward as if he'd been punched, his hand on his heart. "I do *not,* sir, and I ask you to see for yourself."

John rose from his seat, bracing his hands on the desk to stop their trembling. "You," he said, pointing at Zachary. "Stay here. I expect I will be back directly, complaining about a half day wasted."

"Yes, sir," Zachary said, relieved.

*

John was absent for dinner, and so Zachary and Alice ended up eating her preparation of sausages and stewed cabbage in gravy alone, the seat at the head of the dining table conspicuously empty. "Might you know what errand engages my dear husband and your benevolent master this afternoon?" she asked.

"He's gone out to—to the Tofts' home." Zachary felt strangely embarrassed, as if he were confessing misbehavior, even though he himself had done nothing wrong.

"Oh, *really*," said Alice.

The two of them continued to eat, the corners of Alice's lips turned upward in private merriment, the room silent except for the occasional clink of a fork against a dish.

"Would you like to hear a secret to a happy marriage?" said Alice finally. "No need to blush: of course you would. It is this: that a wife must not *repeat* herself. If one's dear husband is deaf to the truth the first time it's spoken, repetition will only stop his ears more tightly."

Zachary, confused, merely nodded.

"One would prefer not to be labeled a harridan," Alice continued, speaking half to herself. "A termagant, a fishwife. One must not *harangue*. Deliver the message once and have patience; wait for time and the Lord to confirm it."

Zachary tried to smile in a manner that matched Alice's, seemingly knowing and self-amused, but the cocked eyebrow he received in response signaled that he'd advertised his befuddlement about the direction of the conversation rather than concealing it, and so he gave up the charade.

Alice put down her fork. "One must be prepared for the degree of equanimity required of a woman to be immeasurable, beyond belief." She stood, and began to clear the dishes.

*

John returned to the office in the middle of the afternoon, haggard and distraught. He clutched his leather satchel of tools in one hand and held in the other a crumpled, stinking, bloodstained bundle of once white linen with something inside, weighing it down.

Wondering what had happened, fearing to hear the news, Zachary wordlessly followed John into the surgery room. Dropping his satchel carelessly in the middle of the floor, John dumped the bundle of linen on the operating table and released its corners, letting its contents tumble out in full view. He beckoned Zachary over to look; then, with a drawn and bitter expression on his face, he stood aside and gestured expansively toward the array of objects, like a traveling merchant advertising the rarest of wares.

The boy's gorge rose at the sight of another rabbit's head, this one with white fur, while the fur of the rabbit that Mary Toft had birthed last week had been dark brown. A fly perched on the surface of one of its sightless, sky-blue eyes, rubbing its front legs together. Next to the head lay a pair of clawed hind feet (one with white fur; one with brown); a long, pink, translucent string of intestine that held a series of black pellets suspended within it; and a hunk of burgundy meat that Zachary guessed was a liver.

John retrieved the medicinal gin from a cabinet, along with a pair of glasses. He poured a dose for himself, carelessly splashing the booze over the edges of the glass, and downed it immediately; then he poured a second shot for himself, along with one for Zachary. Zachary gingerly accepted his glass and quickly tossed back its contents in imitation, grimacing as the stinging gin slid down his throat.

Arms folded, John Howard stared down at the rabbit parts spread on the cloth before him; then he turned to Zachary. "We won't be able to ignore this, I'm afraid," he said quietly. "I was a fool to ever believe I could. A single occurrence such as that we saw last week might be called an anomaly, and might let itself be wished away, no matter how strange. But twice begins a pattern, and so we cannot turn from it: we must now prepare for the third instance that is sure to appear, and soon.

"It may be that the guidance of the usual medical authorities may not suffice in this instance," John said as he served himself yet another glass of gin. "We may have to stray from well-marked roads; we may have to head down darker paths."

*

A half hour later, feeling a little more relaxed, a bit less terrified and anxious, Zachary leaned over John's desk, peering at the title page of the slim volume that John had pulled from one of its locked drawers—the surgeon hadn't kept it shelved with the other books that a curious apprentice might easily browse. *"Aristotle's Compleat Master-Piece,"* he read. *"Displaying the Secrets of Nature in the Generation of Man."*

"Not actually written by the great philosopher, of course," said John. "A borrowed mantle of authority, meant to give credence to a survey of the folk wisdom of midwives. But the knowledge here has on rare occasions stood me in good stead, in cases where works with more storied reputations have failed me."

The illustrations that Zachary saw as John leafed through the volume were bizarre, and unlike the fussily precise diagrams of the medical texts with which Zachary was familiar—these seemed more fanciful, in a manner that would be suited for a book for children, were they not so grotesque. One page depicted what looked like a boy of about six years of age, covered in thick black hair from head to toe, including the insides of his ears, the tops of his feet, and the surfaces of his lips; another boy who wandered naked through a stylized valley sported four arms and four legs. All of his limbs were equally strong, none of them withered; his feet were identical to his hands, with fingers in the place of his toes. The look on his face was oddly beatific, as if he were the benevolent god of a foreign nation.

"Here," said John. "This chapter." He tapped the heading with his index finger: "Of a Mole, or false Conception; and also of Monsters and monstrous Births, with the Reasons thereof."

"Monsters," Zachary said. "Like those at the exhibit we saw, except we weren't sure whether what we were looking at was real, or some kind of trick."

Surgeon and apprentice scanned the pages together. The first half of the chapter addressed the unusual incident of a pregnant woman giving birth to a *mole*—not a living, thriving child, but a mindless, soulless, featureless mass of tissue, a dead lump of matter. "True cause therefore of this carnous conception *which we call a mole,*" said the anonymous writer who'd taken Aristotle's name, "proceeds both from the man and from the woman, from corrupt and barren seed in the man, and from the menstrous blood in the woman, both mixed together in the cavity of the womb, and Nature finding her self weak (yet desirous of maintaining the perpetuity of her species) labors to bring forth a vicious conception, rather than none, and not being able to bring forth a living creature, generates a piece of flesh."

"Horrible," said Zachary.

"But only loosely related to the case before us," John replied. "See here: three tests to determine whether a conception is true or false. A mole cannot be said to be an animal; it cannot be said to be human; it cannot bear a resemblance to its mother. Toft's issue passes the second and third tests, but fails the first—though it should not be able to be produced by her body under normal circumstances, it is clearly recognizable as an animal. But let us read further."

John flipped forward to the second half of the chapter, which switched to the subject of monsters. " 'Monsters are properly depraved conceptions,' " Zachary read aloud, " 'which are defined by the ancients to be excursions of Nature, and are always vicious either in *figure, situation, magnitude,* or *number.* ' "

"Vicious in figure," John said. "A woman birthing a beast. Vicious in situation: its components ripped apart instead of a single creature, whole. Vicious in number: two, mere days apart. We are closer now. Here: a description of the cause."

" 'As to the cause of their generation,' " read Zachary, " 'it is either divine or natural: The divine cause proceeds from the permissive will of the great Author of our beings suffering parents to bring forth such deformed monsters, as a punishment for their filthy and corrupted affection, which let loose unto wickedness, like brute beasts that have no understanding.' "

"God's condemnation, visited on sinners," John summarized. "But this seems most likely to result in creatures recognizably human, though the child might be missing an arm or a leg, or have one arm or leg too many. However. Look: farther down. The list of manners in which the woman's womb might be at fault. The third."

" 'The imaginative power, at the time of conception, which is of such force, that it stamps a character of the thing imagined upon the child.' " Zachary looked up from the page at John. "Like the creatures at the exhibition."

"Yes," John said, only the shadow of reluctance in his assent. He continued reading from the page where Zachary had left off. " 'So that the children of an adulteress, by the mother's imaginative power, may have the nearest resemblance to her own husband, though begotten by another man.' " At that he made a sound that, to Zachary, sounded something like a strange cross between a cough and a clearing of the throat. "And I believe," John continued, "that we are forced to at least consider the possibility that this powerful facility of female thought might, in rare cases, allow the woman to imagine something not only human, but other than human."

*

The rest of the chapter was a series of examples of monstrous births from France and England and Germany, from the previous three centuries (including a story about a woman with two heads "from the time of Henry the *Third*" that churned Zachary's gut: according to "Aristotle," one of the sisters outlived the other by three years, and was forced to drag the inert, decaying corpse of her sister behind her—"for there was no parting them"—until she herself succumbed to illness. He thought about the woman he'd seen behind the curtain at the Exhibition of Medical Curiosities; he wondered whether she knew what fate awaited her. Perhaps her two heads had made a pact with each other, in case one of them passed—surely in such circumstances God would not consider suicide to be a sin).

At the end of the chapter was a short didactic poem:

Nature does to us sometimes monsters show,
That we by them may our own mercies know:
And thereby sin's deformity may see,
Than which there's nothing can more monstrous be.

John closed the book, placed it back in the desk drawer, and locked it away. "Though to believe so goes against the instincts I've acquired over many years," he said, "I am increasingly sure that we have encountered a problem we will never solve if we choose to rely only on the body of knowledge exclusive to the surgeon's craft. More wisdom is required: we will have to speak to another authority.

"Zachary: tomorrow morning, would you visit your home and ask your father if he is available for a consultation with me? Bring him back with you, if possible: make it clear that the matter is urgent."

CHAPTER VI

MARY'S DREAM.

An errand to another parish for a baptism prevented Crispin Walsh from attending the birth of Mary Toft's third rabbit, two days later—John Howard supervised the delivery, with Zachary reluctantly accompanying him for observation. But the minister was present at the Toft house for the delivery of the fourth, on the morning of Friday, October 21.

By now John justifiably felt that even though he had only a few days of experience, he was right to consider himself the world's foremost expert in human-leporine midwifing, and so he approached the birth with the manner of an old hand. Zachary was proud of himself for maintaining his composure when the mangled parts of the creature were produced (this one with ink-black fur, except for a few spots of white that decorated the tip of the nose and the severed paws), and he felt a small, shameful sense of satisfaction when his father ran from the house after John extracted the expected pile of rabbit guts from the woman: the gagging and splatter of the minister's retching soon followed, easily heard from outside. When Crispin returned, stifling coughs and splutters and attempting to act as if nothing unusual had happened, Zachary and John merely offered him wordless nods of recognition—there was no need to embarrass him further. The cleric had been made well enough aware that he did not know every single thing that went on under heaven.

*

On the long walk back to John's practice, Crispin was apoplectic. "After the woman's churching, I thought you were mad when you told me what you'd witnessed," he said to John. "Or that I'd misheard. Or that you somehow wished to approach the borders of blasphemy, by telling obvious falsehoods within the church's doors. But I did not believe you, not at first—only, truly, now, do I believe, after I have seen. I offer you my apologies, for what little worth they may have to you."

"We have not always seen eye to eye on matters of midwifery," John said, and once again Zachary had the feeling that there was a past history shared between John and his father that they both thought was best only looked at sideways. "But in this case I concede that my expertise has its limits. Your voice is wanted here. It is needed."

A story there, to be sure.

*

Crispin's belief cemented itself further still at the birth of the fifth rabbit, the following Monday. Joshua's knock at John's door that morning had almost been expected, as if a predictable schedule was becoming established—however, on entering, Joshua said he had the impression that Mary would not deliver the rabbit until that afternoon. She seemed troubled, and she sometimes muttered nonsensical incantations and wept an occasional bloody tear that her husband dutifully wiped away, but she was not exhibiting the raw anguish that suggested the birth was imminent. This fortunately gave Zachary enough time to return to his home, collect his father, and meet John at the entrance to the Tofts' home, where Mary was, at this point, in a seemingly indefinite state of lying in.

The three men entered the bedroom. Mary lay on her back in a nightgown, eyes glazed, breath wheezing, stray damp locks of hair pasted to her forehead. Her husband sat at the head of the bed beside her, gently wiping her brow with a folded piece of cloth; as John entered, he raised his hand to show him the dingy square of fabric, and its faint smears of pink. John merely nodded in response, as if to speak openly of the woman's malady in her presence might somehow make it worse.

Margaret Toft sat opposite Joshua on the bed, her back to the door, a teacup held in one hand and a chipped saucer cradled in the other—as Zachary passed the threshold, she suddenly swiveled, looked over her shoulder, made unerring eye contact with the boy, and, as the attention of all others in the room focused on the patient, her crinkled face screwed itself into an exaggerated wink, the corners of her blade-thin lips curling cruelly. Then, as Zachary's breath caught and his heart stuttered, she turned away, and took a quiet sip of her tea.

Placing a hand on John's back, Crispin gently steered the surgeon back out to the front room of the house, where they spent a few minutes in quiet conference. (Zachary, left out of this, stood against the wall opposite the bed, hands behind his back.) The minister entered first when the two men returned. "Mr. Toft," he said, "I might ask something of you that may provide some useful knowledge. I—I would like to listen to your wife's stomach. With your permission."

As Mary muttered meaninglessly and kicked her legs in a quick flurry, the frayed hem of her nightgown riding up past her knees, Joshua slipped his hand into hers and gave Crispin his quiet assent. Once she calmed down, Crispin approached the bed, awkwardly leaned over her, and, clumsily bracing himself on the bed as if to touch her as little as possible, rested his head on her abdomen, the thin cloth of the nightgown between his ear and her flesh. He closed his eyes and concentrated.

There was silence in the room for a minute or two as the minister listened; then, quietly, he said, "I hear it."

Then, once again, more firmly: "I hear it."

He stood, turning to John Howard. "I have never encountered anything as strange as this," he said. "Inside her, in her stomach, I heard the sounds of . . . *opposing forces*. As of enormous rocks grinding against each other, deep in the bowels of the earth. And beneath those grinding noises, what, for a moment, sounded like a scream, of an animal being slaughtered."

"The creatures have always come out in pieces," said John.

"A possible consequence of whatever is compelling this poor woman's body to do what it was never meant to do," Crispin responded. "I believe that the forces that are materializing these beings inside her are also tearing them apart."

Mary screamed then, a throat-ripping wail that to John had become a familiar signal, even as it stabbed a needle into his ear. "Speculation will have to wait," he said. "It's time—we should take our positions."

*

Afterward, when the rabbit had been delivered, its parts wrapped in a cloth that John had brought with him—he would take it home where it would join his collection of three others of the five rabbits birthed thus far, tightly sealed in glass jars, suspended in spirits—John and Joshua led Mary into the other room of the house, where she settled herself in a chair by the window, her joints stiff. "She lies on her back now more than she sits or stands," Joshua said quietly. She looked through the curtains into the yard beyond, at the boy James running around in merry circles, making himself dizzy. A faint, exhausted smile crossed her face.

Placing a stool before her, John sat down so that he could look directly into her eyes. "Mary," he said, leaning toward her, hands clasped together. "I believe that we approach a hypothesis that may explain your condition. I must ask you—have you had any dreams? Dreams that play out in the same manner each night, their content unusual, but predictable?"

She continued to look out the window for a moment longer, bathing her face in the sunlight. Then she slowly turned to John, eyes heavy-lidded, mouth slack, and spoke, each word a labor.

*

Night after night. Every night.

I have to harvest the hops. It has to be done tonight. What isn't saved tonight will be ruined by the locusts at dawn. I have to do it alone. No one else understands.

I am in the hop fields with the scythe. Sky full of twinkling stars. Blood-red full moon. Red light on the fields. Red light on my skin.

Sometimes the swarm of locusts crosses in front of the moon and it blocks out the light. They are waiting for the sun, and then they will come down and feed.

I tried to tell the others but no one else would listen. All they wanted to do was sleep.

Swinging the scythe in the red moonlight. Back and forth. Back and forth. I must cut faster. No time to look. No time to aim. Soon I will make a mistake. But if I don't finish the harvest the world will starve.

The blade bites into flesh instead of flying quick through the stalks like it should.

I look down and a dead rabbit lies on the ground. Head cut off of its body.

Every time I have the dream I know I've had it before. I know I shouldn't swing the scythe when I do, and I do it anyway. And the rabbit always dies.

Its mate is next to it, and it comes up on its hind legs, like it's a man. Its paws have five toes, but not fingernails. Claws. It speaks. It says, You killed the queen. Now you're the new queen.

I say I'm a woman. It says, You killed the queen, and now you're the new queen! You're a God-damned sinner and you're the queen. Now you have to go into the cave.

Then I see the entrance to the cave. A dark wet slit in a sheer wall of rock. Inside it, a thousand glittering eyes, like a thousand stars.

The rabbit points with its paw that is a hand and says, Go. You're a sinner! Go!

I walk toward the cave, and the entrance spreads open for me. The ground shakes as the rock shifts.

The entrance shuts behind me as I walk through, and all the lights in all the eyes go out, and now it's dark.

Then there is fur. Everywhere, all over me, as the rabbits swarm me and chew through my clothes with their teeth and drag me down. Fur, brushing against my cheeks, smothering my face, pushing against my secret places. Pressing me down, with more of them piling on top, and more, and more, and more. Clothing damp from rabbit piss. Sharp stink of rabbit shit, so strong I can't breathe.

I cry out as one of my ribs cracks from the weight, then another. A rabbit stuffs its paw into my mouth to stop my scream, and I choke as it shreds my tongue into ribbons.

I'm a queen with a mouth full of blood. And they're going to silence me. They're going to make a home inside me. They're going to crush me. They're going to kill me. Every night. Night after night.

Then I wake.

CHAPTER VII

FOOLSCAP.

Zachary spent the following afternoon and evening—of Tuesday, October 25—with his parents, at his father's request to John Howard. The minister had seemed shaken over the events of the previous few days, and in any case John would not have denied the poor man the solace of family. Besides, he had his own work to do, a letter to write: a draft, a revision, and four fair copies, those last to be dispatched to London on tomorrow morning's coach. If he was lucky, the intended recipients would have them in hand by Thursday afternoon.

John removed a sheet of foolscap from his desk drawer, folded it neatly in half, and drew the blade of a letter opener down the crease, splitting the paper in two. Placing one half to the side, he dipped quill in inkpot and began to scratch at the other: *Dear Sir: I am a surgeon in the town of Godalming, who has come upon a most unusual case that may reward your attention.* He paused, drew a line through *unusual,* and in smaller letters, wrote *notable* above it; then he drew a second line through *notable* and wrote *significant* in its place, in smaller letters still. "Momentous?" he said to himself; then he looked up to see Alice, standing in the doorway to his office, the smallest of smiles on her face.

John saw that she held a ledger. Reluctantly, knowing what was coming, he put down his pen.

"Love," she said, entering as she pointedly ignored his unvoiced gripe, "the month of October nears its end, and I harbor concerns. I ask you not to look at me as your usual dream of a helpmeet—brimming over with wit and charm; skilled before a stove; still lithe and nubile in her middle years—but as a bookkeeper, severe and humorless, head full of naught but numbers." She placed the ledger on the desk and opened it to its most recent entries. "And *most displeased.*"

She tapped the page with the tip of her index finger. "Toft, Toft, Toft. Once every two or three days. Visit after visit, but no fee charged, no income *gained*—"

"I have, in fact, been giving them money," John said quietly, eyes still on the paper before him. "Not much. A shilling or two, each time. They seem to need it."

"One might easily deduce my opinion," replied Alice evenly, "that even if they are in need of charity, they do not deserve it from us."

John's eyebrows arched as he looked up at her. "They will," he said firmly, "receive our charity."

Alice stepped back, exhaling, and John thought he heard a single word carried on that breath, something like *tool* or *fool,* but could not be sure. No matter. He was not deaf: if she did not speak clearly, she did not mean to be heard.

"Are you writing a letter?" Alice asked, her voice suddenly cheery and light. "To whom?"

"Certain persons of distinction," said John. "In London."

"Are they distinct enough to have been granted names of their own?"

"They are surgeons of considerable esteem," he replied. "Perhaps one or two will pay a visit, and you will learn their names then."

"I see," said Alice, the sparkle leaving her voice, "that you are determined to follow this path until it reaches its end."

"I am. I cannot do otherwise. And I do hope that I will eventually convince you to join me, or at least not to stand in my way."

"Oh, I would never *dream* of standing in your way," said Alice, backing away from the desk with her hands clasped before her, in a manner that John could not help but feel was slightly mocking. "I presume young Zachary will be at his parents' for supper this evening," she continued, changing the subject. "Shall I throw together something simple for the two of us then? I've skinned a rat that might be nice, sautéed."

"Whatever you please," John said. His attention had already drifted back to the paper before him, well before his wife had finished speaking. *A most magnificent case?* No. But: *important.* Yes. *A most important case.*

*

The pile of meat that Zachary's mother ladled onto his plate for supper was more of it than he'd eat in three days at the Howards'—the boy's bowels quivered at the mere sight of all those hunks of mutton, heavily peppered and slathered in gravy. It was as if Clara Walsh somehow believed that Zachary was forced to subsist on air and dreams when not in her presence, and had to make up the lost nutrition whenever he could escape from beneath the Howards' watchful gazes.

Crispin, on the other hand, devoured his food, delivering his customary supper monologue to Zachary and Clara as he chewed. "I had my doubts about you becoming an apprentice to that man," he said to Zachary. "We've had our disagreements. But I admit my error—I must concede that God's ways are often inscrutable, even to a man who has dedicated his life to their understanding. I never—never!—expected the Lord to reveal himself to me so clearly, beyond doubt."

"I confess," Clara said, "that I do not understand why the Lord would select such a strange and troubling manner of revelation. I would think he would speak in plain English instead of riddles and rebuses, if he wished to be sure of being understood."

Eyes on the plate before her, she continued quietly: "And I know not what message to read in a rabbit birthed of human flesh, other than the news of my own fright, my own confusion."

Crispin snorted, shaking his head at Clara dismissively. "Shall I remind you of the tale of Belshazzar's feast? The Babylonian king hosts a meal for a thousand lords, who stuff their bellies with fine food and drink themselves stupid, swilling wine from goblets looted from the Temple of Jerusalem. Then a hand appears, holy and glowing—it carves four words into the stone wall with the tip of its flaming finger, and it vanishes. The Babylonian wise men cannot interpret the message, and so the king summons Daniel, who proves himself wiser than them all when he pronounces: *Mene, mene, tekel, upharsin. A prophecy. Belshazzar: your kingdom is dying. You are judged and found wanting. Your lands will be split between the Persians and the Medes.* Now: why did the Lord not write in a language that the Babylonian wise men could understand? It would have been a simple thing for him to do, to make his meaning plain as day to the king." He looked at Zachary and at Clara, who both chose to say nothing.

"Because he wanted to remind them that Daniel, as a Hebrew and a true man of God, was *necessary*," Crispin answered himself, as expected. "That even if the Lord's wisdom is ultimately available to all, he takes care to choose those to whom his ways remain a mystery, and those to whom he speaks clearly, trusting them to act as his interpreters. The strange nature of the message *is* the message—don't you see? John Howard was presented with the mystery, but it was rightly left to me to unveil its final meaning. Surgeons know much, but do not know all; men of God know things that no others can know. It is good for all of us to remain aware of this."

"How was Daniel able to understand the entire prophecy from just four words?" said Zachary. "How could he have been so sure?"

"Daniel could decipher the prophecy because he was wise," replied Crispin, and the scrupulous attention the minister began to pay to his meal signaled the conversation's end.

*

On Wednesday morning, John Howard handed his letters personally to the driver of the mail coach passing through Godalming on his way back to London, stressing the urgency of the message. Tipping his hat, the kindly, red-nosed coachman said he'd let his horses know, and gave John his solemn guarantee that his dispatches would arrive in London just as quickly as all the others, and not a moment slower. With a sharp, showy snap of the reins the coach creaked into motion, heading down Godalming's main street and out of the village. John stood in the center of the road, hand shading his eyes from the morning sun, and he watched the coach until it vanished out of sight over a hill, as if his gaze could impart a motive force to it, compelling it to travel faster.

When the coach disappeared, John returned to his office, unable to restrain himself from imagining the letters entering the city, their distribution through London's coffee houses, their delivery to their intended recipients, the hands breaking their seals and opening, the heads of the readers jerked backward by the revelation as surely as if some kind of explosive had been hidden inside. As he performed the sixth delivery of Mary Toft the following day (dropping two more shillings into Joshua Toft's palm in exchange for the rabbit that he brought back to his office, preserving it in spirits along with the rest), he thought of the missives passing from man to man, of the information being disseminated in quivering voices among all those wonderful Persons of Distinction.

And in a corner of one of the back pages in the issue of the *British Journal* published in London on the morning of Friday, October 28, was a brief notice, its details distorted by two days of feverishly relayed hearsay, but the essence of the message still preserved:

> They write from Godalming, that a woman working in a field,
> saw a rabbit, which she endeavoured to catch, but she could
> not, being with child at that time: she has since, by the help of
> a man-midwife, been delivered of several things in the form of
> dissected rabbits, which are now kept by the said man-midwife
> at Godalming.

Thus did John Howard's troubles begin.

PART TWO.

CHAPTER VIII

NATHANAEL ST. ANDRÉ.

The ongoing presence of the miracle in the midst of the people of Godalming did not prevent them from going about their daily business that November: most of the locals had yet to learn about it, even as the first notice of the event appeared in a newspaper published sixty miles away. For John Howard and Zachary Walsh, the delivery of the creatures from Mary Toft became a matter of routine—on the mornings every two or three days when her husband Joshua arrived at Howard's office, Joshua no longer even bothered to state his business. John merely nodded, while Zachary retrieved his surgeon's satchel; then they were off. Conveniently, Mary's parturitions never occurred on Sundays—Crispin Walsh only half jokingly cited the rabbits' respect for the Sabbath as further proof that the pregnancies had a clearly divine nature.

Those villagers who weren't birthing animals several times each week continued to experience the expected garden-variety afflictions: runny noses; racking coughs; vicious rashes; broken bones. With steps so slow that even Zachary himself was not entirely aware of the progression, he began to become more than a mere apprentice to John, even as his voice finished the breaking that had taken the whole summer, settling down into a rich baritone that would need its own training, in time. (As it was, he spoke indoors at the same volume as he did on the street, and his whispers would make teacups tremble in their saucers.) He handed tools to John Howard without needing to first hear their names; he bandaged Howard's patients with a nearly perfect combination of care and efficiency. Though he kept his opinion to himself, Howard believed that even if there were procedures whose ultimate mastery lay years in Zachary's future, in perhaps another six months the apprentice would be able to sometimes stand beside the surgeon in his own light, rather than huddling in the master's shadow. Now was as good a time as any to begin acclimating the people of Godalming to the ministrations of another, younger practitioner, to reassure them that in all but the most dire cases, they would be as safe in Zachary's hands as with Howard himself.

The perfect opportunity for Zachary's public trial by fire came on the first Monday in November, about six months after his apprenticeship had begun—the coincidence seemed almost like a deliberate product of fate. That morning Phoebe Sanders, the town crier, appeared at Howard's door, her son Oliver's wrist clasped firmly in her hand. "His *breath*," she said to the surgeon. "It would shrivel butterflies to ashes. And he can't speak in a way that any man alive could understand—everything's a mumble." Oliver entered the office behind his mother, sallow-faced and enervated in a manner that could not entirely be attributed to the burden of being Phoebe Sanders's son.

The diagnosis was, of course, self-evident, though Howard made a brief show of puzzlement after he ushered the two of them into his office and seated them. He sat behind his desk, stroking his chin and humming idly to himself. "Oh, it could be any number of things," he opined, and Phoebe's face dropped as she seemed to imagine a prescribed series of increasingly rigorous and absurd curative regimens, all of which were doomed to fail as the child wasted down to a skeleton.

Then Howard turned to Zachary, who stood silently against a wall beside the door, waiting to be acknowledged. "What do you think?" he said. Phoebe turned to him, as if she had only just realized he was there.

"Quinsy, I believe," he said, not skipping a beat. Good, even if he'd picked up on Howard's playacting.

With a gesture, Howard beckoned Zachary over toward Phoebe's son. "Take a look."

Zachary approached Oliver, who seemed a bit confused, but who at least did not have the dawning expression of distress that was appearing on his mother's face, which Zachary was clearly doing his best to studiously ignore. "Tip your head back, and open your mouth as wide as you can," he said, standing over the other boy, looking down on him (and as Howard watched, he saw Zachary realize that Oliver was becoming, at this very moment, Zachary's first real *patient,* dependent on him for healing, and therefore willing to accept his commands).

Zachary peered down Oliver's throat, squinting, and winced and drew backward as one of Oliver's exhalations hit him in the face. "I see the abscess," Zachary said. "Next to the tonsil."

"I do believe you are correct," Howard said, leaning back in his chair, hands behind his head. "Now that you say it, it seems quite apparent."

"My breaf ith haw'ble," Oliver said, with what might have been a small amount of pleasure.

"Does this call for scarification?" Zachary said, perhaps too eagerly, his voice at that last word slipping up into one final childish squeak.

I wish he hadn't tipped our hand so early, John thought, but there was nothing to be done about it. "Come with me across the hall for a consultation," he said to him. "Mrs. Sanders, Oliver—sit comfortably. We'll return shortly. I promise we will effect a cure of your son within the hour; there's no need for alarm—"

"Scarification?" Phoebe Sanders said, hands clutching the armrests of her chair.

"Sit comfortably, I said. Zachary: come with me."

*

Once in the operating chamber across the hall, Howard shut the door behind him and turned to Zachary. With the two of them alone, it was clear that the boy finally felt the weight of the moment on him—he'd gone pale and wide-eyed, drawing his arms around himself as if to protect himself from the future. "I believe," said Howard, "it is time for you to have your first experience with wielding a knife. Do you feel ready?"

"Yes," Zachary said, stepping back from Howard.

"That was a well-meant lie, and a good one to tell," said Howard. "You don't feel ready, but trust me—you never will until after you make the first deliberate cut, and you see with your own eyes that wounding a person is often the first necessary step toward healing him. Then your mind will become calm, and all your fears will vanish. And this is a simple procedure—you've seen me do it, and because you have had it performed on yourself, you will have an instinctive knowledge of the method, and a sympathy for your patient that will make it easier still." *It may actually make it more difficult,* Howard thought, *but the boy need not know that.*

"Easy," Zachary said, nodding slowly, talking himself into it.

Howard approached his cabinet of tools and began to prepare a tray for Zachary, just as Zachary had for him on a hundred past occasions. "Imagine that the surgery is already completed, sometime in the distant past, and you are merely reenacting the event, retracing the steps that led to your success. The procedure was simple. The patient lay on his back and you looked down his throat. You saw the abscess; you pinned down the tongue with a wooden paddle in your left hand, and inserted the knife in your right hand down the patient's throat. You did not warn him of what you were doing beforehand, because you wanted to rely on his initial surprise and terror to keep him still. You acted with precision, but also with speed, because you were confident, and because you knew that with each passing second, the patient's panic ran the risk of overwhelming the sedation provided by the gin—he might have begun to thrash, and that would have led to disaster. You did not think of what you were doing as *cutting,* precisely. You did not think of letting blood. You merely inscribed three quick lines on the abscess with the knife, as if you were writing with a pen on paper, and your inscription effected a cure. You withdrew the knife and the wooden paddle from the patient's mouth. The procedure required no more than fifteen seconds.

"Do you remember all of this? How it happened? How easy it was for you? How silly it was that you could have ever considered it difficult?"

"I do," said Zachary.

"Good. Take this bottle of gin and this glass out to the patient," said John, handing them to him. "One dose quickly, all in one swallow, and a second dose fast behind that. Make idle conversation with the mother for ten minutes—soothing the relatives of the patient is an inconvenient but necessary component of our craft. Then bring him in here, and begin."

Zachary looked up at John, and, with a single slow nod, he turned as Howard opened the operating room door for him. Howard remained behind as Zachary crossed the hall alone, and he smiled to himself as he heard Zachary say, "Here: drink this. Quickly. Because I'm going to do it."

"*What?*" Phoebe shouted.

Well, perhaps Zachary wouldn't be able to handle the mother entirely by himself. He couldn't leave him alone to do that.

*

There was a brief moment, as Zachary was escorting Oliver into the operating room, when Howard saw Zachary's tight grip on the woozy patient's arm, as if he were leading him to the gallows instead of to a surgery, and thought that he had made a bad bet, that it wasn't yet the young man's time. But to his relief, Zachary executed the procedure perfectly, and exactly as Howard had envisioned it (largely because Howard had convinced Phoebe to stay in his office alone, and not to watch: if she had, Howard was certain she would have tried to valiantly sacrifice her own flesh to spare her son from the blade). When Zachary and Oliver entered the office afterward, with Howard trailing respectfully behind, Phoebe jumped from her chair, ran toward her son, and clasped him in her arms, pushing his head deep into the crook of her shoulder. "Will he be well?" she asked Zachary accusingly. "I heard screams."

"Those may have been yours," Howard replied. "We promise that your son will be in full health inside of a week. One shilling, please."

Phoebe let her son go and began to rummage in the pocket attached to her waist, feeling for the proper coin. "I hear there is a new guest in the inn," she said, idly. "A most mysterious figure. Seems to think he owns everything he sets his eyes on—this is what Amelia Glasse told me. She spies on every person going in and out of that place, you know: when someone catches her eye, she's quick to ask questions."

"Where from?" said John.

"*London,*" Phoebe breathed. "He's a *surgeon.* He brought an apprentice, a smart little man dressed just like his master. Supposedly," she said, edging closer to John, "the fellow was dispatched here by none other than *King George himself.*"

Quickly, Phoebe cut her gaze back between John and Zachary, noting the apprentice's open mouth and the startled expression on his master's face. "Now," she said, firmly pressing the shilling into John's palm, looking him dead in the eye. "I wonder what sort of events might be occurring in this little place, of note enough to convince the king of all England to send a surgeon here, of all places. He is a man of your illustrious trade—might you be able to offer a supposition? Yes?"

"This is a surprise to me," said John as Phoebe rolled her eyes— she apparently felt no need to disguise her disappointment at such a weak attempt at subterfuge. "But if you happen to hear something of his business, or even his name, please do not hesitate to tell me. Now, I have . . . urgent business. And as much as I would like you to stay, I must regretfully ask you to leave."

"I expected as much," said Phoebe.

*

The mysterious figure of whom Phoebe had spoken arrived that afternoon, announcing himself with a rap on the door so loud and persistent that Howard feared his visitor had left a dent in the wood.

Zachary opened the door, only to find that he had to quickly lift his arm to guard himself against a knock on the head by the oaken cane, tipped with a sphere of ivory, that the man was using as a drumstick. The door had its own knocker, but the gentleman seemed to have judged it inefficient for his needs.

"Oh, goodness, *there* you are," said the visitor as Zachary yelped and clutched his forearm, which would surely develop a bruise. "No, wait: you're not the man I seek. Too young; too young to be the future legend."

(Behind his desk, Howard's ears perked up. Exaggeration, to be certain, and perhaps it was meant to be overheard, and meant to flatter. Even so, the fact that someone considered him to be one whom it might be worthwhile to flatter was, to Howard, its own good sign.)

Zachary looked the man before him up and down—his voluminous and heavily powdered horsehair wig; the cocked hat folded under his arm; the waistcoat of a stylishly different color than the rest of his ensemble, deep blue in contrast with the green of his coat and breeches. Blue knitted silk stockings covered his breeches at the knee, and the blue and white silk shoes that completed the outfit had some of the tallest heels Zachary had ever seen. Behind him stood a boy who appeared to be a copy of the man in miniature, with a similar wig and similarly coordinated three-piece suit, though the heels of his shoes were not so absurdly large. The boy vacillated between glaring at Zachary with an affected imperiousness and gazing pointedly at the sky, as if insulted that Zachary had the gall to look on him in return.

"Forgive me," the man before Zachary said, "I forget that I am no longer in London, where my visage usually suffices as my entrance pass. Please notify your master that the surgeon Nathanael St. André has arrived, at the request of the king of England, to observe his most notable medical case for himself. My eyes are his eyes. And Laurence," he continued, speaking to the boy who was presumably his apprentice, "would you return to our inn and arrange to have our baggage delivered here? Considered relative to the surroundings, this residence is positively palatial, and will suit the two of us just fine."

*

"Would you believe," said Nathanael St. André at the Howards' supper later that evening, "that the surgeon's trade in London is so mercilessly competitive that an attempt by a still unidentified professional rival was once made on my very life? That I was *poisoned*?"

"My goodness," said Alice Howard, "I can't imagine who would even consider such a thing."

"Few who have made my acquaintance could," said St. André, placing his hand to his chest as he suppressed a belch. "But as a close confidant of mine has said—I will admit that he has expressed an earnest desire to become my biographer—I am a most uncommon man, and so I must suffer a life filled with most uncommon incidents."

This was the first time since Zachary had become John Howard's apprentice that Alice had served five at supper. John sat in the lone chair at the head of the dining table, with Alice and Zachary on the bench to his right, and Nathanael and Laurence seated opposite. Despite the unexpected guests, Alice had been able to throw together a meal of fried pork sausages and sliced apples, along with some stewed cabbage—though when serving himself, Nathanael had fastidiously picked through the dish of sausages and loaded his plate with almost all the meat, leaving the apple slices and the cabbage to feed the rest. Zachary was unused to supper being a race—he sensed that this night, the lullaby that sent him to sleep would be sung by his grumbling stomach.

Nonetheless, John Howard favored Nathanael St. André with a gaze most often associated with those in the early days of a love affair, and Nathanael's tale—which showed evidence of having been polished and enhanced through repeated retellings—held John enraptured. "I was seated in my office when I received a visit from a stranger who seemed to be in desperate straits—surely he would have been, to approach me directly instead of arranging an audience through the well-known proper channels. I am famous, I should say, for my red-hot flashes of rage at breaches of protocol. However, this night I was in a forgiving mood, and due to his clear agitation I determined to hear his entreaty. He claimed that his wife suffered from a venereal disease that none of the doctors he had enlisted had been able to identify, that she stood before the underworld's gate, and that I was his last resort. I sensed a rare challenge to my talents, and so I followed this fellow through London's labyrinth, finally reaching a two-room apartment, strangely unfurnished, its bedroom door closed. The man offered me a cordial, which I thought strange, but accepted out of politeness—the drink was so foul that I could only manage two sips of it, but that was enough to serve this fellow's dastardly purpose. My eyelids became heavy, and I collapsed."

Zachary looked across the table at Laurence, who seemed to view him as some sort of rival; for what reason, he couldn't fathom. Between bites of food, Laurence lifted his chin and stared down his nose at Zachary, making his most valiant attempt at a haughty glare. What strange London fashion, dressing children as tiny adults—Laurence seemed to think that the clothing granted him years and authority, though Zachary guessed that the boy was a year younger than himself; moreover, he found Laurence's ensemble ludicrous. There was time enough in life to shave one's head and don a powdered wig; Zachary preferred to postpone that day as long as possible.

"I have heard conflicting tales of the time between then and when I found myself in my bed the following morning," Nathanael continued. "One person said that I had been dumped unceremoniously in an alley, drooling and insensate; another that I was wandering the streets, disheveled and raving. It matters not. For two weeks I fought the poison, as my body alternated between ice and fire, and my mind blended reality and nightmare. But a man such as myself is not easy to kill: in addition to my naturally strong constitution, a diet rich in meat and small beer has made me a man of iron." He belched again. "After a fortnight I returned to my feet, as hale as if I had never been poisoned at all. I have not been troubled by such attempts since; presumably, my enemies now know the nature of the star that shines on me."

"Were you ever able to determine who perpetrated the crime?" Howard asked. His meal had gone mostly untouched, as if he'd been too distracted by St. André's tale to eat, or thought mastication rude in the presence of such a guest.

Zachary stared forlornly at the last available sausage as St. André forked it into his mouth. "I have not," Nathanael said, speech muffled by his chewing. "The man who called on me was unfamiliar, and I was taken to the apartment where I was poisoned by such a twisting path that I would never be able to find my way back. He might have been an agent of anyone in the trade who had cause to envy my position, or who perhaps wished to usurp it: Ahlers; Davenant; perhaps even Manningham, though I would not expect him to stoop so low. Which brings me to a new subject: when I read the notice of the recent events in Godalming in the *British Journal,* I knew that I was in the presence of yet another *uncommon incident,* of the kind that acts on me as a lodestone. How was this news transmitted from here to there? Whom did you contact, initially?"

"Nichols," said Howard, thinking. "Stillingfleet. Douglas Hammond. Caryll." Then, sheepishly: "Davenant."

"Ah, well, Davenant is no one to fear," said Nathanael. "Avaricious, perhaps, but avarice is powerless without an ambition to match it. He is a lazy, provincial fellow—one might as well propose that he visit the Continent as that he leave London. And this case will likely not draw Manningham's eye: it is too out of the ordinary, and he fears risk, preferring to keep his reputation intact by concerning himself only with quotidian matters of medicine. Ahlers is the one we must watch out for, friend. Risen to an undeserved station despite his mediocrity; unwilling to let any scruple stand in the way of advancing his interests. If Ahlers arrives in Godalming, we *must* be on our guard."

At that, St. André rose, and Laurence with him. "And now, my hosts, it is time for us to retire," he said, licking the tips of his fingers. "Tomorrow, John, we will visit your dear patient. I expect it will be a historic day, the first of many for us all. I tell you, in ten years this little town will be noted by Chinese mapmakers. Now. Madam," he said to Alice, "have you prepared our room? If not, will you do so promptly? I long for a bed, and digestion is aided by lying on one's back."

Alice gave St. André the blackest of looks, to which he seemed determined to appear oblivious. Then she turned to Zachary. "Come with me," she said, "and assist me with this woman's work."

*

"I have so very many questions," Alice said to Zachary in one of the otherwise empty rooms on the house's top floor as they stretched the sheet over St. André's straw mattress. "Which I will merely voice into the air, as if I am talking to myself: no need for you, apprentice of the legendary John Howard, to respond. Though you might overhear something you wish to consider, to reflect upon with your master in your own time."

"Certainly," said Zachary.

"First. How is it that a man in the employ of King George chooses to lodge himself in the house of a stranger, presumably at no cost, and that he leaves a perfectly well-appointed inn in order to do so? I am sure the king would not mind the expense. One might also wonder why such a man wears a wig of horsehair, rather than human hair. It is quite interesting! Zachary, look under the bed to see that the chamber pot's there: place it where it can be easily seen. Who knows what he'll do if he can't find it at a moment's notice."

Zachary got down on his hands and knees and retrieved the chipped ceramic pot from beneath the bed, wiping the dust off its surface with his hands. "Who would have thought that man-midwifing was a profession of such drama and intrigue?" Alice continued. "Though those most often given to speak of conspiracy are also the most likely to try to dream it into being. I expect he gave the wrong warning regarding whom to beware, but what do I know: I am not Ahlers, or Davenant, or Stillingfleet, or Manningham, et cetera, et cetera. Hand that here."

Zachary passed the pot to her, and she turned it over, inspecting it as if it were a valuable piece of art she was considering purchasing. "Do you think it's large enough?"

Zachary looked at the receptacle in Alice's hands. "It seems the same size as any other, ma'am," he said, and donned the appropriate expression of perplexity on his face that he believed Alice was hoping for. *Let her make her joke.*

"Well, keep in mind," said Alice, "that it also has to hold all the shit coming out of his mouth."

CHAPTER IX

Confirmation of the Preternatural.

On the following morning, of November 9, a column of a half-dozen men made the march from John Howard's practice to the Toft home: Joshua Toft; Nathanael St. André; Crispin Walsh; John Howard; and the surgeons' apprentices, Zachary and Laurence. Joshua and Nathanael were at the head of the procession, a fair distance apart from the rest; though the rest of the group could not hear what they discussed, Nathanael's expansive gesticulations suggested that he was regaling Joshua with a tale of yet another "uncommon incident." Crispin and John walked behind them, deeply engaged in a private whispered conversation, as they often seemed to be these days whenever together; seeing them from the back, side by side with their heads inclined toward each other, Zachary was reminded of the two-headed woman of the Exhibition of Medical Curiosities, and what he imagined to be her—their?—endless oscillation between argument and harmony.

Zachary and Laurence brought up the rear. Once again, Laurence was dressed like a miniature version of his master, in a black waistcoat accented with golden trim, along with a burgundy coat and breeches. His swaggering stride was an affectation that seemed intended to convey some kind of manliness, but so much effort went into the swing of his arms and the occasional toss of his bewigged head that he appeared to be constantly stumbling forward, as if perpetually rescuing himself from falling on his face. Occasionally he would glance sideways at Zachary to verify whether Zachary was looking at him in turn, which Zachary often was, primarily to avoid an inadvertent clout by his windmilling arm.

Eventually, perhaps due to exhaustion, Laurence settled down into something approaching an ordinary gait; then he spoke, directly acknowledging Zachary's existence for the first time since his arrival in Godalming. "How long have you been an apprentice?" he asked.

"A little more than six months," said Zachary.

"And," said Laurence, "how much have you *learned,* in that time?"

"Oh, quite a lot! Mr. Howard has a great library, and I've read through almost all of it. And I've attended most of his surgeries, as an assistant—I performed my own first surgery, just yesterday. For quinsy."

Laurence made a show of concealing his amusement. "Were you to see the library of Mr. St. André, in London, you would be embarrassed that you ever thought of a library as something that one could *finish reading.* He has enough volumes to keep a man occupied for centuries, and he has read them all."

"I did not know that your master was a Methuselah in disguise," said Zachary. "I myself don't expect to live longer than a single century at the most, and so a library of such size is of little use to me. Mr. Howard may not have all the volumes of Mr. St. André, but I am sure he has the most useful ones."

"Hmph," said Laurence.

They walked along together in silence for a while, and then Laurence said, "Quinsy. That is not much of a surgery. It is something that your master let you perform because he knew you could not fail."

"It is more difficult than it might seem," said Zachary. "When making the initial incision, you must be careful to draw the blade across the proper place at the wrist. Too close to the hand, and you will kill the patient."

"Of course," said Laurence after a brief pause. "Though an experienced surgeon would know that it is best to make the incision perpendicular to the wrist, rather than parallel."

"I see that knowledge of medicine must be greatly advanced in London."

"It *is*. I have no idea how one learns anything out here."

Zachary turned away from Laurence with the slightest of smiles.

*

It took some doing to cram everyone into Mary Toft's lying-in chamber who had a plausible reason to be in the presence of the patient: the six men who'd walked over together, plus Margaret Toft, who, one could easily infer, would not leave her station at the head of Mary's bed even if asked. But after some rearrangement, with people moving in and out through the doorway and occasionally colliding with each other, the congregation came to an arrangement: St. André, the honored guest, at the foot of the bed, seated on the stool where John Howard normally sat during deliveries; Howard and Crispin Walsh on either side of him; Joshua Toft at the head of the bed, on the opposite side from his mother; and Zachary and Laurence standing behind their respective masters, peeking around them at the woman, whose labor pains increased sharply as soon as the men had settled themselves. James had been sent outside to amuse himself however he could, as he always was during these events.

"We begin," Nathanael announced, and went to work. The rabbit he brought forth from Mary only ten minutes later was beheaded, missing its legs, and stripped of its pelt; to his credit, he did not have the violently nauseous reaction that Zachary, John, and Crispin had had when they were first present at one of Mary's deliveries, though Laurence, unsurprisingly, gulped and quickly ran outside. Perhaps Nathanael had in fact experienced so many "uncommon incidents" that he'd become inured to the kinds of sights that would normally shock a man. Seeing his equanimity in the face of such grotesquerie, Zachary felt unexpectedly reassured.

With a smile, Nathanael held the gory rabbit trunk aloft as if presenting it to the mother for viewing. "Magnificent," he said. "Astonishing. I assume that, in this specimen, the lungs are fully formed and intact. John, have you performed a close examination of the lungs of any of the others? We should excise a piece from one of them, and place it in water to see if it floats—if it does, it will tell us that air has become integrated with the flesh, and therefore the rabbits are breathing when inside her."

"I have preserved most of the specimens in spirits," John said, "but I have admittedly done little else in the way of experimentation." He sighed, and in that sigh Zachary heard a quiet, reluctant ceding of authority and control. "Beyond preservation, I have been at a loss as to how to proceed."

"A perfectly understandable loss! But that is why I have come," said Nathanael, handing the rabbit trunk to John. "Please wrap this in cloth, and return it to your practice: tomorrow, we'll examine this one in addition to the others you have thoughtfully saved, make some anatomical comparisons, and determine if the nature of the births has changed in some manner over time. And perhaps that will be the first step to a cure. Because, Mary," he continued, reassuringly placing his hand on her leg near her ankle, "we *will* cure you. I, Nathanael St. André, promise this to you." He lifted his gaze to meet the eyes of Joshua and Margaret Toft in turn. "I promise this to each of you," he affirmed, his voice trembling. Joshua nodded his solemn recognition of the vow; Margaret merely offered the surgeon a thin slit of a fleeting smile.

As Laurence returned to the lying-in room, coughing and sweating, his complexion pale, Nathanael stood. "Now," he announced, "enough pleasantries. We must examine the patient just after delivery, to determine if there are any anomalies in her reproductive organs that may show evidence of themselves only at these particular moments."

He pulled Mary's legs flat and approached the head of the bed. "With your permission," he said to Joshua, who once again nodded his assent. Then with a single quick motion he yanked the covering sheet off the bed, revealing the woman's naked body to the world. "No need for delicacy here," he said as Zachary and his father both glanced away. "We don't want to deprive ourselves of valuable information in the name of an unnecessary sense of decorum." Looking at Crispin, he continued, "If we are to be agents of God, who will cure this woman just as surely as he has chosen to afflict her for his own inscrutable but no doubt just reasons, then we must attempt to look on her with the same unsparing scrutiny of God, yes? We must not conceal what can be seen; we must not embrace ignorance out of propriety." This reasoning seemed to satisfy the cleric, who returned his gaze to the bed.

"Good," said Nathanael. "Good." Bending over Mary, who lay still and insensate, her breathing fast and shallow, he spread apart the lids of her right eye with thumb and forefinger and peered into it, then did the same with the left. He commanded her to open her mouth and looked inside; with the tips of his fingers, he then rubbed the glands of her neck. He cupped and then kneaded one of her breasts, then the other. Then, with splayed fingers, he began to press upon her stomach with particular care, gently, then deeply, then gently again, moving back and forth across it. "Yes," he said to himself after a minute or two of this, alternating between the left side of her stomach and the right. "Yes. Howard. Come here." Eyes still pinned to the patient, he reached out a hand and beckoned him.

"Place your hand here, as you have seen me do," said Nathanael. "Then here. Left side, then right. You feel the difference?"

Howard moved his hand from one side to the other as St. André asked, frowning. Back and forth, once, and once again.

"The right side," Nathanael said, as if he were a teacher giving a student a hint to a challenging question. "It's harder to the touch. More resistant."

Once more Howard felt both sides of Mary's stomach, pressing down with his five extended fingers. "I feel it," he said, eventually. "Yes." He looked at Nathanael, who nodded, and he nodded back.

"An irregularity in the Fallopian tubes, no doubt," said Nathanael. "The right one is larger than the left, and thicker. My conjecture, which I'm sure will be proven true, given enough time: the rabbits are bred not in her uterus, but in her right Fallopian tube. Thus, no placenta accompanying the birth. Her initial painful agitations are a signal that the rabbits are being dispensed into the uterus, and being violently torn apart in the process. From there the delivery proceeds as would any ordinary birth, barring the timely manner and the exceptional speed."

Retrieving the bedsheet from the floor where he had tossed it, Nathanael shook it out and draped it gracefully over the bed once again, covering Mary up to her neck. "I feel," he said, "that we are doubtless in the presence of the preternatural, and that this promises to be the most challenging case of my career thus far. Busy days are ahead of us, friends and colleagues—busy and exciting days. But I tell you this: tomorrow, we begin to inscribe our names in all the world's history books."

Nathanael turned to John Howard, grasped his hand, and, with a beaming smile, shook it firmly, clasping his other hand tightly over it. Then, surprisingly, he took Howard in an embrace, firm, close, and warm. As the other men in the room dissolved into relieved laughter, Crispin grinned and began to clap—Zachary and Laurence joined in, then Joshua, while Margaret continued to stand in the shadows, silent.

From her lying-in bed, Mary Toft offered a sympathetic moan.

Zachary could see his master looking over Nathanael St. André's shoulder and down at him—amid the merriment and applause, his eyes shone with tears. There is no rarer and more precious comfort than this: when a man who is the sole possessor of a truth, and who feels himself misunderstood by all the world, looks into another man's eyes and finds, at last, that another believes what he believes, and he is no longer alone.

CHAPTER X

The Seat of Imagination.

By Saturday, November 12, 1726, the day after Mary Toft delivered her twelfth rabbit, there were at least nine people in Godalming who knew of the strange events going on in her household, and in London, the notice that had been printed in the *British Journal* had been circulating among interested parties for over two weeks. In other words, there was more than enough tinder to spark a rumor in the town: it was perhaps a miracle that it did not happen earlier.

In Godalming, the genesis of the gossip appeared to be spontaneous, as if once enough people knew of a particular set of facts, a distorted version of those facts would manifest in the minds of those nearby, without the need for speech to convey them through the air. Or perhaps Nathanael St. André's tongue became loose after one too many pints of beer at the local inn, or Crispin Walsh made the rare decision to confide his innermost thoughts to his wife, or young Laurence walked in his sleep to the town center and proclaimed the news aloud. Whatever the cause, bits of hearsay began to float from person to person, in beds and markets and church pews, accreting details as they traveled, and becoming full-fledged narratives that were just as likely to support as conflict with each other.

And so the gossips of Godalming felt a smug and doubled pleasure: they believed themselves wise enough to know a tale to be factual that those less wise than themselves would consider self-evidently silly; meanwhile, they also considered the equally incredible tales of others to be ridiculous, and thought themselves smarter than the benighted fools who retailed them as truth. When Mary Mitton crossed paths with Phoebe Sanders on Godalming's main street (with Phoebe plainly looking up and down at Mitton's figure, to assure herself that the money she had given Mitton to retrieve her stays from the pawnshop had been put to its intended purpose), Phoebe breathlessly relayed the story she'd heard from a reliable source whose identity she would not divulge: that poor Mary Toft had gone insane, and now kept a pet rabbit, a young kitten, that she believed to be invested with the spirit of the child she had miscarried earlier in the year. "It's why she hasn't left her home in weeks, why she was churched for a second time last month, and why the surgeon Howard and the minister Walsh pay a visit to her almost daily," Phoebe said. "Though neither prayer nor medicine has yet to offer a remedy for her madness. She constantly cradles the little thing in her arms—she sings lullabies to it, and won't let it go. It's the saddest thing I've ever heard."

Mary Mitton nodded in silence, thinking that it would be indecorous to correct this insufferable know-it-all by relating the true and revolting tale of Mary Toft in daylight. The account *she'd* heard from Amelia Glasse was of a freakish event that admitted of no explanation besides the preternatural: one night earlier this month, when Joshua Toft had returned home after a bout of heavy drinking, he'd demanded of his helpmeet that she satisfy his amorous inclinations. Finding his inebriate entreaties rebuffed, he'd threatened force; his wife had responded by lifting her skirts, standing with her legs apart, howling like a wounded dog, and dropping a litter of a dozen scurrying field mice. The sight of that certainly shrank Joshua's yard, of that you could be sure—when a woman has no desire to dance Adam's jig, it's wise to leave her be.

The word circulating among some of the men of Godalming was that Mary had had a tryst with a blackamoor, one of the members of the Exhibition of Medical Curiosities that had come through town back in September. The fact that there had been no such black person in Nicholas Fox's exhibition did not prevent the rumor from traveling, of course: after enough telling and retelling, the fantasy of his dark-hued skin, ink-black eyes, and shimmering golden robes became a

memory, and some even found themselves able to recount the charming African's dulcet seductions word for word. That such a rendezvous
would not sufficiently explain why Mary had not left her house in over
a month was of little relevance, nor did anyone trouble themselves
with wondering why such an exotic specimen of masculinity would
bother to debauch a wife and mother who could only be described as
plain-faced on her best days—on the street, Joshua's friends greeted
him with the particular expression reserved for cuckolds unaware of
their own natures, half sorrow, half mockery. Joshua, for his part,
seemed oblivious to the chorus of whispers, and no one was reckless or
foolish enough to confront him directly: though a quiet man, he was
a large one, and verification of the allegations wasn't worth having his
meaty slab of fist collide with your face.

*

Along with the rise of local rumors regarding the Toft family
came the appearance of strangers in Godalming, two or three arriving
each day, identifiable on sight as Londoners. Fed almost from birth on
an urban diet of meat, they were taller than the native villagers; they
moved through the streets with the long strides of giants, their big,
fleshy bodies swathed in layer after layer of fine clothes, dyed in colors
rarely seen beneath God's sun. They had a tendency to gaze rapt at
the ordinary, as if these rural English were of a different nation altogether than city folk. They stopped in the middle of the road, paused,
and drew in deep breaths with their eyes shut, as if the very air of the
village had some strange and novel perfume; they stared unblinking
at passersby of both sexes, following them with their eyes until their
heads threatened to twist themselves off their necks; they pointed and
smiled at sheep. In the market, Alice Howard had to step backward
with her hand ready to slap when one of them reached out to touch
her linen cap.

The Godalming citizens sometimes found the speech of Londoners difficult to understand; when approached by one of them, it
was generally easy to pick out enough words from his rapid patter

to determine that he sought directions, or lodging, or sausages, but conversation beyond that could pose a challenge. The way they pronounced words made one want to suggest they speak more loudly or be more careful with their enunciation. It was easy to mishear them, and in addition, they seemed to express unusual ideas; some were perhaps not entirely in their right mind. For instance, Michael Burwash, the town's local farrier and veterinarian, swore that one of the visiting Londoners told him he had come to Godalming because there were reports in London that one of its residents, a woman whose name he didn't yet know, was a performer of miracles: she had been blessed by God with the ability to give birth to rabbits at will, as often as once a day.

Clearly the Londoner could not have meant what Burwash heard him say, or was more than half mad. The very idea was absurd: most reasonable people would call such an affliction a curse, not a blessing. But the Londoner had paid good coin to Burwash to have his horse newly shod, forgoing bargaining even though the farrier had looked at his clothing and decided on the spot to charge a fee double his usual rate. His money would spend the same as anyone else's, and so far as Burwash was concerned, he was free to believe what he would.

*

In the meantime, John Howard and Nathanael St. André began to consider possible cures for Mary Toft's unfortunate condition. The two of them stayed cloistered in Howard's office that Saturday, bent over the proliferation of open volumes that covered his desk. "Despite the age of his writing, the work of Descartes may illuminate a path forward," Nathanael said. "It was he who identified the pineal gland in the center of the brain as the seat of imagination, and, as you point out, the good anonymous author of *Aristotle's Master-Piece* suggests that our poor patient's births may be caused from an irregular operation of the patient's imaginative faculty. Might her pineal gland be overactive, or perhaps swollen? Needless to say, the poor woman would not survive a direct investigation into the matter! But we can act under the suspicion that the patient is suffering an inflammation, and treat her as such—phlebotomy ought to reduce the swelling."

"I fear I can't agree," said John. (*I should have just said* I cannot agree *and been direct,* he briefly thought, but nonetheless pushed forward. Still, he found himself ceding ground to Nathanael by inches.) "She has undergone twelve births in the space of a month—an ordeal never before experienced by a human woman. Her constitution simply won't allow it."

Seated behind John's desk, Nathanael looked up from his volume of Descartes's *The Passions of the Soul* and offered John an indulgent smile. "But does not the very fact of her frequent, repeated births suggest that she has been gifted by God with a stronger constitution than that of an ordinary woman?" he said. "Is this not, indeed, an essential characteristic of the preternatural phenomenon? And whatever the suffering that might be induced by the bleeding, it is nothing when compared to the deliveries she is subjected to several times a week—moreover, if the bleeding has a chance of relieving the pineal gland's inflammation, thus bringing these deliveries to a quick and welcome end, we have a moral obligation to take that risk. Do we not?"

*

They returned to the Toft home that afternoon, the two of them, to bleed the woman: John felt it unnecessary to bring Zachary along, and Nathanael left his apprentice Laurence behind as well. Since they speculated that Mary suffered a disorder of the head, John and Nathanael agreed that the site of the bleeding should be a jugular vein, and John preferred to execute the operation himself. In her lying-in chamber, John lifted up Mary's head while Nathanael wrapped a handkerchief around her neck, yanking it tight and tying the knot. Tears formed in her eyes as her breathing dwindled to a slow rasp, but soon enough the vein in her neck was turgid and ready for the lancet.

"You must act neither with rashness nor with timidity," Nathanael said in a low voice as John approached the vein with the blade, hand steady. "In either case you run the risk of—"

"Quiet, please," said John.

"But—"

"*Quiet.* And have the vessel ready."

"I merely offer advice," said Nathanael.

Thankfully, Mary fainted the moment the lancet pierced the vein. Blood spurted from her neck in a fast hot jet, spattering the floor before Nathanael was able to catch the flow with a large ceramic bowl, in which John also placed the lancet. They drew what John estimated to be two or three pints; then, as the stream began to lose its vigor, John pinched the wound on Mary's neck shut with the thumb and forefinger of his left hand while he applied a compress with his right. ("So much of the surgeon's craft involves growing a third or a fourth hand when necessary," he said to Nathanael, who stood by watching, holding the bowl of blood.)

After John had finished bandaging Mary's neck, he retrieved the lancet from the bowl and wiped it down, while Nathanael cavalierly dumped the rest of the bowl's contents out the window. Then the two surgeons entered the front room of the house, where Joshua sat waiting. He held his son, James, on his lap, who slept with his head tucked against his father's chest. (Margaret Toft had chosen to take her taciturn disapproval elsewhere this afternoon, it seemed.) "We have executed the operation flawlessly," Nathanael said. "Your wife will awake directly. And perhaps we will find soon after that our ordeal has, at last, reached its end."

"I certainly hope so," Joshua said, weariness evident in his voice. "This has been difficult for all of us."

He lifted his head, slowly, as if it were double its usual weight. "When I look on her, lying in that bed," he said, speaking quietly so as not to disturb the cheerfully snoring boy, "sometimes I no longer recognize her for the woman she once was. As if some strange demonic creature has taken her shape, or wears her skin. Often when I speak to her now, she does not respond: she just stares at me, or she whimpers, or she screams to wake the dead. This morning I had to put my hand in her mouth to stop her from biting off her tongue." He presented his hand to Nathanael, who held and examined it: there, across the tips of three of his fingers, were a row of teeth marks, angry and red.

"I don't know if she can ever return to the person she once was," said Joshua, taking his hand back from Nathanael as James stirred in his slumber. "But I ask you, please: do what you can. If these monstrous births end and Mary still somehow retains her sanity, I swear I will count myself lucky."

*

Zachary was in his loft, that afternoon, lying on his bed and drifting in and out of sleep—these days he took his rest when he could, for his sense of unease often kept him awake long past midnight. Increasingly, he found himself wondering if becoming a surgeon necessarily involved learning things that he would have preferred not to know. It might have seemed to others that he'd become acclimated to the sight of Mary Toft's deliveries after twelve of them, but that only meant he'd developed enough reserve to prevent his terror from showing on his face: the images still rose in his mind when his head hit the pillow each night, of shrieking women and beheaded rabbits stripped of their skins. He wondered if becoming an old surgeon meant becoming *haunted,* in the way an old soldier might be by the memory of unspeakable deeds committed on a battlefield. He was uncertain that the rewards of a surgeon's career were truly worth becoming haunted in that way, witness to devils dancing in daylight that only he and his accursed like could see.

He was awakened from his thin, unsatisfying twilight sleep by a soft, tentative knock on his door. Rubbing his eyes, he rolled out of bed and answered the door to find Nathanael's apprentice Laurence standing before him, dressed in a neatly fitting suit of burgundy and gold. In his hands he held a wooden box; a band of bright red ribbon ran around its lid, and it was kept shut by a pair of brass latches. "May I enter?" he said.

Zachary stood aside and waved him in, sneezing at the smell of the starch from Laurence's freshly powdered wig. The boy entered, looked around him, and sat down on the edge of the bed—here, outside the presence of his master, he somehow seemed more childlike, even more a person in costume. "I want you to try something," he said. "Come sit next to me." Zachary could swear that Laurence's voice had a slightly different pitch than usual, and that this voice was his natural one, while the lower register in which he spoke when in the presence of adults was a performance.

Zachary sat down on the bed next to Laurence, the mysterious box between them. With reverence, as if there were some sort of ancient reliquary inside, Laurence opened the two latches and lifted the lid, inviting Zachary to peer within.

In the box was a pile of white hair that, as Zachary stared, resolved itself into a wig, just like the one Laurence wore. "I believe our heads are the same size," he said, "though you really are meant to shave your head when wearing one of these. You should try it on."

"Oh, my, no, I—"

"It has no lice—I guarantee it. My master and I had all our perukes boiled by the wigmaker before we left London: this one hasn't been out of its box since."

Zachary edged away from Laurence on the bed. "I—"

"You needn't be afraid of it," said Laurence. "It isn't alive. Just try it on. No one will know but you and me, here in this room. Aren't you curious? Don't be a *coward,* Zachary."

The accusation of cowardice got under Zachary's skin, just as the mere suggestion that Zachary was curious brought that curiosity into being. As if he were picking up a cat by the scruff of its neck, Zachary lifted the wig out of its box, clouds of powder blooming as its horse-hair locks tumbled down.

He held the wig up before him, turning it, examining it. "How do I—"

"Oh, goodness, let me," said Laurence, taking the wig from him. He oriented it, gripped it in both hands, reached toward Zachary as if to embrace him, and jammed the wig firmly atop his head. Then he adjusted the fitting, looking at Zachary from one angle and then another, running his fingers through the locks in a gesture toward combing. "There," he said. "Do you not feel twenty years older?"

Zachary straightened his posture, as if the thing perched on his head required balancing. "I feel . . ." He brushed a lock away from his eyes as Laurence stared at him expectantly. "In all honesty, I feel ridiculous."

"And you also *look* ridiculous," said Laurence. "But not as ridiculous as I do in this town of yours, with this wig on my head and a full suit to go with it."

Startled, Zachary's mouth dropped open. "Well, now you are attempting to trap flies, and you look sillier still," Laurence said.

Laurence kept an admirably straight face as Zachary smirked, then giggled, then fully surrendered to his laughter, throwing himself back on the bed and kicking his legs in convulsive glee; only then, finally, did Laurence join in. They chortled in harmony for what seemed like minutes: once they would calm down, Zachary would reach up to feel the peruke on his head, and it would set him off again, which would send Laurence into a paralytic series of guffaws. It seemed that the amusement would never end: there was a dark thing that the laughter was allowing Zachary not to think about, but Zachary could not remember what it was, and to recall it would break the fragile, temporary spell.

Eventually, Zachary sat up again and yanked the wig off his head, hand on his hurting stomach. "A good joke," he said, catching his breath. "A good joke."

"In London," Laurence said, "ridiculousness is the height of fashion. Garments in six dozen colors; wigs that tower to twice the height of the men who bear them on their heads. I just want you to be prepared, for the time when you come."

Laurence sidled closer to Zachary. "I fear I have cut a strange figure, here in Godalming."

"You have: that's beyond doubt. But all is forgiven, Laurence. I am glad, very glad, to name us friends."

"That is a relief," said Laurence. "You will come to London sometime, yes? I expect we will not be here much longer, a day or two at the most. My master is perhaps a strange person, and something of a showman and a braggart, but I do believe he is a genius, and I have seen him perform remedies that both patients and other men of medicine have deemed almost miraculous. It's highly likely that, today, he has effected a cure, and is already writing a triumphant notice for the London journals."

"Perhaps," said Zachary quietly, as a shadow descended on his mind once again. "I suppose we'll see, soon enough."

*

On the morning of Monday, November 14, 1726, Mary Toft gave birth to her thirteenth rabbit.

CHAPTER XI.

SOME UNANTICIPATED VISITORS.

The first patient to visit John Howard's practice the following day, Tuesday, was an unexpected surprise. His small stature, rotund build, ruddy-cheeked face, and swaggering gait seemed inexplicably familiar, but it nonetheless took a few moments for John and Zachary to recall where they'd seen him before. It was the suit, the same deep green from head to toe, that finally clued them in: Nicholas Fox, the proprietor of the Exhibition of Medical Curiosities that had passed through the town back in September, a time that now seemed to Zachary as if it were a century ago.

Fox entered Howard's waiting room, with the young woman with the birthmark following behind. (She was pretty today, thought Zachary, in a dress of sapphire that contrasted pleasantly with her father's suit of emerald, her long blond hair tied loosely in the back with a white lace ribbon. She glanced at Zachary as she passed him, one of her icy eyes shining amid the crimson splotch that spread across her face, responding to the smile he gave her with a haughty sniff.) The four of them settled in Howard's waiting room, where Fox told John and Zachary that his tour of south England had come to an end a few weeks ago. At the exhibition's final stop, in Glastonbury, he'd paid off the participants and sent them on their separate ways, so that those who had homes and families to return to could reach them before winter arrived in earnest. Meanwhile, he and his daughter Anne were returning to London. In late spring, those exhibition members who were willing to sign on for another six-month stint would reconvene there, along with any other newly added and sufficiently unusual specimens of humanity whom Fox had chanced across in the meantime, and the show would set out again.

When John asked Nicholas what business brought him to his door on his way back to London, he expected that Nicholas had heard of the local rabbit-related goings-on, and John readied himself to rebuff any of Fox's attempts to draft his afflicted patient into his traveling show. But either the Toft phenomenon was as yet unknown to Nicholas, or he knew of it and did not care. Nervously, Nicholas made an attempt at crossing one leg over the other, though his legs were too stubby and his thighs too large to fully allow it. "In Glastonbury," he finally announced, drumming his fingers against the frame of his chair, "I had a grand adventure."

"You need say no more," said John abruptly, standing and glancing briefly at Anne. "Mr. Fox, you'll come with me across the hall for an examination—this won't take long. Zachary: keep the young woman entertained? I'm sure you can manage that." With a brief, weak smile, he escorted Nicholas out, leaving the two of them alone.

When he heard the door shut across the hall, Zachary turned to Anne, who squinted at him steel-eyed, wrinkling her nose as if she smelled something bad. Zachary briefly thought that John had taken the easier job for himself; nonetheless, he soldiered on, pulling his chair closer to Anne's so that the two of them were but a few feet away (and half believing that the sound of the chair legs sliding across the wooden floor covered a high-pitched yelp from Howard's operating chamber. But perhaps he was hearing things).

"What a long trip you've been on," he began. "It must be wonderful to see so many different towns in England. My duties keep me here—I can only dream of travel."

"No, it's not wonderful; it's awful," Anne replied. "Ever since my father and I left in April, I have been counting the days until we return to London. These people, in every town we pass through: they're all so *provincial*. They know little if anything of what goes on beyond their village borders, and what's more, they seem not to care. They are uninterested in the miracle of candlelight—when the sun sleeps, they sleep with it, wasting time when books might stir their spirit of inquiry or make them wise. But a person could live and die without leaving London and still be a person of the world: the city is the whole world, rendered in miniature."

There was a knot in what Anne said that Zachary could not quite untangle, but he decided to let her comments pass. He chose to change the subject, realizing that now might be an unlooked-for opportunity to satisfy his curiosity about a conundrum for which he'd resigned himself to living without a solution. "I have a question," he said. "When my master and I attended the Exhibition of Medical Curiosities—afterward, when we walked home, we could not help but ask ourselves—"

"How much of it was brazenly fraudulent?" Anne interrupted. "Whether my father and I are the unscrupulous leaders of a traveling gang of cheats?"

"I didn't mean to pose the question in quite so harsh a manner," said Zachary, startled, "but—yes, we did wonder how much of what we saw was as real as it seemed."

"Forgive me, then," said Anne. "I should not have spoken for you. But it's a question I receive quite often, and it irritates me no end. Though I suppose that, since your master is treating my father's illness, you're entitled to an answer. How much of the exhibition you witnessed was real: that is your question?"

"Yes—that's it." Zachary leaned forward expectantly.

"Well, to begin with," Anne said, "I *myself* am not real. I, Anne Fox, daughter of Nicholas, am an *illusion*—in your mind; in the mind of your master; even in the mind of my own father. And in the minds of our provincial audiences I am not even my father's daughter, but a creature of unknown origin, perhaps fathered by Zeus."

"Somehow I find myself doubting that," Zachary replied.

Reading her absurd claim as an invitation, he reached out to touch her arm as if to verify her corporeality, but she quickly snatched it away. "Stay back, I tell you! You will have to believe me when I say that your hand would pass right through me, and neither of us desires that. Ghostly as I may seem to you, the space that my body occupies is mine; asserting my God-given title to it, though, requires a constant vigil."

"You are at a loss to prove your illusory nature, then," said Zachary, feeling that somehow he wasn't interpreting this situation correctly. He intended his words as harmlessly flirtatious endearments, meant only to while away the time, but they seemed to be twisting into something else as they traveled between his mouth and Anne's ear, for reasons he couldn't understand—in fact, the more Anne spoke, the less he understood her.

"Consider this," said Anne. "My dear father is now in consultation with your master, after having been on what I'm meant to believe is a 'grand adventure.' I am perhaps expected to think that while I slept one evening he journeyed to the moon, engaged in a sword fight with one of its six-armed inhabitants, and needs his secret wounds treated by a surgeon now that he has returned to earth. I know quite well that his 'adventure' took him no farther than a Glastonbury bagnio, and that as a result of an encounter within its walls, he now whimpers and mewls when he pisses. But were he to realize that I was aware of this, he would wonder how an innocent creature like myself came by such knowledge of the world—which, I assure you, resulted merely from keeping my ears open in public places: men seem to think that if they are not looking at me directly, I do not exist—and his idea of what I am would vanish. His daughter would disappear before his very eyes. Just as the version of myself that existed in your mind a few moments ago is vanishing, the one who looked like this—"

Anne slowly waved her right hand in front of her face, fingers spread wide, palm turned inward, like a magician performing sleight of hand. Once it had passed, Zachary saw that her expression had changed: the squinting stare that he was admittedly finding intimidating—he was starting to feel as if he were made of glass—was replaced with a wide-eyed gaze and beaming smile, the look so different that Zachary felt almost as if the very shape of her face had altered, becoming rounder and more angelic as the bones beneath her skin shifted.

"Witness a series of physiological wonders of which I am the *very* least," Anne said, her voice high and trilling and mocking; then she waved her hand in front of her face again, in the opposite direction, and the expression that Zachary found piercing and uncomfortably austere returned. The trick, if trick you could call it, seemed to make her age five years. "Are you confused?"

"Most certainly," said Zachary.

"Here, I've taxed you unduly. Let me relent." She passed her hand before her face once more, her eyes now sparkling. "Oh, goodness, whatever do you think the 'grand adventure' might be to which my dear father referred?" she asked. She giggled, looking away from Zachary as her eyelids fluttered, and Zachary felt a sudden warmth rush to his heart, even though he knew, and had been told directly by the woman just a few moments before, that this was all performance: the look, the ingenuousness, the laugh. Sitting next to Anne he felt baffled, frustrated, stupid, and embarrassed by his own evident stupidity, and the sudden sharp rap at the front door to Howard's offices came as an unexpected relief.

Anne smiled at Zachary with a deliberate blankness, her slim, long-fingered hands politely clasped in her lap, as he leapt out of his chair to welcome the guest.

*

The man at the door had the look of the Londoners who had been proliferating in Godalming these past two weeks, seeming somehow alien even though they hailed from the same nation. He pushed past Zachary as if his welcome onto the threshold were a foregone conclusion; once inside, he turned to face Zachary, offering his hand. "Cyriacus Ahlers, Surgeon to His Majesty's German Household. I have business with your master—I've been sent here by the king to inquire into an unusual case of his." Ahlers presented a handsomely polished appearance that stopped short of foppishness—his suit was of various shades of gray, accented with gleaming silver buttons; the black cocked hat clamped under his arm was embroidered along its brim with an unostentatious silver lace; and his wig was full and voluminous, with fine, lustrous locks that looked as if they'd be a pleasure to pass one's fingers through.

"Your master," Ahlers prompted. "Where is he?"

"He's with a patient," Zachary said, "but you're welcome to wait." He escorted him into Howard's office, where Anne sat with the same enigmatic smile, looking at the men as they entered. Ahlers offered Anne a slight bow, little more than a tip of the head, gracious in its subtlety.

John Howard and Nicholas Fox entered slightly after Ahlers had seated himself, Nicholas looking somewhat pale. "You're in luck, if luck you can call it," Howard was saying, hand on Nicholas's shoulder. "Butcher's-broom is still in bloom, though it's near the end of the season—in London you ought to be able to find a conserve of the berries easily enough. Thrice daily on bread. Fluids should be plentiful and tepid. Never mind the running; the running is the cure—" As Anne rose to her feet to greet her father, Howard stopped in mid-sentence, startled to see the new guest, who nodded at him knowingly.

Anne crossed the room, locking gazes with her father despite the three other sets of eyes on her as she walked. She took his hands in hers. "You're well?" she asked.

"Better," said her father. "The good surgeon has provided a temporary relief at a reasonable fee; the science of medicine advances apace. But the final stages of my convalescence are best achieved in London; we ought to return there posthaste. Good day," he said to Ahlers, then turned and made his way out, Anne following.

At the last moment she turned to look at the room of assembled men: Howard, Ahlers, and Zachary Walsh. After a bit of playful darting from one man to the other, her scrutiny fell at last on the apprentice. "Zachary?" she said.

"Ma'am?" He felt himself blushing.

"Come to London," she said, the corners of her lips lifting. "Perhaps there are still other versions of myself I have to show you; versions of yourself you haven't seen."

Then, as John Howard put his fingers to his mouth and looked discreetly at the floor, the woman in sapphire glided out of view.

"Quite an invitation you've received, young man," said Ahlers.

"It sounded like a command to me," said Howard. "Be wary, Zachary. Alice spoke to me in that voice, once, when I was young."

*

"Now," said John to the new visitor, "I haven't had the pleasure."

"Cyriacus Ahlers," said Ahlers, striding across the room with his hand offered in greeting, taking clear pleasure in the melody of his own name. He gripped Howard's hand and pumped it with three firm, carefully measured shakes. "I am honored to hold the title of Surgeon to His Majesty's German Household, and the king thought it fit to dispatch me here to learn in person about a most unusual case of yours, so unusual that despite his repeated, energetic confirmations, I fear I have misheard. '*Das Kaninchen*,' he says, but surely this must be some strange German idiom, whose meaning has not yet crossed to England's shores." Ahlers squinted. "Rabbits? Surely this refers to babies that are born prematurely: unusually frail, perhaps, or particularly endearing—"

"Rabbits in the most literal sense, I am afraid," said John. "Torn apart during the birthing, beheaded or stripped of their pelts, but rabbits all the same, and recognizable as such. Three each week on average. Arriving between nine and noon, regular as clockwork."

"That," said Ahlers, frowning, "is . . . most interesting."

"I have been tending to this woman since the middle of October," said John, "and despite our strenuous efforts her condition remains unchanged; nor has the phenomenon shown any signs of ceasing. We are both gravely concerned, Nathanael and I, and I find it reassuring that the king has chosen to send a second—"

Ahlers put up a hand. "Second? I am the *second* surgeon sent here by the king, you say? Who, may I ask, was the first?"

"Why, Nathanael St. André, of course. His assistance in this case has been of inestimable value thus far."

"Interesting. I have had . . . business . . . with Mr. St. André before," said Ahlers. "London is a small town in some ways—those who share rarefied circles within a profession often cross each other's paths. Whether St. André genuinely belongs in the circles in which he has irreversibly entrenched himself is, among his colleagues, a frequent subject of debate—"

The rap of the knocker cut Ahlers off mid-sentence, followed soon after by the door flinging open as if the visitor felt there was no need to wait to be welcomed. It was Nathanael St. André himself, along with Laurence. "A most unpleasant experience as I approached your door," Nathanael said to John as he entered the room. "In the company of a tubby little dandy was a woman whose face was spoiled by a birthmark—it covered half the poor creature's face. She might have been quite lovely otherwise. The look she gave me as she passed had clear intent to hex—"

He stopped, startled. "Cyriacus?"

Ahlers, beaming, extended his hand once again. "So *great* to see that you enjoy good health." He gave Nathanael's hand the same three quick vigorous pumps he'd portioned out to John, though Zachary got the impression that Ahlers's handshake in this instance caused St. André some slight pain. "The king, to whom I spoke in person *just yesterday,* sends his regards, and offers his hope that the mysterious case of this Godalming patient has not proved too thorny for a surgeon such as yourself to manage."

"I am certain, knowing my reputation as you do, that you assured him there is no cause for concern," said Nathanael. "Indeed, when I spoke to the king in person *myself* before I set out, he idly mentioned his intent to dispatch another person in my wake sometime later, to offer me some small assistance that he judged might be necessary. I assured him that such precautions were unneeded, but he is ever headstrong, and chooses to plan for even the most unlikely of contingencies. So here you stand, and we must make use of you—perhaps you might even be able to make one or two worthy observations as this case reaches its speedy and salutary conclusion."

"Oh, there will be many an *observation,*" said Ahlers, "of that you can be sure."

Meanwhile, Laurence had edged around the room until he was close enough to Zachary to talk in a whisper. "I sense trouble," he said as Ahlers and St. André spoke, the volumes of the two men's voices rising.

"I do not mean to cast aspersions on your master," said Zachary quietly, "but I feel compelled to ask whether he is sometimes given to lying."

"Lying outright, no," said Laurence after some consideration. "Stretching the truth to serve what he sees as a good end: on occasion."

"Which of these two is lying now, do you think? About having spoken to the king?"

Laurence looked back and forth between the two of them, their faces red; both of them had now begun to lay emphasis on their words by tapping the chest of the other with an extended index finger. He shrugged. "Neither? Both?"

At last, John placed his hands on the men's shoulders, silencing them. "Gentlemen," he said, "is there any need at this point for such heated discussion? Should not the health of the patient be our only focus until she is cured? I propose we delay our arguments until the crisis has passed. Yes?" He looked at St. André (who was breathing heavily) and Ahlers (who was biting his lip). "Yes?"

"Yes," Nathanael said, after a deep breath.

"Yes," Cyriacus said, straightening a stray lock of the hair of his wig. "John, it was a pleasure to meet you. I have a room at the Silver Hart—tomorrow morning I shall return, and I'll want to examine the specimens you've preserved thus far."

"Certainly. In addition, we have heard nothing today from Joshua Toft, the patient's husband—given that Mary tends to birth a rabbit every two or three days, it's likely that you will have your first chance to witness the phenomenon tomorrow. So prepare yourself."

"I shall," said Ahlers. "In the meantime, I believe I will explore this charming little town, and experience the novelty of air free of the city's smoke. Good day, all."

As Ahlers exited, St. André hissed to Howard in a stage whisper, "And while he takes the air, I would like to offer my studied opinion on *another case* of yours, John. I believe we must find a means of *stemming the infection*, before it *runs rampant*."

CHAPTER XII

THE SHEARING EFFECT.

The group of seven men who journeyed to Mary Toft's home to attend the delivery of her fourteenth rabbit, on the morning of Wednesday, November 16—Joshua Toft; Cyriacus Ahlers; Crispin Walsh; Nathanael St. André and Laurence; John Howard and Zachary—found themselves constantly jockeying for pride of place at the head of the procession. The apprentices excepted, each of them had their own ideas of the hierarchy of Toft's various attendants; each of them saw themselves deserving a place at or near the front of the line, and there were too many men for them all to be correct.

But who could definitively say which of these many men was most important? Joshua Toft was the woman's husband; John Howard was the surgeon who had the most experience with the case, and therefore the most intimate and intuitive knowledge; Nathanael St. André was the first surgeon from London to discover the case; Cyriacus Ahlers was the newest arrival in Godalming, and held an official title, bestowed on him by the king himself; Crispin Walsh was the only man of God in the group, and thought the Lord had no regard for earthly titles. Zachary and Laurence stood in the shadows of those to whom they were tethered, and thus acquired a portion of the eminence of their masters. None of these men could justifiably be pushed aside or dismissed. And so when Ahlers looked to his left to see St. André fast overtaking him, his strides long and exaggerated, he cut off his conversation with Crispin and Joshua to pick up his pace as well; Laurence trailed behind his own master, stepping once or twice on the heels of others, though this was surely not deliberate;

Zachary, seeing this (and though he viewed Laurence in a different and more favorable light than when he'd first arrived in Godalming, he was not at all inclined to cede any authority to him), began to walk more quickly, exerting a small pressure on John from behind to walk faster too. By the time they reached the Toft house the group had assumed a gait that, if not quite a run, could be reasonably described as a vigorous trot.

They had some difficulty entering, what with the front door not being quite wide enough to fit everyone abreast who wanted to pass through it at once, but after a brief comedy of crushed toes and grumbles, all of them eventually managed to fit themselves into the front room of the house. However, then came the larger problem of entering the lying-in chamber, which had a bed that took up a great deal of it, not to mention the space occupied by the patient who lay on the bed, which might have otherwise gone to the man most willing to break social convention; in addition, Joshua's mother, Margaret, occupied her usual station, standing beside the head of the bed, and with her sallow face and grim expression she looked the type to cause a scene if asked to move. Joshua absolutely had to enter the lying-in room: it would be strange for so many men to be in the company of his wife while he waited outside. Crispin had to accompany him, for the miraculous nature of the event required his presence and authority, beyond doubt. Ahlers surely had not come all this way for nothing: he had to observe the delivery at the very least. This left Nathanael and John, and as Nathanael turned to John and gently placed his hand on his arm, as if John were a distant, rarely seen cousin suffering bereavement, John realized that he had lost a game that he had not even realized he was playing.

"John," Nathanael said, "just this once, would you be willing to wait outside while this business is completed? It's far too close in there for all of us. And given certain *new arrivals to our party*, I am perhaps best suited to observe any *unexpected occurrences*. Yes?"

John quickly nodded, loathing himself for feeling warmed by Nathanael's answering smile. Nathanael turned and entered the lying-in room, Laurence following; at the last moment, Laurence looked back to make eye contact with Zachary, and the two of them shared a simultaneous cringe that Zachary found oddly comforting—if Zachary perceived that this situation was getting out of hand, its path unforeseeable and its conclusion unpredictable, then Laurence realized it too.

As Laurence wedged himself into the room and Nathanael shut it behind them, John and Zachary glanced at each other, seated themselves in the dim room's two rickety chairs, settled themselves, and waited.

Soon enough, through the door they heard the screams that heralded another birth, the familiar opening melody of a harsh, unsettling song.

*

Later that afternoon, Ahlers, Howard, and St. André returned to Howard's offices, where Ahlers undertook an examination of the fourteenth rabbit to be delivered from Mary Toft: a head, a torso, and both hind legs, along with a collection of viscera. "Strange," Ahlers said, seated on a tall stool before Howard's operating table, the rabbit parts spread out on a bloodstained cloth before him, prodding at the little pile of intestine with the tip of a knife blade. "I am no veterinarian," he said, "but this seems like a longer amount of intestine than ought to belong to even an adult rabbit. Perhaps twice as much, even."

"An unusual aspect of the phenomenon throughout the series of pregnancies has been an unpredictability in the number of components," said John, who stood behind Ahlers, next to St. André. "Only rarely have we seen a rabbit with a full complement of parts in their correct number, even if those parts are torn asunder. Either there will be too many legs, or not enough, or no head, or some other irregularity. As if the making of offspring requires a kind of instinctive knowing, of the body rather than the mind; and in her instance the knowledge required to bring such creatures into existence is misremembered, or not entire."

"There is more about this that occasions my interest," said Ahlers.

With a nimbleness of fingers that belied his age, he speared one of the thin, translucent ropes of rabbit gut with the knife tip, lifted it high so that it uncoiled, and stretched it out on the table as straight as it could go. "Pellets," he said, indicating with the knife. "Here, here, and here. Feces."

"Not ordinary feces, but meconium, certainly," said St. André, looking over Ahlers's shoulder and peering at the intestine. "Every mammalian fetus produces a modicum of solid waste in the womb; there is no reason for these to differ, monstrous as they might be."

Ahlers sliced through the intestine with a quick stroke of the knife; then, using the blunt side of the blade, he squeezed one of the pellets free. "Not dark enough for that," he said. "Meconium is almost black. This is lighter. Not viscous enough, either: this is solid. To my eye it seems to be derived from digested plant matter. Curious, don't you think?"

"Since the creatures this woman births appear to have the size and physical features of adult rabbits," said John, "it seems reasonable to conclude that their digestive systems would behave as those of adults. Perhaps some preternatural reconfiguration of the patient's digestive organs allows the fetuses to be delivered solid food, a portion of that which she consumes daily."

"A fine and credible conjecture," said Nathanael.

"Perhaps," said Ahlers, seeming to consider. "Let us move on to another interesting feature. Look at this hind leg, which we delivered detached from the torso, which followed on later. The severing here—it isn't ragged, as one might expect if the rabbit had been torn apart within the woman during its birthing. It's clean: a nearly level plane. Almost as if done with a knife."

"I've observed the shearing effect with a few of the other births as well," said Nathanael, as John looked at him in perplexity.

Ahlers turned on his stool to look up at Nathanael. "Shearing effect?"

"Yes—we, John and I, conjecture that as the rabbit passes from the Fallopian tube into the uterus prior to delivery, its parts are often sheared neatly away from each other, killing it in the process. Crispin

Walsh was the first to observe the audible sound of the rabbits being ripped apart inside the woman: I myself have since confirmed it. The regularity of the separation is, we believe, due to the fact that the fetuses are more malleable when passing into the uterus—they must be, in order to make their way there in the first place—and become less so once they arrive."

"That is a most bold claim, Nathanael; I would hazard that such physiological anomalies are unheard of, in all the literature."

"Boldness is warranted, I think: extraordinary evidence requires extraordinary claims. You are bound to accept the initial premise, unless you choose to disregard your own direct observations. You delivered this rabbit with your own hands, just as John and I delivered the thirteen rabbits previous; you examined her breasts, and found that one of them produced milk."

"A thin liquid substance," Cyriacus said, "watery, and not much of it, but . . . milk, I suppose."

"It could be nothing else," said Nathanael. "To continue: if you accept the premise, then you are bound to consider all conclusions that can plausibly proceed from that premise. We must not deny the evidence supplied by our own eyes; we must not delude ourselves in a futile attempt to cling to what is familiar, and comforting. Don't you agree, John?"

"Yes," John said quietly.

Ahlers put down the knife and rubbed his eyes. "How bizarre all this is," he said. "Here is what I propose. John, I would like to take this rabbit that, as Nathanael correctly points out, I delivered myself, back to London, along with two other of the specimens you've preserved in spirits: one from the first set of five, and one from the second set. I might be able to observe some kind of change in these creatures over time. And I might be able to shed more light on this once I can consult my library."

He stood. "I'll leave on tomorrow morning's stagecoach bound for London. I will report my findings to the king, and return if he judges it necessary. But it is difficult to see how all this will end: given the increasing amount of discussion that this case is occasioning among medical circles in London, and the heated nature of that discussion, those with a close association with it might find themselves in a place that is likely unexpected."

Cyriacus gripped John's right hand in both of his, and looked directly into his eyes. "Take care, friend."

*

"I find myself relieved that our *friend* Mr. Ahlers chose not to remain for much longer," said Nathanael at dinner the following afternoon. "John, as this enterprise proceeds we must be sure to choose our associates with care. In particular, given its extraordinary novelty, we must beware the company of those who wrap themselves too tightly in the mantle of their *expertise.*"

Alice had made a sweet veal pie for dinner, stuffed with forcemeat, potatoes, raisins, currants, candied citron, and lemon peel, covered with a feather-light puff pastry crust. She meditatively chewed a forkful of food, taking quiet pleasure in her own work; then she said, "I can only speak for myself, but I quite enjoy the company of experts. For instance: if there is a thing I do not know, and I am lucky enough to befriend an expert in the subject, then I might exchange words with her, and when our conversation ends, I will know a thing I once did not."

"Would that the trusting of experts were so simple, and so seemingly wise," said St. André after a mirthful chuckle. "But in some cases the expert can become corrupted by the very process by which he acquires his expertise—thus, he becomes shackled to orthodoxy, and will defend it against any challenges at all cost. Such a man can be identified because of his strenuous attempts to *look the part*—he may have fine clothes, or may repeatedly inform you of his long and august-sounding title—but to the wise man, such attempts merely betray his insecurity, his ossified state of mind."

"Oh, goodness, I see the peril, now that you've pointed it out," said Alice. "If by misfortune I am to cross paths with one of these pernicious people who knows entirely too much about the field he has chosen to spend his life studying, how can I best avoid him, and seek out someone who knows much less?"

"Seek the man who wears his learning lightly, who does not take an undue pride in his knowledge," said St. André, as Zachary glanced across the table at Laurence and risked the flash of a half smile. "Seek the man who prizes not mere quantities of specialized knowledge, but versatility, imagination, an openness to new possibilities. The man of *vast* learning is ever to be preferred over the man whose body of knowledge is miles deep, but only inches wide."

"I don't agree," Zachary said quietly.

Nathanael turned to look at Zachary. "Who speaks?" he said, as if it was somehow not quite clear to him who was speaking.

"I don't agree," Zachary repeated, a little more loudly. "If I were to agree, there would be no point in me being an apprentice. If expertise matters little, or if the man who calls himself an expert poses some sort of danger to society, then it seems that every man would be entitled to call himself a surgeon, regardless of whether he'd practiced for years. Surely you do not believe that yourself, sir? You have your own titles, which proclaim you as an expert. You speak of the king with familiarity, while the rest of us here cannot: his title in your mouth gives your own presence weight."

"Ah, see," said Nathanael, "I adopt the use of titles bestowed upon me by others because I know the social custom—they are a burden I am forced to bear, and it is true that on occasion they can convince others to listen when I speak. I would be foolish not to take advantage of that when necessary. But I am wise enough to know that in a moment of crisis my titles are worthless, mere conventions: I cannot cure a dying patient merely by declaring my titles." He turned to John. "Is this not so?"

"I would *love* to know what my husband thinks about this matter," said Alice, her gaze swiveling to John.

He was paying studious attention to the remains of veal pie on his plate, pushing pieces of potato aimlessly with his fork, leaving curving tracks through the sauce. "One might see it one way or the other way, depending on circumstances," he said. "Sometimes an expert's opinion might be wanted; sometimes not. Too much knowledge can sometimes be a problem when just enough will do."

Nathanael nodded; Alice and Zachary frowned.

*

Later, after the meal was finished, Nathanael, Laurence, and Zachary said their goodbyes and went up to their rooms. John had a feeling that he was expected to remain behind, though the events of the past few weeks had slowly eroded his trust in his own intuition—he no longer believed he could reliably look at faces and interpret the thoughts that lay behind them, or comprehend the secret messages that sometimes lay in the silences between supposedly innocent words. And he was tired.

He sat in the chair at the head of the dining table, slumping, half drowsing, waiting, chasing the ragged fluttering fragments of his own thoughts, and then Alice sat down and took his hand in hers, gently rubbing the pad of her thumb against his palm, rhythmically, back and forth. The simple, familiar gesture brought back years of memories of a mind that had once been in harmony with his, and unexpectedly, he felt himself on the edge of sobbing.

He clenched his teeth and looked into his wife's eyes, fearing she would spy the watery shine of his own, but she did not—or if she did, she chose not to acknowledge it.

"If you think I'm going to play the agreeable mate," she said quietly, still gliding her thumb across his palm, "eager to accept all her dear husband's pronouncements on the state of the universe without question, I suggest you think again. I've given my honest opinion on this, and I haven't changed my mind. I can't imagine what would make me do so."

"I would expect no less," said John.

"I see a glimpse of the wise man I married, then. But I want for your happiness—the strings of my heart are too knotted together with yours by now for me to ever desire otherwise. And short of dis-owning my own convictions—which you know I will not—I do not know what action to take.

"My love," she said, "you tear me in two."

"Even a fortnight ago I was so sure of my path," said John. "But now I can no longer distinguish up from down."

"I see," said Alice.

"With my own eyes I've witnessed the thing you call some kind of lie, again and again," said John. "Participated in it, firsthand. It cannot be a trick."

Alice said nothing.

John shook his head and wiped his free hand across his face as Alice gripped his other hand tighter. "Am I leading the way forward, or being pushed forward from behind?" he said. "In all honesty, I no longer know."

"Believe me, if I could solve this for you, I would. I can't think of what to say that I haven't already said."

"I may have received a quiet warning yesterday, from a man who believed me a lost cause. But who thought he might offer it anyway. Perhaps only to salve his own conscience."

"There is something on your face," Alice said, wiping at John's cheek with a maternal roughness; John did not ask what it was, and Alice did not say.

He bowed his head as if in silent prayer, his eyes closed, and Alice turned her hand over and caressed his cheek with the backs of her fingers; then he stood. "I need sleep," he said. "And perhaps tomorrow all this will start to come clear. Perhaps a hint of the last destination carved into a signpost, if not a glimpse of the end of the road itself."

He kissed her on the cheek and, exhausted, rose and went upstairs, his climb as slow as if his shoes were weighted with lead.

CHAPTER XIII

THE KING AND THE THREE IMPOSTORS.

By Monday, November 21, 1726, everyone in Godalming knew, or believed they knew, the details of Mary Toft's condition; everyone knew the reason for the influx of well-heeled Londoners into the village, crammed two or more to a room in the full-up Silver Hart, lodging in every spare accommodation in the town they could find.

Everyone knew someone who knew someone who'd seen the blackamoor passing through town that fateful September night, though one had to keep in mind that the details of his appearance and demeanor had probably become embellished in the retelling—certainly, he could not have been seven feet tall, which indicated that Rufus Richardson, the weaver who had openly claimed to have seen the fellow with his own eyes, was either an outright liar or a poor judge of size. Six feet was far more plausible—larger than many, but certainly not a giant.

Most people agreed on the coach pulled by six horses with shining black coats from which he alit when it stopped in front of the Toft house, sometime after midnight (though another detail of the story that had obviously been exaggerated into ridiculousness was the nature of the outerwear he wore—it was probably not a fur coat long enough to sweep the ground, sewn together from the pelts of three dozen rabbits, their heads left intact, the eyes of some of them roving wildly as if the creatures were possessed by nightmare). Most people also agreed that he strode up to the Toft house and rapped on the door with the ease of familiarity; Richardson, again, said that the black had stood outside the house and serenaded its occupants with

an ominous melody performed on a theorbo, which seemed like an
ordinary lute in his enormous hands. This was self-evident embroi-
dery. A mere knock on the door would have been enough to summon
Mary, who boarded the coach with the black fellow and left for parts
unknown, returning to her husband late the following morning, bab-
bling with her head addled, a small silken bag clutched in her hand
that held a dozen golden coins, minted in a foreign nation. Supposedly she had not spoken an intelligible word since, and began to give
birth to animals soon after, one or two clawing themselves free from
her each morning as soon as she awoke: rabbits, mice, and cats, but
mostly rabbits.

Just as everyone knew someone who knew someone who had seen
the blackamoor abscond with Mary Toft, everyone also knew that the
tale of the blackamoor was probably false—when one person relayed
it to another, which by this point was happening quite regularly, it
was with the understanding, decorously left implicit (because why
would one insult one's audience by spelling this out?), that this was
what *other* people were saying about Mary's condition, and that telling the story was meant to clarify the state of mind of Godalming's
citizens in general, not necessarily to make specific, true claims about
events that had occurred in the life of one specific woman. It did
not cause confusion or disquiet, this simultaneous knowing and not
knowing, believing and not believing. Indeed, it was quite possible for
a man to hear Rufus Richardson spin a wild story, of an ebony giant
whose head was wreathed in a cloud of mist illuminated by flickering
sparks, and judge it categorically false; then that man might tell the
same story himself—minus the silly facetious details—and believe it
true in his own mind as he was doing the telling; then, alone in his
bed at night, he would think to himself that the only place one could
come across a black person in Godalming was in one's dreams, or in
the illustrations of books.

It was also possible (and perhaps this pointed to the genuinely
miraculous nature of the Toft case) to hold that Toft's condition arose
as a result of her encounter with the mysterious black man, and also
hold that one of the rabbits she had birthed hosted the spirit of her

miscarried son—though, again, that story had been embroidered through retelling as well, and the belief that the rabbit invested with her son's soul had developed a rudimentary ability to speak, and could tell you the day of your death if you asked, was laughable. For those who observed it from a distance, the Toft case acted as a kind of vortex that drew facts and falsehoods into it and stirred them together, so that all things were true and none were true. And if considering the case might give one the feeling that the ground was unsteady beneath one's feet, that the world was filled with fog, then it also challenged one's long-held preconceptions of the world's true nature, and opened one's mind up to myriad possibilities previously left unconsidered. For this reason—some might have said, if asked—it was wonderful.

*

Late during that Monday, John Howard and Zachary Walsh returned to Howard's offices after attending the difficult delivery of a child who, for a change, was human. (The birth was breech but expertly turned by Howard's sure hand, so there was no need to break any of the baby's limbs, or do worse still to save the life of the mother; the child, a girl, had ten fingers and toes and was perfectly, blessedly normal. Man-midwife and apprentice left the new family, the woman exhausted, her husband relieved, their daughter red-faced and wailing as if to alarm all the devils in hell.) Once inside the offices they found that a gentleman had somehow gained entrance ahead of them, and had made himself at home in Howard's waiting room, seated in a chair and paging idly through the copy of Locke he'd lifted off Howard's desk.

He looked as if he were about to deliver the eulogy at his own funeral—skeletally slender, dressed in black from head to toe, his wig a lightly powdered white. His face was long and gaunt, with paper-thin lips and a narrow, aquiline nose; his eyes were a dark brown that seemed almost black, his eyebrows mere suggestions. "You've gotten rather a bit farther than most in this, it seems," he remarked as he snapped the book shut, replaced it on Howard's desk, and rose. "Greetings," he said, crossing the room and offering his hand, which John took (it was cold and limp, the shake unvigorous). "I am Sir Richard Manningham, Fellow of the Royal Society and Licentiate of the College of Physicians, and I come at—"

"—the request of King George?" said John.

"Yes—it seems you find this unsurprising. I've been preceded, I believe, by several others. You might imagine that my colleague Ahlers's report was . . . most unusual. St. André must still be here. And other observers, unassociated with any of us or with the king, appear to be arriving on their own initiative. Which leads me to my next point. I fear," he sighed, "that the local inn is full, and I have no place to stay. Your abode looked to me as if it might have some space you might offer, for which I'd be quite grateful."

*

If Ahlers's presence had occasioned a bluster from Nathanael St. André, Manningham's brought on a not entirely unwelcome silence—St. André was the quietest of the six who sat at Alice's table for dinner that afternoon. She served a turkey dressed in the German style, stuffed with forcemeat and roasted chestnuts, accompanied with turnips and sausages sliced and mixed together; Manningham chose to content himself with a single turkey leg on an otherwise empty plate, as if he endeavored to eat the minimum necessary to keep his soul tethered to his body. "My compliments on the dish," he said to Alice, surgically removing each bite of meat from the leg with precise, fastidious movements of his fork and knife, stripping the bone completely clean, occasionally sawing futilely at the bone with the knife, as if he wished to cut through it to get at the marrow. "You may have guessed, incidentally, that due to a superstition suddenly in vogue, rabbit rarely appears on London plates as of late—our poulterers find themselves tossing coneys away unsold. And there is now some debate in intellectual circles—facetious, one would hope—

concerning whether rabbits have souls. Some would have it that we may have been mistaken about the creatures, all this time. That we unwittingly committed the direst of sins whenever we enjoyed a rabbit fricassee." A rasping sound came from his throat that seemed intended to approximate a laugh.

"A strange vision of heaven," Alice said. "Seraphim tripping over hordes of the creatures bounding underfoot. Imagine the stink."

That grating rasp from Manningham, again—he seemed as if he'd made the decision early on in life to embrace the power of his physiognomy and demeanor to unsettle, and yet that did not entirely explain St. André's sudden onset of diffidence. "I should clarify my stance on this matter," Manningham said. "It is, you may have guessed, skeptical, and my skepticism is supported both by my years of prior experience and my status as perhaps the preeminent man-midwife in London."

"And if you persist in your skepticism, you will find yourself standing alone," St. André said finally, his sentence ending in an unmanly squeak. He cleared his throat and then continued: "You have seen the groups of people arriving here. Hundreds, now, who all believe. They cannot all be incorrect. And tomorrow morning, when you witness one of her births firsthand—"

"The arrivals can be predicted in such a timely fashion? Within a few hours? Odd."

"Yes—it's merely another part of the miracle. You will see it for yourself, and then you will have no reasonable choice to believe, as the rest do. As does he, and he, and he." He pointed a finger at John, Laurence, and Zachary.

"I can't help but notice that you've left our wonderful hostess off your list of adherents."

"I continue to keep my own counsel," said Alice.

Zachary and Laurence ate quietly, heads bent over their plates; John looked placidly at his wife, his face a plaster mask.

Eventually, Manningham reclined in his chair, his long-fingered hands steepled as he gazed at the ceiling. "For some reason, I am strongly reminded of a fable that my mother heard from her father, who, family legend has it, received it in turn from a Spaniard noble-man, passing through London on his travels. Transformed in the tell-ing and retelling, perhaps; distorted by translation in addition. All the same, it is a good story—I offer it as payment for my seat at this table. My mother called it 'the tale of the king and the three impostors.'"

"I love a good tale," Zachary spoke up, finding Manningham's offer unexpected, but thinking that a story might mitigate the unwel-come tension at the table.

"And your title already promises something more agreeable to the ear than the endless chatter of these other fellows," said Alice. "Please: begin."

*

"In a tiny kingdom whose name is lost to history," said Manning-ham, "three impostors approached a king, presenting themselves as weavers with the rarest of talents. They claimed to be able to manu-facture a cloth that was unparalleled in its beauty, exquisite in its design—moreover, it had the ability to distinguish those men who were legitimate sons of their fathers from those who were bastards. To the bastard, the cloth would be invisible; only a legitimate son would be able to see it and appreciate its magnificence.

"The king immediately saw the value of such a cloth, for the kingdom's laws declared that bastards could not inherit the property of their cuckold fathers, and in such instances the property of the deceased would go to the state. He showered the impostors with sil-ver and gold, assigned them a wing of rooms in his palace where they would not be disturbed, and set them to work.

"The impostors stayed in seclusion for seven months, only dis-patching occasional requests for servants to bring them sweetmeats and wine; eventually, the king sent his lord chamberlain into their private wing to observe their progress. The impostors, who had become surprisingly corpulent and red-faced since anyone had last seen them, with ruptured veins coloring their noses, escorted the lord chamberlain into the chamber where they went about their labor. In the midst of disorder—plates with sauces dried to crust; half-full glasses of beer; discarded women's undergarments—was a loom, and on the loom, saw the lord chamberlain, was nothing.

" 'Is it not wonderful?' said one of the impostors, gesturing at the empty loom. 'So beautiful that one might be blinded by it, were one to look upon it for too long. You must take care: avert your eyes if you begin to feel faint.' Of course, the lord chamberlain began to recall a few moments in his youth when he had spied his mother closeted in conversation with one of the family's gardeners and she had protested, perhaps a touch too vehemently, that she was doing nothing wrong, and that what he saw was best forgotten. 'It *is* wonderful,' said the lord chamberlain. 'So stunning that I can barely believe my eyes.'

" 'You notice the intricate weaving together of spun gold and silver threads?' The impostor lifted nothing in his hands and held it toward the lord chamberlain. 'Supple and smooth to the touch, yet it would turn away an assassin's dagger thrust. Do you wish to feel it?'

"The lord chamberlain retreated. 'To touch such fabric is a privilege I do not deserve: it must be reserved for the king. I am content merely to look. I am quite satisfied that the work is progressing apace; I leave you to your labors.' The trio of impostors sent him on his way with a long rumbling belch in three-part harmony."

Nathanael St. André interrupted at that point. "I find myself puzzled by your choice of narrative," he said. "Its ribaldry might be judged unsuitable for the company of a woman; moreover, it threatens to touch on the topic of *fraud,* and I worry that it may lead you to stray into unintended and undeserved insinuations that you would later recall with remorse."

"Oh, I've heard worse," said Alice. "I've *said* worse. Please don't concern yourself with my womanish sensibilities, good Sir Richard."

"I shall not," said Manningham, "and as for the matter of fraud, those who do not commit it—which, presumably, includes all of us seated here at this table—have nothing to fear from a tale that features it. But perhaps fraud is not the story's principal concern, in the end? Let it unspool in its own time.

"To continue."

*

"The impostors worked on the fabric for another year, and eventually, the king became impatient. Rousing himself from his throne, he entered their private rooms and found them in the chamber where they labored: to his surprise, he found that twelve months of meats and pastries had enlarged them astonishingly, making them tiny-eyed and triple-chinned; moreover, they were completely naked, and stood before him without shame, innocent as Adam. Before the king could declare his shock, anger, and disgust, one of the impostors approached him, head bowed, flesh quivering, and with a tremulous voice he made a confession: that as their bodies had grown and their original clothing no longer fit, they had used the special fabric to make three suits for themselves. 'We realize that only a king deserves to clothe himself in such splendor,' the impostor said as, behind him, the other two turned in circles with their arms raised, modeling nothing but their own folds of fat. 'I hope to restrain your justifiable anger with the news that we have, just today, completed a fourth suit of this material for yourself: your native resplendence will only serve to amplify the beauty of the fabric, casting the three of us in shadow.'

"It was impossible to even consider the possibility that the three impostors would be so bold as to exhibit themselves naked before the king and tell a flagrant lie: such impertinence defied belief. And so the king knew, or thought he knew, two things: that the fabric functioned as the impostors had advertised, and that he himself was a bastard, unaware of this until now. As for the latter fact, no one else needed to know—in fact, the knowledge had to be kept secret, lest a pretender to the throne appear and the nation plunge into war. As for the former: well, it was high time for all the other bastards to unwittingly reveal themselves, so that their so-called parents would fill the king's coffers. Praising the impostors' workmanship and thanking them profusely, the king ordered the suit they had made for him to be boxed and brought to his living quarters, and commanded that a day in the following week be set aside for a grand procession, at whose head he would appear; no one would work that day, and attendance would be mandatory. He would wear the miraculous suit, display it to the populace, and in the reactions to his wardrobe he would see what he would see."

"It sounds as if our poor king has quite the embarrassment in store," said John, chuckling.

"Perhaps," said Manningham.

*

"On the day of the grand procession," Manningham continued, "a tradesman, whose name is also lost to history, closed his shop as the royal edict demanded and took his young son to view the parade. They were among the first to arrive along the route, and they staked out a spot at the side of the road where they could have a clear view.

"The tradesman's loves could be counted on one hand, but they were simple and pure: he loved his family, and he loved his nation. If pressed, it would be difficult for him to say which he loved more. Family provided benefits that were immediate and constant, real and easy to cherish—the warmth of your wife's embrace, the merry laughter of your daughters, or the way in which your only son looked up at you with a mother's inherited eyes. But family, wonderful as it could be, was precarious, and ephemeral in the great scheme of things. A human life was but a moment, measured against the life of a nation. No one knew when death might steal one's wife or son or daughter away, but a nation's love for its citizens would last forever; the nation had existed long before the tradesman had been born, and it would remain long afterward, to safeguard the livelihoods of his descendants after he himself had passed. To have a wife look into your eyes provided a small, daily, dependable reassurance that you were loved, and that you deserved love. But what would that be compared to falling, even briefly, under the kind scrutiny of a king who embodied the

nation that granted succor to so many? Even a short glance would
serve to affirm a man's sureness of his worth for decades. And to meet
the king's eyes as a boy might set that boy on the path to becoming
a great man.

"Such was the thinking of the tradesman who pulled his sleepy-
eyed son out of his bed at sunrise, to wait for the king's appearance;
he thought it best to let his daughters sleep.

"As the time for the parade approached the crowd became larger,
and larger still, the noise of the thousands in garrulous conversation
behind them becoming louder and louder. The sun was high in a
cloudless sky; the weather was perfect, with a slight cooling wind to
counteract the heat of bodies pressed together. The tradesman and his
son were at the very front of the throng; they would not have to crane
their necks or bob their heads to see the king as he passed, clothed in
what was rumored to be the most fantastic royal robe that man had
ever laid eyes on, in all of human history. The robe had become the
foremost topic of conversation among all the nation's citizens; they
spent sleepless nights attempting to imagine that which was beyond
imagining.

"At noon sharp the tradesman heard a cheer in the distance, the
roar rising in volume as it came closer, and he looked down the road
to see the royal procession approaching: lines of soldiers marching in
spirited step, their legs kicking high; flautists and trumpeters and
drummers playing the national anthem; flags and pennants flapping.
The tradesman's heart began to hurl itself against his rib cage, as if
it wanted to burst free of his chest and flop down on the road before
him, offering itself up to be trampled.

"At the front of the procession was the king himself, standing
proud in the rear of a wagon towed by six white horses, arms akimbo,
grinning with his chin jutted forward and held high. And as the
tradesman looked on the king, he squinted as if blinded, not quite
trusting his eyes—

"And then he saw the robe. He saw it, and he freely wept. It shimmered; it shone; it *altered*. Sometimes it appeared as the colors of the
national flag, in sumptuous shades of crimson, ivory, and ultramarine;

sometimes it appeared as if the king had shrouded himself in a thousand ribbons made of rainbows. The sheer magnificence of the king's clothing threatened to bring the tradesman to faintness, but with a strength of will, the cheers of the crowd around him resounding in his ears, he managed to stay upright, keep his head, and direct his son to look.

"The young boy's eyes widened as his mouth dropped open, and he first began to chuckle, then to laugh without restraint, his high-pitched *haw-haw-haw* cutting through the applause. The tradesman became confused: was laughter the expression of the child's awe? 'Do you see it?' he asked. 'Isn't it wonderful?'

"The boy laughed, harder still, and pointed. 'He's naked!' he shouted. 'The king is naked!'

"And at that, the wagon with its six white horses slowed, then stopped, as the cheering of the crowd began to be shot through with murmurs of consternation. Puzzled, the tradesman looked up at the king and, to his alarm, found that the king was staring directly back at him with a cruel, confident smile, and, worse, he was in fact as naked as he'd been on the day of his birth, with drooping old man's breasts, a sagging, wrinkled bottom, and a limp, shriveled yard, crowned with a tangled gray thatch of pubic hair. And yet he seemed unembarrassed; the smile remained on his face with its knowing twist, as if the king was waiting for the tradesman to realize something, and to take a necessary course of action. The king seemed strangely unworried that the crowd behind the tradesman was becoming enraged, the clamor of their shouts developing a nasty edge—it was only the child who was consumed by gay, mocking laughter, and as the tradesman felt a hand grasp his shoulder from behind, perhaps in threat, perhaps in reassurance, he looked up into the naked king's eyes, and he knew what he had to do.

"Standing behind his son, he bent over him, and he whispered a brief, heartfelt apology in his ear. Then, with an ease surprising even to himself, he snapped the child's neck."

(At the dining table, Zachary started, for it seemed to him that he had somehow *heard* the break of the boy's neck just as clearly as he had heard Manningham describe it; before his eyes he saw the child's head canting at an unnatural angle, his face going slack as he collapsed to the ground like a marionette cut loose from its strings. Then he saw that as Manningham had spoken, he'd taken the turkey bone from which he'd stripped every last string of meat, held it in both hands, and broken it in two. Later, thinking about it, Zachary would realize that the whole time Manningham had been working away on the turkey leg, he'd been quietly scoring the bone with his knife blade—he'd begun the dinner with the intent to tell this story, to create this dramatic moment.)

"The tradesman looked up at the king again, and the monarch smiled down at the tradesman with pleasure. And the robe the king wore had become, somehow, even more dazzling: its fabric had manifested as a rippling mirror, which reflected the tradesman back to himself as what he imagined himself to be, and as he once was, and as he would become. For a brief moment the tradesman had experienced what one might call a vision, some sort of devilish illusion, the details of the matter too embarrassing to repeat; but that cursed vision was gone now, and the hurrahs of the crowd grew ever louder and more frenzied as the team of horses pulled the king's wagon onward.

"The tradesman loved his nation, and in the king's beatific gaze he felt that love affirmed and justified. He had only one regret: that he did not have a son with whom to share this day, for such a sight was the kind of experience that might set a boy on the path to a fruitful manhood, all in a moment.

"But alas, the tradesman's wife had only ever given birth to daughters."

*

In silence, Manningham let go of the halves of the turkey bone he'd been clutching in his hands, so tightly his knuckles had gone white. He rose, tall, thin, and ghostly, and looked down on the rest of those seated at the table. "I believe I will take the air," he said; then, not waiting for any kind of acknowledgment, he unceremoniously left the room.

Alice leaned forward once Manningham was out of earshot and said, "He is certainly the most unsettling of all the fellows who have come marching through here since this whole affair began," she said. "I find him strangely refreshing."

"I have crossed paths with him in London many times before, as I have with Ahlers," said St. André. "I will not lie, or underestimate him: our minds are not in harmony, but his is cunning, and quick. For all that his demeanor might recall the newly dead, he has, it is true, saved lives that other surgeons and man-midwives would have considered beyond rescue. Though I worry about his open profession of skepticism—he may be a judge who has already come to his verdict before the trial has barely begun, and who sees the consideration of evidence as a mere formality."

"He will have to witness one of the births himself," said John, "as you and I and Ahlers have. Surely he will not reject the evidence of his own two eyes."

*

That evening, as Zachary lay in bed, he heard a quiet knock on the door that he'd been half expecting. He opened it to find Laurence, who entered without speaking and sat down on the end of Zachary's bed, looking out of the loft's lone window at the night sky.

"I couldn't sleep," he said eventually. "Because of the story we heard this afternoon. When I do fall asleep, I expect nightmares."

"Me too," said Zachary.

Zachary reclined on the bed and stared at the ceiling; he sensed that Laurence was not yet done speaking.

"There was one thing I did not understand," said Laurence quietly. "The robe, in the story. Was it real, or not real?"

Zachary thought about it. "Well, from the perspective of those of us sitting at the table this afternoon, none of it was real: neither the robe, nor the king, nor the three impostors. All of it was a temporary illusion to which we acceded, for our entertainment. But from the perspective of the people in the story . . ." He left the thought unfinished; he had no idea how to complete it.

"Surely the tradesman in the story would not have been willing to kill his own son unless what he saw was real," Laurence said. "But killing the son was what made the robe real, and then the son wasn't real anymore. It's strange."

"It was only a story," said Zachary, yawning as his eyelids drooped.

But Laurence was determined not to let the matter drop. "Wake up, Zachary. Consider this. What if the tradesman had left his son behind when going to see the procession? He, and all with him, would have seen the king in his wonderful robe. He would have returned home and described the robe to his son—the son might have regretted missing the experience, but otherwise his life would have proceeded as normal. He would have gone on to live a full life, with no harm done except for the possible delusion."

"But that's not the story we heard. Your version is easier to digest, but somehow . . . less honest. Not so true—insofar as it makes sense to talk about the truth of a story like that."

"Perhaps," said Laurence, thinking on it, "it doesn't matter whether the king's magic robe was real or illusion. Or perhaps the story's moral—unintended, but still present—was that boys who wish to stay alive need to learn when to speak, and when to stay quiet."

Suddenly, Zachary felt himself snap wide awake again.

CHAPTER XIV

A STRANGE CELEBRATION.

Thursday, November 24 (three days after Manningham had told his unsettling tale at dinner, and two after Manningham had delivered Mary Toft's sixteenth rabbit), was the day when Zachary realized beyond doubt that events had escaped the control of Howard, or St. André, or Manningham, or Mary Toft herself, or anyone. The story of the Toft event had become its own creature, dragging the people associated with it in its wake, moving forward to who knew what end.

He awoke, that morning, to the sound of cheers and the ringing of what sounded like a dozen tiny tinkling bells—he'd been dreaming, just before, of the crowd waiting for the king in Manningham's story, finding himself in the throng of supplicants, seeing the impossibly beautiful robe, screaming so loud with unrestrained joy that he began to spit blood. When his own yells awoke him, the echoing holler from his throat dying out as his eyes opened, the applause of the crowd in the dream continued to ring in his ears, making him wonder if he had merely stepped out of one dream and into another; then he roused himself from bed, the haze beginning to clear from his mind, and went to the window of his loft to look down on the street below.

The road was filled with marchers, what looked like at least a hundred, all headed on the path out of town that led toward Mary Toft's house. Most of them were Londoners, rotund and red-faced, though more than a few of the local townspeople had mingled in with the gathering out of curiosity. Flanking the crowd were two small girls in brilliant gowns, striped in jewel-toned reds and greens, running gaily alongside the procession with their beribboned braids streaming behind them; before them, they held bells attached to long wooden sticks, whose chimes harmonized with their trilling laughter.

What on earth was this? Even before he asked, he knew, and though Zachary thought that all of this was amiss for reasons he couldn't articulate, he felt the urge to join the procession below. His reservations barely won out, and only because, close to the head of the throng, making wide gestures of speechification, his grand pronouncements made unintelligible from this distance by the crowd's din, was none other than Nathanael St. André. Young Laurence trailed behind him, dressed as usual like St. André in miniature, dragging his feet in exhaustion.

Zachary frowned as he realized that he'd bitten his tongue in his sleep, as well as the tender inside of his cheek: the little wounds would nag him for days. Still wondering where the girls in red and green had come from, how they had obtained the bells they rang, and by what means they'd been designated proclaimers of what must be the forthcoming miraculous birth—a conundrum for which, even after this was all over, he was never to receive a satisfactory answer—he pulled on his clothes and, still drowsy, made his way downstairs to Howard's offices.

Despite the noise outside, Zachary found Howard sitting quietly at his desk, intently reading Locke. He sat down in a chair opposite. "No word from Joshua Toft this morning?"

Howard looked up at Zachary, his feigning of surprise at the question unconvincing. "Joshua Toft has not appeared this morning," he said. "I would take it that my patient is not in need of my care. Though *patient* is, perhaps, an inadequate word for what she has become."

He closed the book. "It seems there's quite a commotion outside," he said. "Shall we see what that's about?"

*

Two days before, Joshua Toft had arrived at Howard's offices as expected, summoning Howard, St. André, and Manningham for a delivery. It had seemed to Zachary, and to Howard, that while St. André had regarded Cyriacus Ahlers with a barely restrained antagonism, he somehow wanted to ingratiate himself with this newest emissary of King George's curiosity—despite his condemnations of authority and expertise once Ahlers had returned to London, Nathanael appeared entranced by Sir Richard Manningham, and approached him with an attitude of solicitous deference. As they walked over to the Toft house, Manningham and St. André were in the lead—Manningham strode purposefully with his hands clasped behind him, while St. André walked beside him, gesticulating whenever he spoke and responding to Manningham's terse responses with exaggerated nods of approval. Howard could not help but feel forsaken, and as the usual press to fit Mary Toft's myriad attendants into her lying-in chamber left Howard and Zachary stuck outside once again, Nathanael's apology was perfunctory, and Howard accepted it with resignation, and without complaint.

The subsequent routine was, to Zachary, depressingly familiar—as he sat in the front room of the house with Howard he could, with reasonable accuracy, predict the pitch and duration of Mary's screams through the wall—and so, figuring that he had at least a few minutes before the delivery was over, he asked his master's permission to step outside. Besides, he'd wanted to investigate a small gathering of people whom the group of men attending Mary Toft had passed on their way inside the house—the surgeons in consultation had paid them no mind, but Zachary thought they merited a second look.

When he stepped outside he saw a white blanket spread out on the yellowed grass of the yard in front of the house. Seated on the blanket, with cheerful smiles and pink cheeks as if they were having a leisurely afternoon outing in high summer, were two London women, wearing fur hats and leather gloves and layers of wool to guard against the November chill. One of them was dandling the little Toft boy, James, nuzzling him and cooing: "You're a *monster*. You're a dirty little *animal,* and I'm going to *eat* you." She bared her teeth and playfully bit into James's neck as he squirmed and giggled and pushed at her face with his tiny hand.

"Look here," said the other woman, glancing at Zachary. "Here's another one: too large to be devoured in one sitting, I fear, even for the two of us."

The first woman pulled her nose away from where she'd been rubbing it in James's ear. She smacked her lips in mock desire. "Now here's some mutton: richer in flavor, to be sure, but I expect he'd protest if we got out our carving knives. Not like my little lamb here," she said, tickling the laughing boy as he futilely tried to slap her hands away. "Good only for eating is what you are, you *awful* little thing."

"Though I hate to disappoint, it's true that I've grown old enough to become fond of keeping my flesh," said Zachary. "Might I ask why the two of you are here?"

"We are the Sisters Snelling," said the second woman, "famous only to ourselves, perpetually nomadic, beholden to no man, forever inseparable. I am Frances; my carnivorous companion here is Henrietta."

They did not look like sisters in the least. Henrietta was small, ginger-haired, and chubby, pale-skinned with a dense band of freckles crossing the bridge of her nose; Frances, on the other hand, was tall, slender, and dusky, with a single curling forelock of white hair amidst a mane that was otherwise jet black. They certainly behaved in a sisterly manner, though, with a playful warmth between them that was easy to see, and that suggested a fellowship forged over decades, and so Zachary saw no harm in taking the two of them at their word.

"As for what brings us here," Frances continued, "in our search for adventure beyond London's environs, we have heard a rumor about the woman inside that house that defies belief: we would scarcely credit it, were it not so often repeated." And as Henrietta covered the little boy's ears, Frances beckoned Zachary to lean over so that he could hear her whisper.

"We have heard," said Frances with a wink, "that the woman inside has *bunnies* leaping forth from her *cunny*."

"Rabbits, yes," said Zachary reluctantly, feeling his face turn hot. "Though not alive—severed into parts, in fact."

"She ought to do better, then," said Henrietta as she removed her hands from James's ears. "If a woman goes to the trouble to engage in such business in the first place, she ought not to settle for half measures."

"I'm sure she's doing the best she can, Ettie," said Frances. "Please do try to be less censorious?"

"My apologies, Fanny," said Henrietta desultorily, as if she apologized to Frances a dozen times a day.

"We came," said Frances, "because no matter the truth of events, we could sense that *something was happening,* and we wanted to witness it firsthand."

"There are other Londoners here as well, filling up your beds and tossing money about—as Fanny and I do in London, we try our best to avoid them—but at present they possess too much propriety to approach the scene of the event," said Henrietta. "We have no such silly scruples, and so we are first. Why come all this way to the village and fail to travel the last mile out of shyness?"

"And we thought that perhaps we might get a glimpse of the woman," said Frances. "Speak to her even, if there's a chance of it; find out how she feels. How does she feel?"

The question puzzled Zachary, even as he realized that perhaps it shouldn't have.

"We would *love* to know how she feels," Frances prompted. "Is she thrilled or troubled? I can't begin to imagine my state of mind, were such a thing to happen to myself."

Henrietta grabbed the belly fat of the boy in her arms and gave it a vigorous pinch. "And what has *this* poor creature done," she said, "to deserve such an unending litter of devilish brothers and sisters? Shame on you, child. *Shame.*"

"Stop," the boy said, giggling.

"Putting the obviously necessary rewrite of the woman's last will and testament aside," said Henrietta, "surely she must have offered her own opinion on the state of things, given the extent to which her very own body is involved in this matter." Zachary thought it unwise to disappoint the women, to say that the first thing that anyone would notice when in the presence of Mary Toft was a face that clearly indicated her dull-eyed, bovine stupidity—if anything, she seemed to the men who served as her doctors to be her body's hostage, rather than its owner. He could offer nothing in response but a noncommittal shrug.

"Well, when you return inside," said Frances, "please do make it known that there are those out here who have her in their thoughts, and are concerned about her well-being."

"I'll do so," said Zachary, turning to leave as, down the road, an apparent foursome of husbands and wives approached, the two women gaily chattering to each other, one of the men holding a bundled blanket beneath his arm.

*

If Manningham had retained his skepticism after delivering Mary Toft of her sixteenth rabbit, he had kept his cards close. When they returned to Howard's offices later that afternoon (as they'd left the Toft house, the gathering of people waiting outside had grown to a dozen), Manningham reported that he had examined the woman with close attention, and despite his "vigorous efforts," he could find "no evidence of imposture." ("Vigorous? I should say so," complained St. André to Howard later that day, when Manningham had busied himself with study of the prior specimens that Mary had birthed, and the two of them were closeted alone. "He not only scrutinized every inch of the woman, but the bed in which she lay, getting on his hands and knees to peer under it, sliding his hand between the mattress and the frame. As if he were searching for the concealed mechanism of a magic trick! I thought to make a joke about how his peculiar notions of childbirth were at odds with the literature, but kept it to myself.")

Manningham did discern some medical irregularities in the

patient, other than the obvious: as had Cyriacus Ahlers, he noticed a liquid leaking from her breasts, similar to milk, but too thin and watery to be nutritive; when palpating her stomach he felt a slight hardness on her right side, which St. André triumphantly announced was consonant with his own observations. Looking at her neck, slightly bruised and displaying the dot of an old needle prick, he inquired as to whether Mary had undergone a phlebotomy, and Nathanael replied that he had performed it, with Howard's able assistance—that it was one of the first things they'd considered, and that it had not produced even a temporary cessation of the anomalous births: a new rabbit had continued to appear every two to three days, on schedule.

Manningham concluded, then, that there was nothing to do but watch and wait. The group of people holding a vigil in front of the Toft house (fifteen arriving on the morning of Wednesday, November 23, swelling to thirty by that afternoon) appeared to have come to the same conclusion, but what they were all waiting for, none could say; nor could one say whether they were all waiting for the same thing, or whether each was waiting for something entirely different.

*

John Howard locked up the entrance to his offices—he did not expect that anyone would come calling with urgencies for the next hour—and he and Zachary joined the procession marching to the Tofts' home. There was an undeniable *joyousness* in the crowd: a gay laughter erupted, now here, now there, above the din of a hundred people in lively conversation, and occasionally people broke into cheers and clapped their hands for who knew what reason—perhaps no more than sheer pleasure at being alive, at a time and in a place that held such wonders and promised still more. Zachary felt his heart lift in happiness even as he found himself suspicious of that happiness's cause; he felt the boundary that separated his own mind from those around him becoming porous, as the unrestrained delight of the crowd worked its way into him. How lovely it would be to believe, as all these people seemed to; the object of the belief was not important, merely that one believe in something, wholeheartedly, without question, to let that belief grant you its unadulterated jubilation—

Zachary felt Howard's firm hand on his shoulder. He stumbled as he was jostled by the person next to him, a grinning Londoner seemingly as wide as he was tall; then he heard Howard's voice in his ear. "We need to get closer," Howard shouted, jabbing his finger in the air in the direction of the head of the crowd, where Nathanael St. André was holding forth.

They worked their way forward as best they could without resorting to ruthless elbowing. As they approached Nathanael, the volume of the surrounding crowd began to drop, as those immediately close to the surgeon bent their ears to hear his exuberantly delivered monologue: "—*more things in heaven and earth than are dreamt of in our philosophies,* to paraphrase the great man, yes? I have always regarded myself as a man who balances pride in the depth of his hard-won knowledge with humility, born of an awareness of how little he knows compared to the Lord, who knows *all.* How wondrous it is to see one's expectations of our very existence defied so plainly! No word short of *miraculous* can truly describe what we—John! Look here: it's John Howard, my friend and colleague, and his young assistant. Come here. Come!"

As Howard stepped forward, Nathanael greeted him with a hearty clap on his back. "I must acknowledge to you all, and it is in fact my *pleasure* to acknowledge, that the first tentative steps along the path on which we now find ourselves were taken by this local gentleman, who, in the absence of the kinds of resources available to myself, relied on his native instincts to carry him as far as he could. Moreover, he was wise enough to summon aid from afar when those instincts reached the limits of their usefulness. As the leader of the team of surgeons who now cares for this poor benighted woman, I offer all of you the same promise that I have offered this woman and her family—that all of us will persist in our attempts to comprehend the monstrous malady visited upon her; that we will not rest until it is cured—"

Zachary heard his name shouted, and turned to look behind him, where he saw his father waving at him, trapped behind two strangers from out of town. Working his way backward through the throng as his master took up a reluctant position directly behind Nathanael, he greeted Crispin, whose lips were pinched close as he stared at the backs of St. André and Howard ahead of him.

"You're well, son?" Crispin said. "I haven't seen you in a number of days."

"I'm fine," said Zachary, puzzled by his father's pretended equanimity in the midst of this situation. "And yourself?"

"I find myself wondering about poor Mary," said Crispin. "I haven't been in attendance at her past few births, though I've heard news of them: whispers in the pews. But I am no longer notified of these events directly." There it was: a familiar fatherly anger, peering out from beneath the politesse.

Zachary thought of what to say and rejected the first thing that came to mind: that he had found out about the birth in the same manner as everyone else, from the cheers in the streets. (Why had Joshua Toft not notified John Howard that this birth was coming, as had been his previous practice? How had St. André received the news without John knowing? For that matter, how had he seemingly gotten out of the house before John and Zachary were even awake? So many questions.)

"Too many preachers spoil the conclave, I suppose," said Crispin, sparing Zachary the effort of an explanation. "Though I do—I did— serve a purpose! Listen to these people: the word *God* falls from their lips so easily. But to what ends are his name being used? Who benefits from all . . . *this?*" With a wave of his hand he indicated the whole gathering, and with that his unspoken wish that all these people might someday find themselves assembled beneath a church roof instead of the open sky.

Zachary thought of the afflicted woman herself, whom he hadn't seen with his own eyes in over a week, only getting as far in recent days as the front room of the Toft house—the more surgeons who became involved in the case, the more Howard found himself distanced from it, and Zachary along with him. Somehow, the matter of her health had become less relevant with each passing day. The last (and, really, the only) attempt made at curing her had been the phlebotomy, which had accomplished nothing; since then, all involved had decided to watch and discuss, as if mere observation and conversation were enough. It occurred to him that, though they would never admit it to themselves, those in the crowd around him might *desire* the woman's illness, want it to be prolonged, want its renown to grow, so those now in the middle of this small procession might soon find themselves near the head of a larger one; that the procession, rather than serving the woman, or the God whose name it so easily invoked, might serve, in the end, only itself.

*

As Zachary pushed forward through the crowd once again to rejoin John, the group began to veer off the main road toward the Toft house, where a number of people had already settled down with blankets in the dead grass, having arrived ahead of the rest to stake out spots at dawn. Standing out in front of the house as the procession began to disperse in the yard was Joshua Toft, arms folded as if he were guarding the people inside from overly curious trespassers. Behind him, John and Zachary could see Manningham (how had he already arrived here, even ahead of even St. André?) and, even more surprisingly, Cyriacus Ahlers (when on earth had he come back from London? Why on earth was he here once again?), each peering around Joshua, out at the crowd. (Was there a conspiracy to keep John Howard ignorant? Had it been openly articulated, or was it the result of people acting independently and intuitively, in silence, out of guilt?)

Nathanael St. André broke free from the crowd and strode across the empty stretch of yard between the gathering of onlookers and the house, with Laurence, John, and Zachary trailing along behind him. When Nathanael reached the door, Joshua stood aside, letting him and Laurence pass; but to John's consternation, Joshua chose to reoccupy the door once the London surgeon and his assistant had gone through, and stared down at John as if looking straight through him, or not recognizing him.

John looked up at Joshua with bafflement, and then over his rather large shoulder at Nathanael, who seemed to have found something extremely interesting to examine on one of the empty walls of the dim room beyond. Zachary, behind them all, caught Cyriacus's eye, saw clear pity there, and felt a brief, intense stab of shame, because he knew that Cyriacus was correct to find him pitiable.

Cyriacus spoke Joshua's name, and Joshua turned to look at him: a quick conversation conducted entirely in glances took place between the men inside, and then Cyriacus said, at last, "He's one of us." As Joshua stood aside and let John and Zachary enter, Cyriacus offered Zachary a weak flash of an apologetic smile.

"So wonderful to *see* you once again," Nathanael said to John with a forced warmth, as if he had not just greeted John minutes before, as if Nathanael and Laurence were not lodging in John's home. Nathanael and Manningham seated themselves easily in the room's two chairs, leaving the rest standing; from the lying-in room, Margaret Toft entered, squinted at each of them in turn (reserving a singularly hateful stare for Sir Richard), and said, "I think she's about to begin. In a few moments, perhaps." Then she withdrew.

"Nathanael," said Manningham, "would you like to do the honors?"

"Um—certainly," said Nathanael. "I thought that perhaps John might also—"

"I'm sure you can handle this alone, or with Laurence's assistance," said Cyriacus. "Besides, I would like to inform John about . . . recent events, while we have the time and the relative quiet."

"I expect there will be few such opportunities from here forward," continued Manningham.

With a sigh, Nathanael rose. "Come, Laurence," he said, as the men heard Mary's first hoarse, quivering wail through the wall.

As Nathanael and Laurence stepped into the lying-in room, Cyriacus edged over to gently close its door behind them; then, gesturing for John to sit in the empty chair, the remaining men in the room huddled closer together, and began to speak quickly in low voices as the screams in the other room grew louder and longer.

*

"I've returned from London," Cyriacus Ahlers said, "where I had an audience with the king himself, two days past. I stood before his throne and presented him with the evidence of my observations; I displayed to him the rabbits preserved in spirits that I borrowed from you, John. I merely described what I saw, without making pronouncements on its truth or falsehood."

"And his curiosity only deepens," said Manningham.

"Based on his response, I believe him skeptical," said Ahlers, "but he does not dismiss the possibility outright that all is indeed as it seems. In fact, he has requested—and we have not informed Nathanael of this yet—that Mary Toft be transported to London, and given lodging somewhere."

John made to jump out of his chair, then stopped himself. "So that he may observe her firsthand?"

"He, or more likely, one of his agents. Though it is difficult to say—he is a creature of whim, even if each of his whims has the force of command. Also, London's nobility finds the woman particularly interesting. They are powerful, but provincial, and have no desire to leave the city; therefore, Mary Toft must come to them."

"You have no idea the extent to which the minds of Londoners can be captured by dazzling baubles," said Manningham.

"They've gone mad," said Ahlers, shaking his head.

"With a particular variety of madness that sometimes leads people like our erstwhile colleague to seek fame and profit," said Manningham, nodding toward the lying-in room.

"You've attended the woman the longest," said Ahlers. "She will have a comfort with you that she does not with us."

"We need you to accompany us, to London, when she leaves," said Manningham. "The day after tomorrow. We will leave a day ahead of you to make arrangements for your lodging. We must take Mary with us. The king will not be kept waiting; capricious though he may be, it is not wise to gamble that he will forget his desires."

(And as Zachary's face lit up, Ahlers leaned over to him and whispered, "You are coming, too," with a benevolent smile.)

*

From the lying-in room came a long, labored howl. "They're almost done," said John.

"You must beware Nathanael St. André!" hissed Ahlers to John. "Given the chance, he will center himself and push you to the margins."

"I must admit," said Manningham as he looked up at Ahlers, "that he is charismatic in a way that we are not."

"Speak for yourself," said Ahlers.

"I merely speak the truth," Manningham shot back as the yells in the other room wound down to silence. "In the eyes of the common man, even the longest, most precious titles count for little against a man who cuts a fine figure. And he is a shapeshifter: a common man when it pleases him to appear as such, and one of the elite when it does not. His opinions change as the wind. If this Toft phenomenon does prove beyond a doubt to be other than it seems, he may act against the evidence, to stoke the public's collective delusion instead of dampening it—whichever action he believes best serves his own ends."

"I see your point," said Ahlers. "We are all vulnerable, then; we must, the three of us, take care—"

At that, the door to the lying-in room slammed open, bouncing backward on its hinges with a crying creak. His eyes straight ahead of him, Nathanael St. André marched forward, toward the door out of the house; Laurence chased behind, his face all worry and horror.

Nathanael's hands were stained red to the wrists; in his hand he held a bundle of burlap, heavily spattered with crimson.

"Too much blood," said Manningham.

"Good Lord," said John, rising.

"Cyriacus and I will handle this," Manningham said. "John: *watch Nathanael.*" With haste, the other two surgeons went to attend to the patient.

Together, John and Zachary followed Nathanael outside, to see him standing before the assembled congregation, quiet spreading through the crowd from front to rear as people ceased their conversation and turned their gazes toward him. Those seated on blankets began to come to their feet; children eagerly approached him, the carefree native Godalming boys mixed in with the Londoners, who, like Laurence, resembled middle-aged men in miniature.

From behind, Zachary saw Nathanael go through the motions of unwrapping the bloody cloth he held; then he reached into it with one hand, rummaged and tore, and raised that hand to the sky, as if in triumph.

In the hand held aloft was a rabbit's head, severed and misshapen, its skull crushed.

"Gentlemen! Ladies!" Nathanael bellowed. "The miracle."

And he tossed the head to the gaggle of boys.

One of the Londoners caught it by leaping into the air, his agility overcoming the encumbrance of his clothing, but upon landing he was greeted with a quick punch in the jaw by a Godalming boy that surprised him into tossing the head out of his hands. Two more Godalming children pounced on the head before it hit the ground, tussling and coming to blows, tearing the thing apart.

"This is all wrong," John said in a shaking voice, so softly that only Zachary could hear. "All of this has gone wrong."

As the assembled crowd began to cheer, the roar growing, and Laurence turned to look back at Zachary with an expression that was a strange mix of terror and glee, Nathanael began to dig into the flayed-open rabbit corpse with his fingers and fling bits of it at the boys before him, who were already beginning to bruise each other in battle: the guts; the feet; the pelt; the heart.

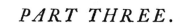

PART THREE.

CHAPTER XV

MARY'S SOLILOQUY.

L isten to me: this hurts.

*

For reasons known only to the Lord, when I reached the age of thirteen he chose to grace me, all at once, with wide hips, bountiful breasts, and the face of a fool. (No need for you to lie to me out of pity: any mirror will show me this weak chin, this slack jaw, these cow's eyes.) Ever since then, men have seen me as a vessel meant only for making smaller versions of themselves, and whatever words I've spoken to them have gone unheard: I might remark on the conversation these surgeons are having between themselves, here on this rickety wagon headed for London, and they would act as if my sentences had no more meaning than birdsong, or the howl of a dog hit by a thrown rock. In a man's eyes I am meant for motherhood, and that only; otherwise I may as well be mute. Tongue cut out; lips sewn shut.

*

Poor Joshua. Ha—poor me when I saw him naked for the first time, for when I laid eyes on him in all his lack of glory, I foresaw a childless, pleasureless future. Such a meager yard, I thought, could never bring about a woman's shiver, and a man's seed cannot find purchase in untroubled ground. And yet he gripped the thing in his hand

as if its weight was a terrible burden to be borne. "I hope," he said as
he approached me, "this does not hurt."

I let him read ignorance on my face that wedding night; I pretended his little needle was a club; his low chuckles as I lay beneath
him suggested that my pained wails were convincing enough. One of
God's cruel jokes, to hang such a little thing on such a large man. But
I loved him, so I lied, or I let him lie to himself.

*

That need to hurt as one does nature's duty; that need to hear it
hurts. That need of his to occupy the space inside me, claim it as his
own. Tiny one-eyed miner barely able to breach the cave's entrance,
and yet if he didn't get screams from me one way, he'd get them
another. Back of the hand against a cheek: a strange kind of kiss.

I learned soon enough that when he looked at me in a certain way,
I was to huddle in a corner and mewl; then he would loom over me
while I stood in his shadow for a few moments. In the end, he'd turn
away from me and leave me be, with a look over his shoulder to let
me know that, at the last, his mercy had only narrowly won out over
his disgust.

But in daylight? The two of us together? Oh, sunshine and dreams
then; melodies and candy. He had a way of *shrinking* himself when he
wanted, to gain another's confidence—his big meaty hands suddenly
become delicate; his voice needing an ear trumpet to understand; his
very shadow fading, as if sunlight would shine through every person
so weak. A man half his size would look up at him and think himself
a giant. And, shameful to say, his sorcery works on me as well, no
matter how many times I see the trick. His whimper never fails to
drive from my mind the memory of his curse, and once I forget, I am
ready to be cursed again.

Am I bitter? Yes. Pained: yes. Cursed: yes. But do not think that
I do not know how to love. I love him, even now. Tell me I'm a fool
and I'll spit in your eye.

*

Despite the long-held lore of midwives, I was great with child soon enough. (Though I was rarely brought off when in Joshua's arms: I thank you for your concern.) James, that first child, had my eyes embedded in his father's face—somehow in a young boy the eyes I despise when they look back at me in a mirror become beautiful. As he grows older, they will soften a face that would otherwise be too hard.

That hard-edged boy hurt, coming out of me—I screamed in awe at myself, that he did not tear me in two as he escaped. Do you know what carrying a child inside you does to your idea of space, of what you *own*? Even the poorest man takes for granted that he holds clear title to the space inside his skin. Oh, but ask a man about a woman, and he'll tell you that her body is so very different from his, that it holds empty spaces that stretch and hold mysteries, that measure time with strange and bloody clocks—whose empty spaces *are* those? Who holds their precious title? Ask a man again, and he'll argue that the case is not so simple when the sex is switched. The mere pockets of air inside men that erupt in belches and farts are of little account, but the spaces inside women are meant by God for so much more that women's ownership of them is clearly only ever provisional. Those empty spaces cannot be left unoccupied for no reason—they are intended to be penetrated, colonized, stuffed to bursting. The rule of men: all spaces must be filled. And so Joshua shoves his little prick against me beneath the bedsheets.

*

Pained and cursed. Two daughters followed James, but the small-pox took them before the spaces inside them had any value. Faces and arms and legs stippled with boils, puking night and day, complaining of aches in their backs as if they were ten times their age. Clara lasted thirteen days against it; Bridget died in eleven. Then, in spring, came the creature, the misformed fourth, a hot mass of flesh tumbling out of me five months early. Dear God, did that one hurt, from gut to heart.

Joshua made himself small to press his case, after that, and it was such a relief, that he made himself small instead of big, that I could not help but agree. He laid his heavy, enormous head on my lap and looked up at me, his ear against my stomach. "Whose is this?" he asked, and I knew what *this* he spoke of, even as I knew I would give him the wrong answer, to give him the chance to correct me in turn. That was his true request—for me to do wrong, so that I could be put right.

"Whose is this?" he said.

"Mine."

"Whose is this?" he said again.

"Ours."

"Whose is this?" he said a third time, the voice of the other, harder Joshua rumbling beneath that of the softer one before me.

"Yours." The answer I knew he'd wanted all along.

"Might it be," he asked, his voice oh so very caring, "that you were a poor steward of what was mine?"

I told you: do not think that I do not know how to love. "Yes."

"The smallpox would not have taken Clara and Bridget had they not come out of you with imperfections that we could not yet see, that took their time to flower."

"Yes."

"And you would not have experienced the early birth of the monster, had you bent your mind daily to the task at hand."

"Yes."

He was silent then, as I ran my fingers through his hair.

"God speaks to us, speaks through you, and damns you for your failures," he said. "But we might obtain salvation for you, if only you could speak back."

"Yes," I said, not yet afraid, too dumb to yet feel the terror I should have.

"Prayer will not do," he said. "The Lord's ears are stuffed full of prayers, so many that he cannot understand a single one. But I know a better way."

*

And so I am becoming, not myself, but a mixture of the dreams of others, of the many pleasing lies they tell themselves: my husband, and the surgeons, and those to whom the surgeons speak, and those who overhear their words. But you must understand that this is not a transformation, not a disappearance, but a recognition. And I am no different from you, despite what my ever-growing collection of caretakers might choose to claim, despite that you can speak while I go unheard.

Have you ever been fortunate enough to be loved? At the beginning of a romance, you saw yourself mirrored in your lover's eyes, a better person than you knew yourself to be—cleaned of stains, free of filth and shining. Did you speak to correct her foolish assumptions, out of a need for her to know the truth at all costs? Did you list all your flaws, show her your scars? Or did you stay silent, keeping your own counsel, granting your lover the sweet gift of her self-deception, for just one moment longer, and another, and just one more, and then another.

Well, then. Now you know why I would hold my tongue, even if I believed I'd be heard if I spoke. When my husband shoved his fingers in my mouth and yelled, *Bite me, bite me you idiot bitch, harder, they have to see the mark,* then the taste of the blood I drew from him was the sweet and hard-won declaration of his love. And it is good to be loved, and to love in return.

*

Oh, dear God: listen to me.
This hurts.

CHAPTER XVI

MOLL FLANDERS.

In the future, thought Zachary, every man would travel by pegasus. The signs of this evolution were already clear to see: if it were possible for a human woman to give birth to rabbits, then the barriers between species that were once thought inviolable were more permeable than mankind once thought, and all manner of crossbreedings might occur with God's tacit permission. The secret was perhaps locked up inside the very patient that he and his master had been attending for the past two months—once it was discovered, it would only be a matter of time until men bred sows with the minds and demeanors of dogs, eager to obey and easy to command; or they might cross horses with swans, to create ponies with majestic, feathered white wings that could carry themselves aloft on zephyrs of their own making. Six of such wonderful creatures, towing a sleigh behind them crafted from the light wood of linden trees, would let a man fly in comfort through the air—the ride would be as smooth as if he were sitting in his own chair at supper, the only indications of movement being the wind against his face and the landscape scrolling by beneath him. There would be no more need in the world for roads and wheels.

But this was the winter of 1726, not the far-off nineteenth century. Here, in this moment, Zachary was stuck on a stagecoach headed to London, and as its wheels rolled over the rutted, rocky road his brain jostled around in his skull, and his teeth clacked together, and his guts churned, and he was deeply miserable. The journey by stagecoach from Godalming to London took about seventeen hours, counting two stops to change horses; they had left well before sunrise, and would arrive in London at night. By noon, Zachary found himself wishing he had chosen to walk the sixty miles instead. This day would last a year.

John Howard sat in the coach next to him. The three London surgeons, St. André, Ahlers, and Manningham, had left for the city the day before, along with Mary Toft and her husband; Margaret Toft had remained behind in Godalming along with James, the child. Crispin Walsh had stayed behind as well; as much as he might have liked to pretend otherwise, there was no immediate need for him on this journey (for which Zachary was secretly glad—John was likely to be a less attentive chaperone).

Sitting across from John and Zachary were two passengers who had both been on the stagecoach when they boarded—the first, an elderly man who reminded Zachary somewhat of his father, had gotten up from his seat and moved to the other side so that master and apprentice could sit together, greeting them with a taciturn nod of the head. He did not seem to be a minister—though his gray suit had Crispin's sense of austerity, the gold rings on his fingers gave the game away. A lawyer, perhaps.

Next to the likely lawyer was a woman, traveling alone. She seemed magically able to preserve her stillness in a place of ceaseless movement: while the men were constantly swaying back and forth (and as the gentleman across from John and Zachary did his best to keep himself as far away from the woman as possible), she somehow managed to sit ramrod still, as if her body were in fact engaged in an invisible, elaborate series of compensating countermovements to the vehicle's regular jolts. The glances of the men in the carriage toward her went unreturned, for she kept her eyes on the book she held up before her, as if to screen her face from their gazes.

The book she read, Zachary saw, was a popular one, and had been for a few years: *The Fortunes and Misfortunes of the Famous Moll Flanders, &c.* He hadn't read it himself—he did not prefer to waste his time with novels, and neither his master nor his father displayed such volumes on their shelves—but had spied enough copies of it in the hands of women, and overheard enough conversations about it, to feel a secondhand familiarity with its story of a woman who seems to dedicate her life to committing every conceivable crime, before the final few pages that (so Zachary had inferred) offered the reader a fig leaf of redemption.

The silence in the coach was a heavy, velvet weight: Cyriacus Ahlers, before leaving for London himself the day before, had told Zachary that one of the (apparently few) pleasures of stagecoach riding was that the forced close proximity to random strangers over the course of a day gave no other choice but to engage in conversation, and such conversations were often entertaining in a peculiar way that those between longtime friends were not. But John and Zachary were bound together in a bizarre confederacy, its nature heretofore unheard of, and to speak of the subject most likely to spring to their lips would surely alienate those not in that confederacy who would overhear. And the woman wielded the book before her as both veil and shield: it seemed that she would see any attempt to engage her in discourse as a bother.

Nonetheless, John Howard made the first sally at small talk. "What brings you to this stagecoach, ma'am?" he asked.

After a moment, as if to realize that she was in fact the *ma'am* that John was addressing, the woman lowered the book just enough for her eyes to peer over it at John. "Returning to London," she said. "I was visiting my sister in Witley."

She raised the book again.

"You have a sister in Witley?" John asked halfheartedly.

"Yes," the woman said, not even bothering to lower the book this time. "She's ill."

Not wanting to follow two clearly unwanted and begrudgingly answered inquisitions with a third, John lapsed back into silence, leaving the passengers to once again listen to the rhythmic clopping of horses' hooves ahead of them as they dealt with the rocking of the stagecoach (except for the woman, who continued to appear as if an invisible mechanism kept her vertical).

It was after the first stop, after the passengers had stretched their legs and had a meal at the way station where the stagecoach's horses were changed, when the other gentleman made the second attempt to speak to the woman. "I don't approve," he said, into the open air, seemingly not intending to address anyone in particular, though Zachary and John knew better.

When no one responded, he said again, turning his head ever so slightly toward the woman, "I don't approve."

The woman lowered her book again. "Of *what*," she asked. "If you speak of me, I fail to see how I offend."

"Not you—a woman such as yourself clearly could not cause offense to a gentleman, even if you sought to." The elderly man made a deliberately casual gesture with his index finger toward the volume. "The book. It seeks to deceive."

"How so?"

"First, it is the work of a man, choosing to speak in a woman's voice, purporting to speak about ways of women he could not know. His first deception, but not his gravest. Second, the book pretends at morality, but any honest man can see that its true purpose is titillation, nothing more—sure, there are a few fine phrases tacked on at the end, meant to absolve the reader of taking pleasure in sin second-hand, but only after hundreds of pages of the most scurrilous, debased actions, recounted in the most depraved detail. Prurience, for its own sake."

"You have a surprising familiarity with the work you're condemning as scurrilous," the woman said. "One might think you wouldn't have desired to dirty yourself."

"Oh, I know of her tutelage in pocket picking, her pretended widowhood, her bigamy, her incest. My wife has read it twice, and describes its events to me as if they were recent news, real instead of imagined. I do not like the light in her eyes when she does this—it's unseemly."

"Well," the woman replied, "I have also heard the rumor that this tale is written by a man. And to be frank, I do not believe it. A woman's honesty, laid out as bare as it is here, without apology, causes discomfort to those not of the so-called 'fairer' sex, it seems: better for men to consider it a fantasy, so that they can continue to imagine that the women with whom they spend their lives remain innocent of the world's vast variety of sins. Why else would you choose to ignore the bare evidence of the title page, that this is 'written from her own memorandums'?"

"I have heard that, too," John Howard put in. "That the author of the book is a man. Though it's not known who. He hasn't come forward. There are similar rumors about that other popular book, *Roxana: The Fortunate Mistress.* Perhaps it's even penned by the same man, who saw a second chance that was liable to be as good as the first."

The woman gave John a gentle smile. "Do you have any evidence for that?" she said.

"Well, *no,* not here in this carriage," John stammered, "not in my pockets."

"Then here in this carriage," said the woman, "it seems that Moll Flanders must be judged as real as you or me, just as she is everywhere else. For in our little game, I have a hand with one very good card"—and she indicated the book, which she'd opened to the title page—"and you have no worthy cards at all: not one. Though if the supposed true author of this piece chooses to reveal himself, I will be happy to change my mind. But not before then, I am sorry to say.

"Now then. Moll calls."

The woman returned to her reading, and the travelers rode on in a silence that the men suddenly found preferable, until the second stop for a change of horses.

*

For the final leg of the trip, as evening came on, Zachary rode outside the stagecoach, next to the driver, whom he'd managed to befriend at the inn while the horses were being changed. The driver was a stout fellow, his faded clothing threadbare, his chin covered with salt-and-pepper stubble, his wig a dingy bird's nest. "Our bodies change to suit our professions, new young friend," he said to Zachary as he snapped the reins of his horses in punctuation. "As a chairman develops large, strong calves, the better to convey the rich through London's streets so that they are not soiled by dirt, and as those same rich have withered legs that wouldn't carry them a mile, but gigantic, swollen heads, the better to enable the constant, rapid totaling of their pounds, shillings, and pence, so I myself have developed a large and generous arse, the better for sitting upon in comfort as I drive these teams of horses back and forth across God's England. Three healthy servings a day of the finest meats and beers: indispensable necessities of the job. Along with coffee to keep my eyes open, during the final miles of a run like this, when I long for sleep." He graced Zachary with a yawn that transformed into a long, rumbling bass of a burp, following it with a gap-toothed grin that Zachary answered in kind.

"And your future occupation?" the driver said. "What do you see yourself as, in ten years' time?"

"I am a surgeon's apprentice," said Zachary.

The stagecoach driver's eyes widened in mock surprise. "Oh, a surgeon, are you? Good on you, and the Lord knows we can use you and a hundred more like you, but I pity your fate. Your guts will transform to clockwork, because when you split a patient's belly open that's all you'll see inside: a broken device, in need of repair. The tips of your ten fingers will transform to scalpel blades; all the women who love you will be cut by your caresses!"

The boisterous laugh that the driver favored Zachary with as the boy shrank away from him seemed half apologetic. "I joke, with a new friend," he said. "If I believed you less than human I would not let you sit here beside me, on this last leg of the journey before you are swallowed up."

"Swallowed up?" Suddenly, Zachary found himself trading one kind of alarm for another.

"In order not to go stark raving mad as you enter London, overwhelmed by the sheer size and variety of it," the driver said, his japery now turned most of the way to seriousness, "it is best to think of it not as a collection of hundreds of thousands of people, each with his own mind and desire, but as a *single living thing,* of which you will become

a tiny component during your tenure here, just as your finger is a part
of your own body. Though you have your own thoughts and desires,
once you become a part of the city you may find that it bends you to
its will, that it makes you have thoughts and aspirations that you will
believe are your own, but are in fact the city's as it sings to itself. I tell
you, it lives and breathes and it has its own cycles." He lifted his nose
and sniffed. "Do you smell that? Even here, when we are still six or
seven miles away?"

Zachary inhaled in imitation: certainly, there was something different about the air here when compared to the air of Godalming,
though the scent he detected was so faint as to be nearly impercep-
tible, the merest rumor of a stronger odor.

"Smoke, mostly, is what you're smelling," said the driver, "but the
discerning nose will note the undertones: the sweat of bodies unable
to escape from each other, and beneath that, shit and piss. Even the
most brilliant of London's minds are unable to abscond from their
flesh, much as they might long to. They must shit; they must piss;
that shit and piss must go somewhere. And so, the evening ceremony
of the removal of night soil, when men who are no less necessary to the
city's life as its scientists and bankers collect the contents of hundreds
of thousands of chamber pots and convey them to a secret place, out of
sight and out of memory. The city has its own bowels, young friend;
those bowels have a rhythm, as do yours.

"And it *grows*. Stealthily, but it grows. Do you see these houses
here? Their lovely views, their pastoral surroundings?" The driver
waved his arm to take in the scenery—a half-dozen mansions visible
in total, each surrounded by vast swaths of denuded landscape, dotted
with dead tree trunks. "Londoners, all, who thought to escape the city,
hoping that their riches would allow them to enjoy bustle or silence as
they chose, not realizing that they themselves were the city's agents of
expansion. Because first they had to bring their servants. Then they
brought a road with them, wide and nicely paved, because they also
wanted to be able to choose between meditation and mayhem with
ease and *speed*—without wonderful arses such as mine they cannot
enjoy the journey from one place to another for its own sake. And now

they complain because the city reaches out to them, spoiling their view; they gripe that others use the road they thought was meant for them alone. Not realizing that in fact they were the city's vanguard, the first tentative expression of its desire."

The driver's low chuckle was freighted with menace. "It drew you to it," he said, "and when you leave you will take part of it with you. Your mind is already undergoing its first subtle, irrevocable alterations, the better to carry out London's ambitions. Soon the grasping creature will cover this entire island; then it will find a way to leap across the water to the Continent, and then what will stop all the world from becoming London, every square inch covered with it? Think on that as you come closer; show caution and respect, in the presence of this great and monstrous thing. Pray that its usage of you is kind rather than rough, for you *will* be used: no avoiding it. Best accept it."

Turning slowly to focus on the road ahead of him with just the smallest amount of theater—there had been other friends on other journeys, Zachary sensed, who had heard this monologue before—the driver left the surgeon's apprentice to his thoughts, as night descended and the city approached.

CHAPTER XVII

DR. LACEY'S BAGNIO.

Zachary could not have imagined the extent to which London's storied marvels would exceed his expectations the moment he saw the city in daylight.

He knew of the Thames River that cut through London; he knew of the single bridge that spanned it, the artery that led to the city's beating heart. But he had somehow remained unaware that on that bridge there were buildings, cleverly constructed four-story structures with archways cut through the middle that conveyed a constant flow of horse and foot traffic in both directions, and that people made their homes in these structures, that a few people were lucky enough to live on this most majestic of the world's bridges.

He had been so exhausted when the stagecoach arrived in the city that he could hardly stand upright. It was clear enough through his drowsy haze that the three London surgeons who'd gone on ahead of them had made arrangements for Zachary and John's lodging, though when the stranger who greeted them as they stepped down from the coach led them to the place where they'd stay for the coming weeks (the female passenger and the lawyer who'd shared their journey going on their separate ways without a word; the stagecoach driver saying goodbye to Zachary by screwing his face into a cartoonish wink), Zachary soon gave up on any attempt to keep track of his path. He became a sleepwalker. He gave himself over to the overwhelming conglomeration of signs advertising inns and shops and pubs, the miasma of smoke, and the glimpses of light in darkness, from candles and stars and the pale-faced boy in a trim, tiny golden suit and wig of curled and powdered locks who preceded them through the urban maze, solemnly holding a lamp aloft to illuminate their path through the ramshackle buildings that loomed over them. He entered a hallway; he climbed some stairs; he was led to a bed on which he fell asleep; his dreams were tangled and uneasy, with their details easily forgotten, though all of them were filled with the sound of moving water—pouring bottles, emptying bladders, rushing rivers.

He awoke the following morning, unsure where he was: the ceiling above him was too close to his head, and the sounds of the room were not his own. There was a man here with him, snoring: a light, self-contented wheeze that Zachary soon realized was John Howard's.

Morning light shone muted through the room's lone window as through a scrim, and as Zachary arose from his bed and padded over to it, he saw that the veil was not in the window, but in the sky: the rising sun was dimmed by the city's smoke to a muted orange circle, easy to look at without squinting.

Then, beneath it, he saw the river.

It was the first body of water that large he'd ever seen in his life, and it surged and tumbled beneath the bridge with astonishing ferocity (and only now did he notice the constant low tremble in the floorboards beneath his feet). The watermen who shot the bridge (and Zachary could see the boats emerging from the bridge beneath him, each one flying as fast as a bullet from a pistol) seemed to be on comfortable speaking terms with disaster, if not death—each successful shooting, and there was one every minute or two, was accompanied by gay laughter that drifted up to Zachary's ears as the boat made its way into relatively calmer waters, while the occasional overturned boat (that sometimes dumped a passenger too reckless to take to solid ground before the bridge and reboard afterward) was greeted with a chorus of mockery by watermen in boats nearby, and the audience watching the never-ending show on shore.

Beyond the bridge, farther down the river, Zachary saw the Port of London, with more varieties of boats than he knew existed, clogging the waterway so tightly, even as they danced around each other in a nautical ballet, that they might have served as a second bridge— Zachary thought that a goat might have a good chance of crossing the Thames farther downstream merely by jumping from one deck to the next. The galliots and barques and catamarans maneuvered delicately between each other when they were not tied together, unloading their cargoes onto fleet lighters that conveyed the goods to shore. If, as the loquacious stagecoach driver had said, the city was best thought of as a single living thing with its own unique anatomy, then the Port of London was its enormous mouth, the enabler of its gluttony. Merchandise from a dozen countries fell into its maw, and the lighters might be seen as agents of digestion, sorting the various goods and delivering them to the places where they could best satisfy the city's need for nutrition, the copper and iron and hemp and flax and sugar and hundreds of other things that keep the city running, that would be placed aboard these same or other ships again in weeks or months, transformed by nimble hands in the meantime into other shapes that gave them more value—iron to nails; flax to damask—or merely held in a dark warehouse until the economic weather changed.

How could a person keep his mind on a single subject in this city, with so many sights to distract, and so many ideas to consider that lay behind those sights? He could have spent hours watching the watermen shoot the bridge, envisioning the biographies of each one, wondering about the choices that led them to take up such a dangerous profession; he might have thought of the histories of each ship milling about in the port beyond, the histories of each nation that sent each ship to London, the lives of all the sailors on all those ships. A man with enough imagination could keep himself forever entertained by staring out of a window, as stories yielded other stories and none of them ever reached its end. But that man would starve, unless he could somehow feed himself on dreams and digressions.

With some regret, he turned away from the window: he would try to take in as much of this wondrous place as he could by glancing out of the corners of his eyes, but his focus would remain on the task at hand, the job for which he had come here.

*

He found, as he left the window, that there were four envelopes scattered just in front of the door to the room—they'd been slipped under it. He'd heard from John about the postal delivery system in London, a miracle of communication that seemed to function with a high reliability largely through coffee houses and word of mouth, but even then, its efficiency was a surprise. The news of their arrival seemed to have preceded them (though if the London surgeons knew where they were staying, it seemed logical that others would know, soon enough).

Two of the letters were for John Howard, from Cyriacus Ahlers and, surprisingly, from Nicholas Fox; the other two, Zachary was even more surprised to find, were addressed to him. He handed John's to him as he arose from the other bed in the room; then he seated himself on his own bed to read.

The first letter was from Laurence, the writing cramped and pinched, the lines like the scratching of a chicken in the dirt; Zachary had to squint to read it.

Dear Zachary—

My master tells me you and your master should have arrived in London by now, and so I send greetings, so that you do not feel alone in the city. (A place as large as this can quickly breed loneliness: one of its tricks.) I fear that for the near future we will be occupied by events of the day, but I do hope to take a moment for quiet conversation, or to show you an interesting sight or two, something that will distract us from current events and give an indication of London's true nature (though you have likely already gathered it is impossible to fully survey the place in so short a visit). We will cross paths again soon, most likely at Dr. Lacey's (I do not know why the patient has been housed in such a place, except that someone in the king's employ has thought to make a joke, too oblique for me to understand).

Yours with affection,
Laurence.

The second was in a woman's hand, bold and clear despite its loops and curlicues. The script filled both sides of the half sheet of foolscap, and seemed designed for mockery.

Oh, dear Zachary.

What a wonderful world of coincidences this is—this letter to you accompanies one to your master from my father, thanking him for services expertly rendered some days past, the exact nature of which I remain ignorant (note: I most certainly do not). How was I able to contact you so readily, so soon after your arrival, you might ask? My father returned yesterday from a visit to one Dr. Lacey, the nature of whose practice is unfamiliar to me (note that I lie again: it is, and your master's skilled ministrations are the reason my father can so readily pay this other doctor such regular visits). He was quite excited to tell me of a woman who, it seems, gives birth to rabbits almost daily, and who finds herself staying in this same Dr. Lacey's residence! Such a wonder of nature seemed peculiarly attuned to his chosen occupation, and so after a day of feverish inquiry in the local coffee houses regarding the woman's history, we discovered that a team of London surgeons was in league with none other than the great John Howard of Godalming, who had treated my father so ably (and whose apprentice had been admirably tight-lipped *about a conversational subject that would have been* sure to elicit a certain woman's interest).*

You must come see me: an audience grows outside Dr. Lacey's even as you read this, sitting vigil, and on occasion I may be a part of it. (I trust you will remember my face, as all men do.) I want you to be my guest at one of my father's winter performances. The caravan of curiosities he brings to the villages outside London is small beer, for you provincial folk are amused easily enough: for more jaded eyes he must offer *stronger, darker entertainments.*

Yours,
Anne.

Well, perhaps Zachary would not be able to concentrate solely on the patient he had come here to assist in the care of, not entirely.

He might still steal some time for pleasure and curiosity, here and there.

*

The bagnio where Mary Toft and her husband had taken up lodging was in Covent Garden, a district of London whose days as a desired residence of men with titles was decades behind it—it was now largely known for the bustling marketplace that occupied its central square, its burgeoning theaters, and, most notably, its prostitution. Truth be told, John Howard was initially as puzzled as Laurence by the fact that his patient had been housed in a place whose repute was certainly dubious, if not entirely ill—to be sure, it was conceivable that one might use a bagnio as a kind of hotel without partaking of all the benefits it offered—but eventually reasoned that she'd been placed there because the building had the convenience of running water, a precious rarity, even here. (Such a place as this would have customers who'd want baths both cold and hot: there was some thinking to be done about how sexual predilections were a secret driver behind the expansion of luxuries from the very rich to everyone else, but it seemed somehow predictable to John that out of all the buildings that could have used plumbing, Dr. Lacey's Bagnio would be one of the first to receive it.)

On arriving at Dr. Lacey's that afternoon, John and Zachary (the boy still bleary-eyed and sore from a long day of stagecoach travel) found the Tofts installed in Room No. 1 of the bagnio (the sign on its door named it "The King's Head"). The place was quite well appointed. Two wide curtained windows filled it with light and overlooked the piazza below, the hawkers of goods outside loudly doing business among a tightly packed conglomeration of ramshackle wooden stalls. The room was furnished with a card table with a marble surface, whose inwardly curved legs, painted in gold, each ended in a clawed three-fingered talon clutching a sphere; a dining table of richly colored, highly polished mahogany; and several chairs scattered through the room, plushly upholstered, with their frames carved from walnut. The bed that dominated the chamber was enormous, large enough to let a half dozen sleep in comfort (or engage in other, more strenuous activities if the mood caught them, one supposed); Mary Toft seemed lost in its middle, face chalk white as she stared at the ceiling, her head nestled among a pile of embroidered pillows, her hair a matted tangle, her body buried so deeply beneath layers of blankets that one could not reliably make out its shape.

Joshua Toft, Nathanael St. André, and Laurence were waiting for John and Zachary when they entered, and Joshua rose from his chair and approached the three of them, his hand offered in greeting. There was a moment, not much more than an eyeblink, when Zachary thought that Joshua seemed thankful for his own good fortune, but then the shine in his eyes vanished, to be replaced with the grave and downcast aura of concern that one would expect.

On the other hand, Nathanael's grin as he sprang from his chair was wide and unsuppressed, and seemed intended to make up for Joshua's deficiency of joy. "You are well, all of you? Recovered from the journey? Bones all settled back in their proper places? Good. Good."

"How is the patient?" said John.

"Oh, quite lovely, all things considered. No impending births, it appears: perhaps the regular cycle of fetal maturation has been disturbed by the journey, but I'm sure it'll start up again soon enough. A slight expansion and toughening of the hardened area of her stomach in the vicinity of her Fallopian tube, but that is to be expected as her body becomes inured to the traumatic processes it regularly undergoes. She moans sometimes. Again: expected."

From the bed came a low, tortured whimper in answer.

Meanwhile, Laurence had greeted Zachary with a gentle hand placed on his elbow. "You look well," he said. It had to be said that Laurence, in his usual wig and coat that matched his master's, looked more suitable here in his native context: though the claw-footed table and walnut chairs were not to Zachary's taste, Zachary could admit that Laurence belonged among them, and looked at ease. He somehow seemed taller, more of a man, even as he appeared to have decisively given up the manly affectations that had made him initially seem out of place back in Godalming. Shortly after, it dawned on Zachary that in the clothes he thought of as normal for a boy of fourteen, he'd be the odd one out, but reasoned that there were so many sights in this city, and so many styles of clothing on so many different people, that he would be unlikely to draw any real notice—

"Some might observe that you look like a beggar," Laurence said, looking him up and down, "but pay such rudely expressed opinions no mind. You and I know better. I continue to be proud to know you." Surely the sentiment was well meant, but if it was intended to reassure Zachary, it didn't help.

"I'm glad you arrived here in one piece," Laurence followed up quickly, perhaps in response to Zachary's sudden blanching. "The time before us is . . . fraught, you might say? But we will have some time for touring, you and I."

"There's someone else—" Zachary blurted, his mouth leaping a regrettable half second ahead of his brain.

"Someone else?" Laurence prompted, as if he were briefly considering the bizarre possibility that someone to whom he'd extended an offer of friendship might nonetheless choose to have more than one friend.

"There's a woman," Zachary said, and Laurence's face twisted in a strange way. "A girl, I mean," Zachary continued, and Laurence's mouth seemed to briefly exchange places with his nose.

"A girl," Laurence replied, once his features resumed an approximation of their original places.

"Someone I met. Passing through town with her father. Twice this year."

"Passing through town," Laurence said.

"And she said she wants to show me the city, too. I received her letter at the exact same time as yours—can you believe it?"

"Astonishing," said Laurence drily.

"And perhaps the three of us could amble about together, I thought," Zachary stammered. "I think you two might enjoy each other's company, even. Though you are, admittedly, quite different."

"Some of London's sights that I had in mind for you would not be suitable for a woman's sensibilities," said Laurence.

"Oh, I'm sure she has no such scruples at all," said Zachary, as Laurence raised an eyebrow.

*

Zachary and Laurence, and their masters, were interrupted in their conversations by a knock on the door, unexpected and authoritative. They all turned at once to find, standing in the doorframe, one of the most extravagantly dressed persons that Zachary had ever seen—if Laurence's style of clothing was a copy of Nathanael St. André's rendered in miniature, then this fellow was the sort of person whom St. André was attempting (and mostly failing) to imitate in turn. His wig seemed to grow directly out of his own head, while also subtly signaling its own artifice through the regularity of its locks, as if a wholly convincing simulacrum of lustrous ringlets would not be recognized as the expensive work of an extraordinarily talented artisan, but would be unwittingly confused for hair that was natural, and therefore cost nothing. Beneath his arm was a three-cornered hat of black beaver fur, ornamented with a single sapphire; the waistcoat of his suit (snow white, embroidered in gold) had a collar that came higher up his neck than those of any other Londoner that Zachary had yet seen, and he could tell that this was meant to mark the stranger as a setter of fashion that other men would emulate, always a year too late.

The man strode into the room on the heels of his black leather shoes; though the oldest person in the room, he had the demeanor of a man decades younger. He moved with the ease of someone who took it for granted that the space directly in front of him was always his to enter, and who was happy to fill the eyes of those who looked on him, for he saw the care he took in his appearance as a matter of generosity to those less fortunate.

As he watched the newcomer, Zachary was startled to find that Nathanael St. André was behind him, hissing into his and Laurence's ears. "Do you know who this is? It's *Lord M——*," he whispered. Then, as if the word *Lord* might not have been enough for Zachary to comprehend, "The *Duke of R——*."

With the practice of someone for whom hearing his own name while pretending he hadn't overheard was a common occurrence, Lord M—— turned after a moment to face Nathanael, giving St. André a chance to stand and step back from the two boys. "Is this the . . . patient?" he asked. "Though that seems too inadequate a word for someone so reputedly wondrous."

"She is my patient, yes," said Nathanael as John opened his mouth and then shut it.

"Our patient," said Zachary, stepping forward as John glanced toward his apprentice in surprise.

"Oh?" said Lord M——, looking down on Zachary (and in the clear eyes of Lord M——'s wrinkled face Zachary sensed a challenge, offered almost offhandedly—he knew he had to return the gaze and do precisely that, no more, no less. To shy away would be cowardly; to attempt to intimidate would be foolish; Lord M—— had deigned to grace Zachary with the exact amount of respect due to one human being from another, and if Zachary caviled or bristled in response, the favor would be just as quickly withdrawn, never to be proffered again).

"Ours," said Zachary. "My master was the first of her doctors; the three others joined later. And the two of us"—he indicated Laurence—"are apprentices."

"There are four surgeons who tend to her, yes," Nathanael said, though no one had asked.

Lord M—— gave Zachary the slightest of smiles, barely noticeable. "A strange apprenticeship for you, friend," he said. He turned away, still smiling, as if giving Zachary a chance to show his relief unseen; Lord M—— had silently acknowledged Zachary as human, which, Zachary imagined, Lord M—— did not do for everyone, and rarely for people of Zachary's age. That was another test passed, but when would his life become anything more than a seemingly never-ending series of unexpectedly sprung trials? (Perhaps never—perhaps every day carried its little challenges of intellect and character, until the last respite of one's deathbed. The very thought made him weary.)

Once again Lord M—— looked down on the woman, whose wheezing, labored breathing had suddenly grown louder. "May I sit?" he commanded, taking a chair at the marble table next to Joshua, who had escaped his notice entirely. "It would please me much," he said, "to sit here in vigil for a time. If this is in fact the miracle that is advertised, then to spend a short while in its company might lead me to some kind of enlightenment, of a manner granted to few, and that I expect is not to be found in even the most learned texts."

His eyes shone as his face formed a smile that its creases and wrinkles, acquired through fifty years of imperious frowning, strained against. "And it would be one of the greatest honors of what has been, thus far, a long and fruitful life."

*

In the square outside the gaudy, pseudo-Turkish facade of the bagnio, amid the constant rumble of the merchants and customers of the Covent Garden Market, appeared a person who had no earthly business to transact, followed by another, and then another. They were not nearly as well dressed as the lord who waited two stories above, whom propriety prevents from identification by anything more than an initial; if Laurence were to see Zachary standing next to them, he in his naïveté might have noticed similarities in their style of clothing, though they themselves would have been wiser, and marked out Zachary as one not of their own.

They stood before the bagnio, looking up at its faux cupolas whose gold paint was flaking away: two men, one woman. They had all resigned themselves to the realization that they would never get close to the woman that Lord M——, two stories above them, gazed upon in meditative contemplation; nor, in the end, did mere physical proximity matter. For Mary Toft was becoming an inhabitant of the minds of those who imagined her, as much as, or more than, the creature of flesh and bone who lay in the bed of the bagnio's finest room.

And if Lord M—— was a person who'd worn the mantle of power as easily as a second skin since his days in a crib, not all varieties of power were his to command: those standing outside the bagnio had more power than he did to decide how those who lived in the world perceived its shape and nature, if only because there was only one of Lord M——, and so very many of them.

Another woman came out of the crush of laughing and cursing buyers and sellers to join them, and, looking up at the window, the four of them continued their intense collective dreaming.

CHAPTER XVIII

A Coffee House Meeting.

The Blackamoor was one of the most popular coffee houses in Covent Garden, though its good fortune was only recent: under its previous name as the Rusted Anchor, it had consistently seen its star eclipsed by Rawthmell's, across the road on Henrietta Street, in the same location since the beginning of the century. In the spring of 1726 the Rusted Anchor had closed its doors for two weeks, ostensibly for a "change of management," but that change was a fiction: the establishment's operators merely reupholstered some of its furniture and, more importantly, changed the sign that hung above the door out front.

The old sign for the Rusted Anchor had been exactly that, an anchor once rendered in gold, but flaked and worn by years of rain and smoke and wind until it was hardly visible against the wood; at that point, the sign was more a cue for regulars to recall the symbol it had once displayed rather than an advertisement to newcomers of a place of business. The new sign, once unveiled, was more detailed and less abstract, commissioned from a portrait artist who'd studied at the Academy at St. Martin's Lane. It was of a charming black fellow with a welcoming smile, holding a steaming mug of coffee in his hand, dressed in a neat suit of dark blue with a tri-cornered hat in the same shade. Cleverly, there was no word hovering above his head to indicate the new name of the coffee house—the proprietors kept their faith in human nature, and it was only a day or two before customers began to refer to the place as the Blackamoor instead of the Rusted Anchor, though the new title was written down nowhere.

It was a stroke of genius on the part of the owners: watching from the window, one could occasionally see passersby walk past the sign swinging on its pole above them, slow to a halt, and gaze up at the beaming black man for a moment or two as if in reverie; then their feet would swivel to a new path almost as if they were briefly spirit-haunted, leading customers through the establishment's doors. It helped that the portrait artist had graced the black gentleman on the sign with a smile that, warm as it was, had an impish twist to a corner: it seemed to promise that the liquid in the steaming mug might offer a stronger, more unpredictable drug than one expected.

But it also helped that, in this year, in this city, black people were everywhere and nowhere, and could thus be everything to everyone. A Londoner who kept to his well-established daily paths, eyes on the ground, might go for days without seeing one in the flesh, and even then only at a distance; if he did happen to speak to one, the conversation would be brief and its form prescribed, for it was most likely that he would be answering the door at the home of a merchant of means (his skin meant to advertise the nature and extent of those means before negotiation with the merchant even began), or running a delivery errand for a duchess, or reciting lines on a theater's stage. But the *image* of the black person, the continued reminder of his existence in a place out of direct sight—ah, that was everywhere, from the engravings displayed for sale in shop windows in which a black man might appear in the background of an assemblage of carousing drinkers or card players, merely watching, a curious and unexplained interloper, to the newspaper notices about escaped slaves that meticulously listed names and heights and shapes and scars.

The black person was often out of sight, then, but never out of mind, and thus any shop that could find a reason to hang a portrait of one above its door could proffer an implicit promise that was all the more delicious because it was inchoate, and that could only benefit from not being openly expressed. The image lent an aura of the new and unfamiliar to that which otherwise could be nothing other than mundane. An engraving that might have sat in a shop window until the men who'd inspired it went to their graves would fly out the door in a patron's hand, his pocket lighter; a coffee shop that had once spent its days half empty would find itself bustling, and if the coffee served was still made from the same beans in the same manner, with a noticeable bitterness that differentiated it from the brew at Rawthmell's, then the lingering memory of the black's face above the entrance might distract a customer from the unwelcome wince that accompanied the first daily sip.

*

Like all the most popular London coffee shops, the Blackamoor was a thriving node of the great city's distributed brain. A dozen copies of each of London's newspapers were delivered to the place each morning, along with letters sent to London's citizens from the rest of the island, or the Continent, or parts still farther flung. After the first hour of opening, the proprietors of businesses that did not depend on having a strictly physical location set up shop in one of the array of booths that lined the Blackamoor's back wall, where they would trade the stocks of companies, or shares in ships on their way to India; or sell subscriptions to mutual protection ventures meant to preserve businesses against loss by fire; or insure the lives of loved ones (or ones who were not so loved, or perhaps only barely heard of). At high noon a man could walk in alone, sit at a table with a cup of coffee before him, close his eyes, and listen to the city talking to itself, certain words burbling up out of the conversations, repeating themselves and detailing the city's obsessions.

On this Monday, November 28, if the words *Mary Toft* were not on everyone's lips—no single name could be; this city had too many names for even a king's or a god's to dominate a conversation for long—you could hear it now and again, at one table or another, spoken in horror or followed by a laugh. The one place where one could *not* hear it was at a table in the back of the coffee house, where the surgeons who attended the woman were ensconced in council: St. André, Howard, Ahlers, and Manningham, with Zachary also there, his chair wedged in between those of John and Nathanael. They spoke only of "the patient," for they needed to do no other. (But their mere presence seemed to spark curiosity. Zachary noticed that at least a few people in the shop kept glancing over at their table: a man in a nearby booth who, Zachary gathered, was engaged in the business of purchasing a life insurance policy from a rotund, gaudily dressed gentleman who had something of the cast of a sharper about him; and, drinking coffee alone at an adjacent table, a young man whose eyes were more on the surgeons than on the days-old newspaper held limply in his hands. In Godalming it was impossible to step out of one's door without encountering the regard of others, to be sure, but the town's small size nearly guaranteed that the person who greeted you was known to you, even if that person did not necessarily have your best interests at heart. Here, though, in this enormous city, to be stared at by a stranger made one singularly uncomfortable—more so when those strangers were several, and failing to disguise their furtiveness.)

"I believe that the most pressing order of business is the issuing of pamphlets," Nathanael St. André was saying. "There is a danger of public misperception of the simple facts of the case, and of their subsequent medical, religious, and philosophical implications: we must, each of us, do what we can to ensure that the public has a collective understanding of the truth that is as close to our own as possible. I myself have a facility with prose that has brought me some small acclaim in literary circles, and am putting the finishing touches on my own publication that will be issued shortly; for those of you who may have less of a comfort than myself with wielding the tools of language, I offer my services as a discriminating editorial hand." And indeed, Nathanael had a sheaf of papers in front of him, the top one of which had a title handwritten in large enough letters to be read at a distance: *A Short Narrative of an Extraordinary Delivery of Rabbits, perform'd by Nathanael St. André.* Nathanael had written his name in larger letters than the rest, the first name taking up one line, the last another.

"The title of your proposed work is . . . interesting," said Ahlers as Zachary, squinting at the pages before Nathanael, began to count on his fingers.

"An effective title describes the work and nothing more, with no writerly trickery to be revealed in the reading," said Nathanael. "The work must be *short,* so as to not unduly tax the attention. It must promise the pleasure of a *narrative,* rather than other, less engaging forms of discourse."

"It must be termed *extraordinary,*" said Manningham, "to differentiate it from the myriad ordinary accounts of rabbit delivery that bend the shelves of libraries."

St. André sniffed. "The learned gentleman attempts a jest—"

"Ten," said Zachary, raising both his hands with his fingers extended.

Ahlers looked across the table at Zachary, smiling. "Ten?"

"The number of rabbits that Mr. Howard and I delivered from the patient before you arrived, Mr. St. André. Ten, out of a total of seventeen." He turned to John. "Do I have the number right, sir?"

John Howard turned to see Zachary's gaze steadily meeting his and gathered that there was something more going on here than the mere confirmation of a fact, that there were other questions lying beneath the question, and that one answer would do for all. "Yes," he replied, hoping the noise of the coffee house was loud enough to cover the slight hitch in his throat when he spoke. *Yes, I should have been the first to speak the words you did; yes, you are now an apprentice in name only, and we will talk further about this when we return.*

"It would seem that among us all here, Mr. Howard is the principal surgeon on the case, with the longest tenure," Ahlers said.

"I would say that I have brought a significant degree of knowledge and instinct to this case that would otherwise be absent—to disavow this would be to sell myself short." After this bristling, Nathanael paused, and seemed to deflate under the stares of the other surgeons, Manningham looking daggers at him over the tilted rim of his coffee cup. "I shall retain authorship of this document, naturally," he said, more quietly, "but John, you may rest assured that in its title I will give you the credit that is your due—"

"Excuse me," a new voice intruded. The surgeons looked up to see a man standing over them, the gentleman from the booth who'd been purchasing a life insurance policy. "I couldn't help but overhear," he said. "I would guess that you are the surgeons for the woman Mary Toft? Just arrived in London?"

"Yes! Yes, we are," Nathanael said, before anyone could think to stop him.

The man's eyes brightened. "I'm torn between admiration and wishing you ill luck," he said. He brandished a paper before him, a legal document with the ink of its signatures still wet. "I've just purchased a policy on her life—I expect to find it the smartest decision I've ever made."

"Are you related to her?" said Manningham, frowning.

"Oh, not in the least," the man laughed. "And neither are the dozen others that have bought the exact same policy from that fellow over there since business began this morning. But twenty shillings against a thousand pounds is a fair risk in this instance, yes? Look at all your sallow faces—I should say so!" Uninvited, he pulled over a chair from a nearby table and, reluctantly, the surgeons made room for him. "Matthew Richardson," he said, sitting down. "I have a cousin in Godalming—his name is Rufus. He sent me a letter detailing the most absurd story I've ever heard—it can't be true. But it gave me the idea."

The story, Matthew took pains to make clear even as he delighted in telling it, was not one that Rufus himself believed, but one that he had heard and thought worth passing on, as it indicated something of the nature of the town, and the predilection of its residents toward gossip. The word was that Mary Toft had been abducted by a mysterious black person, who arrived outside her house at midnight astride a snorting, slavering stallion with an ebony coat that shimmered in the starlight, the largest horse that anyone had ever seen. She had been found by her husband lying naked outside the front door of the house the next morning, confused and with no memory of what had happened to her the night before, "and you wouldn't believe what happened next," said Matthew.

"She began to give birth to rabbits, one after another?" said Manningham.

"Yes, that, of course, everyone knows that, it's in the newspapers, but also—and here is what is truly shocking—she began to *change*. Her hair began to curl; her skin began to darken, as if she spent her days beneath the sun of a hotter clime instead of our feeble English light. Rufus says that the story he commonly overhears in the town is that the woman will be a full-blown coffee-hued black before the year is out, and that this is the reason no one has been permitted to lay eyes on her except you fellows, right here before me. The medical conundrum is such that the king of England himself has shown some interest, which is why she has been summoned here.

"As I said, a silly story," Matthew said, leaning back in his chair with his arms folded. "But such stories often spring from a seed of truth, yes?"

"If I had more of a *facility with prose*, I might detail exactly how silly that story is," Manningham said, "but at the moment words escape me."

"That," said Matthew, "is exactly what one would *expect* you to say, if you had a secret to keep. But whether it is true or not is, in the end, neither here nor there. A woman who finds herself the subject of so many unusual stories, who finds herself in seclusion and attended to by an army of surgeons, some of whom are quite famous, cannot be long for this world."

He stood. "I hope you do the best for her that you can. But not so well that you prevent me from my thousand pounds. Good day, gentlemen."

CHAPTER XIX

The Keepers of the Vigil.

History does not record how the first people began to gather in front of Dr. Lacey's Bagnio, arriving one or two at a time, mostly alone, occasionally hand in hand. There was no organization, no leader, no advertisement publicizing the assembly—they just came. They would join the formation that silently rearranged itself to take them in while keeping its constant geometric order; they would leave when they were at last called home by the intruding consciousness of earthly duties or the grumblings of their stomachs. No single person stayed for more than two hours, but the gathering itself persisted, replacing those who drifted away, shrinking as night fell and growing as the sun rose, its numbers increasing every day.

Perhaps they were peculiarly attuned to the city's unending song of itself, and could hear the strange, arrhythmic melody that it hummed in the vicinity of Covent Garden, a tune that offered a new kind of beauty to those who had the ears to hear it. Perhaps they could somehow sense that, in a room within the bagnio, the fabric of reality was slowly turning from cloth to lace, and so they found themselves drawn to a place where the truth was mutable; where, if you pushed at facts, they would kindly move aside for you instead of pushing back. Their dreams and wishes were small, perhaps, and usually meant for themselves alone, but a thousand such contrary-to-fact imaginings, working in quiet concert, might bring about a new philosophy, or a new nation.

*

Robert Swale was a proud Englishman and a prouder Saxon, tracing his lineage all the way back to the hardy invaders of the island's southern shore in the fifth century (though it was perhaps true that the farther back one went in Swale's family tree, the more that genealogy became less a science and more an art, a matter of intuition and feeling). One did not need documentary evidence to be sure of his ancestry, or so Swale thought—it could be seen in his sparkling gray eyes and broad forehead, in his height and his stoutness, in the beard that bloomed on his face mere hours after shaving. A hardy creature was Robert Swale; a lover of gustatory pleasures; an eater of many meats.

Robert Swale had gout—at least, this is what his surgeon said. But that had to be a misdiagnosis, if not an utter lie meant to convince Swale to undo his purse strings still further. There was something *wrong* with the big toe of his right foot, to be sure, but it was a temporary problem of the kind that crops up as one ages, soon to sort itself out once said toe recalled the hardy nature of the Saxon body to which it belonged. His surgeon had tried to push a pamphlet on him, an excerpt from the memoir of a merchant named Thomas Tryon, who felt that "flesh does breed a great store of noxious humours," and suggested a diet of "milk, pulses, grains and fruits," but Robert Swale was not a child, not one to leave the dish with pride of place at the center of the table left untouched while other men of weaker constitutions loaded up their plates with roast beef. This body of his needed stronger nourishment. The idea of forgoing meat altogether seemed strangely cultish, possibly irreligious, certainly un-English.

Still, though—that God-damned toe. During his days it throbbed and hated shoes; about an hour after supper its ache invariably turned into something mean and stinging, as if an invisible asp had latched its fangs into it and was filling it with poison. Just last night it had woken him up with a stab so strong that it revealed to him a peculiar clarity of mind, its variety unknown to him before, that lay on the other side of the most extreme pain. *I should just cut the damned thing off,* he thought serenely. *A carving knife will do the job—a few tough moments, some quick work with a bandage, and it's done.* But in the morning light Swale thought that was perhaps too radical a solution as of yet—larger shoes might suffice.

He had just purchased those shoes in Covent Garden and changed into them in front of the merchant right then and there, unembarrassed to do so, and was carrying his old ones in his hand while his new ones annoyed him with the constant slipping of their heels. On his way out of the Garden he noticed a group of eight people in two rows of four, standing patiently in front of a bagnio with a mock-Turkish facade, looking up at one of its windows. He sensed a certain tranquility about them, and, curious, he stood next to one of the men in the gathering and said, quietly, as if he wished not to disturb, "What's this?"

"There's a woman in there," the man replied, not taking his eyes off the window. "She gives birth to rabbits."

Swale believed he'd misheard, and leaned closer. "Rabbits?"

"Rabbits," the man repeated, his voice intense and just higher than a whisper.

Swale stood next to the onlooker for a moment, observing the window—he saw a silhouette of a man behind the curtains, looking down on him in return, but could not make out his face. He had the distinct impression that he was somehow a person of import, though, a lord or a man of science.

"What are you all waiting for?" Swale asked.

"Hard to say," the man next to him replied. "But whatever we wait for is sure to come along, soon enough."

And, just like that, even before Swale realized that he was thinking he might change his plans and stay awhile, if only to satisfy his curiosity about these strangers, the group of onlookers shifted itself around him where he stood, so that he found himself in one of three rows of three, at the corner of a square that held the man to which he'd spoken in its center.

Swale stared up at the bagnio window in silence, and as he stood there in the formation, turning his thoughts over in his mind, the throbbing in his foot began to diminish, its angry pulses becoming weaker. Within a half hour, the ache was gone, and he knew without a doubt what was true. The shoes that he had just purchased fit his feet as neatly as if they'd been made just for him: this was true. He was a Saxon man of iron: this was true. And it was true that he knew no pain.

*

Something was happening to Erasmus Charnock's wife, Caroline—not all at once, but over months, over years. It wasn't happening to him, or to them, but to *her.* Caroline's eyes were fading; her face was falling; the beginnings of a knob of her spine were protruding from the back of her neck; new strands of dingy gray wove themselves into her raven-colored hair each night. Her hands were cold when he touched them, dry and papery; her voice had the beginnings of a quaver, or perhaps her once forthright demeanor was giving way to a tremulous timidity in the face of her own speedy aging. That was the problem. He wasn't aging; she was. She was aging and becoming uninteresting, her tales, when she told them, a monotonous, meticulous recounting of the past day's events, of her endless cleaning, and her cooking, and her eating, and her breathing. One does not expect love to persist through all the thousands of days of a marriage, nor even true joy—no wise man expects those, thought Erasmus. But Erasmus felt that instead of melancholy, he at least deserved a neutral contentment to go along with a youthfulness that had extended well into his forties, a vigor that showed no signs of flagging. Look at this man! Look at his shining eyes. Look at that mouth full of teeth, ten years since the time when an ordinary man would start to have them yanked out. Listen to that voice, its sonorous rumble that sounds as if it comes from a cello's body. He grows a day younger with each passing day! Soon he will appear to be standing next to his mother, not his wife, when the two of them are out in public. Who, in such a situation, would call himself content?

Erasmus and his wife were in Covent Garden, purchasing foodstuffs from a stand—he thought that perhaps if he pretended love, then love would return, and a thing that a person does when in love is accompany one's wife on errands that could be accomplished alone just as well, as if her presence were a pleasure no matter the mundane nature of the duty it entailed. But it was hard to see her selecting spinach and potatoes without thinking about how that spinach would be served before him, butterless and nearly raw, how the potatoes would be boiled too long (and cooked without beef fat, for Erasmus's wife had gotten the absurd idea from somewhere that eating animals was, if not an outright sin, something that decent people should not do). It was difficult to look forward to the conversation that would take place over supper, which would be about the purchase of these same vegetables he was eating, describing in minute detail the very transaction at which he'd been present.

Nonetheless, Erasmus Charnock persevered. As the money was exchanged and they began to leave the Garden, they walked past a group of ten people in two rows of five, standing in an easy formation, staring up at the window of a bagnio with a mock-Turkish facade that looked out onto the marketplace. It was impossible to tell why these people were here, and so Erasmus approached a gentleman at the end of one of the rows, a big, blond fellow whose flesh hung heavy on him, in shoes that were comically large for his feet. "May I ask," Erasmus said, "what it is you are gazing on?"

"There is a woman inside the room up there," the man said, pointing his stubby finger at the bagnio window, "who gives birth to rabbits."

"Rabbits," Erasmus said.

"Yes," said the blond fellow. "Another is due any moment now."

"That," said Erasmus, "cannot be."

"Perhaps," the blond fellow said, and turned away from Erasmus to look up at the window once again.

The dismissal infuriated him. How could he be so certain? And yet, in the back of his mind, the fact that the blond man in his ridiculous shoes seemed so sure of himself, and that others seemed sure of themselves as well, kept Erasmus rooted to the ground on which he stood.

Silently, his wife took his hand and stood next to him, and, without noticing, the group rearranged itself into four rows of three, with Erasmus and his wife in the back, the large blond man standing next to him.

And, slowly, as he stood there meditating, Erasmus felt a love bloom in his heart, an ember that turned into a fire. This world seemed full of possibilities, and he felt he had the power to describe its shape. If this were true, this absurd thing, then *anything* might be true.

He looked down at his wife to ask her: *Do you realize?* And he saw that, once again, she was young, and her hand in his was warm, the blood within it surging.

*

It was important to understand that nothing had happened to Lucy Addison, nothing at all: if something had happened to her, then that would have made her a *victim,* and a victim she was certainly not. When she looked in a mirror she did not see a cowering, sniffling victim looking back at her; when she examined her hands they were steady, not a shaking victim's hands. She did not have a victim's troubled dreams; each night she slept like the dead.

She was not a victim, for being a victim entails activities and duties that she felt no obligation to perform. It means that people who come across you in the street will look at you with pity in their eyes, and smug thankfulness in their own good fortune will lie behind that pity. In the moment they will conveniently forget their own secret tragedies; they will not realize that they are no more fortunate than you are, that calamity comes for every one of us, and assumes the shape that will be sure to hurt us most.

And so there was a thing that did not happen. No grabbing of the wrist as she passed her landlord on the staircase up to the second floor of the building where she had her room, no sudden surprising twist, no foot slipping, no realizing that he'd planned to do this here on the staircase where no one would be likely to see and where she could easily be pulled off balance. His smile, when she saw him after, was a genuine smile that was well meant, with nothing nasty hiding in its corners. He was not someone who would engage in a small act of secret cruelty, meant to grow in a woman's mind into the threat of something far worse that could have happened there, on the staircase, where no one could see. His comportment was one that commanded respect, and he was an owner of property, and because the thing did not happen, and she was not a victim, she could see the same thing in him that all others saw, and believe in it as everyone else did, and everything was easier for everyone.

Except that the thing that didn't happen kept coming back. Her mind repeated the story of the thing that didn't happen to her every night as she dropped into a dead person's sleep, and every morning when she awoke; sometimes the sudden, unasked-for recall of his face stopped her in mid-stride in a city street, and whenever that happened she felt as if some knife-wielding spirit had snuck up behind her and stabbed her in the nape of her neck. This was the kind of thing that a victim's mind did to itself. But a victim she was not. To speak of the thing would make it true, or so thought Lucy Addison—best, then, not to speak of it.

She was walking through Covent Garden; she had to get home, had to walk up the staircase to her rooms (where the foot of the man of good comportment had not shot out and tripped her heel, where he had not smiled and said, "Yes? Good" as she fell). She was not a person who feared ascending a staircase, not a person who made excuses to herself to keep from returning to the place where she lived, wandering the city idle instead—

What was this? A group of fifteen people, in a formation of three rows of five, standing before the facade of a bagnio that looked out on the marketplace, all of them staring up at one of its windows. How strange. It was hard to tell what they were looking for, and not at all obvious. She sidled up next to one of the onlookers, a woman holding the hand of a man who was presumably her husband, and said, "Might I ask what this is?"

The woman raised her free hand and indicated the window up above them. "Inside, there is a woman, performing a miracle," she said. "She gives birth to rabbits."

"Rabbits," Lucy said.

"Rabbits," the woman affirmed matter-of-factly. "If we wait long enough, perhaps it will happen again."

They were all of them oddly silent—and the woman turned away from Lucy, as if even that short conversation was a distraction best brought to an end, for there was important business to attend to— and Lucy's confusion slowly shaded into curiosity. She had no reason to return home immediately, and so she stood and waited with them (and, as she waited, she found herself, almost insensibly, integrated into a group of sixteen in four rows of four, the husband and wife on her left, and a portly, ruddy fellow with ridiculously enormous shoes on her right).

She gazed up at the bagnio window, imagining what might be inside, and slowly, her mind cleared and became tranquil. For she realized that here, in the midst of this group of people standing vigil, was a place of wonder; in a place where anything could be true, anyone could be a writer of history, rather than a mere reader. An unpleasant page could be wiped clean of its ink, ripped out and burned, its ashes scattered (Lucy thought, as she felt a happiness she hadn't in weeks, the weeks since the thing that hadn't happened hadn't happened).

Best to forget, then, to burn the nagging little memory away.

*

The woman standing next to Caroline Charnock looked as if she'd seen something bad, or done something, or had something done to her. Even if she fancied that you couldn't see it in her downcast face, you could. And perhaps in the end she would be better off speaking of it, even if it hurt her to do so. But she did not have to tell her secret here, and in fact Caroline had no wish to hear of it, not now. This was a space where it was easy to live with one's secrets, for a little while. There was plenty of room for everyone, and no inclination to judge.

She was glad that Erasmus had brought her here, for this was a good place for him—she could see the change in him, looking out the corner of her eye. Their marriage was one from which the pleasures had been diminishing, and that was due in no small part to changes in him that she had been too circumspect to mention—his constant trumpeting of his persistent youth and virility were at odds with all the evidence, and yet he did not seem to be aware that he was less of a man than he had once been, when the two of them had found each other, long ago. It was no pleasure to see one's partner through life aging two years for every year that passed, while you yourself were still able to catch a stranger's eye. His eyes, once shining, were becoming blurred and milky; his back had developed a stoop, and she feared that in twenty years he would make his way through the streets by staring at his feet. If he ate meat at supper he held his hand to his mouth for hours afterward, a sure sign that he would be better off with some of his teeth removed, but he took so much pride in them that he seemed to prefer the pain that came with them—thinking that he might be happier with food that was not so challenging to chew, she'd begun serving him vegetables at supper, offering a change of heart regarding the eating of animals as an excuse. Erasmus may not have believed her—she wasn't sure—but whether or not he did, he was still a gentleman, and a gentleman always accepts the truth of a woman's well-meant lie.

But here, in the midst of these people keeping vigil, he seemed . . . if not younger, exactly, then stronger, and nearly as virile as he claimed to be. If his visage had not changed, there seemed to be a new kind of life behind his eyes, and with it a calmness, an acceptance that growing older might mean exchanging one kind of beauty for another. Recently she had come to dislike taking his hand in hers—it was always hot and wet and clammy, as if a furnace inside him were in a hurry to burn itself out, but now, standing here among the group of people that had grown to twenty-four, the temperature of his palm had cooled to match her own. And this was good.

And look—here comes another, making his way across the marketplace to join them. And another, and yet one more.

CHAPTER XX

SECTS.

"W"ould you look at this?" said Lord P—— to Joshua Toft, pulling aside the curtain to Mary Toft's room and peering outside
at the market below. "It's patently ridiculous. Never a shortage of fools
in this world: one falls victim to his own idiocy and two more come
to take his place."

Lord P—— was a friend of Lord M——, though to Joshua the
two noblemen were interchangeable, for they paid him the same
heed, which was little. There was something strange about the very
rich, Joshua was finding, this being his first exposure to them and,
he had come to hope, his last: they seemed to regard those not of
their circles as, not so much lesser people than they were, but not
even entirely human. Not animals either, not dumb beasts, but no
more than ghosts, or rumors. When Lord M—— or Lord P—— or
Lady E—— deigned to talk to Joshua, they looked at him as if he
were not as plainly *visible* to them as were others of their kind—as if
he were a mirage of their own minds, one so convincing that it was
best to humor it so that it would disappear all the faster. And yet the
lords and ladies adopted this haughty attitude with such surety that
when they addressed him, Joshua half expected to see through his
own hand, were he to hold it up before his eyes.

There were twenty-five people standing out front of the bagnio,
looking up at the window where Lord P—— had stood before, and
what was unusual about them was their regimented *order*, in the midst
of the Covent Garden Market's noise and swirl. They stood in five neat
rows of five: some of the men and women had the disheveled look

of the perpetually indigent, though there were several of the mid-
dling sort whose clothing suggested that they'd decided on impulse
to shirk an honest day's work. They seemed indifferent to the weather,
this close to December. They did not speak; they did not move, and
the crowd merely moved around them. They all held the same easy
stance, hands loose at their sides, feet spread slightly apart. Sometimes
a few of them would close their eyes and open them again after a few
moments, as if they were offering up an unvoiced prayer. They waited.

"Who do you think they are? What reason would they have to
gather here?" Lord P——— said, and Joshua realized that he was not
being asked the question, really, but that Lord P——— thought he
was conversing with the man he considered the wisest in the room:
himself. (John Howard was also in the room with him, but he was
so immersed in the book he was reading that he was dead to all the
world.) "Perhaps they're all from some strange religion or other?" Lord
P——— speculated, not waiting for Joshua's response. "Muggletonians,
most likely. Muggletonians, or Diggers, or Fifth Monarchists, or one
of a half-dozen other crack-brained sects. You know the type: apt to
see signs of the end of days in everything from the beheading of King
Charles to the pattern of mold on bread." He chuckled. "Perhaps they
believe they have at last found a thing on which they can all agree."

He turned away from the window. "They only *think* they know
what we have in here. But I know."

*

Since Lord M———'s first visit to the bagnio two days ago, Joshua
and Mary Toft had not had a single spare moment to themselves.
After Lord M——— had sat in his chair for two or so hours, looking on the afflicted woman in silent contemplation as an occasional
beatific smile bloomed on his face, another imperious rap at the door
to the room had announced the entrance of Lord P———, whom Lord
M——— greeted effusively: their ensuing conversation, to Joshua,
sounded as if it were entirely composed of a list of places that only rich
people were permitted to enter, along with confirmation that both

Lord M—— and Lord P—— had been in those places in the recent past, though regrettably not together. After some consideration, Lord M—— and Lord P—— deduced that since they had independently found their way here simultaneously, this signaled that this room in the bagnio was, *de facto,* also one of those suitably exclusive places, even if a few of the other people present—most notably the patient and her husband—were not rich, and yet could not be gotten rid of without robbing the spot of its value altogether.

Lord P—— immediately assumed the vigilant position vacated by Lord M—— once Lord M—— had somewhere else to be and had gotten his fill of the enlightenment he was clearly experiencing, even if Lord M—— did not, or could not, articulate the exact nature of that enlightenment. Lord P—— stayed there for the rest of the afternoon, only breaking his silence to order hot tea from the bagnio's harried porter (and Joshua shared a smile of acknowledgment with the porter, which Joshua presumed must have looked to Lord P—— like two spirits recognizing their ephemeral natures, their tenuous presences in this material plane). Lord P—— sipped his tea and considered, and occasionally nodded his head in approval when Mary brought forth a particularly wrenching wail. Eventually, he turned away from the woman and stared at Joshua, in an intense manner different from the way that Lord M—— had ever looked at him, or, before this moment, Lord P—— himself: he seemed to need Joshua to be temporarily corporeal.

"When do you think it will happen again?" Lord P—— asked. "The miracle."

"It . . . is difficult to say," said Joshua.

"I've heard that it happens to her every two or three days on average. So it must be due soon. Yes?"

"It may be . . . that the effort of traveling here has upset her. That it has delayed whatever is going on inside her."

Lord P—— considered. "True enough that no woman with child should brave the rocky roads to London," he said. "But given what her body has already experienced, she must be preternaturally resilient. She will recover from the journey shortly. Yes?"

Why did Joshua have the feeling that Lord P—— did not find it too out of the ordinary to instruct a pregnant woman to give birth on command? "One would hope," he said.

"I understand that these events cannot be predicted to the minute," Lord P—— said with exasperation. "But I hope to be present when the event does occur. I want to know what her surgeons know—"

There was another knock at the door, and Lord P—— rose to greet Lady E—— and her young female companion. Lord P—— and Lady E—— had the same conversation about the secret moneyed places of the world that Lord P—— had had with Lord M—— earlier in the day, and then, without ceremony, Lord P—— went on his way while Lady E—— made herself comfortable in his vacated chair, with her companion sitting next to her. Lady E—— stared intently at the woman in the bed, while her companion pulled some knitting from a silk bag and began to rhythmically work the needles; neither of the women made the faintest acknowledgment of Joshua's existence, and he felt more invisible still to himself, not even sure that his own thoughts were real.

*

As evening came and the din of the market outside dimmed, the bagnio's porter brought Joshua some food: nothing more than five shriveled pork sausages on a plate along with a fork and knife, but enough to keep soul tethered to body. "I will be quite busy for some time tonight," he said in a low voice. "But you seem as if you and your wife could use this, and I wanted to provide it when I could." Joshua gave the porter his sincere thanks, and the man (old, gaunt, and stooped, dressed in an embarrassing outfit that, like the bagnio's facade, was meant to be "Turkish," with faded purple pantaloons and a full, billowing blouse) replied, "If you are unfortunate enough to find yourself awake an hour before sunrise, join me for a glass of gin in our lounge: it is how I celebrate the end of my 'day.'"

"I will," said Joshua, as Cyriacus Ahlers entered the room unannounced, with Sir Richard Manningham just behind. Would Joshua ever have a moment of privacy? It seemed not. "Has there been any change in the patient?" Manningham asked, shrugging himself out of his coat. "We thought to look in, and spend some time observing: it's been a few hours. Lady E——," he said, with a slight bow.

"Sir Richard," said Lady E——, standing as her companion rose with her and packed up her knitting. "I am relieved to discover that this grievously afflicted woman is in the care of London's finest." Turning to her companion, she said, "He saved my life, three years ago. My poor daughter was lost—during the birth she presented sideways—but it was either one of us, or both."

"I continue to wish I could have done better," said Manningham. "The longer and more storied a surgeon's career, the more troubled his soul becomes."

"You did what you could," said Lady E——, "and every day I have remaining is your gift to me. Come, Torie: let's leave these men to their business. Sir Richard, we will return at some point tomorrow, or possibly the day afterward, and perhaps I will see you again."

"No change," said Joshua as Lady E—— and Torie left; he seated himself on the side of the bagnio's bed with the plate on his lap and began to cut the cold sausages into pieces, ravenously stabbing one slice into his mouth with the fork and then feeding another, carefully, to glass-eyed Mary.

"I think," said Manningham, approaching the bed and standing over Mary and Joshua, "that now that we are in London, one or the other of us surgeons ought to have a presence here as often as we can manage it. Which, now that we have Mr. Howard settled and have dispensed with any business that accumulated in our absence, ought to be always. There are four of us—we can take six-hour shifts. Occasionally we will have to keep hours more appropriate to the establishment in which we find ourselves than to polite society: as I've concocted the plan, it is only fair that I am the one to keep his eyes propped open this first night."

"And I will relieve you," Cyriacus Ahlers said, "until Mr. Howard arrives in the morning."

"Leaving Mr. St. André to lie abed, as is likely his wont."

"On my way out," said Cyriacus, "shall I ask the porter to bring you anything?"

"Coffee, please, as close to boiling as you can manage," said Sir Richard, seating himself at the little marble table, "and a deck of cards. Solitaire helps pass the time for minds too exhausted for more rigorous endeavors. And do please ask if and when the services of a messenger are available—if a birth is about to commence, the king must be alerted immediately."

"My pleasure, Sir Richard," said Cyriacus, pronouncing Manningham's title with good-humored teasing. "Until tomorrow."

*

Night fell, and the market's silence was replaced by a collage of sounds from the bagnio's dozen rooms and the lounge on the floor below, coming muffled to Joshua through the walls: bursts of laughter that erupted with the suddenness of pistol shots; guttural strings of curses; the percussive patter of men engaged in gambling, the shouting of numbers and cheerful slapping of cards against tables; the rhythmic rapping of headboards against walls; occasional wordless arias of pleasure, which seemed as if they were practiced. He lay next to his wife, drifting in and out of a drowse, and she slept little at all.

Manningham had positioned the card table so that he could sit behind it and watch Mary and Joshua, and whenever Joshua arose from his twilight sleep he found Manningham staring at him, unblinking, seemingly able to play solitaire without glancing at the cards, laying them down in precise arrangements as he speared Joshua with his pinpoint gaze. "I hear that Lord P—— visited here briefly today, as well as Lord M—— and Lady E——," he said. "Lord P—— is an acquaintance of mine. I sometimes move through those circles, if only because my surgeon's satchel serves as an entrance pass."

He laid one card down, then another, then looked down at the table, frowned, swept the array of cards together, and shuffled it with a nimbleness that suggested extensive experience with the deck.

"Court and parliament are positively *abuzz* with the news of your wife and her presence here at the behest of the king," he said, once again dealing the first few cards out. "You can safely bet that if Lord M—— and Lord P—— and Lady E—— have all paid a visit here, then all the Houses of Lords and Commons will want to pass through this place, all the dukes and barons. They will want to be here, and will want to be seen here. Their unending knocks will wear a hole in the door."

He covered a king with a queen, and he smiled.

"You realize," he said, "that until Mary gives birth to another rabbit, you will have no rest, no solitude? Not a single second? And when she does deliver again—why, who knows what will happen? Sensation and mayhem! Hustle and bustle! Why, I can't even begin to imagine the coming hubbub."

"I believe I will wander down to the lounge to refresh myself," said Joshua, rising wearily from the bed.

"You do that," said Manningham. "No need to invite me along. I am content to wait here, with your wife, until you return."

*

Joshua stayed in the bagnio's salon until it emptied out, sprawled on a worn-out couch, watching a last few gamblers as their fortunes shifted and nursing a dram of spirits provided to him by a sympathetic whore. Eventually, the bagnio's porter sat down next to him, a bottle of gin filched from behind the bar in one hand, a glass in another. He carelessly filled his own glass until the liquor splashed over the edges, drank it down in one long stinging gulp, refilled it, and poured a dose into Joshua's empty glass as well.

"You would not believe the things I have seen," the porter said, lying back with his eyes half closed, exhausted. His pantaloons sagged about his thin legs; a stray wisp of white hair on his mostly bald head poked awkwardly upward. "Each night brings a new and unwelcome surprise. Because I am not real for them, they have no shame before me. Look: here is my withered arse; here is my limp prick; bring me some tea. Bring me *oysters,* porter—I need to fuck and bugger to feel alive."

"They are bastards," said Joshua.

"Bastards and sons of bitches," the porter agreed.

They drank to that.

"And I don't like the way these rich men look at my wife," Joshua said.

The porter's ears perked up. "How strange to see people who would never choose to darken this establishment's doors traipsing through here, one after another," he said. "The whores and I have laughed about it. The very Lady E—— stepping in here with her nose up just as if this were Saint Paul's Cathedral. One never would have thought.

"You," the porter said, leaning closer, "have pulled off some kind of strange trick."

"No trick at all," said Joshua. "No illusion: the surgeons we will never be rid of will tell you as much."

"No trick?" said the porter, topping off Joshua's glass.

And as Joshua took a sip from the newly filled glass of gin, he looked into the aged porter's kindly, milky eyes, set in twin nests of wrinkles, and his heart opened.

The two of them finished the bottle of gin, trading jokes and stories until morning sunlight began to peek through the lounge's curtains and the tumult of the market began again. Then they parted, the porter dragging himself home to sleep until afternoon when he would have to return, and Joshua returning upstairs to collapse in the bed in the King's Head (a room that, it dawned on him, was as much a prison cell as a place of comfort), snoring for hours under the watchful eye of Cyriacus Ahlers, blissfully unconscious, his dreams no more than blurs of color and vague suggestions.

*

As Lord P—— went to the window to look out of it again, hours later, a new person arrived to join the group of people standing before the bagnio as silent sentries, a woman who might have been pretty had her face not been ruined by an unfortunate birthmark. Without a word, the group began to rearrange themselves, changing from an array of three rows of five to four rows of four; then they resumed their gaze up at the bagnio window (and though the eyesight of Lord P——— was not the greatest in his old age, he believed he could see a smirk on the new woman's face, as if her purpose there was to tease all the others without their realizing).

"I am half inclined," he said, "to go down there and join them—if only to find out what they believe they see, up here with me. Perhaps I'm wrong about them, and distance and imagination allow them a more perceptive view. But I suppose we shall see, soon enough."

CHAPTER XXI

The Proof.

W hen John Howard and Zachary Walsh arrived at the Black-amoor for their daily meeting with the other surgeons on Thursday, December 1, Ahlers was absent, for he was on his six-hour shift observing the patient (who had not birthed a rabbit for seven days, though she ran a fever and her pulse was rapid. Orange tea would treat the fever, Cyriacus thought, bringing her pulse down in turn). Nathanael St. André had a stack of papers assembled before him, a proof of the manuscript that was due to be published in a few days, and he'd changed the title as promised: it now read *A Short Narrative of an Extraordinary Delivery of Rabbits, Perform'd by Mr. JOHN HOW-ARD, Surgeon.* (Beneath that, in smaller letters, was printed *Published by Mr. St. André, Surgeon and Anatomist to His Majesty.*) "Does this title meet your approval, John?" Nathanael asked as Howard sat down. "I assume that you will want to publish your own, more comprehensive account of the case—this only details my personal experience, coming into it later as I did. If you agree on all points, all the better; if our stories conflict in parts, there is no harm, though I doubt any such conflicts will be more than trivial." He pushed the papers across the table to John. "We will all want to take oaths attesting to the truth of what lies in these pages, to be appended to the narrative before its publication—"

"I will do no such thing," said Manningham, "and I believe I speak for our colleague Ahlers when I say he will do no such thing either. Not when the facts of this case are so far from being settled."

"Well, perhaps Toft herself will swear to what Ahlers said in her presence," said Nathanael, leaving it at that. "I will speak to her *personally* about this when I tend to her this afternoon."

John turned over the title page. The one beneath it featured only a single centered sentence: *The account of the delivery of the eighteenth rabbit, shall be published by way of appendix to this account.*

"I feel certain that there will be at least one more delivery, though she has not produced a birth in seven days," Nathanael explained. "There will have to be an appendix published for each successive birth, and in addition I am planning to produce a separate publication, with drawings from life of the preternaturally produced rabbits, comparing their anatomies with those of ordinary rabbits so that the reader may see the difference—"

"How much do you plan to charge for all these publications and appendixes?" said Manningham.

"Not very much at all!" said Nathanael. "My aim is to inform the public rather than to accrue personal gain; profits, if any at all, will be modest."

John leafed through the proof to find that the letter he had sent to Nathanael and a few other surgeons, back in late October, was reproduced in full here and signed with his name—its appearance there surprised him, but then again, there was no explicit reason to expect Nathanael's confidence, nor to keep the correspondence a secret, and the letter, once Nathanael had received it, was his, not John's, to do with as he wished. And he stood by what he said in it, still. He knew that others held their suspicions of St. André—the other surgeons sometimes seemed to tolerate his presence out of professional necessity, and Alice had not concealed her dislike of him during his stay in their home—but this new and scrupulous willingness to grant credit where it was due signaled that it was sometimes profitable to revisit one's initial assumptions about character, and that people, when encouraged, could change.

Most of Nathanael's text detailed the nature of the rabbit parts that he'd delivered from Toft himself, comparing them to those that Howard had delivered before St. André's arrival in Godalming and preserved in spirits, and his descriptions struck Howard as pleasingly, meticulously observed:

> All the heads which I examined had their complete number of teeth, but they appeared not in the least worn nor stained, as the teeth of other rabbits are by mastication.
>
> The nails of the paws were most of them exceedingly sharp.
>
> The skins were of several colors, as to their fur, which was exceedingly long, and in one particularly, that part which covered the head was curled.
>
> From all these considerations I was fully convinced that at the same time that the external appearance of these animals was exactly like such creatures, as must inevitably undergo the changes that happen to adult animals, by food and air, they carried within them the strongest marks of *fetuses,* even by such parts as cannot exist in an adult, and without which a *fetus* cannot possibly be supposed to live. This, I think, proves in the strongest terms possible that these animals were of a particular kind, and not bred in a natural way; nor will there be any doubt remaining (even with the least knowing in these matters) when those parts which are subservient to the circulation of the blood, and nourishment between an adult creature and its *fetus* are brought away; which I am fully satisfied must shortly happen, or be the cause of this woman's death.

John looked up from the pages at Nathanael. "Death?"

"We need not deceive ourselves," said Nathanael. "The fellow we spoke to two days ago, who took out a policy on her life, had the right of it. Whatever is happening inside her must be the result of a highly irregular constitution—her womb is at war with the rest of her body. If we believe that this is the result of God's direct intervention, then there is no reason not to believe that he will withdraw his favor once his message, inscrutable as it may be, has been relayed in its entirety. And then, unless we ourselves can work a miracle and remove her irregular womb intact, she will die.

"But perhaps the four of us, working in concert, will be able to manage it. If there is any hope for her life at all, it lies in our hands."

"We will *not* cut this woman open," said Manningham, his coffee cup trembling in his hand.

"I sincerely hope," said Nathanael, "that it does not come to that. But I fear that it will. With each passing day it becomes more difficult to see another way out."

CHAPTER XXII

A Principle of English Law.

As the meeting at the Blackamoor broke up, with St. André headed to the bagnio to relieve Ahlers at his vigil, Zachary took Laurence aside. "Do you think your master could do without you for an afternoon?" he asked. "I spoke to the friend of mine with whom I promised to spend some time—she has been occasionally joining the vigil outside the bagnio, and yesterday I spied her from the window."

"Does she stand with the madmen?" asked Laurence, arms folded. "With the shambling madwomen?"

"Not *with* so much as *among*, I think. It's hard to tell what she thinks of anything: everything with her is laced with teasing. Nonetheless, I thought the three of us might head forth into the city together tomorrow afternoon. Her father is an entertainer of sorts, and she can gain us entrance to his show tomorrow evening. She promises something strange—beyond that, she won't say."

Laurence paused for a moment, and his face was difficult to read, as if he were making a calculation to which Zachary was not meant to be privy. "I suppose," he said eventually.

"Excellent! Then we will all meet tomorrow afternoon, after Mr. Howard finishes his morning shift with the patient."

"And there is somewhere I'd like to go with you all beforehand," said Laurence. "Not such a mystery—it is quite blunt about what it is—but I believe you will enjoy it all the same."

*

And so, on the afternoon of Friday, December 2 (as Mary Toft went into her eighth day without giving birth to a rabbit, and her husband assured the lords and surgeons who kept her constant company that a birth was surely due shortly; and as Cyriacus Ahlers sat at the desk in his study and wrote in his diary that "one way or another this horrible business will soon near its end—I dearly wish I had never encountered this woman, for I am coming to believe I know what must be done, and have not the will to do it"; and as Nathanael St. André's pamphlet went to the press with a last hurried addition, a record of the patient swearing under oath that when in Godalming, "Mr. *Ahlers* [had] examined her breasts, and found milk in one of them," followed by "The Mark of *Mary ‡ Toft*"; and as Lord P——— considered the menu for the supper at which the storied Sir Richard Manningham would be his single guest, and thought that even if Manningham was not the sort to appreciate a good joke, this would not stop Lord P——— from telling it; and as Nicholas Fox made the last few arrangements for the evening's entertainment, taking delivery on a box of fireworks, a bull whose breeding days were long behind it, and a pair of shrieking, mange-ridden feral cats), Laurence and Zachary met Anne outside Dr. Lacey's Bagnio, where the group of people holding vigil had swelled to twenty-four. (When she stepped away from the formation of four rows of six to greet the two boys, the remaining watchers began to rearrange themselves, swirling around in a restless, agitated mass for a few moments until two other strangers drifted out of the market's crowd to join them. Their arrival soon settled the rest down, and soon enough they were standing in five rows of five, staring up at the bagnio's facade, continuing to wait in silence.)

It occurred to Zachary that it was odd how the memory of a woman you had anticipated seeing after a long absence could enlarge her beauty as she stood before you at last. She was wearing nearly the same clothing as she'd been the last time he'd seen her, as she and her father passed through Godalming on their way back to London—the same blue dress that rhymed with her eyes, though her hair was now loosely tied with a ribbon of red silk that drew attention toward her

birthmark, rather than away from it. Somehow the deliberate choice
to emphasize the port-wine stain transformed it into something stunning, and as Anne greeted Zachary by looking into his eyes and briefly
clasping his hand, he was reminded of the other times she'd favored
him with her gaze, azure twinkling impishly in the midst of scarlet.
Even beneath today's smoky overcast skies, she shone.

"I have something to whisper to you," said Anne, and as Zachary leaned forward and Anne brought her lips close to his ear (and
he smelled some kind of lovely girlish scent he'd never encountered
before, a fragrance distilled from a plant whose name only women
were permitted to know) she said:

"Zachary. Your hands are sweating. In December."

"Oh!" Zachary pulled his hand away from her and wiped it on his
shirt, chuckling nervously, hearing his own chuckle and regretting it,
wondering why he cared about it, what had changed to make him so
prone to cringing—

"And this must be your friend," Anne said, mercifully rescuing
him from his spiral of self-doubt. "Aren't you a funny one," she said to
Laurence, looking him up and down. He was dressed in a sharp slate-
gray suit of ditto with golden buttons and accents, his wig freshly
powdered. She was two inches taller than him, but he smiled at her
with an ease that gave the impression that he considered height no
matter—again, Zachary had the idea that Laurence was a different
creature in his native element, with social rules he knew. Anne briefly
clasped Laurence's hand as she had Zachary's, and smiled, and said,
"I have something to whisper to you, too." And she leaned down to
speak a few words in Laurence's ear: Zachary could not hear what she
said, but whatever it was made Laurence's eyes widen as he suddenly
felt the need to clear his throat.

Zachary thought that it was good of her to be kind to Laurence
in this way, and not show clear favor to either of them (though he was
certain that she had not touched Laurence's hand for as long as she'd
touched his, nor held it as firmly, and he found himself hoping that
Laurence's hand had been clammy, too. Surely, it must have been.
Surely whatever she'd whispered in his ear was trivial, was nothing,

was something un-girlish and uncouth, meant to shock and unsettle, meant to create a healthy distance between her and this new stranger before the question of distance had even been posed. Yes).

"I've arranged entry for the three of us to my father's Cavalcade of Forbidden Wonders this evening," Anne said, withdrawing. "It's also in Covent Garden, not far from here—not quite in a *theater*, but . . . well, you'll see. I promise that what you witness tonight will positively make the blood *surge* in your veins. But we have a little time beforehand—Laurence, Zachary said you had an idea for somewhere you'd like to take us?"

"I thought we might go to a dram shop," Laurence said. "There are aspects of London that the city would not think, or choose, to display to visitors: a dram shop is as good a place as any to see them."

Delighted, Anne sidled next to Laurence and looked at Zachary side-eyed, playing at conspiracy. "And which of these lovely establishments did you have in mind?"

Laurence frowned, considering. "Bambridge's?"

"We're likely to run into my father there—it's one of his haunts. He's a nervous man, and needs liquid courage before stepping on a stage. Defour's?"

"Isn't that place sometimes a bit . . . indecorous? It has a reputation for occasional violence—"

"Yes it is, and yes it does," said Anne. "We're agreed, then: Defour's it is. Good choice, friend."

"I have a question," said Zachary. "If I'm to be dragged into this. Is it . . . I suppose, permissible, for us to walk into a dram shop and just—"

"Order glasses of gin as if we are adults, with sons and daughters our own age?" Anne finished. "Is there a law prohibiting us from entering such places, or proprietors from taking our money? No, there is not. Everything which is not forbidden is allowed, Zachary—if we're going to spend any time together at all, you must learn that and take it to heart. Now off we go."

*

Anne led them down an alley branching off from the Covent Garden Market, into the city's labyrinth. She stepped sure-footed through the twisted streets, steady on the uneven cobbles, tenaciously asserting her right to spaces on sidewalks, deftly avoiding puddles and mud and horseshit, and the two boys with her soon found that the wisest choice was to travel close behind her, in her wake. The air was filled with a mist that occasionally coalesced into rain, and by the time the three adventurers reached their destination, a seemingly unmarked door draped in late-afternoon shadows, Zachary felt as if he wanted to go back to his apartment on London Bridge and wring himself dry. But one soon learned to accept the brute fact of London's pervasive smoke and dampness—Zachary saw a few women with umbrellas, but no man would want to be seen wielding such a frivolous device instead of keeping a hand ready for better use.

"Defour's," Anne announced, and pushed the door open, revealing the dimly lit interior beyond. The place was small and closely packed, its air thick with the fumes of alcohol; the clientele was mostly male, seated in rickety chairs at canting tables or standing at the bar that lined the back wall, playing cards or trading stories. Scattered amid the men were a few women, their laughs merry and melodic and rising above the conversation, loud as it was, and another group of children like themselves, three boys huddled at a table in a corner, making themselves invisible in a manner that was likely to work on adults, but not other children. Zachary and Laurence spied them, caught their eyes, shared a quick moment of confidence in their glances of recognition, and dutifully looked away to avoid drawing further attention.

In Anne's company, Zachary and Laurence had no such chance at anonymity; nor did Anne seem to desire it. She marched straight through the crowd of men toward the bar, her deep blue dress a sharp contrast to the grays and blacks and browns favored by the assembled drinkers, and as Zachary followed behind he could see the men's faces, some smiling, others turning away or stifling sputtered laughs, but none of them indifferent to the face of the young woman they saw.

She reached the bar as the men parted before her, rummaged in the pocket of her dress, and firmly slapped threepence on the table. "Drunk for one penny; dead drunk for tuppence; clean straw for nothing," she said, quoting the sign in the window of every dram shop (and indeed, behind the bar lay a scrawny, elderly man on a bed of straw thrown onto the floor, shirt stained with vomit, unwitting of the world). "So: drunk, to begin. Dead drunk if your gin is of quality and your claims of fine straw aren't lies."

The publican was an awesome pile of old and seasoned flesh, acquired pound by pound over decades spent seated in front of plates of mutton and mugs of beer. His pale, bullet-shaped head was shorn completely bald, and his eyes were tiny and dark. As he turned to retrieve a bottle of gin from a high shelf behind him, his thick, stubby fingers and the sweaty rolls of fat on the back of his neck put Zachary in mind of links of sausage.

"You never pull that bottle down for me, Keith," said the man standing at the bar next to Anne, smiling.

"Because, Michael, you are not a pert young minx who strides through my door to offer a *challenge*," Keith replied in a booming baritone as half the dram shop erupted in a long, rolling roar of laughter. "To her, and her two young friends who are clearly in *well over their heads*," he announced to more raucous guffaws, "I give my rarest ambrosia, brought here from the Continent."

He decanted servings of gin into three tiny glasses, stopping each pour just before the rim, and Anne carefully passed them back one at a time to Laurence and Zachary, taking the last for herself. Zachary immediately tossed his back in one long gulp, as he'd done with every glass of gin he'd ever had before this one (all of three, each handed to him by John Howard, and never for pleasure). It didn't taste much different from every other swallow of gin he'd taken—it stung his tongue and felt warm going down his throat—but afterward he noticed that a few of the other patrons were looking at him as if he'd done something embarrassing.

Keith, the publican, blanched. "That wasn't made by amateurs, friend," he said quietly.

Meanwhile, Laurence and Anne had both taken small sips,

enough to ensure that the gin wouldn't splash out of the glass, and were deep in concentration—Anne's eyes focused on nothing in particular, while Laurence's were completely closed. "Not much juniper," he said, "though it appears later."

"What's that at the beginning, though?" said Anne.

They both took another small sip as Michael beckoned Keith, leaned over the bar, and whispered something in his ear.

"*Cardamom,*" Laurence and Anne exclaimed simultaneously, as Keith nodded.

Laurence laughed to himself. "French."

"Interesting," Anne said, "and I like it, but I wouldn't make a habit of it."

"It *is* interesting," said Zachary, too late.

*

While Anne and Laurence finished sipping their servings of gin, Zachary played aimlessly with his empty glass—humiliated, he'd found that he'd wasted something rare, and showed himself as unworthy of a second helping (which he thought he wouldn't have been able to handle anyway: he felt light-headed, and the good cheer he usually associated with alcohol was muted by a shame that might not have been so potent if he'd been sober). Laurence and Anne continued to compare their impressions of the gin, a conversation that threatened to become interminable, due in no small part to Zachary's intoxication. It seemed to Zachary as if, for Anne and Laurence, drinking gin was like having a story told to one's tongue, with flavors in the place of words. To Zachary (and, Zachary suspected, to most of the other people in the pub) gin was a means to an end, not an end in itself, but Keith probably did not retrieve the special bottle on the top shelf for those people (and again, he felt a stab of shame at having wasted a gift that he had failed to recognize as one). He wondered if this was some kind of trick or delusion—if Anne and Laurence were genuinely tasting all the things they said they were, or were just fooling themselves or, worse, lying—but each description of the drink by one was met with enthusiasm by the other, and their impressions appeared to agree.

As Anne collected the glasses and handed them back to the publican, she asked for something "a little more ordinary" (and Zachary felt a final irritation at the reminder of his *faux pas,* for she seemed to imply that, if not for uncouth present company, she might have preferred to continue on with drinks that tasted like parades of herbs and flowers). Keith retrieved a bottle from a lower shelf, smudged and half empty, less august than the first, and refilled the glasses: "These are courtesy of the establishment," he said, his tone tinged with apology, as if someone who could discern the hint of cardamom in the first sample he'd offered should not have to pay good money for mediocrity, even if they'd requested it.

What sort of person Anne's age would be knowledgeable about such a subject? How strange this woman was; how strange the place in which this woman lived. Zachary took a small sip from his newly filled glass, which tasted more or less exactly like the first to him. "This is fine," Anne said after a taste. "This is fine," Laurence agreed; then in unison, the two of them tossed the shots back, Laurence grimacing while Anne shivered like a wet dog.

And then Zachary did not know what to do. He tried a method of drinking that he intended to be a cross between sipping and gulping, which resulted only in splashing some of the gin on his shirt, and was regretting that he'd even set foot in this place—the dram shop patrons in his immediate vicinity were making a big show of not looking at him, which made him feel even worse than if they *had* looked at him—when he turned toward the door and saw a most astonishing sight.

There, at the entrance, coming toward the bar, approaching Zachary, was a black person.

It took him a moment to realize it: at first, he was just startled. Almost all the images of black people he'd seen in life had been in monochrome, in engravings and the illustrations of books, and the heavy lines of woodcuts could not capture the true hue of the skin— a dark, rich brown that colored his face and the backs of his hands.

He was dressed in unusual finery—his velvet coat was slim-fitting and trimmed with golden lace, and strapped to his hip was a sword, the blade polished to a shine, its point sheared off so that it seemed to signal that its owner was a gentleman, but not one prepared to do violence. In his hand he carried a trumpet, slender and long, made of bronze. He seemed not to fear that someone would try to take it; it appeared to be an emblem of some kind of power, if only the power to make music, or to herald an important man's arrival.

He passed through the crowd of drinkers, smiling and nodding at those he recognized, and as he reached the bar Keith poured him a glass of gin from a bottle that, Zachary gathered, was his regular choice. He drank it while carrying on a conversation with Michael, whom he seemed to know, and Laurence sidled over to Zachary. "You're *staring*," he hissed.

Zachary shook his head as if he'd been slapped. The black man finished the glass, placed it on the counter, made a show of digging in his pocket (which cued Keith to say, "Your money's no good here, friend": this, too, seemed like a regular ritual), and then, saying good-bye to a few people on the way out, left the way he came.

Once the door had shut, Keith erupted in a loud series of chortles. "You should have seen this fellow," he chuckled, pointing at Zachary with one of his thick, short fingers. "Fellow from the country, never saw a black before. Eyes about to fall out of his head. Asking himself *what magic is this?*"

"World's full of wonders," Michael chimed in, as Zachary blushed still more.

"I'll need to pour you another drink to get over that, it looks like," Keith said. "That, my friend, was William Douglas, the Black Prince. One of the King's Trumpeters. One of the kindest men you'll ever meet as well."

"I like the blacks!" Michael proclaimed cheerfully. "Both that one, and the other one who comes in here sometimes—never caught his name."

"The blacks are good people," Keith said, passing the glass to Zachary, who felt obligated to take it and drink it even though he'd had more than enough alcohol at this point. "Neither papists nor Christ-killers: if they come here of their own free will, they try to fit in. Might get called *smoke Othello* once or twice, walking down the street, and that can't be pleasant. But they try to fit in; they try to make a go of it. Even marry one of ours and have those kids you don't know what to make of, looking at them: pretty girls and handsome boys, but you can't tell where they come from—"

"Ha—have you heard the stories about that crazy woman holed up in a Covent Garden whorehouse?" said Michael. "Brought here from some village? Rumor has it she had congress with one of the fellows, and it's afflicted her with all sorts of unheard-of maladies—"

"Nonsense," Keith pronounced. "Lies spread by ignorant people afraid of what they don't understand. I tell you that fellow who came in here has the same blood in his veins as the rest of us. And he tries to fit in. Now, if one of them brought ninety-nine brothers and sisters over from one of those hotter lands, and they started speaking some other language to each other instead of English, then I expect we'd have a problem—something would have to be done."

"But they don't do that," Michael said. "They're smart about it. Not like the Jews: soon as the ban was lifted they poured into London, they set up shop, they started moneylending and selling rags and bones."

The conversation had taken a strange turn and, drunk as he now was—the drunkest he'd ever been—Zachary still thought he detected something dark lying beneath Keith and Michael's seeming joviality. They seemed to mean harm to no one, or at least they thought they did not, and yet he felt himself on edge, as if the possibility of harm was in the air, or was already being done unwittingly. Anne and Laurence had quickly become friends, as people do who find they share a private language, and they had, for the moment, cut him out of the conversation—indeed, they were both huddled together and diligently trying not to see the publican and the man at the bar, in a similar way to the men who sometimes made a studious pretense of not seeing Anne, and this bothered Zachary. This dram shop had become a place of unveiling, and he did not like it. If you started to see that worms lurked behind the eyes of everyone you saw, it was only reasonable to deduce that they'd made a home behind your own, living in their little tunnels in the mind, silently altering what you see and how you see it.

Michael caught Anne's eye and offered her a friendly smile, and she uttered a skittish, nervous laugh, turning at last to Zachary. "I don't have room for another glass in me, and we ought to arrive early to get the best seats for the performance," she said. "Shall we go?"

"Yes, let's," he and Laurence said together, a little too quickly, and they turned and made their way out, through a crowd of men that seemed to press a little tighter, through air that had become a little heavier.

Once out into the street, the light having become dimmer in the brief time they'd been inside, his head felt slightly clearer. It hadn't all been a bad experience—the part where he'd seen a black person had been interesting. It was so strange how he took himself for granted, as if he thought the only thing that made him unusual in the eyes of others was the regalia he wore and not the skin beneath it. Though he lived in his own skin daily and, most likely, no longer found it fascinating, if indeed he ever had. In the bath he probably looked down at his own body with indifference. It was almost, Zachary thought, disappointing.

*

If he had not been able to retain his sense of direction when Anne led him through London's streets sober, he surely would not be able to do so now, and he trusted himself to merely follow in the path of the woman in sapphire who flew ahead of him. An errant footstep splashed something nasty on his trouser leg, and he felt London accreting on him like another layer of clothing or a film on his skin, a patina mixed from smoke and ash and stink and shit. He thought they were heading west, and eventually they found themselves in a wide street again, Haymarket, lined with theaters and cafés, along with a few bagnios with tackily ornamented facades, much like the one in which Mary Toft was being lodged in Covent Garden.

For some reason Zachary felt anger in the air, more intense than the mild impression of aversion he'd felt in the dram shop, an unrest that made the hair on his arms stand on end. And indeed, in front of the entrance to the King's Theater were assembled two groups of people, facing each other and taking turns screaming an indecipherable chant, apparently waiting for a final catalyst to send them over the edge into riot. The groups had about two hundred people each, and together they had almost entirely stopped traffic through the street. They wore tokens that indicated their allegiance to whoever had inflamed them, or who had honor in need of protection—half had red ribbons or buttons or scraps of fabric pinned to their chests, the other half green. About a third of the people on both sides were women, and they seemed just as enraged as the men, if not more so.

"We're just going to have to push through them," Anne turned to shout behind her, and she dove into a huddle of incipient rioters bearing green badges, somehow growing extra elbows and knees, the better to shove people aside. "Stay close behind," she yelled. Zachary obeyed, close enough to keep his hand on her back (and she seemed, subtly, to lean backward into it, to welcome the touch, though he may have been reading an interpretation into it that couldn't be fully supported). He felt Laurence's hand between his own shoulder blades in turn, the answering press of his palm as he was unexpectedly shoved backward, keeping him steady.

The two groups, red and green, seemed to be engaged in a series of chants that responded to each other in turns, which would have been cheering were it not so clearly hostile. In the distance Zachary could hear the shouted name "Bordoni"; then, all around him a few moments later, the deafening cheer "Cuzzoni!" Some of the people near seemed to sing the name rather than speak it, and so the violent declamation had a pleasing harmony beneath it nonetheless.

"Bordoni!"

"Cuzzoni!"

"Bordoni!"

"Cuzzoni!"

"Opera fanatics," Anne yelled back to Zachary and Laurence, as if that explained everything.

As they pushed their way through the crowd of Cuzzoni loyalists in front of the King's Theater, the press of bodies grew tighter, the crowd more agitated. The people around Zachary seemed to be having a discussion about opera, and though the matter they were discussing was trivial—something about whether Bordoni or Cuzzoni had given a better performance during the recent run of an opera, *Alessandro,* whose composer lived in the city—they were going at it with the seriousness of people who thought those who opposed them had committed a grave crime, or were guilty of a heinous moral failure. It was important that those people who wore red tokens come to understand that Bordoni was not fit to empty Cuzzoni's chamber pot—it would have been self-evident if those lovestruck fools would take a moment to clear the wax out of their ears—and if fists rather than words had to be the method of convincing them of the truth of the matter, that would be regrettable, but the end (the proper glory of Cuzzoni) would justify the means (a few bruises; some loosened teeth).

Slowly, he felt a fog creep into his thoughts; he felt the boundaries of his self becoming porous, as if he were sharing some room in his mind with those around him, while borrowing some space in theirs in turn. To his drunken puzzlement he found himself *caring* about Cuzzoni, despite never having heard about her ten minutes ago, and never having attended an opera; he was certain, beyond doubt, that Bordoni was not merely an untalented singer who had somehow tricked her way onto the King's Theater stage to torture listeners with squawks like those of a wounded chicken. The woman was worse than incompetent: she was actually *evil,* capable of all manner of malice in the service of besmirching Cuzzoni's hard-earned and well-deserved good name. Even a newborn babe could tell that there was no reason for Bordoni to perform in a world where Cuzzoni existed; if an opera required two sopranos, better to have Cuzzoni take both parts than to have to hear Bordoni at all. Something needed to be done about her tin-eared, deluded supporters; by God, something needed to be done about *her*—

The three of them broke through into a narrow no-man's-land between the armies of red and green, and Zachary turned around to see undiluted, wild-eyed panic on Laurence's face. The chants were equally loud in this space, their tempo quickening—"Bordoni! Cuzzoni! Bordoni! Cuzzoni!"—and on either side of the otherwise empty strip of street in which they found themselves, the men were squaring their shoulders and glaring across at each other, while some of the women turned over rocks in their fists that they'd picked up off the ground.

Anne turned back to look at Zachary and Laurence, and her eyes shone with delight. "London, eh!" she shouted, pounding Zachary on the shoulder. Then she pointed gaily at the wall of red ahead of her. "Through!"

She pushed ahead. Zachary thought they probably had Anne's serendipitous choice to wear blue, rather than red or green, to thank for their lives this afternoon. For a moment he felt traitorous or as if he had something to hide, as if his love of Cuzzoni, already fading, had tattooed the soprano's name across his forehead. "Bordoni!" a woman near him shrieked, tears running down her face. "Cuzzoni!" came the answering echo, smeared as it traveled to his ears.

The blue dress chased ahead of him through the tumultuous sea of red badges, and he did his best to follow, his hand outstretched to stay near the woman, grasping, clutching, missing. Suddenly, he felt that fog again, sensed himself turning stupid and angry as his mind once more became strangely *porous*. He found himself becoming outraged, on Bordoni's behalf; he had the vaguest, flimsiest memory of a time long past when he would have stepped in front of a pistol's barrel for Cuzzoni, but the fever that lit up his head would not even let him fully recall it. Which was a mercy: what person with two ears to hear could not plainly discern the superiority of Bordoni's voice compared to the unholy squeal of Cuzzoni's? The farts from Bordoni's arse would make for better music than the howls that tore their way out of Cuzzoni's gullet—anyone who'd heard both the singers in *Ales-*

sandro would know that for sure. Those fools with green tokens of love pinned to their chests were obviously mad, or deaf, or under some kind of fiendish spell; if it took a few broken bones to relieve them of their misapprehensions, then the pleasure of having the deliciously agonizing beauty of Bordoni's voice unveiled before them would more than compensate them for the pain they suffered—

The crowd became easier to move through as they approached its edge, and Zachary suddenly inhaled deeply—he hadn't been aware until then that he'd been holding his breath, and had no idea how long he'd been doing so. The rapid hammering of his heart slowed, and the mist lifted from his mind as the fire cooled in his lungs. He felt no affection for either Bordoni or Cuzzoni—he had no opinion of their talent, having never heard either of them onstage and knowing nothing about opera to boot, but he figured that if he had to listen to them sing while he was blindfolded, he wouldn't be able to tell them apart. Were both those mobs of people out of their minds? How could they possibly care so much about something so trivial?

Anne turned around to face Zachary and Laurence, breathing heavily, cheeks glowing red as she grinned at them both. "I suppose we could have taken side streets and gone the long way around instead of pushing right down the center of Haymarket," she said, "but you wouldn't have *seen*. Wasn't it *wonderful*? Didn't you get so *angry* for a moment?"

"Inconvenienced, severely," said Laurence, straightening his wig. "But angry: no."

"Liar," said Anne. "You felt the rage, the same as the rest of us! Your blood boiled and you *loved* it." She giggled.

They had left the throng of opera fanatics behind them, and Zachary gave them one last look. The chants of the sopranos' names had now become so fast and frenetic that the words began to overlap and echo. Suddenly, a man's wail cut through the crowd's strange music, high and tortured and surprised at itself, making Zachary's hair stand on end. And silence fell.

Unexpectedly, Zachary felt someone gripping his forearm, hard, and looked down expecting to see Laurence's hand, searching for a panicked reassurance. But it was Anne's, clutching at him with a man's strength.

"Wait for it," hissed Anne. "Wait."

The quiet stretched out, second by second, as the tips of Anne's fingers dug into the muscles of his arm—that night, when he removed his shirt he would find five faint bruises—and Zachary dared to believe for a moment that the whole thing might be over, that these temporarily crazed people might drift back to their homes and places of work as the dark magnetic bonds that held them all together weakened and disappeared. But the scream was followed by a sound that was an unsettling cross between a yelp and a gulping cough, and the mob of red-badged people began to first walk and then run away from Anne, Laurence, and Zachary, rushing pell-mell toward their green-badged enemies, colliding with them, punching and kicking, shoving thumbs into eyes, sinking teeth into flesh.

Anne let go of Zachary's arm, and he resisted the impulse to rub the sore spot where she'd grabbed it. "Enough of that," she said. "You've seen one riot, you've seen them all, and there are more interesting sights in store. The venue's just ahead. Down this alley. The afternoon's entertainment is not entirely aboveboard, though remember what I said: *Everything that is not forbidden is allowed.* Nonetheless, to witness it we must step into a space that is not on London's maps. Come."

*

She walked down the nearly empty stretch of street, indifferent to the rising din of the riot they'd left behind. Then she came to a halt between two theaters, the pair of three-story buildings separated by a space not more than fifteen inches wide. There was no sign that the gap between the structures was special in any way, but "here we are," Anne said. "I hope you don't have a fear of tight spaces—if you do, it'll be over soon enough." She turned sideways, and, clasping her skirts close, she slipped nimbly into the dark space and disappeared into shadow. Laurence followed, with Zachary taking up the rear.

Zachary edged along the narrow path, the wooden panels of one of the theater walls sliding past just before his eyes, the other wall brushing against his back. The sharp ammoniac smell of cat piss filled the air and made his eyes water, and he heard a nasty squelch at his heel as he stepped on something unpleasant—he reasoned that looking down to see what it had been would probably be harder to bear than his present ignorance. Not for the first time did Zachary think that God had never intended so many living creatures to make their homes together in such a space. He thought about the conversation he'd had with the stagecoach driver who'd brought him to the city. If his prediction of the future was accurate—that London was an enormous living thing that would someday grow to cover all the world—then clear skies and clean streets would someday only be a memory, and only a fantasy once those people old enough to remember passed into history. This would be a world of ash.

He continued to move. The passageway seemed as if it was never going to come to an end, that he would be sidling down it and becoming increasingly filthy until he was brought down by the colony of feral cats that most likely made its home here, until all at once it opened onto a wide space exposed to the gloomy, overcast sky. Here, dead in the middle of a city block, with the mostly windowless backs of buildings looming over it, was a sort of amphitheater. The ground was covered with a mix of sand and gravel (and, alarmingly, Zachary saw one or two dark brown spots that appeared to be dried blood, a day or two old and diluted by light rain, but surely his gin-clouded imagination was running away with itself). A sturdy platform made of wooden planks, about ten feet on each side, was attached to a pulley and suspended above a hole in the middle of the performance space by thick, hempen ropes, rigged so that it could descend and ascend. This platform had a few more dark brown spots that probably were not spilled blood either—it was not really important, Zachary suddenly decided, to speculate on what they were.

The perimeter of the arena was bounded by three tiers of wooden benches, on which about twenty people were seated, lounging easily and engaging in idle chatter in low voices. Most of them, Zachary found, looked rich—they had the same fine clothing, and the same ease in their environment, as some of the visitors to Mary Toft's room in Dr. Lacey's Bagnio. In fact, there in the front row, waving cheerfully at Zachary and Laurence, was the elderly Lord M—— himself, the first of those moneyed gentlemen to pay a call on Mary Toft a few days before.

Once noticed, Zachary felt obligated to join Lord M——, and so he crossed the arena and sat down next to him; Anne seated herself on his other side with Laurence just beyond them, on the end of the bench. "I would not expect someone like yourselves to find your way here," Lord M—— said, the statement half observation, half question. "To even know that this is a place where one could come. But my bold young friend Zachary here is full of surprises." Zachary recalled that first time a few days before when Lord M—— had looked into his eyes, taking his measure—deciding, Zachary thought, whether he was human.

"Nicholas Fox is my father," said Anne. "These two are friends of mine. I wanted them to see."

"Ah," said Lord M——. "In that case: welcome, to all of you—excuse me, one moment." He'd seen someone entering into the amphitheater through that space that, from here, seemed so narrow that a human being would not be able to fit through it at all, and yet this fellow, as well dressed as Lord M——, had strode into the space with a smile as his arms swung jauntily, as if the dirty, cramped passageway had the dimensions of the widest city street. Gaily, the man approached Lord M—— and they shook hands (and Zachary observed that they had the same demeanor, as if two young and energetic adolescents had somehow contrived to occupy the bodies of old men). "I want you all to meet Lord S——," said Lord M——, and Zachary and Laurence nodded their greetings while Anne briefly rose to give the suggestion of a curtsy, one that somehow seemed intended to ridicule the very custom of curtsies. Lord S—— responded to Anne with a comically deep bow that a person half his age would have been hard pressed to execute, the locks of his wig tumbling down to veil his face, though the wig itself remained moored to his head. Anne burst out laughing, clapping her hands with glee.

"How much have you contributed to the pool today?" said Lord S—— as he rose, his smile turned sly.

"Fifty pounds," Lord M—— replied.

Lord S——'s mouth formed an exaggerated *O* of surprise. "You think the *man* will win today?"

"The cat will *always* win," said Lord M——, "but we must continue to behave as if it could be otherwise. And perhaps this day I shall be surprised—at our age, opportunities to be proven wrong grow rarer with each passing year, and I have learned to cherish them when they arrive."

Lord S—— threw back his head and let loose with a gut-busting chortle. "Most excellent," he said. "Most excellent. I could not agree more. Perhaps it's not too late for me to throw in fifty pounds myself. One ought to pretend that there is still hope, in this late season, for astonishment.

"I'll leave you to your young friends, then," Lord S—— said, still chuckling. Bidding the four of them farewell, he went over to a few of the men on the benches on the opposite side of the arena, who greeted him in unison with a joyous shout of his name.

"What was that about the cat?" whispered Zachary.

"You'll see soon enough," said Anne.

*

Eventually, the amphitheater filled up about two-thirds of its seats. There was no one taking tickets, and it was not clear how money was being exchanged for this performance, though it clearly was—money, or some unspecified good or service, or the promise to fulfill a future favor; or perhaps people like Lord M—— and Lord S—— were of such a rarefied breed that their mere presence in the audience of a show was payment enough for whatever entertainment they might gain from it. Most of the audience were men, with a very few women among them. Other than Anne, Zachary, and Laurence, the youngest of them seemed to be in his forties; certainly, the three of them were the only ones in attendance who had not reached adulthood.

There was no apparent advertisement for the performance, either—the news of its existence, its time and its venue, seemed to have been relayed by word of mouth alone. Eventually, with no prior notice, the platform in the middle of the arena began to descend, the pulley's wheel squeaking rhythmically as it was activated by an invisible hand, and at this signal the audience finished its conversations, becoming quiet in anticipation. Sitting next to Zachary, Anne bit her lip, her right knee bouncing nervously beneath her skirts.

When the platform rose again, there was a man standing in its center, and it took a few seconds for Zachary to recognize him as Anne's father, Nicholas Fox. When he'd first seen him months ago, in Godalming, he'd been dressed to dazzle country folk in a neatly tailored green suit of ditto; here, in London, his outfit was clearly chosen to openly ridicule his well-heeled audience. The wig he wore was comically tall, easily towering two feet above his head; a slender tree branch jutted sideways out of the dingy pile of once white locks, and perched on it was a bright yellow canary, dead, prepared, and stuffed. His suit was a mismatched riot of red, violet, and gray, the coat misbuttoned so that it hung on him asymmetrically; as he turned his back to the audience, he revealed a flap that had been installed in the rear of his trousers, hanging down to reveal his pale and sagging bare arse.

At this, the crowd applauded lustily, though Zachary, taken aback, kept his hands in his lap. What could Anne be thinking of this? She looked on with that same inscrutable nervousness, staring at her father unblinking, chewing her lip and digging the nails of her fingers into her palms. Laurence looked on stone-faced as Nicholas Fox bent over and wiggled his flat, naked behind at the cheering spectators; if he was not exactly entertained, he seemed at least unbothered.

Fox spun around and squinted at the audience in pretended resentment. "How *dare* you laugh at the majesty of Lord Q——?" he said, his voice pitched higher than Zachary knew it to be in life, when he'd spoken to his master in private about a disease that needed his curing. "How *dare* you poke fun at Lord Q——, the Baron of Z——?" He stamped his tiny feet in impotent rage, and the audience laughed even harder. Lord M——, next to Zachary, was applauding fiercely. "Oh, goodness," he said. "This man never fails to be *such* a tonic."

During this pantomime, Fox had stepped off the platform, which had lowered again and was now rising—this time it brought with it four dwarves, all of them men, all of them dressed in white. One of them, mugging at the audience, eyebrows raised, tiptoed over to Fox and buttoned the flap of his trousers as Fox, still playing at anger, pretended not to notice; the other three dispatched themselves to corners of the amphitheater, where stools and small tables had been prepared for them. They each carried mechanical contraptions that looked something like conventional oil lamps, except that the jittering flames of the lamps were placed between two plates of tinted glass, one red, one blue.

It was the first time that Zachary had ever seen a dwarf, but, having previously seen a black person for the first time not two hours before, and having reasoned his way through the experience, he was somewhat at ease with the idea that dwarves might also be as comfortable in their own skins as he was in his own. And yet the dwarves seemed to have been selected by Fox with the expectation that those who looked on them would find them strange, and take pleasure in this—it was no coincidence that there were four, out of what must have been less than one hundred to be found in all London, and they were dressed alike. What would it be like to be seen as a signal of the strange if one was not strange to oneself?

"I am so grateful," Nicholas said in his normal voice, abandoning the comic persona of Lord Q——, "that you were able to find your way to this Cavalcade of Wonders. It would perhaps be unwise, perhaps unseemly, to openly advertise this place's existence, but rest assured that if you are here, then you belong here. You are a person who has become jaded by all of the sights that even London has to offer, yes? You've seen everything there is to see beneath God's sun, in this city at the center of the world. How long since all your riches have been able to buy you the shock of the new? Too long—"

"Enough of your windy preamble! Bring us the cat!" Lord S——
shouted, on the other side of the arena: he had been drinking from a pewter flask that he and his companions had been passing back and forth, and they were all becoming increasingly garrulous.

"Bide your time," Nicholas replied. "Trust that, as much as I would like to show you the novel, I would not deprive you of that which is loved and familiar; I would not stray too far from hallowed traditions."

"What is this about the cat?" Zachary whispered again.

"*Quiet!*" hissed Anne.

While the dwarf who had fastened the flap of Fox's trousers had descended on the platform once again, the other three dwarves who had carried the strange lamps began to slowly turn cranks fastened to the lamps' bottoms, which spun the glass plates in circles around the fires that flickered at their centers. The effect was beautiful, for the flames began to shift their colors from red to blue to red again, casting the ground in muted, multicolored lights as the sky darkened. Zachary began to feel as if he were watching one of his own dreams made real—he half expected to turn to Anne to see that she had grown a set of rabbit's whiskers, and a twitching rabbit's nose.

"Before the cat," Nicholas Fox announced as the platform in the middle of the amphitheater rose again, "comes the bull."

On the platform this time was the dwarf who'd descended before. In one hand he held a lit candle raised to the sky; in the other, one end of a rope. The rope's other end was tied around the neck of a decrepit bull, its skin hanging loosely on its withered body. It was a pathetic, tired creature: both its horns had been sheared off to their blunt roots, and a brass ring, tarnished green, hung from its nose. Oddly, the trunk of his body was wrapped entirely in a strange coat that Zachary, at first, could make no sense of—it was composed of brightly painted pieces of paper, pink, red, and blue, that had been twisted into tubes, each about six inches long and an inch in diameter. The tubes themselves were linked together by thin cords of hemp, making a long chain that circled around and around the bull, over its back and under its belly; the tubes of paper had some substance contained in them, possibly sand or some kind or powder, but what it was exactly, Zachary could not tell.

Another thin rope trailed behind the bull like a slender second tail, and as the dwarf led the lethargic animal off the platform by its leash, a recognition of what was about to happen swept through the audience, its sudden murmurs punctuated with a laughter that sounded somewhat bashful, or ashamed of itself. Nicholas, meanwhile, was saying nothing, merely looking at the audience members in expectation.

Then Zachary understood—the rope being dragged behind the bull was a fuse, and the bull's body was encased in fireworks.

He was horrified—first by the realization of what he was about to see, and second by the reaction of those around him. Anne was, inexplicably, *giggling;* Laurence, on her other side, had his mouth discreetly covered, but the crinkling of his watery eyes and his occasional sputtering coughs seemed to indicate that he was stifling laughter as well.

Lord M——, next to Zachary, felt no need to disguise his delight. "This will be good," he said, patting Zachary's knee. "This will be good! The best thing in months."

Anne looked past Zachary at Lord M——. "Since that poor fellow was run through?"

"Yes! That was a wonder—brave of him to turn toward us, to let us watch him bleed. Pure despair in his eyes, wishing for a surgeon, but he stood still nonetheless so we could have our little pleasure. I wouldn't have had the nerve, not for ten times as much as he got. He did survive, yes? Patched up before the life leaked out of him? Guts put back where they belonged?"

"I believe so," said Anne.

"Oh, good," said Lord M——.

As Nicholas put his fingers in his ears and scurried toward the edge of the amphitheater, his face pulled into an exaggeration of panic, the stuffed canary bobbing crazily on the branch sticking out of his wig, the dwarf let go of the bull's leash, picked up the fuse, and, with a grand sweeping gesture, lit it with the candle. Then he dropped the fuse and the candlestick, and ran.

The tip of the wax-coated fuse sputtered into flame as the bull stood in place, tired and indifferent. The fire moved along the fuse with an agonizing slowness; the audience was so quiet that Zachary half believed he could hear, beneath Anne's heavy breathing, the hiss of the flame as it consumed the wick. Laurence's cheeks burned with two spots of bright red.

As the fuse burned down and the flame began to climb upward, approaching the first firework near the bull's tail, the bull walked a few steps forward, as if to escape an insect that threatened to bite. It swished its tail lazily and lumbered forward once more with a sleepy, irritated snort; then, suddenly, it swung to face behind it, frightened, as the spectators tittered nervously.

Zachary wanted to close his eyes; he wanted to be elsewhere. But he did not want to be seen in front of Anne and Laurence and Lord M—— with his eyes squeezed shut as if he were a child getting a splinter removed from a fingertip, and he had neither the will nor the courage to walk out (and, he would think later, perhaps he did not truly have the desire, and wished only to pretend to himself that he had, to spare his self-regard. Perhaps he had truly wanted to see, just as Anne had wanted him to see).

The flame reached the end of the fuse, flared briefly just as it touched that first pink firework, and died out, and Zachary thought for a moment that this was all a prank at the poor animal's expense, or that a dud incendiary would grant it a reprieve. But then the firework exploded with a muffled *pop,* a shower of golden sparks flying as the bull leapt in surprise, and half the audience jumped to its feet and cheered.

Another firework exploded, and another, and two and three and then five more, and within a minute the bull was enveloped from head to tail in a cloud of blood and light, trailing a plume of black smoke behind it as it staggered in clumsy circles, bellowing in a voice that sounded like that of an old man, deep in nightmare. Thick droplets of blood spattered on the sand; chunks of meat flew. Zachary smelled singeing skin and burning hair.

In the corners of the arena's floor, the dwarves who operated the lights they'd brought in with them continued to turn their cranks, stoically staring at the flames before them, coloring the arena in hypnotic, shifting waves of red and blue, red and blue.

At last, as the wooden platform in the center of the arena lowered once more, the golden light died out and the bull collapsed, its head striking the ground before the rest of it, its neck bending at a troubling angle, its bleeding tongue lolling through teeth clamped shut. One of its back legs was broken, and dangled loosely. The bulk of its body was drenched in blood; much of its skin had been burned or torn away, revealing glimpses of pink flesh and exposed bone.

The bull drew three breaths, slow, liquid, and ragged, and died.

The wooden platform came back up, bringing with it eight muscular men dressed in dingy, spotted trousers and leather butcher's aprons; efficiently, they surrounded the bull's carcass, hoisted it at a count of three, carried it back to the platform as its warm blood coated their hands and forearms, and descended once again.

Nicholas returned to the center of the arena, hands raised in a sign that might have been read either as one of victory or benediction—it was hard to tell. "Was that not a special thing to witness?" he said. "Was that not beautiful and rare?" The audience of bewigged lords responded with a cheery round of huzzahs.

"Wonderful," Lord M—— said. "Wonderful."

"There will be an intermission to give us all a chance to catch our breaths," Nicholas said. "And then—the cat."

*

"While we are waiting," said Lord M—— to Zachary, "may I tell you my Theory of the Cat?"

Zachary was not sure he wanted to hear this theory, but felt he had no choice. This was all so different from the exhibition that Nicholas Fox had brought to Godalming—this was raw and ugly, and stripped of scrims and shadows, it left no room to doubt its realness. Nicholas seemed somehow angrier here in his home, too, as if his secret motive were revenge or spite, rather than mere diversion. This was the sort of entertainment a hateful person would concoct for people he despised.

"The Theory of the Cat," Lord M—— said, "is thus. I have quite a lot of money, young friend, so much that, through the peculiarly British innovation of *finance,* it has become self-renewing, growing even as I sleep and idle the last years of my life away. It replenishes more of itself than even a fool could spend, and I am no fool. But I feel no *sense* of it growing, and without this, I feel no *worth.* A man who has only nine pounds to his name is thrilled to get his hands on a tenth, but for a man with nine hundred thousand pounds, another hundred thousand is almost nothing at all. It is just a number: it makes for no material change in life that one can truly appreciate. It is hard for the very rich person to have that very important sense that he is, day by day, becoming more than he was before, when the only record of this is a figure in a ledger, one that ticks higher whether he sleeps or wakes. And that feeling of growth is essential to one's happiness—even, perhaps, to one's sanity.

"In a way, you might say that *finance* is the problem here, even though it provides so many solutions to civilization, for while goods are finite, money is limited only by our ability to dream it into existence. And the money will not be deterred from dreaming itself—it never stops. But do you know what there is a finite amount of, even in this crazed, finance-driven city, the harbinger of a future, finance-driven world?"

Lord M—— winked. "Humanity, Zachary. At any time in the history of the earth there is exactly enough humanity to go around for each human on earth to have one full share of it, to entitle himself to say he is better than an animal because he walks on two legs, and sings, and invents money, and wraps a decrepit bull in a many-colored firework coat. But if I am very, very rich, and you are not so rich: well, then, *I*," Lord M—— said, his hand on his heart, "can take some of *yours.*" And he tapped Zachary's nose with his fingertip. "This is the last thing that money is good for, once you have as much as I do—to make myself *more* human, which regrettably but necessarily entails making you *less* human, by contrast."

Lord M—— retreated slightly, perhaps responding to the alarm in Zachary's eyes. (Meanwhile, Anne and Laurence were huddled close together, talking excitedly in low voices. Since they'd entered the dram shop he'd felt as if their willingness to acknowledge his existence was provisional, to be given or withheld based on rules he didn't know.) "I don't mean *you* in particular, friend," Lord M—— said. "Even having only spent a few minutes in your company, I know you too well to want to see you brought low. And you look enough like me to remind me of what I once was, which occasions my sympathy. But if I did not know you, if I had only heard news of you from a distance, or if you looked different from myself, then I might hit you, or put you in chains, or employ you in some demeaning occupation for a few coins, or hunt you for sport. And that would provide *some* satisfaction, but not what I and my like are truly seeking. If I were to use a woman's mouth as a chamber pot—and you would be surprised how little money it takes to acquire this service, if one has agents in the proper quarters: the money I paid her was replaced in my coffers in the time it took me to finish pissing—then we would both be aware that the perversion was one that required human invention, and so the woman would believe she was a *lesser* person than I am, but she would still consider herself a person. To do what she did is humiliating, without doubt, but it is not a thing an animal would do. Slaves, I imagine, must think the same way, when they see that their chains are forged by human hands, that their freedoms are circumscribed by human laws. They may view themselves as *lesser* people, which would please me, but they would still view themselves as *people,* which is not entirely satisfying. Such a transaction of humanity favors me, but it is not quite as favorable as I would wish: I want a better bargain, and I know I can drive one.

"What I want, Zachary, and what I have yet to see thus far, is to witness a human not merely humiliating himself but doing a thing that he knows only an animal would do, not a human. A final depth of debasement from which one could not return. Do you understand?"

*

"Do you see now," continued Lord M—— as the platform that had carried down the butchers and the bull carcass began to rise, "why I was so excited when I heard the news of the particular affliction of your master's patient? Because it was a possible sign that I was about to reach my apotheosis. Though I must confess I have my doubts about her—I sat and watched her in silence for hours, and though I have not yet witnessed the phenomenon I seek, I am sure that I will know it when I see it. And she still seems human to me— my instincts tell me that she believes herself to be made of the same stuff as myself. I cannot say why."

Zachary felt a hand on the back of his, and turned to see Anne looking at him. "You should let me take over from here," she said to Lord M——, "because the rest of the explanation involves my father's particular . . . innovation."

"Of course," said Lord M——.

And Anne continued, in a voice that seemed to borrow something of Lord M——'s hauteur, in a way that, subtle as it was, Zachary still found deeply unpleasant.

*

"My father is not himself rich, but he knows how the rich think," said Anne. "The opinions of Lord M—— and his like are not unfamiliar to him. So he thought: what sort of entertainment could he offer that would satisfy these people? If not the guarantee of what Lord M—— sought, at least the promise of it. And this is what he came up with—a social experiment that he and the lords have been conducting for four years."

"We are attempting," Lord M—— cut in, unable to restrain himself, "to determine the exact amount of money that would induce a man to eat a cat, alive."

"Good Lord!" said Zachary.

"There is a pool of money," said Anne, "to which the lords contribute. Each month, during the winter season, my father finds a man, most likely a beggar with no roof over his head, and convinces him to take the chance."

"The pool is now greater than seven thousand pounds," said Lord M——.

"Is there a reason," said Laurence, now entering the conversation, "that the fellow couldn't just cook the cat beforehand? Outsmarting the rules, as it were?"

"No preparation is permitted," said Anne. "This includes strangling the cat just before. The cat must die during the process of being eaten; all of the cat must be eaten except its fur and bones."

"The man may not have utensils, for those are human inventions," Lord M—— clarified. "To see a man sitting before a cat's raw remains, dining with a fork and knife as if he were a gentleman in a club, would certainly be *amusing,* but it would not be satisfying in the manner I require. He must restrict his use to teeth and hands. Those must suffice."

"It calls for strategy," Laurence put in. "Best to start with the soft flesh of the belly, and endure the raking claws for a few moments to gain access to the organs necessary for life."

"Perhaps," said Lord M—— politely, in the manner of one who had long ago considered the possibility and dismissed it. "I believe that the man who is ultimately successful will summon the courage to begin not with the belly, but with the face. The teeth would pose a problem, to be sure—those feline kisses would be most unwelcome! But the face offers the surest point of entry to the skull, and to the brain inside—the bone structure there is delicate, and easily broken if you have the will—and so it presents the quickest way to snuff out the creature's light."

The platform had completely risen now, and on it was a man, seated before an enormous desk, mahogany with brass accents, that looked as if it ought to be in the office of a fairly successful lawyer. On the desk was a small cage; in the cage was a tabby cat that looked as if London's streets had schooled it into adopting the predatory habits of its distant ancestors. Scabrous as its fur was, with spots of mange among the black and orange, the cat was lean and muscular, and it prowled in tight circles in its rickety enclosure as if the cage were just a suggestion, to be disobeyed whenever it suited. The man seated before the desk in a plushly cushioned chair was clearly drunk, though his intoxication had done little to mute his distress—his milky eyes wandered constantly, unable to focus on anything as he avoided looking up at the audience, or at the cat before him. He was on his way toward old age, perhaps fifty-five, and was bald and wore no wig, though a few days' worth of beard grew in salt-and-pepper patches on his pointed chin and sunken cheeks.

"Too old to do it," said Lord M——. "Someone younger would be more daring; would not have dietary habits so deeply ingrained."

"Ladies and gentlemen!" Nicholas Fox shouted. "At last, the event for which you have been waiting. The seventeenth attempt in this space of a man to devour a living cat, for which, if successful, he will receive a reward of seventy-two hundred pounds." Nicholas reached into his enormous wig, and, as the audience laughed, he fished out a pocket watch, flipping its lid to consult it. "Sir," he said, "no need for prelude. You know the terms. You have five minutes to begin—once begun, you have as long as you need until you either give up or the task is done. Now: start."

The spectators became dead quiet. The man peered into the cage as the cat inside retreated to its back; then, carefully, the man lifted the latch of the cage's door, opened it, and reached inside to pick up the cat.

Lifting it gently out, hands around its torso, the man held it up in front of his face. The cat, for its part, was limp, gone strangely placid, looking into the man's eyes. They stared at each other for a solid minute, until Lord S——, across the amphitheater, shouted, "No need to romance the damned thing first!"

"Three minutes remaining," Nicholas said. "You must begin. We are all waiting."

The man mumbled something that Zachary couldn't hear—from where he sat, looking at his lips, it seemed something like *Time to get this done*—and then, tentatively, he leaned his head around the cat, gulped, and placed his teeth on its neck.

Things blurred then. What happened in those next few seconds was hard to follow, but it ended with the chair on its back, the man screaming as his arms flailed, and the cat treating his face as if it were a tree trunk, cheerfully scratching and scratching as it yowled with what sounded like a vengeful pleasure.

"Oh, goodness, this is no good at all," said Lord M———. "Anne, please convey to your father that I will contribute five pounds to defraying a surgeon's expenses; more if he loses an eye, et cetera, but perhaps he will come out of this with nothing more than the cat's autograph as a memento."

Lord M——— sighed. "One can, I suppose, hope," he said, as Zachary grimaced and turned his face away.

CHAPTER XXIII

LEAVING THE BARN.

L ater that night, in the room he shared with John on London Bridge, Zachary stared at the ceiling, listening to the constant rush of the Thames River beneath them.

On the other side of the room, John's voice came out of the dark. "How was your day amid the wonders of London?"

"We saw . . . some interesting things," Zachary said.

John said nothing.

"I'm not sure how much I like London," Zachary continued. "The place, or the people in it."

"Not what you imagined?" John said.

He'd left it vague what he was referring to—the city, or the people Zachary had spent time with—but it did not matter. "No," Zachary said.

"Cities are complicated," said John. "They can be both the beautiful thing you believed them to be and the dark thing you did not imagine they could be. The one does not obscure the other."

Zachary was silent.

"People, too," said John more quietly.

*

Apprentice and master pretended at sleeping, but even though John was quiet, the nature of his quiet kept Zachary awake, as if he could hear the noise of the thoughts knocking against the walls of John's mind, even over the sound of the river.

"Are you awake?" said Zachary, knowing the answer.

"No," said John.

*

"I share your concerns about London," John said, a little later. "A troubling city that turns its visitors upside down. I am not sure it was wise for us to come here."

"We were smart to know the limits of our expertise," said Zachary, as John silently noted the *our* where one might have expected a *your*. "Involving the other surgeons was the best course."

"And I believed I was correct to think that the more great minds were brought in to the case, the better it would be for the patient," John replied. "But perhaps I was not entirely honest with myself about my motives. When I recall how I spoke to Alice as I wrote the letters summoning those surgeons, I have a feeling not unlike shame. I spoke with a snappishness that I have rarely offered her, and that she has never deserved. I was a different person then, in the moment, perhaps desiring a fame I might not have ever seen otherwise."

"But sir," said Zachary, "you are already the most famous surgeon in Godalming. What man could ask for more?"

John chuckled at that, and Zachary heard him roll over, his voice becoming clearer as he spoke toward Zachary, rather than at the ceiling. "Perhaps you're right," he said.

*

John lifted himself to sit on the edge of his bed. Zachary would have little sleep tonight, it seemed, but he felt little like sleeping anyway—this city sometimes made one feel as if an endlessly full mug of coffee were being held to one's lips, and could not be pushed away.

"Have they done anything that I couldn't have done myself?" John asked. "St. André; Ahlers; even Manningham? For all their titles and honors? Other than bleeding her once, I feel we've done nothing but *observe*. None of us has even *begun* to offer a satisfying solution. The case is so strange that it offers little precedent for treatment outside of the half-true tales relayed between midwives. So what could a surgeon be expected to say, as knowledgeable as he might be? And your father, for all his study of theology, seemed nearly as baffled as myself as you and I left for London, though he did not advertise it. He posed a reason for the *why* of it, but not the *how,* and the *how* is what concerns us."

John rose and began to pace the floor in the darkness. "Zachary," he said. "Listen to my reasoning, though it takes a strange path. The Lord made us in his own image. It is also true that he made us creatures of reason—our minds are what differentiate us from the animals. Therefore the Lord must also be a being of reason, yes? Which means the Lord's actions might be inscrutable to us, we being not as wise as him, but they would not be *senseless.* If this is a miracle, then it is a strange one, for, if its cause is truly unfathomable, if its sole purpose is to affirm God's existence and force us to admit our ignorance and powerlessness before him, then the only course of action remaining to us is to abdicate the exercise of our reason, and abandon our attempts to comprehend it. Which would involve going against our very nature, as God created us. Which would, in turn, involve going against God's nature.

"As inscrutable as the Lord might be to us, what God would ask such a thing? To deny the very feature of our being that makes us what we are, that makes us what he is? For what reason?

"There must be a *how* to this, Zachary. Even if we cannot perceive it with what we presently know, we must continue to try. We are less than men if we believe otherwise."

*

Zachary thought about his father, left back in Godalming. The last time he'd spoken to him was in the crowd that marched to Mary Toft's house: *Though I do—I did—serve a purpose! Listen to these people: the word* God *falls from their lips so easily. But to what ends are his name being used?* It was only now that Zachary realized that his father had spoken in the wounded voice of a man usurped, who had been robbed of his authority to describe God, and with it, the power to describe the world and have others proceed as if that description were true.

And, if Zachary were to be honest with himself, was that not a small part of the reason he had wanted to become a surgeon? For was not the pronouncing of a diagnosis a means of *description,* to one who, because of his illness, had temporarily resigned his power to describe? It was, as surely as Zachary's father stood in his pulpit and described God's ways to men. Certainly Zachary's training had taught him to identify ailments from their symptoms, but at the moment when he spoke the name of the disease—easy as saying *Quinsy, I believe*—there was a relieved look in the patient's eyes that was almost as satisfying as the successful performance of the cure. It was undeniably wonderful to witness an acknowledgment of the power that lay in your mind and in your hands, from someone who did not hold that power.

Was Zachary any different than Lord M——, who saw humanness as a finite resource, of which he wished to deprive others so he could have more for himself? In his heart of hearts, he felt that he was not—that it was best that some had more power of *description* and *definition* than others in some subjects, to serve the good of all.

But what if a phenomenon occurred that was so impossible to explain that it not only confounded experts, but challenged the very nature of expertise? Would it not (Zachary thought as John continued to pace the floor and talk to himself) give people cause to believe that in such an instance, the power to define and describe ought to be shared out equally, just as humanity would be shared out equally in a just world? And if it was true in that instance, why not in others? Would those who did not possess the power to describe and define see this phenomenon as a sign that it was time to reclaim what was rightfully theirs?

Those people standing in front of the bagnio, holding their vigil, day and night—were they at war? Each of them for their own unspoken reasons, small or significant; many of them for reasons that were understandable or even good; but all of them, nonetheless, at war?

*

"There must be a *how*. What are we failing to understand?" said John. "If the phenomenon is so far outside our experience, does this not suggest that we are failing to comprehend something elemental about it? Perhaps we should not be searching for a new understanding of medicine that builds on our previous knowledge, but attempting to correct a misunderstanding of a first principle, or something close to one."

Zachary looked at John's drawn, dimly lit face in the moonlight; his head seemed to be hovering in midair, ghostlike. "Something so plain that it will be obvious to us once the truth is spoken," he said.

The young man's mind went back to the beginning of the case, when Joshua first set foot in the door of Howard's office, cap in hand; then farther back still. *A phenomenon far outside his experience:* in his mind materialized a scrim, lit from behind, and a shadow behind it, of a woman with two heads.

"Something that would make us wish to kick ourselves," said John.

Afterward, surgeon and apprentice had returned home together, minds aflame almost as they were now. *Only when I had left the barn did I start to question, to consider alternatives,* John had said. *It was as if a spell had been lifted once I had come into the open air.*

"Something that would make all of us brilliant surgeons feel like fools," said John.

In the moment when we were in the barn, looking at the woman as she stood behind the curtain. If all of us believed in her, would not her existence be a matter of fact, and not a—

Zachary suddenly sprang out of bed. "Like—"

"—dupes!" John finished excitedly. "Like *dupes!*"

"Cat's paws!" Zachary said, running across the room on bare feet toward John.

"Gulls!" John said, taking Zachary's hands in his.

"Oafs and laughingstocks!"

"Spectacles and imbeciles!"

Understanding flew back and forth between the two of them as each of them saw their own idea reflected in the other's eyes, and with that understanding came an irrepressible joy. And then, as they saw their sentiments confirmed, and began to consider the consequences, they let go of each other, and backed away, and each sat down on his own bed, and they put their heads in their hands.

*

"Dupes," said Zachary.
"Fools," said John.

*

"She was right," said John. "Alice was right."

PART FOUR.

CHAPTER XXIV

HASENPFEFFER.

There was one lone guest at the dinner held by Lord P—— on the evening of Saturday, December 3, at his home on the out-skirts of London: Sir Richard Manningham, who'd arranged for John Howard to take his shift with the patient. In a capacious dining hall whose ceiling was veiled in flickering shadows, the lord and the sur-geon sat huddled together at one end of a table large enough to seat twenty—though the space near them was candlelit, the other end of the table was cast in darkness, and the only other illumination in the room came from the twin fireplaces needed to heat the cavernous space. On this night, Lord P—— wanted conversation, and though he could have filled the table with a dozen minds as august as that of the surgeon who sat before him, he had found in the past that gathering too many intellectuals in the same room tended to aggravate all their myriad insecurities, and turn discourse into combat. Lord P—— was of the opinion that no more than three people above a certain level of intelligence and schooling should be in the same room at the same time, if all the people in the room were to leave it wiser rather than more foolish; two was best of all, if both were sure of themselves, able to explain the reasons behind their positions, and willing to concede their errors. And concession was something that Lord P—— expected Sir Richard would have to do, this night.

The dish before them tonight was German, starchy and sitting heavy in the stomach. Lord P——'s cook had obtained the recipe from one of the chefs who had come over from Hanover with King George—*hasenpfeffer,* a stew of rabbit cooked in red wine along with bacon, shallots, and garlic, served with carrots and potatoes. Lord P—— had been mostly silent for the past few minutes, attacking the dish before him until the rabbit leg had been stripped to the bone. "Is there a problem?" he said to Manningham, who had eaten the vegetables on his plate but left the meat untouched. "Don't be reluctant— the rabbit's soul gives it a wonderful flavor! Sharp and peppery." He laughed and poured himself a glass of French brandy, from a bottle he'd smuggled in the last time he'd visited to the Continent: while Manningham had predictably chosen to abstain thus far, this drink was Lord P——'s third of the evening, and the first two had made him garrulous. "You'll have some?" he said to Manningham, not for the first time.

"Water suffices for me," Manningham replied, once again.

"You wound my heart," Lord P—— said, hand held over the presumably injured organ. "I tell you this is better than our English gin, distilled from corn and shit and mouse bones, good for getting empty-headed maids between the sheets and nothing more. English gin is a drink for people who think a sin must always be accompanied by its penance.

"You've seen the debates in the pamphlets, yes?" Lord P—— continued, taking a sip of his drink. "Not the publication of your colleague St. André—which, given what I know of him, shows an admirable and unexpected restraint, and restricts itself to what he sees as the facts—but those of the anonymous theologians and philosophers who've chosen to offer up their opinions in his wake. The implications are significant, if you believe in such things: there are *factions*. The Thomists, who argue that Toft's so-called 'children' have souls of a lesser kind than those of humans; the Cartesians, who hold that rabbits have no souls at all. The Thomists think we are in the presence of a monstrous inversion of the Great Chain of Being, that this is a message sent by God that prophesies a coming inversion of the social order—fools in the place of geniuses, beggars lounging on thrones. The Cartesians think this is a plain abomination, an early sign that humanity has reached the end of its tenure on earth."

"And what do *you* think?" said Manningham.

The lord drained his glass. "I think it is nonsense, plain and sim-ple," he said. "I believe that your patient Mary Toft and her husband are purveyors of the purest horseshit. When I visited her, it seemed highly likely to me that the woman was shamming. My dear friend Lord M—— was willing to believe in what he saw, but his mind is full of strange notions, and one might therefore conclude that he is more susceptible to being taken in. And dear Lord S——, who last night was sitting in the very chair where you sit, may have had his reasoning compromised by his . . . perverse notions."

"What do you mean?" Manningham asked.

"I shudder to say it. But he speculated on whether Mary Toft's next delivery, whenever it occurred, might be . . . purchased, at a high price. For eating. That perhaps it would merely taste as any other rab-bit does, or would have the flavor of . . . the species of its mother. That perhaps it would offer the rarest of culinary experiences, while letting one avoid the commission of a sin so black that even a man such as Lord S—— hesitates."

"Revolting," Richard said, pushing his dish away for good.

*

"We might reasonably expect the extremely rich to be gullible, for their foolishness is well documented," Lord P—— continued, nar-rowing his eyes at Manningham, "but I do not yet understand why several well-renowned experts in medicine, one of whom has been knighted, have also been fooled by something that seems ludicrous beyond dispute the moment one speaks of it plainly."

"I believe I will want some of your brandy, friend," Manningham said, and Lord P—— poured him a glass, a healthy serving that rose to the brim.

Manningham took it, drank, paused, and drank again. "I have had my suspicions for some time," he said, "which is why I arranged for the patient to be under an unceasing watch once she arrived in London. And at times it was all I could do to refrain from stating them outright—I thought that silence, for the moment, was the best course of action. But now I am ashamed for not acting as if I were sure. If I had been the first surgeon to encounter her, or the second, I believe I would have spoken of my reservations more quickly, but by the time I was brought into the case there were three other surgeons involved, who did not all know each other before first meeting— Ahlers and St. André were professional acquaintances, but there was no love lost between them—and who I could not believe were all engaged in witting conspiracy. So until I knew more, I chose to stay quiet."

"I will grant you this one concession," said Lord P——. "Any reasonable man would admit that we have no way of perceiving truth other than our eyes and ears and memories and instincts. And so the truth must, in the end, be a matter of consensus. By the time you arrived, the three surgeons had already formed that consensus, which even your title did not equip you to dispute. Just as the surgeon who took on the case before you would have found himself arrayed against two more of his profession.

"I tell you, this hoax is a most strange trap," Lord P—— continued, as Manningham shifted in his chair with an uncharacteristic restlessness. "Once it snares one, it makes the victim into its own agent, and uses that agent to snare another. The cycle repeats; the number of believers grows; the false belief gains a greater purchase because of the accumulated authority of those who profess to believe, or whose silence is perhaps too eagerly read as consent. Over a hundred people now stand in vigil in the Covent Garden Market, outside the bagnio where Toft lies in. They come and go, but the crowd grows larger every day."

"But what about the very first believer?" said Manningham. "St. André is a man I would be slow to trust, but I have spoken to John Howard on several occasions, and he strikes me as honest and intelligent—not as schooled as a London surgeon, but with a solid reputation nonetheless. He is no knave."

"But perhaps, in the end," said Lord P——, "he was not willing to entertain the idea that a woman would desecrate herself in such a vile and unheard-of manner, repeatedly, for so little apparent gain other than perhaps a few shillings here and there, granted out of charity. Easier to believe that a miracle had occurred instead. It was clever of them to approach a surgeon instead of a midwife—I believe a woman would have been far less likely to let herself be deceived. She would have had no scruples concerning the woman's behavior, no delusions of her wondrous nature, having been a woman all her life, and therefore knowing she was just as human as the rest of us, no more, no less. She would not have given consideration to medical manuals of questionable origin that mix myth with fact. She would have known the hoax for what it was on sight.

"But: you said *Until I knew more, I chose to stay quiet.* Has something changed? Has additional information come to light to support our speculations, certain as we are of them?"

"Yes," said Sir Richard, "to my further embarrassment. For once, I am glad to be in the company of one who judges gently, where my cheeks are free to burn red."

*

"I had my shift watching over the patient late last night," Manningham continued. "Prior to my arrival, Lady E—— had come to visit her with her young companion: she was there when I entered, and spent an hour with me engaged in amiable conversation as her companion continued to knit, whispering numbers and commands to herself as she worked the needles, the both of them ignoring Joshua Toft as was their wont. Then, at perhaps an hour before midnight, the both of them said their farewells, leaving me alone with Mary and her husband. I began to play solitaire to pass the time, and around midnight, Joshua Toft arose to take a walk through the bagnio to 'stretch his legs,' as he said. He returned perhaps a half hour later, climbed into the bed next to the patient, and nodded off to sleep.

"A half hour after that, there was an urgent knock on the door (which, I observed, Toft appeared to sleep through). It was the bagnio's elderly porter—apparently, one of the *filles de joie* in the establishment's employ had developed a sharp stomach pain that seemed to require a surgeon's immediate attention. He seemed in a panic, and so I followed him to a chamber on another floor of the bagnio, smaller than the one in which the Tofts lay, where a woman lay on her back in a canopied bed, groaning.

"I feared a ruptured appendix or something worse, but a moment's observation showed that this was not the case: she was not in nearly enough pain. Her symptoms, I was sure, called for nothing more than a few ripe apples and a few hours' wait. I made some ado about her condition for a few minutes—in such cases, a surgeon's mere attention is more than half the cure—and then, after offering my prescription, I returned to the Tofts' room.

"But I did not enter immediately, for as I approached I heard a heated argument, between two people who felt they should whisper but whose anger had pushed them into speaking. One of them said, *I did what you wanted; you didn't say you needed me to cut it up;* the other, *I should have thought that would be plainly obvious;* the first, *I thought she was merely concealing the creatures beneath her skirts;* the second, *You oaf, that would be impossible, and would not trick a child;* and then I entered to see Joshua Toft in conference with the elderly porter, who had in his hands, to my surprise, a full-grown rabbit.

"Joshua immediately stammered out an explanation—*Ah, hm, you see, yes, Mary awoke while you were out and demanded the company of a rabbit, and so I had no choice but to do what I could to comply,* et cetera, never mind that even a place that prides itself on offering the most obscure delights at short notice is not one where one could expect to lay hands on a live rabbit within fifteen minutes of the request in the middle of the night. Mary lay in the bed, eyes closed and silent, shamming at being dead to the world, just as, I realized, the woman in whose company I'd been a moment before had also been shamming. Clearly seeing that the pretense was not worth keeping up, the porter merely nodded at us both and took his leave, carrying the rabbit with him.

"I seated myself at the table with my abandoned solitaire game before me, so enraged I could not speak. Joshua, insistent on keeping up the hoax until the end, said, 'If Mary is calling for rabbits, as she did while you were out, this most likely suggests that the strange phenomenon still has hold of her, and that she will give birth to the eighteenth rabbit within a day or two at the most.' To which I replied, 'I will most certainly discuss this event with the other surgeons on the morrow—then we will come to a decision.'

"Joshua said nothing: he merely closed his eyes, stretched out on the bed, and slept once more. In the morning Nathanael St. André came to relieve me: as I have said, I am slow to trust him, and so I did not confide in him regarding the events just past. Nor have I met with the other surgeons to discuss the issue yet, because," Manningham sighed, "I do not know what to do. I am at an impasse."

"Because there are more actors in this play than ever before," Lord P—— said. "Even if all four of you were to state publicly that this was a hoax, if you were all men enough to admit that you now believed you had been deceived, you would still be at odds with the hundred who stand outside, and the hundreds more to whom they speak. And it is in the best interests of those hundreds to claim that what the Tofts say is true—I would go so far as to wager that they care not a whit whether the woman is in fact birthing leaping litters of rabbits, or whether she lies. If you got one of them alone where he couldn't be overheard and offered him a drink, he'd be the first to say that the idea was absurd! Because they are not engaged in a search for the truth. Their vigil is a purely political act—a rebellion against, and an attempt to usurp the position of, the intellectual elite of this city. They wish to strip the value from your fine certificates, your sheepskin degrees, your years of learning, from the very *sir* that attaches to your name, Sir Richard."

Lord P—— leaned back in his chair, steepling his fingers and looking at Manningham through half-lidded eyes. "Make no mistake," he said. "The truth, as you think of it, does not matter to them. In circumstances such as these, our notions of truth are *quaint*. This is a coup, and the woman, whether witting or unwitting, is its leader. You must tread carefully in these coming hours, lest you look around one morning to find yourself a man in exile on your own soil."

*

"What must I do?" said Manningham. "This ends badly for all four of us, no matter how it ends: Ahlers, myself, John Howard, and even St. André. I see no escape that lets us save face in the public eye. Yet each day we delay worsens the problem, and will make our eventual chagrin all the greater when the day of reckoning comes."

Lord P—— paused, and considered. "There is a possibility that you surgeons are not the only ones who are finding that you are in a situation it would be salutary to escape," he said. "And if all four of you do not presently find yourselves hemmed in, you all will soon. Surely the others must have their unvoiced suspicions, just as you do; perhaps tonight they are having their own private conferences with their own trusted friends. Even if they do not have the direct evidence you do, Mary has not birthed a rabbit in well over a week, and this sudden failure of fecundity coincides with her being under constant watch—each day the conclusion becomes increasingly difficult to avoid."

"And the Tofts themselves must be tired of this charade as well," Manningham considered. "The woman is in terrible health—she continues to have a high fever and a rapid pulse. And she and her husband must feel imprisoned—they must see no exit. In their hearts they must desire an end to this as much as the rest of us."

"There will be no graceful withdrawals for anyone, I fear," said Lord P——, "especially poor Mr. St. André, who rushed to publish his findings and promised more findings still to come. But from where I sit, it appears that the least painful resolution will come to pass if Mary Toft herself confesses—if the vigil keepers outside the bagnio would not listen to you, they would be bound to accept her own confession out of her own mouth."

"But how could she be convinced to do so?" said Manningham. "She is ensnared in the same trap as the rest of us, and, like the rest of us, it becomes harder for her to escape it with each passing day."

The two of them sat in silence, thinking, and each refilled their brandy.

Then Manningham said, "I think I have a way. I would not be able to take the other surgeons into my confidence just yet, and it will not be pleasant for the woman. Nor for Nathanael St. André—in fact, my method involves gambling that events outside our knowledge are proceeding as you speculate, and that he has rethought some of his recently expressed sentiments regarding the case with a clearer mind. But I believe it is our last, best chance."

CHAPTER XXV

MANNINGHAM'S PLAN.

The four surgeons met at their usual table at the Blackamoor the following afternoon, of Sunday, December 4; Zachary and Laurence were dispatched to the bagnio to watch over Mary Toft, with instructions (which Manningham, at this point, secretly thought unneeded) for one of the apprentices to run to the coffee shop to retrieve them all if any of the usual symptoms occurred that, in the past, had preceded a preternatural birth.

They were all, the four of them, tired. The shifts that Manningham had put them on, watching the patient at all hours of the day and night, had interfered with their regular schedules of sleep, necessary as they all believed this watch to be. Ahlers's characteristic bonhomie and serenity was only slightly abraded by his sleepiness, but St. André's normal exuberance had given way to a cranky irritability. Howard had bags under his eyes that were shading further into violet with each passing day; meanwhile, Manningham's face was somehow growing longer, his lips pursing tighter, his eyebrows arching more steeply.

"Mary Toft's last birth was on Thursday, November 24," Manningham said, beginning without preamble. "Ten days have passed, when the rabbits once appeared with a frequency of two or three each week. Yet other than the ceasing of delivery, her condition has not improved—she persists in this lassitude, her fever remains, and her husband insists not that the crisis has passed, but that another birth is imminent."

"I see no reason not to believe that another birth is forthcoming," said Nathanael St. André. "Whatever changes occurred to her body to produce the preternatural phenomenon could not have vanished as easily as that. It seems impossible that one would revert to a normal physiology so quickly and easily."

"Have any of you heard anything from the king?" said John weakly. He looked exceptionally unwell, Manningham thought, but said nothing.

"I am increasingly afraid that the king's fleeting desires brought you to London only to abandon you, friend," said Cyriacus. "His dilettante's mind may perhaps have moved on to another subject."

"Yet the king's whim has the force of command, in practice if not in theory," said Sir Richard. "So here you remain until there is some manner of resolution, even if you have left his thoughts."

They drank their coffee, hoping for it to restore them to some semblance of alertness, but the wakefulness it brought was inadequate—it made them wide-eyed, but did not speed their sluggish thought. The drug was no replacement for a solid night's sleep.

"This has to end, somehow," Cyriacus Ahlers said.

"It does," said Manningham. "And I have been considering our next course of action. I feel that we have convinced ourselves that the situation is not urgent when, in fact, it is—it is likely that Toft's life is in danger, and we might let her die through neglect. In short, though I disagreed with Nathanael at our last meeting, meditation on the subject has brought me around to seeing things from his point of view. I believe he is correct."

"Surgery," Cyriacus said.

"Yes," said Manningham. "Invasive and, given how little we know about what we will encounter once we begin, necessarily improvisational. But needed. Else she will die. As you say, Nathanael, whatever has occurred in her physiology cannot have reverted back to its original form so easily—I would add that it is highly likely that these anomalous organs in her body continue to impede the function of those organs within her that are otherwise normal. Hence her continued lassitude, her fever, and her lack of urination: she makes water once every two days now, and then only weakly."

"As much as I am pleased to hear that such an august personage as yourself sees my reasoning as correct," Nathanael said, "I'm not sure I—"

"No, no, no need for bashfulness," Manningham interrupted. "I feel, in fact, that you should be credited with the decision to perform the surgery: it is, in fact, on your implicit recommendation that we will do this. Granted, if this were a fraud of some kind—and we can all assure ourselves that it is not—then, Nathanael, your name would be attached to a murder rather than a surgery, but thankfully that is not the case, yes?"

"Yes," Ahlers said after a moment's pause. "Yes. I am beginning to see things your way."

St. André blanched. "I don't—"

"Recall your Locke," Manningham said. "If a statement be not self-evident, there must be proof. We have, all four of us, delivered rabbits, or rabbit parts, from Toft with our own hands. But the evidence of our experience is limited—the inner workings of her body are a mystery to us, as is testified to by the competing hypotheses about Toft's condition. Is this the work of God, or is it caused by some other physical abnormality, or are both of these the case? We cannot say conclusively."

"I don't think we should cut her open," John Howard said quietly.

"Oh, but I have *reconsidered*," said Manningham. "Now I think we *should*. Now I think we *must*. Think of what we could learn, were we to set aside our moral scruples for just a moment in the service of a greater good. Surgeons rarely receive the gift of such extremely rare circumstances as those in which we now find ourselves, and we would not want to make the mistakes of those who have preceded us in this profession. Consider that it was only until the last century that we realized such a simple thing as that blood circulates through the heart, instead of being created by the liver. Do you know why? Because Christian doctrine forbade dissection! Think of all the time we spent relying on the medical treatises of Galen to steer our path, when we might have done so much better. Think of all the lives that we failed to save. Because of some so-called *religious obligation.* Do we wish for surgeons of the future to look on us as we do on Galen? Should we give them cause to regret our moral scruples, as we regret those of our forebears? I submit that we should not."

"I cannot help but wholeheartedly agree," said Ahlers.

"We stand at an unfathomably important point in human history," said Manningham. "We must cut her open. What we find inside her will, at the least, advance medicine by a decade. And it may be the case—and I don't think we should shrink away from this idea—that we have before us real, indisputable, empirical evidence of the existence of God. If this is true, there may even be a chance that she survives the surgery! If God wanted to provide clear evidence of his existence, as he may well be doing here; if he is doing what he has never done before, and writing on her body in a manner that is plain for us to read; would he be so cruel as to ensure that his vehicle for this proof would not remain alive through the investigation that he, knowing all, knows we must make? Nathanael, thank you. I believe that in future years historians will find that humankind owes you a debt it can never repay."

"I feel I must object to—"

"Object to your coming fame? Nonsense. If you do not want to take the lead, then you may stand aside—rest assured that Cyriacus and I will grant you the credit that is your due. I will attempt to speak to the king about this tomorrow morning, though in matters of medicine I may act with his authority without prior consultation—either way, prepare your knives for tomorrow afternoon—"

"I'd like to speak to her," said John Howard.

Manningham turned to Howard. "Oh?"

As pallid as Nathanael looked, John looked even paler. "I'd like to spend the late-night vigil with her tonight, if you please," he said. "Alone. We must arrange for Joshua not to be present. I was the first surgeon on this case, and the responsibility of explaining the terms of what you propose falls to me. But I would like to speak with her without any . . . other parties present."

Cyriacus glanced at Manningham.

"If you wish to speak with her alone," Cyriacus said, "then the three of us will escort Joshua somewhere else, for a while."

"Agreed," said Nathanael St. André. "Agreed!"

*

And so, that evening, in the King's Head room at Dr. Lacey's Bagnio, Zachary and Laurence turned to see all four surgeons filing in, one after the other: John Howard, Sir Richard Manningham, Cyriacus Ahlers, and Nathanael St. André taking up the rear. Mary Toft lay on the bed with her eyes closed, as usual; Joshua sat sprawled in a chair, coming alert as Manningham spoke his name.

"We need you to come with us," Manningham said.

"But why?"

"It is not in your best interest," said Manningham, "to protest."

As Joshua rose—there was steel in the old man's voice that brought him to his feet—St. André, standing behind Manningham and Ahlers, beckoned to Laurence. "Come on," he said gently. "You, too."

"Is there something wrong?" Laurence asked.

"No, there isn't. Just come."

Meanwhile, John had pulled a chair beside Toft's bed and seated himself in it. "Zachary?" he said.

"Sir?"

"You'll need to leave, too. You should go to our room at London Bridge, and return here in the morning."

"Come with us," said Ahlers to Zachary as he and the surgeons began to leave along with Joshua, who had the strange appearance of being under guard. "You have nothing at all to worry about."

"I am going to talk to Mary this evening," John said. "For some time. I have a few secrets to share. And perhaps, in the end, she will too."

*

As the surgeons, the apprentices, and Joshua left and Nathanael pulled the door shut behind him, Mary Toft's eyelids fluttered and, slowly, drifted open.

Wearily, John Howard wiped his patient's damp brow with a cloth, sighed, and began.

CHAPTER XXVI

TRANSVERSE PRESENTATION.

M ary.
I would not have imagined, a few months ago, that you and I would end up here, together—I do not know where I thought this would end when it all began, nor did I imagine how far we would travel together, on that first horrific day. But here we are.

You must yearn to end this silence and stillness, yes? Stand, sing, turn cartwheels? You have been on your back for over a week now. It must have been easier for you back in Godalming, when you were not always in our sight. It was certainly easier for me.

We could go back there, whenever you wanted—all you have to do is speak, and this can end.

*

I have been thinking about the slippery nature of truth as of late, as I suppose we all have been—me, and you, and the other surgeons, and the people who wait patiently outside for the performance of your last miracle (but it will never be the last—you must know by now, after seventeen of these, that giving us one only creates the want for another. It seems that a proof of the miraculous can never satisfy). A hoax—and by now I feel it's urgent that we say the word, that we call things by their names, for truly, your life is in danger—requires a first perpetrator, and it is convention to regard all those other believers except for the first as victims or dupes. But I think—and I say this not to salve my own feelings, but because I have truly come to believe it—that something more complex goes on in the mind of those who we say are "fooled." That there is an additional self-deception, a self-victimization. The dupe become both robber and robbed, both living in the same mind, the one constantly deceiving the other.

Because something profound must happen in the mind to convince a man to distrust the common sense acquired over decades, not just once, but continuously. This woman before me gives birth to pulverized rabbits three times a week, despite the fact that neither I nor anyone I know has seen such a thing with his own eyes before; this company has been granted a monopoly on trade in the South Seas that will be quite lucrative, despite the fact that the lands are presently controlled by a nation with which we are at war, and I have no reason to believe that England will ever be able to trade there; this man was born of a virgin, was crucified and arose from the dead, despite the fact that this goes against all I know of human physiology.

Ah, but that last was blasphemy—forgive me. I did not mean it. I merely mean to suggest that when my thoughts turn toward darkness, as they have more often lately, I sometimes consider that the only difference between a hoax and an article of faith is the number of people who profess belief in it. If ten million people were to believe in these miraculous births of yours, rather than a hundred or a thousand, then perhaps there would be no doubt: perhaps it would be as good as if it were true, and the belief would cause no harm, might even do some good, might become a cause that convinced people to join in harmony.

I find myself asking, in my darker moments: what matter is the unproven nature of an assertion if enough people become convinced of its truth?

*

My wife, Alice, did not believe you; she does not, I presume, even now. Why didn't I listen to her, that first night, she whose wisdom I cherished for all the years of our marriage? What strange spirit possessed me?

Were I interested in defending my actions, one might say that we lure more flies with honey than vinegar, and that evening, when I told her of the new case I'd taken on, my whole house smelled of spoiled wine. I married Alice because of her unvarnished honesty, but that night I had no mood for it. She laughed merrily and labeled you an outright fraud; she described the nature of the subterfuge in fine detail, using words I won't repeat, but that are not the accepted medical nomenclature for female anatomy. It seems obvious to me now that she was correct, but at the time, in the heat of the accusation, I could not tolerate the raillery for which I often loved her.

I had a choice, in that moment—as Alice placed her hand on her hip and said, *Good Christ, love, the husband's cutting a dead rabbit into parts and shoving them up her before you arrive, it's plain as day; oh, come now, John, stop with that serious look on your face*—in living in one of two possible versions of the world. Simply put, there was the one in which I was fooled, and the one in which I was not. In the one in which I was fooled, then the woman I loved was married to a fool, and knew me for one; in the one in which I was not, my wife was married to a wise man, and did not yet realize it. And so it was because I wanted the best for her, wanted her to be married to the best person she could be, that I dismissed her, thinking that given enough time, I would be proven right. I chose to believe in you because I wanted not to be ashamed of the reflection of myself that I saw in Alice's eyes. I ignored her because I didn't want to disappoint her.

You only had to deceive me once, but I had to deceive myself an uncountable number of times after that, day after day, minute by minute, maintaining my own constant vigil against an incursion of common sense that I had to force myself to see as its opposite, as a lack of faith. But I have kept up that vigil for too long, and I am tired. Not as tired as you are, I imagine, but tired enough.

*

Was it easier to keep that vigil because we thought, the surgeons and I, that God might somehow be involved? Did our belief in a being wiser than ourselves, his methods forever inscrutable, his true motives inarguably good but only to be revealed on the Day of Judgment, lead us to credulity? I am uncertain. We surgeons, tasked with coaxing God's creatures back from the precipice of death, often feel as if he is looking over our shoulders when we wield our knives, ready to punish us if we fail to play fair.

And there is no time more fraught for us, no moment when we are more likely to feel as if we are observed by a higher power, than the moment when a midwife calls us for a birth too difficult for her to handle. There is a near certainty then that we will be shepherding someone on their first step to a grave, either a child or a mother, or both. Sometimes we make mistakes. Sometimes we do things we regret, because God has his eye on us. And sometimes, in order to satisfy God's requirements, we perhaps perpetrate necessary deceptions upon ourselves, deceptions so complete that we willfully forget they even occurred.

There was a time a few years ago when I was called to a difficult birth, and I had to make a choice to live in one of two versions of the world, just as I did when Alice called a true thing by its name and I chose to ignore her. I cannot say that I wonder if I did the right thing, because whichever version of the world I chose to live in, the facts would alter themselves so that I did. But I do wonder if the God who watched my actions, who sees all and knows all, had the same perception of the world as I did, at the moment I made my decision.

The mother had had rickets as a child, with the consequent narrow hips that often make births difficult. Moreover, as I discovered quickly—I could see it in the midwife's eyes before I saw the patient—the birth was transverse, presenting the left arm rather than the head. A breech birth, feet first, can often be saved through a surgeon's skill with a judicious turning of the baby; a transverse birth is always fatal, though, and the only outstanding question when a surgeon encounters one is how many will die: one, or two. The indicated procedure is to remove the arm of the fetus, turn the fetus so that its head is accessible, perform a craniotomy, and complete the delivery. It is a ghoulish business, and it cannot be begun until the fetus is dead—more likely than not, the fetus will remain alive and kill the mother first, and attempts to save the fetus after the mother dies are often doomed to fail as well.

On seeing the mother I immediately called for a minister—in fact the man who arrived was Crispin Walsh, my apprentice's father, who waited on you on a few occasions back in Godalming. In moments like this, the thinking goes, mere medicine is not enough to save our souls: God, or his representative, must be brought into the room as well, as an observer, and a conveyor of absolution.

So Crispin and I and the midwife waited—there was nothing else we could do. And dear God, did this woman scream. Every few minutes I would examine the fetus, and it continued to cling to life. And so we continued to wait.

The mother cursed us; she begged us to deliver her from her pain, the muscles of her contractions forcing the child against an entrance it would never be able to pass through. The room began to stink, with sweat and shit and the peculiar rank smell of people who are deathly afraid. The mother clamped down on her tongue and bit it, drawing blood, and I rolled a piece of cloth tightly and placed it in her mouth for her to bite. Morning turned to afternoon. The fetus could not work itself free.

Hours passed, and then the midwife, all at once, gave out. She burst into tears, she and the mother wailing together in sympathy. Then she said to me, sobbing, "I thought I was stronger than this, but I cannot take this anymore. I will pray for you, but I am forced to leave you to what you must do." And those words seemed to be freighted with more meaning than she wanted to make explicit. As if everyone were aware that what I must do would be easier if there were fewer witnesses.

Soon after she left, almost as soon as the door to the lying-in chamber shut behind her, it occurred to me that the fetus was dead. It crossed my mind that, in fact, I'd been fooling myself about its life for at least the past hour, confusing a wish with a fact. Once the thought manifested in my mind, it draped itself in the aura of certainty, and I began to see an exit, a door cracking open with a light beyond. The only remaining thing was to ensure that everyone saw what I saw; then we could begin to bring this to an end.

Gently, placing my hand on the mother's shoulder, I gave her the terrible news, and between us there was a moment of recognition: my recognition that she could see into my mind and that any attempt to deceive her would be fruitless, so it was a good thing the child was, in truth, already dead; her recognition that this was not an instance of having to kill her child in order to save her life, that I was not proposing such a horrible thing, for such an act would curse us all, but that the fetus was merely a lump of inert matter that needed to be removed, in the same manner that I might extirpate a tumor. She closed her eyes and turned away from me, and in her silence I saw her agreement and her consent.

But Crispin Walsh, it turned out, wanted to cling to the delusions that the rest of us in the room had cast off. He insisted, in the face of all available evidence, that the child was still alive; he wanted to examine the woman as I had, and that I would not allow, as he had no expertise in the matter. He insisted that the diagnosis required no special knowledge; I countered that things that seemed simple to the layman had nuances that were only apparent to those with sufficient schooling, that many factors went into my assessment, some of which I would not even be able to articulate to myself, much less to someone who was not a surgeon.

We argued, and it became clear that he was not just concerned about the correctness of my opinion, but afraid of the God that he had brought into the room with him. In the absence of that God, the three of us—the mother, the minister, and myself—would have used our senses and our past experiences to determine the version of reality in which we collectively lived, and, once we arrived at a conclusion, we would have contented ourselves with knowing that the world we lived in was the true one, for we could discern no more of the world than allowed to us by these senses, by these past experiences. But the presence of God brought into the lying-in room meant that we were in the company of a being who saw all and knew all, more than we could ever see or know, and who therefore knew that there was one interpretation of events that was true, and that all others were inarguably false. If we mortals all managed to convince ourselves that the fetus was dead, but we had all indulged ourselves in what, in this circumstance, counted as a pleasing deception, then a God who knew better, who knew otherwise, would not care, and would not grant us clemency. For a lie is a lie whether it is told to oneself or to someone else. We would, all of us, be damned.

So we argued, and we kept our silence, and we argued some more, and the woman screamed, and her screams became quieter and farther apart though the fetus did not move, would not come any farther out of her, and I checked the fetus again and again and believed, and was certain in my belief, that it was cooling, that the twitches I sometimes thought I sensed in it were merely my own imagination, and Crispin would not agree that the proof I offered was proof enough, and he said, and I was forced to agree, that God's authority would supersede the authority of even a thousand surgeons, and I would not permit him to examine the fetus myself for I knew that it would only encourage further misunderstanding on his part and further intransigence from him, and we waited for God (or, a cynic might say, Chance or Fate, going by another name) to deliver us from our dilemma.

Afternoon turned to evening, and the mother closed her eyes and her head fell to the side, and her breathing became raspy and irregular, and she opened her eyes once more and they were lightless. So God had made his choice, and I was left to salvage what we could. Unfortunately, Crispin's sudden and feverish bout of prayer was not efficacious, for we found, soon after I commenced my surgery on the mother, that the child was dead as well. Two were lost. It was the darkest moment of my career, exceeding even this moment in which I sit before you, though at least I can say to myself that I am not to blame. The watchful presence of God in the room at least granted me that.

But here is what you need to understand—here is why you are in danger. Here is why you must speak, and why you must not allow us to speak for you. Because history is an act of continuous collective imagining, and the perception of truth is a constant, unending negotiation, with others, and with oneself when one is alone. I think that if the minister had not been there and the midwife had remained, we would have seen something altogether different through the same dark glass: we would have discovered beyond doubt that the child was dead; I would have done the terrible thing I needed to do—cutting off the arm; turning the fetus; splitting the skull open and crushing it; extracting the corpse—and the mother would be alive today. But the minister brought God into the room. And I will tell you this about God—that despite his presumed omnipresence he often arrives in the company of men; that men fear to interpret the world on their own authority when they are aware of his presence, because his senses are complete and perfect and his experiences are unlimited; that the standards for proof are much higher when God is involved, especially proof of life, or of what goes on inside a woman's body; that weighed against God's displeasure, or against a man's feeling that God is displeased by his actions, the life of one woman is no great thing.

*

God came with us into your lying-in chamber once: do you remember? The first time Crispin Walsh entered, and he placed his ear to your stomach, and was sure he heard the sounds of "opposing forces," grinding the rabbits apart inside you? I had been ambivalent about allowing him the access to your body that is the surgeon's by right. And in my bullheadedness I would accept no explanation for what I experienced, other than the preternatural. I let him touch you when I should not have, that time; I let him make a pronouncement that should have been mine alone. He was not the only reason that we find ourselves here, miles away from home with your life in the balance, but he surely sped us on our way.

I fear, and expect, that we will bring God into this room with us once again tomorrow, and that in his presence we will claim a dominion over your body in both his name and the name of medicine. And I do not expect that you will survive the necessary inquisition to satisfy God's rigorous requirements for proof.

But while you and I are in this room alone, without the other surgeons, without your husband, we can decide, together, to shape another history, just as we shaped a history on the first day we met in October. I make no claims as to what goes on within you—I merely say that with a word from you, what is done can be undone. The world you describe will be the one that is. You have that power, but only for a few hours longer. Until morning, at the latest. Then all the men will enter, and we will begin.

So please. Speak. Save yourself, and set me, and the rest of us, free.

CHAPTER XXVII

MORNING.

The next morning found all four surgeons in the King's Head room of the bagnio, standing at the foot of Mary Toft's bed. Her husband was there, too, sitting in a chair in a darkened corner, shoulders hunched in disconsolation; a constable leaned with ease against the wall, hands behind his back, comfortable in his invisibility, waiting to be needed.

John Howard was bleary-eyed; Manningham and Ahlers wore twin expressions of grimness; St. André looked like a chastened child. Zachary and Laurence did their best to represent their masters, but Zachary felt as tired as John looked, and Laurence's drawn face rhymed with Nathanael's dispirited demeanor. (For once, their clothes did not match, for Nathanael remained in the suit he'd worn since the night before—he seemed to have gotten no sleep at all.)

But Mary Toft sat up in the bed, back propped against pillows, her hands clasped in her lap as if she were sitting for a portrait; her cheeks had something of a ruddiness to them, and her hair was combed neatly beneath her white linen cap, though her brow was damp and her breathing fast and shallow. Her eyes were bright, and a smile even seemed to lurk at the edges of lips unused to making one.

She drew in a breath to speak, holding it in anticipation, and Zachary felt ten pounds lighter, as if his heart were buoyed on air. Through the open curtains of the window beyond, Zachary could see the sky above the Covent Garden Market brighten as light from the late-rising sun somehow managed to cut through the city's persistent smoky haze. The market itself was still, the merchants quiet at their stalls; the group of people waiting outside the bagnio, grown to a battalion of a hundred fifty or more, stood staring upward at the window, frozen, as if they were waiting to breathe until the woman breathed.

She exhaled and spoke, her voice thin and small, but clear and needle sharp.

"Gentlemen," she said, "I will not go on any longer thus. I would sooner hang myself."

She breathed in once more, and out again.

"The rabbits were in pieces," she said. "I put the pieces up me."

And the strangest thing—so Zachary thought later—was that when she stated this fact, so plainly, with such crude artlessness, it did not seem as if she was delivering information to the surgeons that they did not know beforehand, but as if she was granting them a long withheld permission to know something that, quite obviously, had always been true.

*

She slid herself to the edge of the enormous bed with the awkwardness of someone who'd fallen out of the habit of using her muscles, threw her legs over the side, and stood. She placed her hands on the small of her back and bent backward, rolling her shoulders, wincing with a grunt. Then she turned toward the window, squinting at the icy morning sunlight, and walked toward it with the slow, uneven gait of one clearly in pain.

She stood at the window for a time, her back to the surgeons, and then she turned to look at the men over her shoulder. "Who are they?"

"The people down there, in neat rows? They've been keeping a vigil for you," said Manningham. "They believe that God works wonders through you."

Mary turned to look out the window for a moment longer, and back to the surgeons again.

"That's silly," she said.

Ahlers spoke then, his voice heavy with melancholy. "They do not seem to think so, Mary, and there are quite a few."

She turned away from the surgeons again, slightly unsteady on her feet, bracing her hand on the wall next to the window. Then, with a sigh and a cough, she threw the window open to the cold December air.

"The rabbits were in pieces!" Mary yelled down to the assembled congregation beneath her. *"I put the pieces up me!"*

Then she leaned forward, took the window by its handle, and closed it shut.

"There," she said, ignoring the other surgeons to look directly at John Howard, the newly found clarity of her voice already fading. "That's done."

*

Mary Toft's words floated down on the winter air, their vowels smeared and their consonants stripped away by wayward gusts of wind, so that by the time they reached the ears of the hundred fifty citizens who stood there waiting below, each of them heard different things, most of them nonsensical—*haven't fir or nieces, hook and seize us from me; Babbitt's fur indecent, foot the least of hunting; habits nor caprices, look to Jesus stop me.* They looked at each other in confusion, repeating their own received messages to each other—*savages and creases? Shoot the easel hungry? Agate interstices? Soot the bees and honey?*—and though each was sure at first that what they'd heard was what she said, it became clear, soon enough, that all of them were wrong. So revisions were made as the people debated, with possible words and phrases selected and discarded as a consensus came closer and the message developed something closer to a meaning—*the habits were indecent, I look to Jesus finally; our rabbits are in pieces, the pieces ask for mercy*—until a woman in the center of the crowd picked the true pronouncement out of the noise and blurted it aloud, blushing furiously as it slipped out her mouth and she realized what she'd said.

And for all those people who heard her, a light in the world went out. They stood there, staring at each other, faces fallen; then the neat regimented lines of the battalion began to fray and blur. At last they were merely a group of people, with nothing in common and no reason to remain together, and so they quietly drifted away from each other, down the side streets and between the market's stalls: a tall, slender woman who drew her arms around her body as if to protect herself from some unknown fear; a heavyset gentleman whose stride was initially sure but whose gait, hobbled by comically large shoes, soon developed a limp, each step of his right foot accompanied by a grimace; an elderly couple who were at first holding hands as if they were a pair of sweetly lovestruck youths but who, slowly, let each other go.

CHAPTER XXVIII

PAMPHLETS.

London's presses were warm and waiting, once Mary spoke and once the constable led her and her husband away. Manningham, Ahlers, and St. André, though of vastly different temperaments, were London surgeons, after all, and knew the rules of the game—they left the bagnio with only the most perfunctory goodbyes to each other and fairly ran back to their abodes to begin writing. Manuscripts could be delivered by the evening of December 5; the typesetting and correction completed the following day; the pamphlets distributed on the morning of Wednesday, December 7.

The pages spat forth from the presses that Tuesday night; by Wednesday morning they were in coffee houses, in homes by Wednesday night, and ground into the dirt beneath the wheels of carriages by the evening of the following day, part of the city's sediment that layered history upon history, its constant, never-ending process of recording and recall and revision, of exaggeration and lying and forgetting.

*

From *An Exact Diary of My Attendance Upon Mary Toft, the Pretended Rabbit-Breeder of Godalming,* by Sir Richard Manningham:

From the moment I saw her, it was apparent to me that the Godalming woman and her husband had perpetrated a vile and monstrous fraud—my chance encounter with the bagnio's porter beforehand had only confirmed my suspicions, and the only thing left to determine before I sprung the trap was which of the other surgeons had been deceived, and which had engaged in active collusion with the woman. I came to believe, during the conversation at the coffee house when I made my threat to execute a surgery upon her that she would not survive, that all of them are honest men: excessively credulous, perhaps, and too willing to exploit in one particular case, but honest all the same. They may have even realized, at this moment, that they had been hoaxed, and merely wanted a means of escape without public embarrassment from the net in which they found themselves ensnared. This I granted them, through my stratagem.

They all behaved as I expected. Ahlers, the most sensible of the group, immediately placed himself in alliance with myself; St. André, the most artful, became terrified when he realized that his artfulness might indirectly result in the loss of a life; and Howard, who had spent the most time with the patient and who was also of a kindly and sympathetic nature, undertook to quietly rescue the woman from the fate I claimed to have in store for her. He proved himself to be a good man, and his gentleness surely convinced the woman to decide to reveal herself as a fraud when the other three of us might not have succeeded, or may not have desired to try.

When she confessed, she did so with the serenity of one who knows that, at last, she is doing good, and laying down the burden that doing evil places on us. She spoke of the horrors that she had done to herself with an even-tempered clarity, as if she were describing yesterday's weather or indifferently flavored food, and this horrified me in turn. For it seemed that from her perspective, such vile behavior was perfectly ordinary, to pass with little remark.

When the constable led her and her husband away—the woman will surely be committed to Bridewell; of the husband, I know not—we four surgeons felt relief that our shared journey had at last reached its end. I do not know what

punishment awaits the woman, but short of hanging, it must
surely be lesser than that which she inflicted on herself daily,
and so it must be counted as a form of liberation.

*

From *Remarks Made After Continuous Observation of Mary Toft, the
Pretended Rabbit-Breeder,* by Cyriacus Ahlers:

After I first spoke with the first two surgeons involved
with the Toft case, John Howard and Nathanael St. André, I
suspected that a fraud of some kind was being perpetrated;
once I "delivered" a rabbit from Toft herself, I was certain of
it, and could barely countenance its vile nature though I saw it
with my own eyes. It remained only for me to determine which
of the people involved with the case were knowing conspirators
and which were dupes, and so I kept my silence and pretended
as if I myself had been deceived, the better to observe the
behavior of the other surgeons as well as of the patient.

Nathanael St. André I did not trust—his reputation, though
storied, was dubious in the circles in which I traveled, and I
briefly entertained the idea that he might be the motive force
behind the conspiracy. But my instincts told me that though
his inclination toward self-advertisement might make him
susceptible to fraud, he would not be a willing party to such a
dastardly act. John Howard himself seemed not to possess the
necessary cunning or perversion—he struck me as a simple,
provincial man whose willingness to think the best of those
around him led him to be taken in, and I could not help but
pity him. I attempted to warn him in a subtle manner, to bring
him around to realizing for himself what I perceived—I feared
that baldly confronting him with the truth would be sure to
drive him further into disagreement and delusion. Either he
did not sense my signals or chose to ignore them; either way,
I dared not risk speaking with the clarity I desired, when

the situation was so precarious and I risked finding myself outnumbered.

When Sir Richard Manningham became involved with the case, I began to see a way out for all of us—with two of us implicitly in league, the fraud might be exposed with some care. I presented the evidence that I had (so-called) to the king, and gained permission for Toft to be transported to London— I expected that the change of location would disrupt the mechanism by which the fraud was performed, and once there, Manningham insisted that she be placed under a round-the-clock watch. From that point, we only had to wait to exhaust the woman's reserves of resolve.

This took longer than expected, and Manningham was eventually forced to feign a threat of a surgery that Toft would be unlikely to survive; understanding what his aim was when I saw his charade, I went along with him. Perhaps by then John Howard understood that he had been deceived, or perhaps he believed what Manningham said—the fact that he was credulous enough to believe Mary Toft argues for it. What went on in his mind makes no difference—I was not privy to the conversation he had with her the following evening, but whatever case he made was undoubtedly effective.

Her confessions are a muddle—I have seen transcriptions of the three she has given, and they conflict, and seem to pull new stories out of the air. At first she claimed that the entire scheme was the invention of a Godalming woman whose husband was a traveling knife grinder, and who said to her that through this she would earn enough money to last her for the rest of her life. But it is curious that she did not appear to recall this woman's name, or seem to think her interlocutors would find it of interest. (She also claimed during this first confession that once I myself examined her and produced a rabbit from her, I promised to ensure that she received a pension—this is in no way the case.) She wished to absolve her husband and her mother-in-law of any wrongdoing, saying that any culpability for the fraud should fall on her and on this mysterious woman, who in subsequent confessions she failed to mention.

In her second confession the following day—"I am ashamed to tell the truth now," she said, "after telling so many lies"— she seemed to want to pretend that she had been deceived just as anyone else, that the hoax itself seems to have appeared out of thin air, without a person conceiving it. She said that if the rabbits did not breed inside her—implying that up to now, she believed that they had—then Mr. Howard must have placed the rabbit parts inside her in collusion with her mother-in-law (that is, after the first monstrous birth that caused Howard to be summoned). This seems impossible to me—either any potential participants in the fraud must have been party to all of the instances of monstrous births, or none. And Howard appeared to be as revolted by the proceedings of which he was a part as any normal person would be, even as he seemed to believe that he was witnessing an occurrence unique in the medical history. My instincts continue to lead me to pronounce him an honest man.

In the third and final confession, she blames the mother-in-law entirely. ("I was unwilling to tell the truth because it lit upon her," she said; "when I have told the truth God knows if I shall ever be forgiven for it.") This also lacks plausibility, for she also says that her husband brought her rabbits, but knew not what her mother-in-law did with them. Surely the man is not such a complete fool.

And so we have one falsehood, replaced with three others at war. They have two things in common. The first is the one thing that must undoubtedly be true—the woman was in pain. "In pain at night." "In pain all the time." She calls it "rack and torture." She mentions her pain so often that it appears to be not just a description of her travails at the moment, but the single dark thread that runs through her life.

The second is not a presence, but an absence—of her husband. He is absolved of all guilt in the first and second confessions, and briefly portrayed as an unwilling dupe of the women around him in the third. Whether or not her fraud managed to convince those who wished to be convinced, anyone who sees all three of her confessions side by side would agree that she is a poor liar, and the truth can often be approached by paying attention not to what a poor liar includes, but what she leaves out. It is likely that we will never know the full tale of his involvement in the case, but he was clearly a witting party to it, and, I have come to suspect, its principal instigator.

*

From *An Addendum to the Short Narrative of a Fraudulent Delivery of Rabbits,* by Nathanael St. André:

The most perceptive readers of my previous publication, *A Short Narrative of an Extraordinary Delivery of Rabbits,* will have discerned what I was wise enough to avoid stating explicitly— they will have understood immediately that I knew beyond doubt that Mary Toft was committing a monstrous fraud, but that for reasons that should be clear, I could not yet reveal my suspicions publicly. It was apparent as soon as I first examined the patient in the company of John Howard, who seems to have been unwittingly fooled—I will admit that at first I believed he had joined with Toft in conspiracy, and thought it wise to pretend to have been duped as well, waiting for the perpetrators of the fraud to make an error and reveal themselves, as such perpetrators always do. But Howard behaved with perfect innocence, and should shoulder no share of the blame.

As the fraud began to ensnare more and more people, including such esteemed colleagues as Cyriacus Ahlers and Sir Richard Manningham, I found that I could not stand idly by— if there is one thing I regret, it is my delay in this matter. I persisted in my pretense longer than I should have, even going so far as to issue a pamphlet describing my "observations," trusting that later events and my revelation of the true facts of the case would redeem me in the eyes of the public. (I also wished to record an impartial recounting of events, in case someone were to claim that they had dissembled as I had, and that I in fact was a dupe—in the aftermath of such an event one can expect those who are unexpectedly embarrassed to attempt to recover their reputations.)

It was I who concocted the gambit that would convince Mary Toft to reveal herself—once I planted the seed of my idea in casual conversation, mentioning that this peculiar case would most likely necessitate conducting a surgery that *she would not survive,* I had only to wait for that seed to sprout. I was startled at Manningham's ferocity once he embraced the idea— bloodthirst is a tendency that surgeons must forever guard against—but it was that ferocity that appears to have terrified Howard enough to speak to Toft directly: she must have seen the terror in his eyes and known that it was past time for her ruse to come to an end.

I know not what will become of her, but I hope that her punishment will be light. For who can condemn a person for deceiving others who were so willing to deceive themselves? Which of us does not have a devil that lives inside of us, whispering not what is true, but what we wish to believe, out of innocence or cupidity or a hundred other reasons? We must stay ever vigilant against that demon, ever on watch against his pleasing music—if the tale of Mary Toft has any moral at all, it is this.

PART FIVE.

CHAPTER XXIX

ZACHARY AND ANNE.

John Howard wanted no part of the manipulation of the public's opinion—he was weary, and even in his weariness he felt that he was correct in thinking that none of it, in the end, mattered. Only God had a truly long memory, and he presumably had greater concerns than the public embarrassment of a country surgeon, who'd gone into a case with the best intentions and come out of it narrowly avoiding criminal charges for fraud (for if the three competing pamphlets of the London surgeons accomplished one thing, it was Howard's implicit absolution).

He and Zachary rose early on the morning after Mary Toft had been taken into custody, on their last day in London. A stagecoach leaving in two hours would have them back in Godalming in two days—there was no need for haste on the return trip.

Once he'd packed the few possessions he'd brought along with him, Zachary stood at the window, watching the boatmen shoot the Thames, listening for what might be the last time to the overwhelming roar of the river. The thrum of the rushing water drowned out his thoughts and replaced them all with its own noise, and this was wonderful, for when he returned to Godalming's silence his own rough memories would make their voices known again, and would chase themselves in circles in his mind until they wore themselves out.

John joined him at the window, and the two of them looked down together for a while at the boatmen. Then John said, quietly, "Are you going to say goodbye to your friends before you go? Laurence and . . ." He made a brief show of not being able to remember her name. "Anne."

Even over the tumult of the river, Zachary heard the noise of fireworks exploding, of an old bull bellowing, of Anne's half-embarrassed giggle that Zachary thought would likely have been a full-throated belly laugh had he not been present. "I hadn't thought about it," he said.

He felt a hand on his shoulder.

"You should say goodbye to them," John said. "To Anne, at least."

*

So for a last time he returned to the neighborhood of Covent Garden, the scene of his master's ignominy and, by extension, his own. He walked there through a light snow that dusted the ground and showed footprints and the tracks of carriage wheels. (In the Covent Garden Market, a few of the people who'd stood vigil in front of Dr. Lacey's Bagnio still remained, drifting aimlessly in slow circles like bumblebees who'd lost their hives.) Anne answered when he knocked on the door of her father's apartment, and the look of surprise on her face—a startled "Oh!" when she opened the door; a single half step backward—put a knot in his stomach that his brain had yet to catch up with: he knew, despite not knowing yet why he knew, that coming here was a mistake, that at this point the only thing to be done was to wait for his mind to comprehend what his gut already knew, but could not yet articulate.

"It's good to see you," said Anne, a flutter creeping into her voice at the end of the sentence. She looked surprisingly well dressed for the morning: she wore a dress that Zachary had not yet seen her in before, a paler version of the blue that was her signature color; earrings of sapphire and silver hung from her lobes, and her hair was done up in an intricate series of braids that confused the eye and suggested strong knowledge of mathematics.

There was an awkward silence, during which Zachary was wise enough not to say, "You look nice," as it would have come off as an inquisition (which, to be fair, it would have been) rather than a compliment. However, he was not wise enough to stop himself from saying, "You look well," which gave the impression that he had not seen her for months or years, rather than days, and that her lack of apparent illness was an unexpected and pleasant surprise.

"Thank you," Anne said, her expression one of sudden dread; then, as she looked over Zachary's shoulder, he turned to see, approaching behind him, none other but Laurence. And Laurence looked surprisingly pin-neat this fine morning as well, his ivory suit magically innocent of the city's smoke and ash, his wig voluminous and freshly powdered. "Oh!" he said upon seeing Zachary, with the same backward half step, followed by a reflexive glance at Anne that made Zachary's poor gut twist again.

"Zachary," said Anne, "would you like to come inside?" She took Zachary's arm. "Laurence, just wait for a moment," she said, and though the *things she said* to Zachary and Laurence were things that Zachary preferred—Zachary coming inside to be alone with her; Laurence left to wait—the *way she said those things* was strangely reversed, so that she spoke to Laurence with a melody that she should have used for Zachary if all was right with the world, and at this realization his dull mind began to catch up with his mute but perceptive heart.

*

Once she had escorted him inside, she shut the door and the foyer turned dim, the light muted by curtains drawn over the windows, the woman's face veiled in half darkness, its port-wine stain indistinguishable in the shadows.

He heard her sigh. "I don't know what to say," she said, "except . . . that I'm so grateful that you thought to introduce me to Laurence. You have done me a great kindness—I can't thank you enough."

"I . . . uh, yes," said Zachary.

"I would not have expected that we would become so fond of each other so quickly, that we would have so many sentiments in common," she said. "Who would have thought that such a fellow as him would have a taste for gin and violence? But it seems you knew the both of us better than we might have known ourselves."

Did she realize how much her delight stung him? But there seemed to be no malice in what she said—she appeared to be genuinely happy, and to want Zachary to share in her happiness. The whole thing was a puzzle.

"I can't thank you enough," she said again, as if the two of them were on a stage and he had missed his cue.

And finally it occurred to him that she was in fact grateful, and that, in her way, she was doing him a service. She was proposing a better version of events than the one in which he believed, one in which they both arrived at a kind of satisfaction, and all he had to do was agree. So much had been left unstated that the slight revision to history would be effortless, forgotten as soon as it was executed. Little evidence existed, and that was weak—a few ambiguous spoken words that had disappeared into the air; a touch that could be interpreted in a dozen ways; a letter that could just as easily have meant one thing as another. And, truly, there was no point in contesting it. When Zachary and Anne went back outside, Laurence would still be there waiting patiently in white, and Zachary would be on his way back to Godalming. No need to leave on a note of spite.

"It was the least I could do," said Zachary, and Anne, delighted, clasped her arms around him and kissed him on the cheek.

"He's adorable," she said, her icy eyes shining despite the dim light. "I wish he were a little doll, so I could carry him around in my pocket."

*

The two of them stepped outside and Laurence stood on the step beneath them, looking up. "I just wanted to tell Zachary how happy I was that he thought to introduce the two of us," she said, and Laurence broke into a smile. "Yes, certainly," he said. "Good fortune that I met you. I never would have expected this, but this is how such things happen."

"How is your master?" Zachary said.

"He will land on his feet, surely—already, he is behaving as if the last two months had never happened. And yours?"

"He . . . will be fine, eventually," said Zachary. "Melancholic, perhaps, but I expect the light will return to his eyes when we leave this place."

He moved away from Anne, and, climbing the steps as Zachary descended, Laurence took his place next to her, his feet fitting neatly in the prints that Zachary had left behind in the snow.

Zachary turned to face the two of them, standing side by side.

"London is not for me, I think," he said.

*

". . . and then she said," he complained to John in the stagecoach, raising the pitch of his voice in imitation of Anne's, *"He's so adorable! I want to put him in my pocket!"*

"It is unmanning to have such a thing said of one," said John distractedly, looking out the window at the passing countryside, the rolling hills dotted by the mansions of the rich, those people who thought to abscond from the city but were in fact its pioneers.

"Yes!" said Zachary. "Yes, *exactly*. If a woman said that about me, I'd be ashamed."

They were lucky enough to be alone in the stagecoach on the way out of the city, the two of them facing each other on their seats as the coach swayed and jostled. John said little—he seemed to be content to watch the scrolling landscape—but Zachary had things on his mind, and could not help but speak.

"None of this turned out the way it was supposed to at all," he said. "I was supposed to kiss a beautiful woman, and meet King George. We didn't even meet the king!"

"I doubt he knows we're gone," said John. "He may have never been aware that we arrived."

"I just don't understand how we could have been so wrong about everything," Zachary said.

John said nothing in response, and the two of them fell into silence again.

*

A while later, once the moneyed mansions had entirely disappeared from view, the hills they saw from the coach's window no longer stripped of greenery but covered with forests of ash and beech, John took a deep breath, held it for a moment, and let it out. "Do you smell that?" he said to Zachary.

Zachary lifted his nose and sniffed. "What?"

"The air," John said. "The air is clearer."

CHAPTER XXX

JOHN HOWARD RETURNS.

When the stagecoach deposited John Howard and Zachary Walsh in front of Godalming's inn, the Silver Hart, the first thing that Zachary noticed was the silence. London's streets were filled with ambient noise that one learned to ignore soon enough, a mix of rushing river and cartwheel and footstep and scream and shout, and when they'd left Godalming last month the town had been filled with Londoners who had brought their clamor along with them, and with it a change to the town's character. But now the only sound this late afternoon was from a slight wind, and from John and Zachary's crunching footsteps through a dusting of snow as they returned to the Howards' home.

It was wonderful, and it made John realize how much he'd missed his home, though part of the reason for that silence was that Godalming's main street was strangely deserted. John had the faint suspicion that he was being watched; the periphery of his vision seemed to indicate a constant procession of observers ducking furtively behind corners or stepping back from windows into shadows. But perhaps that was only because he had feared that the streets would be lined on either side with people ready to jeer at him; surely the news of the Toft hoax had had enough time to travel here from London ahead of him. The emptiness of the road before the two of them seemed to be its own unexpected kind of condemnation—or, possibly, anticipation.

They reached the Howards' home, and, for a moment, John and Zachary stood before the door. John reached up for the knocker and then hesitated, putting his hand down again and nervously wiping his palm on his trousers.

"Look at me," he said, half to Zachary, half to himself. "I'm not a suitor."

Then with one motion he lifted his hand again, grasped the knocker, and gave it three firm, slow raps. *Knock. Knock. Knock.*

Nothing happened at first, and Howard dropped his hand again. "Well, that's done," he said, his voice barely audible.

Eventually, they heard some noise from inside the house, the quiet rustle of someone rousing herself. The footsteps they heard from the other side of the door approached it, becoming louder; then, in front of the door, they stopped, and there was silence on the other side.

John and Zachary continued to stare at the door before them, at the brass knocker in the shape of a cross-eyed gargoyle with a ring hanging from its mouth in the shape of an ouroboros, a snake gobbling its own tail. Then, with a creak, the heavy wooden door swiveled backward, and John saw his wife.

She stood before him with her arms folded and a smile playing about her lips, and John considered his impossibly good fortune, to be so sure of forgiveness, so dearly wanted, so easily asked for and sure to be given.

"Zachary," John said, eyes on his wife, "would you go upstairs, please?"

The boy's happiness at seeing Alice was clear to read on his face: he had news to tell. "I just—"

But it could wait. "Now, please, Zachary," John said.

Without another word, except for a nod at Alice, Zachary left the two of them alone.

She turned to look at her husband, and he stepped forward and placed his hands on her shoulders, the muscles there unexpectedly tense.

"Alice," he said, "I'm a fool. I'm a fool and I should have known better. I'm the biggest ass in all of England—there are a pair of donkey's ears growing out of my skull."

And all at once her shoulders relaxed, and John felt the warmth flood his heart that comes from seeing the person one loves after a long absence. He looked on her face, at the twin lines that decades of daily laughter had carved into either side of her mouth, at the spark of light in her eyes that was always on the edge of flaring into mischievous flame.

She clasped her arms around him and held him close. She smelled like Alice.

"You *are* a fool, John," she said. "Completely. Absolutely."

And all between the two of them was well.

*

A shared moment of collective delusion, here and gone, John had said to Zachary back in October, when this strangest of cases had begun. *In later days we might whisper of the legend between ourselves—perhaps over the drink that will celebrate you becoming my colleague, rather than my apprentice.*

He had not expected the occasion for that drink to come so quickly, but there were many things that had happened since October that John had not foreseen. For Zachary, a year of education in human nature had been compressed into these past few months, and it was clear enough to John that in the way Zachary had handled events, he had become his own man. Perhaps he did not yet have the skills to handle something as crucial and difficult as man-midwifing, but that was only a matter of time; it was safe to say that in the majority of services a surgeon normally provided, Zachary now stood beside John rather than in his shadow, and John had come to see him not as a subordinate but as a partner. So mugs of beer at the Silver Hart seemed warranted, the day after John and Zachary returned to Godalming, if only to establish a sense of normalcy in their lives once again.

They sat at one of the six wooden tables in the room, the only people drinking there that afternoon except for the driver of a mail coach seated alone two tables away—the same one, John thought, to whom he'd handed those fateful messages addressed to London's Persons of Distinction. The coachman didn't seem to recognize him; he probably delivered hundreds of letters a day, and the face of one person giving him a few more would not have lodged itself in his memory. This was fine.

What was less fine was that no one in Godalming seemed to recognize John Howard at all, or to want to let on that they did. He had not even been absent for two weeks, and yet as he and Zachary had walked from his practice to the Silver Hart, all the eyes on him had been strangers' eyes, his nods of greeting gone ignored. He knew these people by the boils he'd lanced and the bones he'd set, and had in the past enjoyed with them a surgeon's peculiar intimacy, the salutations of his former patients always delivered with a quiet, grati-fying gratefulness. But on the street Rufus Richardson and Michael Burwash and Mary Mitton had all seemed to look straight through him, their eyes all steadily on the horizon as they'd passed. Though perhaps he reminded them all of something they'd rather forget, or that they were in the midst of actively forgetting.

This should have been a celebratory moment, but it wasn't, not exactly—there was a sense of relief that the whole thing had ended, but that relief was tainted with the fact that neither Zachary nor John had any idea what would result from the travails they'd gone through. They sat in silence and sipped their beer, staring at their glasses; even-tually the coachman on the other side of the room rose, handed a few coins to the innkeeper (who seemed slightly irritated to have been roused from his doze in a chair by the door), and left the two of them alone. After a few moments, Zachary and John heard the snap of the reins that signaled that the coachman was on his way, bringing his messages to London.

John leaned over toward Zachary and said, quietly, so as not to disturb the innkeeper, "How do you feel?"

Zachary looked up from his beer at him. "Invisible," he replied.

*

Back in John's offices, the two of them sat reading, waiting out the rest of the day—Zachary had at last shown some curiosity about John's volume of Locke, and John had been happy to hand it off to him, feeling that even though he had not completed it, a burden had been lifted off him, or at least given to another to shoulder. John himself had begun reading Alice's copy of *The Fortunes and Misfortunes of the Famous Moll Flanders, &c.,* having had his curiosity piqued by the conversation he'd had about it in the carriage on the way to London. Already, a few pages in, it seemed so sensationalist and sentimental that it was difficult to credit as memoir, and it was a bit too womanish for his usual tastes. But each page nonetheless compelled him to read the next, and he was temporarily able to put his suspicions that the author was a man behind him, or at least decide that the issue of whether "Moll Flanders" was real was neither here nor there.

Zachary looked up with relief at the knock on the door—he'd been frowning so deeply as he puzzled his way through the book in his hands that John was half afraid his face would stick that way. He fairly leapt out of the chair like the apprentice he'd once been; then he assumed the stately demeanor more appropriate to a surgeon (which didn't yet come naturally, but would, in time), and left the office to receive the guest.

Once again, the visitor was none other than Phoebe Sanders, with her son Oliver coming along behind. John closed his book (and placed it in a drawer of his desk, for good measure) and came around his desk to greet the two of them (and he was thankful, for once, for Phoebe's searching busybody stare, for at least it meant that someone in Godalming was willing to acknowledge his existence).

"There is something wrong with Oliver," Phoebe said as she unwound her woolen scarf, "and I'm very much concerned."

"There's something wrong with me!" Oliver affirmed brightly, red-cheeked from the winter weather.

John and Zachary glanced at each other (and John privately noted that Zachary admirably restrained the desire to roll his eyes). "What are your symptoms?" John asked Oliver.

Oliver looked at his mother, and at John, and at Zachary, and at the floor. "Well, I—"

"Oh, you know," said Phoebe, cutting him off, "just a general . . . you know." She made a circular gesture with her neatly gloved hands that was difficult to interpret—it was intended to suggest either the unknown nature of Oliver's affliction, or to imply that said affliction was so dire, despite his present appearance of good health, that its name could not be spoken out of fear.

"Zachary," John said, "would you take Oliver into the other room and . . . examine him?"

"Certainly," said Zachary.

"Yes," said Phoebe with a surprising alacrity, "please do, Zachary."

"And I will keep his mother company," said John with resignation, "while she waits."

*

Was Phoebe Sanders, in some sense, the town's implicitly elected ambassador, here to negotiate the terms of his embrace back into Godalming society, such as it was? It seemed so. He could tell not because of what she spoke of, but because of what she didn't—she gave him the news of Mary Mitton's suspected pregnancy ("she's not showing yet, but a woman can tell"); she mentioned that Amelia Glasse's elderly uncle was visiting from Glastonbury ("a complete nuisance, with too much of a taste for drink, and who knows when he'll leave"); she told him that William Hargreaves, the town's chandler, was doing a roaring trade due to the short, gloomy winter days ("the things are out his door as fast as he can make them—people are nearly grabbing them out of his hands"). But she seemingly had no news to offer of Margaret Toft or, indeed, Crispin Walsh; she displayed no curiosity of where Mary and Joshua Toft had gone off to; she had no questions about how John and Zachary had spent their time in London, nor did she mention any news about them that might have preceded them on their journey back, carried on the coaches out of the city.

The bargain here was as clearly stated as it could be without speaking its terms aloud, and John was eager to accept it. He showed appropriate concern for Amelia Glasse's irritating guest; he thanked Phoebe for her suggestion that he stock up on candles from William Hargreaves; he promised to keep the information about Mary Mitton's pregnancy to himself until it was self-evident. He told no tales of his time away; a person overhearing their conversation would not have known that he had even been gone. Eventually, Mary or Joshua or both of them would make their way back here, and Godalming would have to decide how to deal with them, whether to shun them outright or proffer the same agreement that the town, through Phoebe, was now extending to John, of silence in exchange for silence. But that would happen in its own time.

Once Phoebe's chatter about the townsfolk had died down, Zachary and Oliver returned to John's office almost as if on cue, and the smile on Oliver's face and the crimson flush of his cheeks signaled that whatever mysterious ailment he'd had when he'd entered was most likely cured.

"No charge this time," said John, as Phoebe signaled her thanks with a nod. "It's wonderful to see you, Phoebe—please give Archie my regards."

"Why, thank you," Phoebe replied as she wound her scarf around her neck once again, preparing to face the chill outside. "It's lovely to see you too, as always. I suspect you don't hear this said often enough, but we really are happy to have you here. In Godalming. We wonder what we'd do without you, John."

Phoebe's mouth twitched briefly then, the flash of a grin there and gone. "So lucky we are," she said. "Think of all the talented surgeons in England who make their way to London to earn their fortune, leaving behind the places where their skills would be put to good use. But here, in our little town, is one who practically works miracles."

CHAPTER XXXI

BRIDEWELL PRISON.

No one had known what to do with Mary Toft once she was escorted from Dr. Lacey's Bagnio, but clearly *something* had to be done—the entire idea of what she'd carried out offended the sensibilities, even if no law explicitly governed it, and her acts felt wrong on instinct. Men heard God and Justice and other such personifications whispering in their ears, and so she was branded a "notorious and vile cheat" and sent to Bridewell, a place for those who committed petty crimes, peddlers and pilferers and people who slept in the streets.

She was considered strange, and so she was housed apart from the general population of light-fingered and lewd women, as if she could somehow be a vector for contagion despite the fact that the nature of the hoax that she'd perpetrated was widely known, as if the prison's wardens might arrive one morning to find that all of Bridewell's prostitutes were birthing rabbits by the dozens, whole litters hourly, overrunning the place. And she herself preferred to be secluded—the women's section of Bridewell was known to be prone to gaol fever, which covered your body in a rash, and made your eyes so sensitive to light that you had to squint at candles. Catching it was nearly as easy as looking at someone who had it out of the corner of your eye; the disease would kill you dead as often as not, and after her ordeal of the past few months, Mary was ill enough as it was.

The prison's surgeons saw her not as a possible miracle, but as a mortal woman, and perhaps their lack of illusion led them to be more aggressive with their cures: perhaps once her fever, rapid heart rate, occasional vomiting, and reluctance to urinate could be clearly seen as a result of infection, the means of curing her announced itself. And so, to purge her body, came the antimonial cup—each morning for her first week in Bridewell, she was given a serving of wine that had sat for a day in a vessel cast in antimony, and the small amount of the substance that leached into the liquid was enough to make her puke for hours afterward. She thought, for a time, that the damned cure would kill her; but either through the effect of the purging, or because her body had merely decided it had had enough of illness, her heart's pace soon slowed to something more like a human's and less like a rabbit's, the water she made returned to flowing regularly and freely, and her fever slowly receded.

Things could have been worse—perhaps out of appreciation of her notoriety, the keepers of her cell seemed to have been inclined to attend to her cleanliness, and so she slept on new straw and her clothes were regularly washed. Certain vagrants' faces became familiar to her in the rare moments when she mingled with the rest of the prisoners, appearing every week or two as December passed, and she realized that they saw this place as a home of a kind, or at least a place that offered some of its comforts. If they could not come and go as they pleased, then shelter, food, and warmth were worth the temporary surrender of liberty, and the labor to which they were put had a more reliable outcome than begging.

Once she was well she was put to work. During the days she beat hemp that had been harvested and dried back in autumn, thrashing long, thick bundles of fibers rhythmically back and forth against the ground or crushing them in a simple press, preparing them to be woven into rope. (Men often came to watch this—the prison was wide open to visitors who were willing to pay the guards in coin or gin—and though Mary did not have the street-trained tongue of the whores and thieves she worked alongside, she nonetheless took silent amusement in the witty barbs the women shot back in response to the men's crass sallies.) The work was not so different from the scythe swinging she did during hop season back in Godalming, though it was more prolonged and more strenuous, so much so that it wouldn't let her think, and it was good not to think.

After a week or two of soreness she felt her shoulders becoming larger and her neck becoming thicker, even as the pains of her past experience healed. She looked less ladylike, to be certain, but given her circumstances this was no concern, if in fact it ever had been. For all their professed humanity, the minders at Bridewell had an unwelcome fondness for flogging those they judged lazy, and those same groups of men who came through Bridewell to watch Mary beat the hemp were an ever-ready audience for punishment (though if stripping a woman's clothes off her back revealed her skin to be exceptionally white, a murmur of complaint from observers would convince the administers of correction to make it gentle, a mere caress with the cat rather than an outright whipping). Sometimes, in her little chamber, she'd hear the hoarse, perpetually startled yelps of women who'd never quite realized the body was capable of feeling such hurt; it was better, Mary considered, to have a broad, strong back than one touched by the lash.

She had no idea what had happened to the surgeons who had attended her, or even to her own husband or family. She saw the chance to briefly fall out of history as a gift, and decided to take it. At first she'd overheard her fellow prisoners referring to her as "the rabbit queen," though the nickname seemed to have an odd affection to it, as if they thought the trick she'd pulled was worthy of admiration, if not exactly praise. Then that nickname disappeared, and in the memories of everyone she was washed clean of any name, of any past. There must have been a reason why she was kept alone, but almost everyone seemed to have forgotten it or pretended not to remember, which was a kindness.

She knew that at first the constables had brought both her and Joshua to Bridewell, where they were separated, but she had heard nothing of him since. This did not surprise her as much as it might have. He had his silver tongue and his gift of making himself small,

and he was a man, for all of that. And in all her confessions, no matter
how true they'd been, she had never blamed him, not once, because
she loved him, and because it was right for her to take responsibility
for her own actions. All of that should have been enough to let him
talk his way out of the prison walls, to find his way home.

She soon lost track of time, forgetting to count the days. Christ-
mas announced itself all at once as a burst of color on the edges of her
vision come and gone, the muffled music of hymns through walls, and
a supper that nearly qualified as luxurious—doubled rations of meat,
and a pudding that encouraged the prisoners to play at raucousness
that night, despite the fact that it didn't have enough rum in it to get
a rat drunk. Then December turned to January, and the world went
dim again.

In the meantime, she waited, for history's eye to alight on her once
more. There was no hurry.

*

One afternoon in January, a gruff and portly constable appeared
in her tiny chamber to tell her that she would have a companion,
or perhaps some companions, from now on. "One or two," he said,
"depending on how you count. Either way, you'll suit each other."
This was presumably meant to be a joke, but his words were delivered
with a strange malice. In his face she saw a look that said, *I see you. I
know your face and your name. I remember you.*

She expected that her companion was with child, and that her
keepers believed they would find this pairing amusing, expecting
Mary to frighten the new mother with a singular collection of terrifying stories. But the case turned out to be quite different.

Two men brought the woman into Mary's room with a burlap
sack pulled over her head, and the first thing that Mary noticed was
that the sack was a wrong and troubling shape, filled too much and
stretched too wide. The shoulders beneath it were broad, too much
so—not strong, but ill-formed. The figure was short, perhaps five feet

tall, and her calves beneath her skirts seemed like those of a chairman, thick and muscular; her feet were clad in a surprisingly stylish pair of green silk brocade shoes, fastened with red ribbons.

"You're a monster, right?" one of the men said. "You tried to make us think you were. So we wanted you to meet another monster. This one is real." And he tore off the sack.

The woman beneath had two heads. Both had the same hazel eyes, and the same clumsily cropped brown hair pinned beneath caps; the right cheek of one was pressed tightly against the left cheek of the other. One of the heads stared directly at Mary, as if in challenge; the other looked at the floor with an expression of melancholy that seemed permanent.

The two constables retreated. "Well," one of them said as they shut and locked the door to Mary's cell, "we'll leave you to it."

Mary heard their laughter as they walked away. "The God-damned ugliest thing I've ever seen," the other constable said; then she heard the slam of a door, and they were gone.

*

The three women became fast friends. There was some initial confusion about the sisters' nature, easily alleviated when Grace introduced herself and Patience; once Mary realized that she was in the company of two people who shared much of the same body, rather than one person who had certain body parts that were somehow duplicated, her feelings of disquiet were much relieved. Grace and Patience were understandably used to being misunderstood by strangers, and bore Mary's puzzlement with good humor.

Grace and Patience were also used to short but frequent sojourns in prison. It was impossible for them to find steady employment to carry them through the winter, and so in this time of year, the sisters were often reduced to begging. But their appearance often occasioned a feeling of wrongness in the guts of peacekeepers—though they themselves were comfortable in their shared body and took it for granted, they were forced to accept that others might not feel this way—and so they regularly found themselves escorted to one house of correction or another on a vague charge of "vagrancy," where, like Mary, they would wait until the caprice of England's legal apparatus swung once more in their favor and set them free.

Grace—the sister who'd stared Mary down when they'd first entered, trying to take her measure—was the talkative one, and was friendly once she felt sure that Mary would not be hostile, as so many strangers often were. According to her, this last run-in with London's constables had occurred because they'd knocked on the wrong door asking for charity. "The woman who answered was pregnant," Grace said as Patience shook her head and sighed, her eyes raised to heaven, "and once we saw that, we knew how the story would go from there. Hand on her belly; *my baby, my baby.* Screams and panic. And so forth."

"Pregnant women are *not to be frightened*," said Patience ruefully. "Or their children will turn out to be frights."

"The mind of a woman with child must be kept as untroubled water, not to be disturbed," Grace continued. "A blank sheet of foolscap, untouched by ink." Grace and Patience spread their hands. "So after some hue and cry, here we are. And yourself? What brings you to this fine abode?"

"It is . . . quite a long story," Mary said, "and you may find it unpleasant in its details."

"We appear to have plenty of time on our hands," said Grace with a smile.

"Having told you our story, we would be honored to hear yours," said Patience.

*

As Mary talked, she realized she'd yet to tell the story to someone entire, and it was complicated and dark; after a couple of false starts she realized that she had to go back to her first miscarriage, and beyond that to her marriage to the man who, in this retelling, was not complicit, but merely a witness. It took what seemed like hours to relate the tale—the pain of the first rabbit inserted in her, and her disgust at what she was doing to herself; the surprise of the first surgeon (this part made Grace and Patience clutch their stomach in laughter); her slow creeping dread when she began to realize that the hoax had taken on its own life and would require her to "give birth" not just to a second and a third rabbit but who knew how many more, each sham of a birth drawing in yet more believers; the news that she had somehow gained the attention of the king of England his very own self ("Did you meet the king?" said Patience. "Let her tell her story in her own time," said Grace); her transportation to London; her subsequent installation in Dr. Lacey's Bagnio; the vigil kept by surgeons and lords that seemed as if it would not end; the threat of a surgery that put the best interests of others ahead of her own; the final relief of giving up the pretense at last and making her confession.

"It is a pity that you did not get to meet the king," said Patience, once Mary Toft was done. "Though your recent past has not been deprived of incident, it must be said: an audience with the king is almost too much to expect, on top of it."

"But I do have one question," said Grace. "I do not understand why you chose to strip a rabbit of its skin, cut it into pieces, and insert those pieces into your vagina, to expel them in the presence of a surgeon. Patience and I would not do this to ourselves."

"I hadn't considered the idea until this moment," said Patience, "but after some thought, I would certainly not."

"I want to know why you would do this," said Grace.

*

Mary considered it. She thought of what her husband had said, or what she seemed to remember her husband saying, one evening in the spring. *God speaks to us, speaks through you, and damns you for your failures. But we might obtain salvation for you, if only you could speak back.*

But that couldn't have happened at all, not in that way. Joshua was a kind man, despite what one might think. He had a small voice that came out of a big body; his size was a curse that made people see him as something other than what he was, something nastier and more threatening. It would not have been his idea. He had gone home to Godalming, to earn a living, to care for James, and to return to the life he deserved.

She must have misinterpreted, or misremembered.

"I did it for the money," she stated plainly. "I thought it would make me rich."

Patience coughed.

"Mary," Grace said, placing her hand on hers. "Did you not, during all those long and tortured months, think to yourself that surely there are easier, more reliable ways to swindle a man?"

*

"And everyone believed it," Grace said. "Despite the fact that the idea seems ludicrous the moment you hear it."

"I can appreciate a good trick," said Patience. "And Grace and I have seen people only too willing to believe the ludicrous, just as we have seen people who insist on doubting what is plainly true. One never knows."

"True enough," said Grace. "Can you believe, Mary, that we have had people claim that Patience and I do not exist, even as we stand before them?"

For in the warmer months, Grace explained, she and Patience made a living by joining a traveling caravan operated by a Londoner, Nicholas Fox. "An Exhibition of Medical Curiosities, he calls it. People with unusual bodies, or exceptional talents. Though some of them are admittedly fraudulent—he would not be able to easily enlist enough people for his caravan to give an audience its money's worth, and so a few contrivances must make up the balance."

"You came through Godalming last spring," Mary said. "I didn't attend. But I remember."

"We have long since lost any curiosity about ourselves, having lived in this body for our whole lives," said Grace, "but there is still profit to be had from the curiosity of others."

"However, propriety prevents audiences from seeing us without a scrim to shield their eyes," Patience continued.

"So when we stand before an audience each evening, as the last exhibit on the program, we see them not as individual men and women, but as a blurred mass of colors and shadows."

"But we can hear them. And most of the time, they pass judgment."

"Sometimes we hear a collective gasp of consternation," said Grace, "and though I might wish that these people might be more accepting of what they have not seen before, it signals to us at least that they see us as *true*—that even in that dim light, something of our real nature has been conveyed through the fabric behind which we stand."

"But sometimes the sentiment of the crowd curdles, and it turns to anger. Perhaps because they've seen through that sad pile of poultry that Fox tries to pass off to paying customers as a 'boneless girl.'"

"And they are so certain that Patience and I are *false*—some kind of dishonest illusion. I can feel their rage when it happens—a heat on my face, as if I've opened a stove's door to look in on the flames."

"The curtain that separates us is as much for us as it is for them, you see," said Patience. "It is hard enough to have someone doubt your very existence when you cannot make out his face so clearly—without that, it would be worse."

"To be doubted so strongly leads you to doubt yourself," said Grace, "but when we are alone together, we can count the things that tell us we are real—our own voices; our own skin; our own heart; our own breath. We can do this service for each other, as sisters—breathe life into each other."

"But I don't know what we would do if we were one instead of two," said Patience, and she turned her head to look at Mary with genuine pity.

"Vanish, I suppose," Patience said. "Float away on the wind."

*

The next morning, one of the two constables who'd brought Grace and Patience in the night before unlocked the door to Mary's cell and beckoned to her. "Your case has been dismissed. You're free to go," he said simply, and though surprised at this—she imagined that at the least there'd be some sort of trial, that she wouldn't get out into the world again so easily—she came to her feet.

"We wish you the best of luck," said Grace, and she and Patience folded Mary in a long and warm embrace.

"Isn't this lovely," the constable said. "I find myself wiping a tear away."

*

"Speaking for myself, I find what you did revolting," the constable said to Mary as he led her past the cells of still sleeping women, through the dark maze of Bridewell's halls that led to the exit. "But your body is yours to do with as you wish—there appears to be no statute preventing women from desecrating their bodies in such a particular and peculiar manner. And it is difficult to say that you truly defrauded someone, since you didn't speak a lie—you merely did as you wished, and let the surgeons who tended to you draw their own conclusions.

"Besides," he said as they approached the wide double doors of this prison that, in a century past, had been a palace, "it appears that enough people of station would prefer this tale be forgotten to ensure a lack of will to revisit it in a court of law; any further punishment you receive would be more than matched by the lash of the satirist's pen, directed at those you duped. And so you are free."

He slid back the large iron bolt of the heavy double doors before him and pushed. With a groan of old hinges, they swung open, revealing a crack of light beyond and the noise and stink of a London street.

"What shall I do?" Mary said.

"I don't know," the constable replied, "but you can't stay here."

He'd pushed the doors open just wide enough for her to pass through. She took one tentative step and then another, and she heard the slam of the doors behind her and the shooting of the bolt, and she was free with the sky above her, the city before her.

I don't know what we would do if we were one instead of two. Vanish, I suppose.

She drew her arms around herself in the January cold and thought of Joshua, that innocent victim of her notorious and vile hoax (though was there something that she was forgetting, or willing herself not to know? No—there was not). It was reasonable to think that a man would resent being so ill-used by his wife, so publicly embarrassed, but they were bound by love, and by their family, and by their need to use each other's faces as mirrors, and she knew, if she returned to him, that he would be able to find it in his heart to forgive.

*

So she set off alone into the great city, to try to make it home before she faded.

Acknowledgments

My thanks to my editor, Edward Kastenmeier, and my agent, Susan Golomb, for their support and enthusiasm for this somewhat unusual project. Thanks also to Caitlin Landuyt, Edward's assistant; to Rose Cronin-Jackman, my publicist; and to Janet Hansen for her jacket design.

Certain elements of this narrative resulted from conversations with Micaela Baranello, Stephanie Harves, and Jessica Terekhov.

Thanks to Ann Laver and the librarians at the Godalming Museum for steering me in the right direction at the beginning of my research.

Special thanks to a few people who made the time to read and comment on an early draft of this novel: Brett Douville, Maria Purves, and Drew Purves.

I first encountered the tale of Mary Toft in the fall of 1996, in a class in graduate school at Princeton University taught by Jonathan Lamb ("Representation of the Improbable"). It's been rattling around in my head ever since, and I'm glad I at last found something to do with it.

For a couple of years now my friends have dreaded what happens when a stranger approaches me at a party and says, "You're working on a novel? What's it about?" Thanks for your patience, everyone.

And thanks, as always, to my family, who have supported my writing career from the beginning and continue to do so.

—*DEXTER PALMER*
February 6, 2016
May 6, 2019
Princeton, New Jersey

Bibliography

It will be clear to anyone who reads this novel that I've taken a novelist's liberties with its subject matter: I've condensed and invented characters and freely rendered their thoughts; rearranged locations (most notably moving John Howard's residence from Guilford to Godalming); altered history and created new situations; and imported one event in particular that didn't take place during the exact time period (the "Chelsea Cat-Eater" did not perform the act that earned him his title until 1790; see Jane Moore and John Strachan, *Key Concepts in Romantic Literature* [New York: Palgrave Macmillan, 2010], p. 60). For a strictly historically accurate version of the Mary Toft story, I refer readers in particular to Dennis Todd's invaluable book *Imagining Monsters: Miscreations of the Self in the Eighteenth Century* (Chicago and London: University of Chicago Press, 1995), and to S. A. Seligman's article "Mary Toft—The Rabbit Breeder," *Medical History* 5, no. 4 (October 1961): 349–60. In addition, Dennis Todd's transcript of Mary Toft's three confessions (originally recorded by Dr. James Douglas in December 1726) is available, as of the time of this writing, at https://tofts3confessions.wordpress.com/.

Chapter V incorporates material from *Aristotle's Compleat Master-Piece, in Three Parts: Displaying the Secrets of Nature in the Generation of Man: Regularly Digested into Chapters and Sections, Rendering It Far More Useful Than Any Yet Extant: To Which Is Added, A Treasure of Health, Or, The Family Physician: Being Choice and Approved Remedies for All the Distempers Incident to Human Bodies* (London: Printed and sold by the booksellers, 1728).

The first half of the retelling of "The King and the Three Impostors" in Chapter XIII is a heavy rewrite of the version of the tale that appears in *Count Lucanor; Or, The Fifty Pleasant Stories of Patronio, Written by the Prince Don Juan Manuel and First Done into English by James York, M.D., 1868*. The second half is my own invention.

Chapter XXI incorporates material from Nathanael St. André, *A Short Narrative of an Extraordinary Delivery of Rabbets, Perform'd by Mr. John Howard, Surgeon at Guilford* (London: John Clarke, 1727, second edition). All writing attributed to St. André, Ahlers, and Manningham elsewhere in the novel is my own invention.

I am also indebted to the following works, for reasons ranging from providing a general overview of English history, to supplying useful details of the period about which I was writing, to influencing the way I thought about the characters. Divergences from historical fact are mine, not theirs:

Apple, Jr., R. W. "Much Ado About Mutton, but Not in These Parts." *New York Times,* March 29, 2006.

Bayne-Powell, Rosamond. *The English Child in the Eighteenth Century.* New York: E. P. Dutton and Company, 1939.

Bensley, B. A. *Practical Anatomy of the Rabbit.* Eighth edition. Edited by E. Horne Craigie. Philadelphia: Blakiston Company, 1948.

Black, Jeremy. *The Hanoverians: The History of a Dynasty.* London and New York: Hambledon and London, 2004.

Blackmore, Sir Richard. *Discourses on the Gout, a Rheumatism, and the King's Evil, Containing an Explication of the Nature, Causes and Different Species of Those Diseases, and the Method of Curing Them.* London: J. Pemberton, 1726.

Blanning, Tim. *The Pursuit of Glory: Europe 1648–1815.* New York: Viking, 2007.

Boyer, Abel. *The Political State of Great Britain, Volume XXXII. Containing the Months of July, August, September, October, November, and December, MDCCXXVI.* London: Printed for the author, 1726.

Brogan, Stephen. *The Royal Touch in Early Modern England: Politics, Medicine, and Sin.* Woodbridge, Suffolk, and Rochester, New York: Boydell Press, 2015.

Cheyne, George. *The Natural Method of Cureing the Diseases of the Body, and the Disorders of the Mind Depending on the Body.* London: George Strahan and John and Paul Knapton, 1742.

Cruickshank, Dan. *The Secret History of Georgian London.* London: Random House Books, 2009.

Davidson, Ian. *Voltaire: A Life.* New York: Pegasus Books, 2010.

Davies, Horton. *Worship and Theology in England: From Watts and Wesley to Martineau, 1690–1900.* Grand Rapids, MI, and Cambridge, UK: William B. Eerdmans Publishing Company, 1996.

Defoe, Daniel. *The Compleat English Tradesman.* London: Charles Rivington, 1727.

———. *A Tour Through the Whole Island of Great Britain.* Abridged and edited with an introduction and notes by Pat Rogers. London: Penguin Books, 1971.

———. *Moll Flanders.* Edited with an introduction and notes by David Blewett. London: Penguin Books, 1989.

————. *Roxana.* Oxford: Oxford University Press, 2008.

Dillon, Patrick. *Gin: The Much-Lamented Death of Madam Geneva.* Boston, MA: Justin, Charles and Co., 2002.

Edison Electric Illuminating Company of Boston. *The History of Stage and Theater Lighting.* 1929.

"The Free-Thinker." *Considerations on the Nature, Causes, Cure, and Prevention of Pestilences.* London: W. Wilkins, 1721.

Gibson, William. " 'Pious Decorum': Clerical Wigs in the Eighteenth-Century Church of England." *Anglican and Episcopal History* 65, no. 2 (June 1996): 145–61.

Giffard, William. *Cases in Midwifry.* London: B. Motte and T. Wotton, 1734.

Glasse, Hannah. *The Art of Cookery Made Plain and Easy.* London: J. Rivington and Sons, 1788.

Grano, John. *Handel's Trumpeter: The Diary of John Grano.* Edited by John Ginger, with a foreword by Crispin Steele-Perkins. Stuyvesant, NY: Pendragon Press, 1998.

Harvey, A. D. *Sex in Georgian England: Attitudes and Prejudices from the 1720s to the 1820s.* London: Duckworth and Co., 1994.

Harvey, Karen. "What Mary Toft Felt: Women's Voices, Pain, Power, and the Body." *History Workshop Journal* 80 (September 2015): 33–51.

Hatton, Ragnhild. *George I: Elector and King.* Cambridge, MA: Harvard University Press, 1978.

Heister, D. Laurentius. *A Compendium of Anatomy, Containing a Short but Perfect View of All the Parts of Humane Bodies.* London: Thomas Combes, 1721.

Heister, Laurence. *A General System of Surgery in Three Parts.* Fourth edition. London: W. Innys, 1750.

Hogarth, William. *Engravings by Hogarth.* Edited by Sean Shesgreen. New York: Dover Publications, 1973.

Inglis, Lucy. *Georgian London: Into the Streets.* London: Penguin Books, 2014.

Kuitenbrower, Kathryn. "Mary Toft, Eighteenth-Century Breeder of Story." *Brick* 91 (summer 2013): 140.

Lane, Joan. *Apprenticeship in England, 1600–1914.* London: UCL Press, 1996.

Locke, John. *An Essay Concerning Human Understanding.* Edited with an introduction and notes by Roger Woolhouse. London: Penguin Books, 2004.

Lynch, Jack. *Deception and Detection in Eighteenth-Century Britain.* Burlington, VT: Ashgate, 2008.

Makari, George. *Soul Machine: The Invention of the Modern Mind.* New York and London: W. W. Norton and Company, 2015.

Manningham, Sir Richard. *An Exact Diary of What Was Observ'd During a Close Attendance Upon Mary Toft, the Pretended Rabbet-Breeder of Godalming in Surrey, from Monday, Nov. 28 to Wednesday, December 7, Following. Together with an Account of Her Confession of the Fraud.* London: Fletcher Gyles, 1726.

————. *The Plague No Contagius Disease: Or, The Infection of the Plague Seldom, if Ever, Communicated by Touching of Persons Infected, or of Goods Brought from Infected Places*. London: J. Millan, 1744.

Marlow, Joyce. *The Life and Times of George I*. London: Weidenfeld and Nicolson, 1973.

Marshall, Ashley. "Did Defoe Write *Moll Flanders* and *Roxana?*" *Philological Quarterly* 89, no. 203 (spring-summer 2010): 209–41.

Medical Essays and Observations. Revised and published by a society in Edinburgh. London: T. and W. Ruddimans, 1737.

Miller, Joseph. *Botanicum Officinale; Or, A Compendious Herbal: Giving an Account of All Such Plants As Are Now Used in the Practice of Physick, with Their Descriptions and Virtues*. London: E. Bell, 1722.

O'Donoghue, Geoffrey. *Bridewell Hospital: Palace, Prison, Schools, from the Death of Elizabeth to Modern Times*. London: John Lane, 1929.

Olsen, Kirstin. *Daily Life in Eighteenth-Century England*. Westport, CT, and London: Greenwood Press, 1999.

Porter, Roy. *English Society in the Eighteenth Century*. Revised edition. London: Penguin Books, 1991.

Robbins, Hollis. "The Emperor's New Critique." *New Literary History* 34, no. 4 (autumn 2003): 659–75.

Rudé, George. *Hanoverian London 1714–1808*. Berkeley and Los Angeles: University of California Press, 1971.

Spencer, Herbert R. *The History of British Midwifery from 1650 to 1800*. London: John Bale, Sons and Danielson, Ltd., 1927.

Styles, John. *The Dress of the People: Everyday Fashion in Eighteenth-Century England*. New Haven and London: Yale University Press, 2007.

Tauvry, Daniel. *A New Rational Anatomy, Containing an Explication of the Uses of the Structure of the Body of Man and Some Other Animals, According to the Rules of Mechanicks*. London: D. Midwinter, 1701.

Thomas, Keith. *Man and the Natural World: Changing Attitudes in England 1500–1800*. London: Penguin Books, 1984.

————. *Religion and the Decline of Magic*. London: Penguin Books, 1991.

Tombs, Robert. *The English and Their History*. New York: Alfred A. Knopf, 2015.

Vickers, William. *An Easie and Safe Method for Curing the King's Evil*. London: S. Manship, 1713.

Vickery, Amanda. *Behind Closed Doors: At Home in Georgian England*. New Haven and London: Yale University Press, 2009.

Voltaire. *Philosophical Letters; Or, Letters Regarding the English Nation*. Edited and with an introduction by John Leigh. Translated by Prudence L. Steiner. Indianapolis/Cambridge: Hackett Publishing Company, 2007.

von Uffenbach, Zacharias Conrad. *London in 1710.* Translated by W. H. Quarrell and Margaret Mare. London: Faber and Faber Limited, 1934.

White, Jerry. *A Great and Monstrous Thing: London in the Eighteenth Century.* Cambridge, MA: Harvard University Press, 1995.

Wilson, Adrian. *The Making of Man-Midwifery: Childbirth in England, 1660–1770.* Cambridge, MA: Harvard University Press, 1995.

———. *Ritual and Conflict: The Social Relations of Childbirth in Early Modern England.* Burlington, VT: Ashgate, 2013.

Worsley, Lucy. *If Walls Could Talk: An Intimate History of the Home.* London: Faber and Faber Limited, 2011.

A NOTE ABOUT THE AUTHOR

Dexter Palmer is the author of two previous novels: *Version Control,* which was selected as one of the best novels of 2016 by *GQ,* the *San Francisco Chronicle,* and other publications, and *The Dream of Perpetual Motion,* which was selected as one of the best fiction debuts of 2010 by *Kirkus Reviews.* He lives in Princeton, New Jersey.

www.dexterpalmer.com

A NOTE ON THE TYPE

The text of this book was set in Garamond No. 3. It is not a true copy of any of the designs of Claude Garamond (ca. 1480–1561), but an adaptation that probably owes as much to the designs of Jean Jannon, a Protestant printer in Sedan in the early seventeenth century, who had worked with Garamond's romans earlier in Paris. This particular version is based on an adaptation by Morris Fuller Benton.

Typeset by Digital Composition, Berryville, Virginia
Printed and bound by Friesens Printing, Altona, Canada
Designed by Maria Carella